STEAL THE STARS

STEAL
THE
STARS

NAT CASSIDY

A NOVEL BASED UPON
THE AUDIO DRAMA
WRITTEN AND CREATED BY

MAC ROGERS

TOR

A TOM DOHERTY ASSOCIATES BOOK
NEW YORK

STEAL THE STARS

Novelization copyright © 2017 by Tom Doherty Associates. Based on the podcast *Steal the Stars* by Gideon Media.

A Tor Book
Published by Tom Doherty Associates
175 Fifth Avenue
New York, NY 10010

www.tor-forge.com

Tor® is a registered trademark
of Macmillan Publishing Group, LLC.

The Library of Congress Cataloging-in-Publication Data
is available upon request.

ISBN 978-1-250-17262-4 (trade paperback)
ISBN 978-1-250-17263-1 (ebook)

Our books may be purchased in bulk for promotional, educational, or business use. Please contact your local bookseller or the Macmillan Corporate and Premium Sales Department at 1-800-221-7945, extension 5442, or by email at MacmillanSpecialMarkets@macmillan.com.

First Edition: November 2017

Printed in the United States of America

0 9 8 7 6 5 4 3 2 1

To K. And to Mac, Sean, Jordana, Bart, Marco, and Jen.
We did the thing.

ACKNOWLEDGMENTS

The great acknowledgments cliché is "no one writes a book alone." This is true by roughly a billionfold for a novelization. This book quite literally would not exist without the work of everyone who made the *Steal the Stars* podcast a reality. Thank you to the cast: Jorge Cordova, Brittany Williams, Daryl Lathon, Neimah Djourabchi, Brian Silliman, Kelley Rae O'Donnell, Rebecca Comtois, Christopher Yustin, James Wetzel, Reyna de Courcy, Jason Howard, Abe Goldfarb, Seth Shelden, Hanna Cheek, Autumn Dornfeld, Jennifer Tsay, David Shih, Sol Marina Crespo, Tarantino Smith, and especially Ashlie Atkinson in the central role of Dak. Your talents, your insights, and even your off-mic questions and observations informed this text and made my job of exploring the depths of this story immeasurably easier. The podcast's sound designer, Bart Fasbender, is an evil genius of sonic creation and was able to do in a single cue what took me hundreds of words, but I am grateful to him for making some very out-of-this-world stuff concrete and real. It almost goes without saying—but will not!—that this book is also deeply indebted to the series' director, Jordana Williams, and producer, Sean Williams. There are too many reasons why to list even briefly in print, but one of them is certainly egg rolls. Massive thanks are also due to editors Marco Palmieri and Jen Gunnels for their guidance, their support, their encouragement, and their belief in this project. This is my first novel-length work and, as I've described novelizing as a sort of training-wheels experience, Marco and Jen were the steadying hand on my back as I wobbled down the sidewalk. Humble thanks (and pancakes) to Kelley, for putting up with my writing schedule during a very special time in our lives. Lastly, two more acknowledgments must be given. First, to the listeners of *Steal the Stars*. I hope this novelization has honored your listening experience while also giving you enough new dimensions (and a few fun digressions) to make you glad you picked it up. It's the job of the writer to be specific, but if you spent seven hours listening to our audio drama, then I know you have your own personal vision of a lot of these events and characters. I respect that ownership and I hope mine is able to coexist peacefully alongside yours. And second, and most of all, thank you to Mac Rogers. Thank you for your words, for this world, for these characters, and for entrusting them all in my hands. It was an honor to write by your starlight.

Everyone has the dream their first night after meeting him. Of rushing blackness, a void infinite and unchanging . . . yet still that feeling of movement.

Everyone is left with the thought, the same conundrum:

Am I hurtling toward something alien?

Or is something alien hurtling toward me?

PART ONE

THE DEATH OF DAKOTA PRENTISS

1

RIGHT BEFORE I heard the guy's collarbone break, I remembered a print hanging in my grandmother's house. In the guest bathroom, written in an innocuous font over a pastel flower: "*There's nothing more satisfying than seeing joy on the face of a friend.*"

My grandmother had obviously never thrown a guy twice her size across a room before.

Now, look, I'm not a violent person by nature. I don't actually enjoy fighting. It stresses me out and makes me feel the bad kind of tingly for the rest of the day. But when a guy sidles up to you in one of only a handful of bars you have the option to patronize and his breath smells impossibly of socks and he leads with maybe the tritest pickup line in history, making it both annoying *and* insulting? Well, you make sacrifices.

"Excuse me," he breathed, he *exhumed*, and if I'd had a force shield I would have deployed it. He tried again, his voice low and (snort) sensual. "Excuuuuse me."

I made the mistake of responding. Not much—barely more than a sustained blink, not even looking in his direction—but he took it as leave to continue. It set him up for the clincher: "Was your daddy a thief?"

THE THING nobody tells you about the end of your life is sometimes you have so much damn longer to live afterward.

I'm talking days, weeks—hell, decades—from when your life ends until your body finally gets the message. In my case, my life ended the day after I threw this guy across the bar and I've been running ever since. I didn't even get, like, a five-minute break to mourn.

And it's all your fault, by the way.

Of course, I say my life ended that next day, but the truth is I've had difficulty pinning down the exact *moment* it happened. Believe me, I've tried. I really can't help myself—I may not have been a scientist, but overthinking is something you catch hanging around them, like a disease.

When was the precise moment my hull breached, my engine failed, my horse went tits up? Was it when I looked at your bare chest and realized I could see your heartbeat? Maybe it was before then, that first handshake, looking into those eyes? Maybe it's the most accurate to say my life ended the day I dropped everything and started working at Quill Marine in the first place, signing my life (and all my fraternization rights) away?

Yes? No? All of the above? Who fucking knows? Technically, it's not the bullet that kills you, it's the lack of oxygen to your brain due to the ruptured blood vessels, right? You parse something long enough and it loses all meaning.

Except those eyes. If anything, the more I parsed those eyes, the more meaning they took on.

Anyway. Back to the guy at the bar.

"I'M ASKING, was your daddy a thief?"

I'm asking myself how a guy's mouth can smell so much of feet.

I usually have one drink on the way home. No more and, if there's a just and loving God, no less. I could just as easily have that one drink in my house, but for whatever reason I prefer not to drink in silence.

There are a surprising number of bars around this tiny town—or maybe it's not that surprising, if you've ever lived in a tiny town—but I usually stick to this one, the Heron. It's got a better juke. Also, of course, consistency helps avoid unwanted run-ins with co-workers. Again: fraternization.

"Because he musta been a thief—"

Here it comes.

"—cuz he musta had to steal the stars from heaven—"

Feeeeeet.

"—to put them in your eyes."

Uuuggh. At last, I turn to him, hoping these eyes he's so fond of have somehow found the ability to shoot poison.

"No." I turn my attention back to my glass.

It's a word I'm sure he's heard a lot. It whisks off him like a drop of water off a windshield.

"I, uh, I see you in here a lot, you know." He's rubbing his fingers back and forth across the bar while he talks, absently, clumsily. Like a piss-poor massage. I put my rocks glass down as close to those knobby worms as I can, trying to send out the signal that I'm okay with crushing any part of him that gets too close to me.

"I'm not gonna fuck you." I make direct eye contact once again.

His eyes widen. "Whoa! Who said anything about—? Jesus, I'm just trying to *talk* to you here. Just talk to me for a second! People always look at me cross-eyed but once we get to talking, they like me!"

There's a trace of sullenness there. I've hit a sore spot. And here's my next mistake: I'm a sucker for accidental vulnerability. It fascinates me. It makes me want to stay and watch what happens. So I don't get up and leave. I let him talk a little bit longer.

"So . . . you work at Quill Marine."

"What was your first clue?" I ask, picking up my glass again.

"Hmmmm. The uniform!" he responds with a smug smile. Oh, no, it thinks it's clever. I'm, of course, still wearing the charcoal canvas coveralls that I foolishly hoped would be shapeless enough to render me invisible. Stitched on the arm are the words "Quill Marine."

"That's really impressive," I say.

"Hey." He pulls out the stool next to me and sits down—actually sits down next to me, and somewhere in the back of my mind I'm already preparing for violence. "What is it you guys *do* in there, anyway?"

His voice has dropped to a conspiratorial tone. I match it.

"Are we going to have a problem here?" I ask.

"I mean," he chuckles, "we kinda already have a problem here. You guys . . . you don't hire local. Why *is* that?"

He's still smiling, but poisonous clouds are gathering around the edges of his voice. Another sore spot. I have little doubt he came over here to flirt first, but, if that mission winds up being a failure, he might as well air some grievances. Never underestimate the ability of a spurned man to shuffle emotions like a monte dealer.

I don't respond and he keeps going: "No, seriously. Why is that? It's not like there's a ton of jobs out here. But then there's big ol' Quill Marine, taking up valuable real estate and refusing to let people sign on. I mean, what, we don't make 'em good enough for you guys out here?"

He's still smiling, trying to show me this is all just harmless, charming ribbing, but his mouth has tightened and the look is grotesque.

I don't hear the bar door open behind us.

"I bet I know why," he goes on. "You guys are making weapons in there. That's it, isn't it?" He nods at my lack of comment. "Yeah. You know . . . my cousin made a delivery there once. He says he saw weapons inside. He swears it. Just lying around."

No. No. It's too much. Too stupid, too confident, too goddamn aromatic. I have to respond.

"I can promise you," I finally say, regretting the decision immediately. "Nobody's cousin saw weapons in there."

His face lights up.

"Ah! See, but: now you're interested in me."

Maybe it all could have been defused. This wasn't the first time I've gotten an earful like this from a disgruntled townie. Maybe

I could have talked him down, shit-talked paper tiger versions of my higher-ups or the company that owned Quill. Maybe I could have avoided what happened next. But, then, enter: her.

"*WHAT. THE. FUCK?!*"

The guy blanches and spins around on his stool.

"Janey?!"

"*What the fuck are you doing?!*"

Janey is standing in the middle of the bar, having just walked in and spotted her man, dear old Feetbreath, chatting to the gorgeous specimen in the charcoal coveralls at the bar. Janey is upset. Janey looks like a bedraggled heroine straight out of a Springsteen song: long-suffering, exhausted, ready to snap.

Feetbreath's voice does an impressive switch from wannabe lothario to whiny teenager: "Jeeeeeeeesus, I can't get one minute to myself?"

Janey's not to be deterred. She's probably been practicing this: "You wait 'til I'm asleep and you come up here—you wait 'til I'm asleep and creep out like a fucking raccoon getting in the garbage?!"

"I can't get *one minute* to get outta that shithole and clear my head?"

Meanwhile, I'm draining the rest of my rocks glass into my face. I'll be goddamned if this soap opera is going to rob me of my hard-earned buzz.

But, then, with impressive speed, Janey's on the other side of me, actually holding my arm.

"How long have you been seeing him?"

I almost choke on my whiskey.

"What?"

"He's been with me six years. I bet he didn't tell you that."

Feetbreath pulls her off of me not a second too soon.

"I'm just talking to her! Can't I talk to a person?"

"Has he mentioned me at all?!" Janey is shouting into my ear.

"I can't just get out of the house and talk to a person?!" Feetbreath is shouting at her through my other ear.

"You're supposed to talk to *me!*"

"I can't get a break from your voice for like *ten fucking seconds—*"

"I wash your pants, *I suck your dick*—you wanna talk to somebody, you talk to—"

SMACK!

Okay.

Let it be said, Feetbreath started it. Let it be said, once again, that I'm not ordinarily a violent person, and that very much includes having a zero tolerance policy toward men who strike women. Not that I haven't met a huge amount of women who could easily hold their own in a fight—it's just damn rude to hit someone smaller than you first.

He got Janey in the eye. She stumbles backward, stunned, almost falling. And it looks like he might try for another shot.

So I grab his arm. Hard.

"Huh? Get the fuck off of me."

"Walk out with me," I tell him, calmly, evenly.

"Get your fucking hands off of—you wanna die?"

"I wanna walk out with you. Come on."

He's twisting, trying to get free. Ain't gonna happen.

The bartender has been watching this the whole time, of course. We are far more interesting than whatever catch-the-ball breakdown is happening on ESPN right now. He finally chimes in: "Dak, you need me to—"

"Nope. I'm good," I tell him. "In fact, I'm great."

And it's true. Because at the very least, I'd managed to finish my drink.

MY NAME was Dak, by the way. Short for Dakota. But you know that.

I START dragging Feetbreath to the door. He is actually grunting, "Do you wanna die?" at me, which is possibly the funniest thing I have ever heard.

A few feet from the door, I catch a glimpse of Janey. She's reconnecting with the world, and her increasingly clear eyes catch mine. First with shock . . . then an unmistakable hatred. It actually takes me aback for a moment. Just a moment, long enough to loosen my grip on Feetbreath, who manages to twist around enough to position his free arm exactly where I don't want it.

"Cuz if you wanna die, I'll—"

And he swings at me.

He telegraphs the punch like a year in advance. I have plenty of time to stroll out of the way. He tries and fails again. And this time I engage.

Three rules for winning a fight against someone way bigger than you:

One. Don't let them get a single hit in. I'm stocky and solid, but this guy is lumberjack big and has almost half a foot on me. All the training in the world doesn't protect you from sheer poundage, that's just physics.

Two. Every one of your hits has to count. No chest, no upper back, no shoulder. You gotta aim for solar plexus, kidneys, balls if that's an option. Dirty? Sure, I guess. *Every* fight is dirty. And shame on you if you jump into one you don't plan on winning.

Three. You have about thirty seconds. If you don't put them down in thirty, draw or run.

In this particular case, about ten seconds into the scuffle, he gives me a wide, sloppy cross that I basically use as a trebuchet.

THIS BRINGS me back to my original point.

Sorry, Grandma. There is nothing, *nothing,* more satisfying than throwing a man twice your size—especially one who just hit a woman after sloppily trying to worm his way into your pants—all the way across a goddamn alehouse.

"Satisfaction" is the right word for it. That feeling of his bulk leaving yours, of shrugging him into orbit, handing him over to the gods of gravity as if to say, "This is yours, do with it what you will"? It *satisfies*. It feels like everything is operating the way it's supposed to.

It would be a long time before I got to feel that again.

FEETBREATH IS not trained in the art of being thrown. There's a sickening crack we all hear when he lands, followed by a howl of pain one slow synapse later.

Whoops.

Janey rushes to his side. Meanwhile, the bartender looks at me and shrugs.

"I had to call the cops, Dak. This is your chance to get out of here."

There's no malice in his voice. He's doing me a solid. Rules are rules and business is business. I slap an extra ten dollars down on the bar.

Janey is cradling Feetbreath. The area around her eye is already beginning to swell.

"Look at what you did to him!" she screams at me. There's such hurt in her voice you'd almost think it was her who just snapped a bone.

"In about thirty minutes you'll be able to see what he did to you. Hope you look good in purple."

I mostly mumbled that second part to myself, though. She was already screaming over me.

"It's not your business! It's none of your business!" And then she turns her attention to her wounded, moaning partner. "Baby, baby, are you all right? Baby, I'm sorry. I'm sorry. I'll do better, I'm sorry."

The bartender picks up my ten dollars and says to me, "I'll say it was someone I don't know."

I tell him to go ahead and say it was me. The cops won't give me a problem. I work at Quill Marine.

And with that I head for the door.

On my way out, though, I turn back and survey the scene.

Janey's on her knees, helping her man stand up. She's babbling to him in soft, soothing tones.

"I didn't know, baby, I won't bother you so much, I didn't know. I didn't know I was bothering you so much, I'll stop. Let me get you home."

Snapshot, I thought. *Right there: everything you need to know about love in one handy image. So neat and tidy you could put it on a print and hang it in Grandma's house.*

I walked out of there, shaking my head, suddenly very tired.

THAT'S NOT my last real memory of the woman that was Dak, but it's certainly the most representative. And like I said, by some point the next morning, that life was over.

And like I said, it's all your fault.

But I'm not mad at you. Not for ending that life, at least. That life wasn't all that spectacular to begin with.

Besides, here's something people *have* said about the end: sometimes paradise is waiting on the other side.

It might only last a few moments. It might take a whole lotta hell to get there. But it's there.

So let's fucking get to it already.

2

ASK ME where I worked and I'd tell you: Quill Marine.

Ask me what we did there and I'd tell you: marine stuff.

I could get more specific—why, I could wax for hours about the reproductive cycle of the noble sea urchin and how it relates to the water's tonicity balance; or how phytoplankton secrete an enzyme that helps us produce a more sustainable kind of plastic—but I rarely got the opportunity to go too long. That's by design. And anything I said from that point on was gonna be 100 percent bullshit anyway.

The *real* Quill Marine Labs is protected by layers upon layers upon layers of bullshit, most of it so boring and eye-glazing as to dissuade any in-depth investigation.

Being boring is the most effective guard dog there is.

Still, the naval base is located a few minutes off of the water in a pretty small town in Northern California and, to quote our old friend Feetbreath, it does take up a fair amount of real estate. So people talk. People guess and assume. Surely, *something* interesting must go on in that immense, faceless compound, right? And it must be connected to why they never seem to hire anyone local, mustn't it?

"HOW'S ALL the mind-control stuff going?"

Sam, the owner of the Seaview Diner, asks this as he lays down my veggie omelet and cup of coffee. Every time.

"I knew you were going to ask that," I respond.

"That only proves my point," he tips back.

Every morning I'm on shift I stop by the Seaview, and every morning it's the same repartee. Although that morning was a little different.

"I heard you had a rough night at the Heron last night," Sam tsked.

I heard the sound of Feetbreath screaming, of his clavicle snapping, and wished I could control even my own mind.

People talk. People wonder.

"Miss? Miss? Please, just tell me that there's no chance of a Chernobyl sorta situation over there? Please? I have *children*," a woman once whispered to me desperately at the supermarket while I was standing in the deli section, looking for the tofu dogs.

But honestly, besides the occasional embittered townie who wishes we took his job application, the interest in Quill Marine is mostly circumstantial. Fanciful, even.

Hell, it's not even as if Quill is the only research lab in the area.

Most people who live in the area are commuters—they go inland to work in the Sustain Farms or south to Silicon Valley or up to Trinidad to work for the next closest research facility, Humboldt Marine. In fact, Humboldt, formerly Humboldt State University Marine before its privatization and now known by the enviable nom de guerre "The Bone Factory" for its research in bone regrowth, is one of Quill Marine Lab's saving graces. As far as we know (as far as *I* know, I should say, since somebody always knows more), they're a legitimate research lab, and they do enough actual work that Quill Marine gets to act as a sort of plucky younger sibling—always trying, but never in danger of coming close to the big guy's reputation.

Then again, as someone who worked at Quill Marine, I've learned not to really believe the thing that anybody or anything presents themselves to be. The Bone Factory could actually be the ones dabbling in mind control. They're owned by the same private defense contractors that bought Quill Marine almost ten years ago, after all. They could be manipulating our every thought, constructing our entire reality out of whole cloth. Everything you're seeing right now could have been conjured up by them and you're just sitting in an empty metal room none the fucking wiser!

See? Isn't parsing fun?

Quill Marine has its own covers and initiatives. It conducts marine studies and releases verifiable results. It does a pretty phenomenal job presenting itself as a by-the-numbers aquatic research facility. It has a front. And then evidence behind the front. And then evidence behind that evidence. The only remotely notable aspect of the company is that it chooses its new hires from a very specific, very remote talent pool.

So none of us in Quill Marine ever begrudge, or even take that seriously, the occasional line of questioning about What We're Really Up To. It's more fun for everyone to imagine we're doing something spectacular.

I'm sure you entertained a few fantasies yourself before you found out the truth.

And in this case, it's not like you were wrong.

IT TOOK me some time to get used to life out here. And honestly, a big part of the adjustment was shedding the implications of terms like "California living."

After all, California living was part of how the job was sold to me. I'd be so close to the beach, to wine country—what an ideal place to ride out the rest of your career, they chirped! After war zones and hell holes and Washington, D.C., now it would be surfboards and floral shirts. Sunshine and seagulls. The twang of a Dick Dale guitar lick always just finishing off an echo somewhere.

Life this far north, though?

Replace all your palm trees with firs and redwoods.

Replace all your surfers with lumberjacks.

Replace your sandy beaches with rocky cliffs.

Replace all your fantasies of lounging in the sun next to a cooler full of Coronas with getting caught in a downpour while trying to read a book on how to better handle seasonal depression.

Now when I think of the beach, it doesn't conjure up images of escape. Instead, it's more like encasement. I don't want to mislead, though: depending on the day, that could actually feel like a good thing. After all, one of the first things you learned on incursions in the service was to find a safe place to set your back. Up here, with the sprawling chaos of pretty much the entire continent stretching out before us, the impenetrable rocky shoreline acts less like a getaway and more like a bulwark. I felt cornered . . . but for someone like me that's actually more relaxing than having everywhere to run.

And, sure, sometimes you need to drive a bit longer to get to places. Nearby towns like Trinidad, with its population of around four hundred, don't always have the most recent movies in theaters (they just got a new one called *Kindergarten Cop,* is it any good? Don't tell me). But there are plenty of bars and I could still hear the ocean. It was my own version of California living and, on my best days, I actually cherished how different it was from the one I thought I was getting. I could look at the rest of California, so jarringly different from this one, and it was a little like being the only single friend in a room full of married couples. Yeah, we had our own problems, but we were also untethered from some massive amounts of bullshit.

It's nice. I thought I'd even grown to love it.

I really thought that.

THANKS TO the incident at the Heron and my inability to stop replaying it, I showed up to work at Quill the next morning with the unshakeable feeling that I'd forgotten something. Parker, our guy at the front gate, did his usual thing of studying my ID in his little booth for a full minute, silent (even though we'd both worked there together eight years at this point), giving me plenty of time to sit in my jeep and stew over what it was that I wasn't remembering.

Lloyd isn't ready to try out his new suit just yet, and we're not scheduled to run any more tests on the dogs, thank God. The visit from Sierra's corporate assholes isn't for another couple of weeks. I have plenty of time before the Harp powers up. What am I forgetting?

It was like I'd undergone brain surgery and someone left a nickel in my skull before sewing me back up. I could feel the thing sitting there, but I couldn't . . . quite . . .

"Date of birth?" Parker finally asked in his flat, impersonal voice.

I gave him the answer automatically. January 12, 19awhileago.

"Middle name?"

I told him I don't have one.

"Cool."

He handed my ID back to me, and, with that part of our day dispensed with, his entire demeanor flipped. He leaned out of his booth window like a gossipy housewife.

"So," he clucked. "The guy got here about five minutes ago and I've got him in holding. We taking bets on this one?"

"The guy? What guy?" Then: the realization. "Ah, *shit!*"

Parker chuckled. "What, did you forget?"

I had a rough night, asshole. "Arrgh! When's Power-Up?"

"If it's regular?" Parker checked his watch. "Like, nineteen minutes?"

Plenty of time, right? On a normal day. But on a newbie day? I growled and tightened my grip on the steering wheel. Parker smirked.

"Better get a move on." He pressed a button and the gate slowly trundled open. As I drove ahead he called after me. "So that's a 'no' on taking bets, right?"

I parked in my spot and walked as quickly as I could to holding.

MAYBE *THIS* was the exact moment my life ended.

Then again, maybe not. I mean, I certainly wasn't impressed.

At the very least, this is when the whistling of approaching bombs could be heard.

THE LITTLE waiting room they built near the front gate isn't shitty at all, and that's by design. If there's a mix-up in clearances, a person could be waiting here for hours while we wait to get them vouched for. The coffee's solid. The sofas are comfortable.

And there you were. Not sitting on any of them. Standing in the middle of the room, ramrod straight. Not at all looking like the god of destruction you'd turn out to be. There was no Shiva here. No eater of worlds. Just a tall, skinny young man on pause. Like a horse gone to sleep.

You saw me. And then you actually saluted.

Internally, I pitched a sigh that could've powered a steam locomotive at least halfway across the country.

"Lieutenant Commander Matt Salem, ma'am."

I stared at you for a moment. Then I said, hopefully with not too much malice: "You wanna try that again?"

I could actually see your thought process, rolling over everything that had just happened, and then—oh! there it is!—realizing your mistake.

"Ah, shit."

"Literally everybody does it."

"I'm just . . . Matt Salem. Hi."

"Feels naked, right? Just saying your name all by itself?"

"I kinda hate it."

We shook hands, like normal people do. I looked at your eyes. Big, eager, underneath long, almost feminine lashes. Physically very attractive, beautiful even, but also kinda cute, in a lost puppy sort of way. But I was someone who definitely couldn't own a dog.

"So, listen, we need to get going—"

"Oh, do you need to see my clearance doc? They sent it to my phone, so I can—"

You pulled your phone out of your pocket and my guts fell down around my ankles. It took all my willpower to not smack it out of your hands.

"Don't ever bring a phone here again."

"I'm . . . sorry, ma'am. I just thought I'd need it to identify mys—"

"Don't ever. Bring that. Again."

"I'm turning it all the way off and I will never bring it here again."

I could tell you meant it. I could tell that if I asked you to throw that phone down on the ground right now and do an Irish jig on its shiny face, you'd do it without even a moment's thought.

I considered it. Instead I told you to leave it here, under one of the couch cushions if that made you feel more secure, to be picked up at the end of the day. I was feeling generous.

"*We* identify *you*," I said. "You'll see what I mean in a minute. Come on, we've gotta hustle."

I watched you pat the couch cushion down and I think I experienced a moment of pity. Bringing a phone was a misstep. I was already dreading what I would have to do if there was another one.

It'd be a shame, I remember thinking. You smelled weirdly good.

I pushed open the door to holding and we made our way back outside to the front door of the lab.

I LIKED to think of Quill Marine, the *real* Quill Marine, as a giant, segmented, man-eating insect, and only the right people are immune to its digestive juices.

Maybe what we actually did there prompted me to look at the

world a little more grotesquely, I don't know. For whatever reason, it was hard for me not to think of being swallowed whole and starting on some sort of peristaltic journey every time I clocked in for a shift.

From the outside, of course, it was nothing special. Before Quill was privatized, back when it was just Quill Naval, they tried to make everything look as unremarkable as possible. If it weren't for the fences and guards it'd almost look like a community college.

The main building itself was a pretty standard office building: there were hallways and rooms (which mostly sat unoccupied), offices, innocuous hanged wall art.

You wouldn't realize that this whole area was actually a mouth.

A guest wouldn't notice, but there were teeth there—guards with weapons behind walls ready to deploy and chew stuff up if it didn't actually belong.

Failing that, though, everyone went through a series of steps to make their way through, and the first step was easy enough: a sign-in counter. A tablet embedded in the wall, tilted at an angle for ease of writing, next to a metal door. I thought of this station as, like, the uvula.

Do giant, segmented, man-eating insects have uvulas?

I don't know. Fuck you. This one does.

I signed in.

Your turn came, and as you leaned over to work the stylus over the screen I thought again how good you smelled and how it'd be a shame to shoot you in the back of the head.

I hoped it didn't come to that. And maybe it was the urgency I was feeling to get through all our checkpoints in time before the Power-Up, but I suddenly realized how tired I was of all this security, of all the steps and secrets and, well, the brutality.

With your sign-in complete, the screen processed for a moment, then the door unlocked with an audible *thunk*. You looked at me. There was no real expression on your face at all, yet somehow I knew you were feeling giddy surprise, and even a smidgen of pride. How could I know that? It's like you were a language I didn't know I could already speak.

"So, that's it? We just walk in?"

"Not even close."

ONCE INSIDE there was a winding hallway and another metal door. This door had a Plexiglas window set into it. On the other side, looking very much like some placid mental patient, was Rosh. His dark, receding hair was messy but his pencil-thin mustache was neat. He stood, wearing coveralls and a patient, prudish smile, holding a tablet like a fig leaf, in front of his beloved machine and, surprise surprise, another metal door.

"Wow, what is that?" you asked as we approached the door. The machine looked like a pharmacy blood pressure machine and an old Atari had somehow successfully reproduced. Except instead of a pressure cuff there was a long, white stick with a chin guard sticking up in front of the screen.

"That would be Rosh and his scanner."

"Oh, but I don't have an issued ID yet—"

"You are the ID." I opened the door. "Hey, Rosh!"

"Hello, person I don't yet recognize!" Rosh chirped—then looked at you, eyes narrowing. "Alongside a person I *genuinely* don't recognize."

"Matt Salem. It's his first day—you get his vitals?"

"One moment, stranger, I shall check." Rosh conferred with the tablet in his hands.

God, I hoped this went quickly. Rosh was easy to adore . . . but usually only in retrospect. Probably out of necessity, Quill Marine employs a lot of weirdos. None of us, with the exception of Trippi, the woman who works reception upstairs and needs to sound as normal as can be, are that socially well adjusted (probably means Trippi's the most damaged of all of us). Rosh was one of our more, let's say, indulgent personalities.

"Behold!" he crooned. "Right here in my system, a Matthew

Salem! Will wonders never cease? But is that really *you*?! Why, you could be anyb—"

"Let's run me through first, please," I said, sitting down at Rosh's machine. "Where are we with the Harp countdown?"

"I wouldn't have the first clue what you're referring to, *stranger*," he barked disapprovingly.

I grunted and settled in, placing my chin on the guard, looking straight into the bottomless black of the concave screen. Rosh intoned the directions as if I hadn't heard them a full seventy million times by now.

"Take a deep, fulfilling inhalation!" I did. "Now, without blinking, very gently *exhaaale*." I did. The scan mulled everything over, made an affirmative little beep, and Rosh threw his hands up in triumph. "Aaaand suddenly I recognize you! Quill Marine Security Chief Dakota Prentiss!"

I'd already stood up, smoothing out my legs. It was a nifty little device, what Rosh liked to call a three-in-one: retinal, facial recognition, and vapor biometric scanner. Most places would probably stop their security protocol there, but we had miles to go. "Now can I get the time?"

"But of course, close friend." Rosh looked at his tablet. "That would be fourteen minutes, nine seconds and descending."

"Fuck. Okay, Salem, get over here."

"They . . . already have my information on this?" you gawked.

"Let's find out, Mr. Second Person I Don't Recognize!" Rosh gestured like a showroom model. "Place your chin here and fill your lungs with rich, nurturing air—"

"Less of the funny stuff, Rosh, I gotta get him there before Power-Up."

You looked at me with questioning eyes—"What's Power-Up?" those eyes were asking—but Rosh patted the back of the scanner and tsked.

"Face front. Breathe in. Don't worry. It doesn't hurt. Much."

He burst into a mad scientist cackle and I wished I'd had it in me to have gotten a nice, quiet job at a coffee shop somewhere.

WE HUSTLED down more hallways.

"We're heading to another checkpoint, aren't we?" you asked. "You're walking like we're not even close." I grunted affirmatively. "Jeez. We didn't have security this intense at Camp Victory and people were actually trying to kill us out there."

"Get comfortable, you gotta do 'em all again coming out the other way, too. The Big Bug pukes you out the way you came in."

"What?"

"Never mind."

"We're . . . we're not doing something involving bugs, are we?" There was some actual panic in your voice. But, again, not on the surface. Subliminal. Private. Readable only by me—I was even finding myself starting to respect your ability to mask it. And, of course, me, ever the gormandizer of unexpected vulnerability: I had to smirk.

"Don't worry."

We rounded a corner.

You chuckled. "I'm starting to think we actually do make weapons or mind control here." And that, for whatever reason, made me laugh too. A small laugh, an in-spite-of-myself laugh.

"Sounds like you've spent some time in town."

"Moved in over the weekend."

"Well. Welcome to the jungle." *What*? "It's easier if you mostly stay home."

"Is that what you do? Stay home?"

"Mostly."

The talk of homes, specifically yours and mine . . . Jesus Christ, why was I suddenly feeling weird? Warm in my gut, icy in my extremities.

Then I remembered: the fight. Feetbreath. The bad kind of tingly. I was still on edge from the night before. Ugh. It was like a hangover. Anxiety had flooded my body, and it was seeking a perch, something to land on.

Get it together, Dak. Shake it off. You'll be in the dark soon.

At last, Lauren's booth appeared. Her image—short, cropped white-blond hair, huge, suspicious eyes—was muted and scratched behind layers of thick, ancient Plexi, but I could tell she was already scowling. She looked as refreshing as an oasis.

Her booth was situated on the left-hand side of the wall. The room itself was narrow and in the center was one chair, one table the size of a foldout card table you might find in some amateur poker player's basement, and, draped over both, the Rhinestone Cowboy.

Sadly, Glen Campbell was nowhere to be found. Just the white, shiny apparatus we named in his honor. The Rhinestone Cowboy looked like a jacket that had been attacked by some scissor-happy fashionista. It was basically two large white cuffs to go over your arms, connected garment-like by a net of white wires and electrodes stretched between them, which connect to the skin. Other wires feeding off that mess ran up and around the table, then down into the wall. There was no machine there on the table, save for the cybernetic jacket. All the information went straight into Lauren's booth.

Oh. And, of course, there was the unlabeled bottle of jelly on the table as well.

Lauren's voice crackled over an aggressively out-of-date speaker (one we could have easily updated, but, no, this was how Lauren wanted it). She was staring at you.

Cccrackle. "My manifest warned me." She spoke in her usual weird, flat monotone.

"Yeah. Newbie. Want me to suit up first?"

Cccrackle. "Please put on the apparatus and apply the electrodes to the appropriate areas."

"On it."

I sat down at the table, unzipping my coveralls a few inches and feeling weirdly energized all of a sudden. Grateful for something active to do, I guess. I had this down to an art, like a street magician walking a coin down her knuckles. Slide the cuffs on, squirt some of the jelly onto my skin where the electrodes attach (nowhere exciting . . . but not too far away from exciting), slap on the electrodes themselves, and then the final piece—

"Am . . . I allowed to ask what that is?"

You almost startled me.

"You wear it like a jacket, see? Then the electrodes here . . . here . . . and here."

"What's that stuff all over it?"

"Some of the best lie-detection tech in the world."

"And . . . ?" You were pointing to the last bit of tech: a black metal plate attached, hinged, to some sort of band. No wires.

"That goes last. Like this." I placed the band around my head and brought the plate down over my face. It was like an opaque welding mask; the idea was total isolation, total blackness. Just you and your truth. Louder, I said, "All dressed up and ready to go!" My voice muffled slightly against the plate.

Cccrackle. "Are you here at this facility with the intent of sabotaging or removing any materials or personnel on site?"

"No."

"Haven't you worked here for, like—" you began.

Cccrackle. "Are you here at this facility with the intent of damaging, removing, or otherwise interfering with Moss, the Harp, or Object E?"

"No," I answered. "Speaking of the Harp, where are we countdown-wise—?"

Cccrackle. "Excuse me, *please.* Assessment is in process."

It sounded personal. I apologized. Lauren was someone who liked her patterns, who used monotony as a snorkel to breathe in this messy world. She didn't take kindly to aberrations.

Whatever it is she did in that booth, she did it, and then:

Cccrackle. "Thank you, Security Chief Prentiss. You are cleared to descend to Hangar Eleven."

"Oh, boy," I deadpanned, already swiftly removing the face-plate, the probes, and rubbing the lubricant into my skin. You were watching. Studying.

"Now it's my turn?"

"Unless you want to stay here all day."

You took my place in front of the table.

"Stick your arms out," I said. I slipped the sleeves on. "And now, we gotta apply the electrodes to the . . . appropriate areas." I felt myself getting warm again. *For fuck's sake, anxiety.* I cleared my throat. "Okay, so I'm gonna unzip your coveralls a little bit. By saying 'yes' you're indicating that you understand that this is for the purpose of assisting you in the process of clearing you for duty."

"You're gonna unzip—"

"I need a verbal 'yes,' please."

"Top-secret facility still complies with harassment liability laws. Fascinating. Sorry. Yes, please."

"Hold still."

I unzipped your coveralls a few inches.

Underneath, I could see the light imprint of ribs beneath your skin. The faint divot where your sternum forked. You were maybe the skinniest man I had ever undressed. Like a tree without leaves. Or a really old painting of Jesus. Your chest was utterly hairless.

"It's not harassment liability," I was saying. "It's for the fraternization policy. You read it before you signed it, right?"

I squeezed some of the tube's contents onto my fingers and massaged it onto your skin. That's when I noticed—

I could see your heartbeat. Faintly. Very, very faintly; I probably wouldn't be able to see it if not for my angle and the stark lighting.

Just under your sternum, the slightest hint of movement.

"Oh, right," you responded. "Yes, I read it."

Lauren crackled over her intercom. *Cccrackle.* "Did you *actually* read it? Everybody signs it but—"

"I did, I promise!" you averred.

Cccrackle. "Quote for me the Quill Marine prohibition against fraternization between security team members."

"Is this part of the test? I don't know if I can quote it *exactly*—"

It would have been easy for you to assume Lauren was being cheeky. She wasn't. There was a reason she was the facility's truth seeker—she went after facts like a goddamn Terminator (although Terminators probably had a better sense of humor). I would have actually been impressed to see her engaging in a dialogue—but for the moment I wasn't really paying attention.

Something about your heartbeat.

It was so very . . . small.

I thought about Feetbreath nursing his broken collarbone (not too far a location from where his own heart beat). I thought of how he screamed when he hit the barroom floor. I thought about Janey, probably trying to help him convalesce and probably taking shit for it . . . probably also getting just enough rewards to keep her coming back, too. I thought about idiocy and fragility and love and death. I thought about pain and the futility of living creatures, fighting for life, only to die one way or another. I thought about it in the context of Moss and the questions we had about him.

All this in an instant, looking at a teeny expanding-contracting shadow just underneath your ribcage.

I realized: if today's training went south and I had to do what I thought I might have to do to you?

I was going to quit.

I'd follow through with the protocol, no doubt; I've done it before, I understood its necessity. But if today ended with you failing your final test, with me having to stop that heartbeat . . . I decided right there to tender my resignation immediately thereafter.

Today very well might be my last day at Quill Marine. The end of this life, as it were.

MEANWHILE, DURING my little revelation (no biggie, just potentially pulling the rug out from my entire existence here), Lauren was reciting the fraternization policy, in full, from memory.

I'm sure you were impressed. And probably a little put off. Lauren had both effects on people. But this particular feat wasn't quite so magnitudinous.

Here, see. I can do it too.

Relationships of the same and opposite genders are prohibited if they compromise or appear to compromise supervisory authority or the chain of command, are or are perceived to be exploitative or coercive in nature, involve or appear to involve the improper use of rank or position for personal gain, or create an actual or clearly predictable adverse impact on discipline, authority, morale, or the ability of command to implement its mission. Such relationships are frequently sexual in nature, but this is not always the case, and is not necessary for this prohibition to apply.

Hold your applause.

Did everyone at Quill Marine Labs have this particular passage memorized? No, probably not. I'm sure Lauren crammed every letter of the rulebook into her rapacious, zealous brain, and I'm sure there were a host of other, er, indoor kids on staff who might have done the same (some maybe accidentally, in that way that only eidetics can). But the majority of us, myself included, were less special and more specialized. To say nothing of the fact that almost every single person working at Quill Marine was the sort who preferred solitude to company—an asset ferreted out and encouraged during our initial interviews, no less—so the fraternization policy actually seemed like one of the most redundant and unnecessary sections of the handbook.

I only have that particular passage memorized simply because, after things started to get bad, I read it a lot. I read it over and over and over again.

"CAN WE get this over with? We've got like ten minutes left."

You nodded. "Sorry. I'm—this is all very impressive. And cool."

Cccrackle. "It's not cool. It's basic. It's a minimal requirement. Are you done, Dak?"

"Yeah, almost." I finished applying all the doodads and gadgets and other technical terms onto you.

"Thanks," you whispered.

"You're on your own next time, so—"

"I paid attention. Don't worry."

I lingered. Just a tiny bit. Purely unintentionally. Just studying you for a moment. Maybe enjoying your scent. Lauren rapped on the glass. We both looked at her.

"Ready," I shouted, way louder than I needed to.

"Lauren! The ink on your wrist—" you said brightly as I stepped away. When she'd given the glass her little knock, the most fleeting impression of a faded fragment of skull and crossed oars had been visible on her arm. "You were in Amphibious Force Recon?"

Impressive that you caught that.

Cccrackle. "I will now ask you a series of questions. Your answers must take the form of either 'yes' or 'no.' No other answers are permitted."

"Got it." You slid the plate down over your face.

Cccrackle. "What did I just say?"

"Sorry."

Cccrackle. "Are you here at this facility with the intent of sabotaging or removing any materials or personnel on site?"

"No."

Cccrackle. "Are you here at this facility with the intent of damaging, removing, or otherwise interfering with Moss, the Harp, or Object E?"

"I don't know what any of those things are."

Cccrackle. "There are only two acceptable ans—"

"Sorry, sorry: No. 'No' is my answer."

Cccrackle. "Please remain still and silent until I tell you otherwise."

We waited. And waited.

And waited.

What the hell was taking so long?

Maybe because he's new, maybe because his heart was beating hard, maybe because I'm never going to actually start this day and life is a meaningless—

Cccrackle. "Thank you, Matt Salem. You are cleared to descend to Hangar Eleven."

You removed the Rhinestone Cowboy—not as fast as me, but with reasonable confidence. You even put it right back the way we found it, recapturing the drape of wires over the chair.

"What do I do with—?" you gestured to the goo still on your skin.

"You can rub it in, it's okay."

We made our way to the elevator. The last, and largest, in a long series of metal doors.

I pressed the button and muttered, "Come on. Fuck. I hope the Gnome is in a good mood."

"The Gnome?"

The elevator chimed and the huge doors spread open, up and down. We stepped in: a massive freight elevator with no buttons, only one destination.

"They don't call it Hangar Eleven because we have eight more checkpoints to go, do they?"

"Next up is blood, stool, and sperm. Hope you're a quick shot."

You looked at me with bulging eyes. "Wait. Seriously?"

OBVIOUSLY, THINGS didn't end there, there were definitely more stops to be made on our way down to oblivion, but by the time I realized I'd already somehow gotten comfortable joking with you, that I'd even somehow looked forward to seeing your response to stimuli, the path was set. Like I said before, I'm a sucker for unintended vulnerability, and you seemed to traffic in the stuff.

In many ways I feel like I've thought about nothing else over the past months. I've analyzed, I've overanalyzed, every step we made to get to where we ended up. I can definitely say for sure that by this point, when we stepped onto that elevator, my life was done.

You felt it too, right? A great *priming*. Or maybe you were just thinking about your new job and all its bizarre protocols. Maybe you weren't thinking of me at all yet.

The elevator lurched and dropped down with a rattling roar.

"I like to think of myself as someone who doesn't scare easily," you said. I don't know if you were saying it to me or to the universe in general, but either way I had nothing to say in response.

We made our way down into the stomach, the literal belly of the beast.

We made our way to meet Moss.

3

WE TRIED to, at least. A few seconds later the elevator lurched to a stop. The anodyne soft light switched over to a poisonous red courtesy of one auxiliary bulb.

"Um . . ." you said, after a deathly quiet moment. "I think we've stopped."

"I know we've stopped. Thanks a lot, Gnome!" I snarled at the walls.

"Is that . . . a problem?"

"Is it a problem for you?"

"I mean, I'm not a claustrophobic . . ."

"No traumatic experiences connected to enclosed spaces?"

"Oh, sure, plenty of those. This one time, I had a guy go septic on me when we were pinned down for an entire week in—"

"No proper names," I snapped.

"Right. Sorry. But, no, no, I'm okay," you said firmly. "I would just think anybody is concerned when . . . this happens."

We stood in silence.

I knew the drill. I knew not to betray any nervous energy. We were being watched. But holy shit did I want to pace, twitch, move around, anything to expel some of the anxious energy building up. The red light was making it worse. Of course it was, that was its job.

Finally, I had to say something.

"I had something similar on my second tour."

You looked at me, curious for more. I looked straight ahead, not giving you an in. I yelled to the metal around us. "If it makes any difference, Gnomie, he's a new fish and I'm trying to get him there before Power-Up!"

"Are you . . . talking to . . . ?"

"The Gnome. Works upstairs. His job's to stop people randomly, do redundant background checks, study their reactions."

"Us."

"Yup."

"Even though we *just* went through all of—"

"Yup. If they keep us here when the Harp starts up, though, I swear to God . . ." *We're going to get real intimate,* is how part of my mind wanted to complete that thought. The part that's a real asshole.

"How many background checks do they need to run?" you were asking. "Isn't it always the same stuff?"

"They try different methods. Different data-dives. Swap the variables in and out. Sometimes they find something new. It *has* happened."

Once, about four years ago, we had a contractor make it almost all the way through. By all accounts he was a nice guy, seemed steady enough (Lauren's predecessor would later insist his polygraph showed signs of stress he should have picked up on). They ran one last background scan in the elevator and noticed his brother-in-law had written him a pretty sizeable check within the past month . . . despite the fact that previous scans had shown that same brother-in-law to have been deceased for about two and a half years. A quick investigation into the check revealed the source of the funds to be a bank in Macau commonly used for clandestine transactions. Once the dots were connected, it appeared our new friend was perhaps not so much on the up and/or up. That contractor was vomited back up by the Big Bug in a box.

"And we've gotta do all this again on the way out?"

I nodded.

"Jeez. What's it like if you ever need to get out of this place in a hurry?"

"Eminently frustrating."

I turned and stole a glance at you. On the surface, at least, it seemed like you were keeping your cool handily, scared or not. In fact, in the red light, your face had taken on an older, stonier look. Handsome, in a mature kind of way.

"How old are you?" I asked.

"Thirty."

"Jesus. I remember thirty."

You laughed. "You can't be that much older than thirty."

"Older enough."

You laughed again, quieter, dismissing.

I was getting to know the elevator door in front of me intimately. It was the only thing I was willing to look at now.

One of us needs to say something.

I actually got two words out of my mouth ("Have you—") but then you started in with:

"Okay. So. I'm former SEAL Team Six. You knew that, right?" I did. "And Laura was Force Recon—"

"Lauren."

"Lauren, right." You nodded. "So . . . what were you, Security Chief Dakota Prentiss?"

At this point, I figured we were looking at one of two situations: either we were about to be co-workers, in which case it couldn't hurt to know a little bit about each other (and I did already knew a fair amount about you), or . . . you wouldn't be leaving this facility with any memories to spill or mouth with which to spill them. So, fuck it.

"I'm Rangers," I said. "Seventy-fifth."

Your eyes went wide. "Jesus! Those guys . . ."

"Yeah, we got around."

"So, they're not just pulling from one branch here. They're looking at everybody."

"Five bucks says right now the Gnome's writing, 'Too inquisitive—problematic?'"

But you were undeterred: "So, what do we all have in common?" You sounded genuine, really trying to puzzle things out.

"You signed paperwork, right? For this gig?" I offered back.

You chuckled. "More papers than I've ever seen in my life."

I wasn't kidding. "Binding you. Locking you in for two decades to something *they wouldn't even let you see before you signed.*"

"Right . . ." Your wheels spinning.

"What sorta person would do that kind of thing?"

I could see you were answering the question in your head. In the red-soaked light. The sort of person who would do such a thing—someone with literally nothing to lose, with no nagging connections, with nowhere to go, perhaps due to circumstances beyond their control or perhaps, after combat, after family life, after whatever monster mask their own particular traumas were hiding behind, because they just didn't feel a connection to anything the rest of society had to offer. The sort of person who wanders through this messy, headless quotidian life, after having dined at the table of order, of mission, of purpose, and now finds themselves like someone with a low-grade migraine, ever suffering but only themselves aware of it. Someone no longer of this world, as it were.

Someone like you.

Someone like me.

Quill Marine Labs didn't hire local. But they hired family.

"I think I know the type," you said.

With cosmically on-the-nose timing, the lights restored and the elevator began its graceful descent again. I breathed an actual sigh of relief. I may have even said, "Fucking finally." It's been known to happen.

"Well, okay!" you said. "So, I guess, if we're still going down, that means I passed, right?"

"You can't pass or fail until you've been through the last part."

"And you're not going to tell me what that last part is, are you?"

"Nope. But I'll tell you where it is."

"Where?"

"The other end."

"The other end of what?"

The elevator plied to our destination and the doors smoothly spread apart.

"The other end of this," I said as the opening doors revealed Hangar Eleven in all its dizzying immensity.

I WASN'T always Security Chief Dakota Prentiss. Once I was green Quill Marine Labs Trainee Ex-Ranger Dakota Prentiss. My first day on the job I was met in holding by an officious little military hausfrau named Magnus Russell. His was very much the antithesis of the patient, understanding, downright charming manner I was extending toward you. He had a tight, humorless mouth beneath a massive push-broom mustache that was never trimmed and always resembled a thatched hut, and he was forever waiting to pounce on even the slightest betrayal of anything beyond the most stoic military impassivity.

That's my fancy way of saying the dude was an uptight dick. I needed one question repeated during my polygraph and he actually took out a pen and pad of paper and wrote the transgression down. *He fucking wrote it down.* I half expected him to tear it off and hand it to me like a parking violation.

Anyway. Right before the elevator doors opened, he turned to me and said, "I won't hold it against you if you gasp."

Any other circumstance that would've been about the creepiest thing I'd ever heard in an elevator. When the elevator doors opened, I didn't gasp—I don't think there's an exact word for the tight, surprised exhalation I let out, but at least I didn't gasp.

THE GENERAL murmuring of the scientists and other personnel were a constant in Hangar Eleven, so when you murmured, "Holy shit" as we stepped out of the elevator, it was like you fit right in.

It's a lot. I commiserated (though I kept my mouth shut, because, old habits). After what seems like hours and hours, snaking our way down The Big Bug's cramped and crimped upper digestive tract, through hallways and tiny rooms, to be suddenly deposited directly onto the floor of some wide open warehouse on steroids? It's disorienting, to say the least. But, like all things, you get used to it. By the second or third shift, the juxtaposition becomes almost mundane. Claustrophobic, even.

Don't get me wrong. Hangar Eleven is huge. But it seems even more so the first time you see it. Like stepping out of a suitcase onto the surface of the moon.

"How far does it . . ." you were asking, awed, hushed.

"Equivalent to one city block. Welcome to Hangar Eleven."

Much like a city block, there were all sorts of little businesses and boutiques peppered throughout. In this case, rather than storefronts, there were booths and stations, regularly dotting the floor. Some of them were small, freestanding computer desks with one or two people huddled around them. Others were cordoned off, or shielded by freestanding sheds. It was kinda like a science fair in a high school gym, if the gym in question needed to be big enough to house a few jumbo jets and if half of the student body were automatic weapon–sporting ex-military.

Unlike a high school gym—maybe more like a study hall, but only theoretically, not like any study hall I've ever actually seen—it was relatively quiet. Just that ever-present murmuring of problem solving, of serious investigation. Professionalism hard at work.

"You're slipping, Chief!"

It was certainly quiet enough that we could hear Patty's coarse voice and hard-soled boots while she was still what seemed like light years away. For security, she sure wasn't concerned with remaining covert.

"Morning, Patty."

"Forgot it was New Fish Day?"

"Repressed, more like. What's the clock?"

"Four minutes. Gnome really put you through it, huh?"

"We gotta get that guy laid."

"Ugh. Not it."

I turned to you. "This is Deputy Security Chief Patricia Garber. You call her Patty and you basically live or die by her opinion, got it?"

To continue the high school metaphor, Patty looked about as unassuming as a suburban gym coach, coming in at around 5′5″ and always sporting a ponytail that bounced and bobbed with every move she made. But she was all muscle. More than that, she'd had more combat training than all but, like, a hundred people in this hemisphere. She was gonna make me proud one day.

You held your hand out. "Hi, I'm M—"

She stopped you with a sneer like a slap. "You're nobody to me 'til you do the last thing, bucko." Then she turned to me. "Wanna pass him off?"

I shrugged, playing blasé. I might have dreaded the final test's results, but at this point I felt like I had to know for myself. "Ehhh," I said.

Thankfully, that was enough for Patty. "Sure," she agreed. "I mean, once you've done the elevator with somebody . . ." and she knit her fingers together to show the strength of my bond with my new trainee.

"So, I'm just gonna assume," you said, watching our little repartee with a clinical suspicion born of being sent on dangerous missions by inscrutable commanders, "the last thing, the last test is . . . inside that?"

You were nodding toward the Tent.

WHAT IS it about the military—or the corporate privatized paramilitary in this case—that makes us love giving short, punchy names to things? I'm sure some of it is the precision, but mostly I think it's just because we know everything sounds so much cooler in code.

Let's describe the room a little more.

So, it's big, we've covered that. And, while there are all sorts of stations scattered around the floor, the predominant feeling is still of empty space. It's a cavernous, echo-y place. Sometimes, depending on what lights are on, a person can lose sight of the ceiling, and it feels as if you're on the surface of some sterile desert forever shrouded in night (even though we're actually some three hundred meters under the surface of the Earth, where worms would be flying higher than condors).

The desert analogy isn't accidental, either—we call the general area where all the stations live "The Bazaar," for its resemblance to an open air market. Instead of hawking baubles, though, top scientific minds are conducting experiments on a dizzying array of subjects—biologists, physicists, quantum theorists. The sheer amount of concentrated genius gave the air a weirdly metallic smell (we also had strict hygiene policies in place, because that's not always otherwise a priority for minds like those). There were even a few regular old marine biologists on staff, working on various low-level side projects as well as more specialized ones, and providing mooks like me with all sorts of useful information about, yup, the noble sea urchin, phytoplankton, et cetera.

Even though it's easy to forget once you're in the middle of it, there are walls to Hangar Eleven. Coming out of the elevator, directly to your left, is a door and a whole lot of reinforced Plexi (in case something blows up, I guess) looking into Conference Hall, or the Hall, for short. This is where we hold our meetings and feel all important. It looks like a pretty conventional meeting room—table, chairs, a few monitors, a jug of water, an ever-increasing collection of dead pens put back in holders when they should have been thrown out—and inside this room is another door leading farther into a more private meeting area.

Going past the Hall, down that wall is another elevator with a much shorter track than the tracheal one we came down. This elevator takes you up a few dozen yards to the area designated Bird's Eye: the observation deck and control room overlooking the entire Hangar. Bird's Eye looms above the proceedings, watching all while being far enough away to not really affect anything. I'll let you make your own jokes about religion here.

Beyond that elevator are the bathrooms (we're only human), a small break room and kitchen (humans gotta snack), and then, all the way down, tucked into the corner, there's one more door. This one leads into an area we call "The Slammer." You don't want to end up there.

This is all just one part of Hangar Eleven.

To the right of the main elevator, beyond the Bazaar and around a slight bend so it's not directly in your line of sight when you first enter the Hangar, is an enormous wall of fairly opaque plastic sheeting.

The Tent.

YOU WERE nodding toward the Tent.

"No," I said. "That's the second to last test. The last is *inside* the thing inside the Tent." I let that hang and turned back to Patty. "Four minutes?" She nodded, her ponytail flopping about like a half-dead inflatable eye-catcher outside a car dealership. I looked at you. "Start walking. I'm right behind you."

With a smart nod that might as well have been a salute, you headed off in that direction. Once you were out of earshot, I spoke low to Patty.

"I didn't get to stop by Lockup."

"You need a sidearm?"

"Please."

She handed me a weapon. A lightweight FN Five-SeveN. I was able to slip it into my pocket and barely feel it.

"Usual deal with Turndown Service?" Patty asked.

I nodded. "Have 'em on hold but don't give them the go unless I say."

"Go catch the Power-Up. I'll see you on the other side."

Amazing how the vibe can change so quickly, isn't it? I was suddenly very tired. A low, ominous hum began to churn in my ears.

I caught up with you easily, our shoes clicking resoundingly as we moved. The murmuring of the Bazaar suddenly felt very

far away. I don't know if you really understood it or not—my suspicion is you did—once we walked through that plastic sheeting,
there was no going back.

We entered the Tent.

I LET you walk in first, ahead of me. I didn't care about seeing
your face—they'd get that on the cameras and I could watch
that later if I wanted to. I was more interested in your full-body
response.

After all, it's not like you could miss it when you walked in.

True story: the first time I saw it, this two-and-a-half-meter-
tall dark, dull oval, cragged with dents and scrapes, my immediate thought was, "Holy shit, that's the biggest walnut I've ever
seen."

It was not, in fact, a walnut.

YOU DIDN'T stop walking right away. You slowed down . . . then
eventually stood still.

Your head seemed to rise independent of your neck, like a
balloon given a little slack. But beyond that, there was no noticeable physical reaction. In fact, there was the conspicuous lack of
reaction.

Again I found myself awash with anxiety, hoping you passed
your final test. I had been starting to feel confident, which brought
with it all new worries. What if I'm misreading you? What if I'm
wrong?

This very well could be the last time you do this, Dakota.

Would you shut the fuck up and concentrate, please?

*I'm just saying, he could be having a mental breakdown right now,
he could be not moving because his mind has—*

"So I'm guessing," you said, ". . . Object E." Your voice was
flat.

"Keep walking," I told you. I wanted to see if you were still
with me. "Straight at it."

You started walking again, musing quietly as you did so.

"Now if that was a thing we were building . . ."

"Head around to the side," I instructed.

Your flat, emotionless analysis continued, ". . . it wouldn't look like it had been dragged across a canyon. It would look new."

We stopped, near a long, thin vertical scar in the broadside of the giant walnut.

"Which means," you went on, "we didn't build it. We . . . found it."

I nodded. "Right here, in fact. Built this place around it. Eleven years ago, the night it crash-landed. Would've been Arthur Quill Naval base then. Didn't privatize until two years later."

"And nobody . . . noticed it?"

"A lot of people noticed it. Made a pretty loud noise when it hit ground."

"And everyone who noticed it . . ." You were reaching your hand out toward it. Toward the hull.

"Works for us now. Or is living pretty good somewhere quiet." *In many cases, somewhere very, very quiet,* I didn't say. "You can touch it."

You did. It was rough to the touch, like the hide of an elephant. Similarly, if you pressed on it, you'd have found that it actually gave a little. It was lacking the structural rigidity of metal, yet it was unmistakably solid and formidable. Your brain would have conjured up all sorts of comparisons—(*it's like foam it's like flesh it's like wood it's like lava*)—but it's like using an English letter to describe a character in Cyrillic or Mandarin, finding superficial similarities between two things uniquely foreign to each other. Uniquely alien.

"Okay," you muttered to yourself. "I'm passing the test, I'm passing the test, see how I'm passing the test—"

"Hey." I put my hand gently on your shoulder. "The crack down the side?"

You looked. It was faint, a slim darkening of the already dark exterior.

"It doesn't look like it at first," I went on, "but if you turn sideways you can fit in."

"And that's what we're going to do?"

"That's what we're going to do."

This time I went first.

YOU'RE NEVER aware of the most basic ambient noises until they're gone. I mean the really subtle ones—the room tones, the sound of air just *sitting* against the walls.

When we entered the ship, those sounds . . . changed.

There was still ambient noise, but it was like the barely perceptible echoes of the world were turned off. Things didn't reverberate the way they usually did. Noise became purely information, no longer experiential.

And, of course, the other thing that changed: the light.

The entryway was tight enough that, as we squeezed our way through, the world went momentarily dark. But once we were standing fully inside, the darkness almost inverted. There was no sense of light bleed from the outside, no sense that there was anything within the ship but deep and total darkness, especially considering there were no windows of any kind, but still the darkness took on different colors and textures. Shadows separated themselves from shadows, except . . . there were no shadows. There were a few clip lights we set up, hanging from various amenable surfaces inside, but the light, like the sound, behaved differently than usual. The way light does in mist, only there was no mist—rather than spreading throughout the room, the yellow light seemed contained to relatively small pools.

Yet still we could see each other. The interior of Object E glowed, an almost incomprehensible blue-green pulse that rendered everything visible. The spectral equivalent of a low hum. All around us.

"So this is the cockpit," I said, in the weirdly dry atmosphere. "Can you see okay?"

"Yeah, it's not so—" But before the last word was out of your mouth, you saw the main attraction.

HOW TO describe Moss?

I guess . . . picture Danny DeVito.

That's 100 percent *not* what Moss looks like—quite the opposite, in fact—but you know how your mind went straight to an image of the great Danny DeVito, unquestionably himself no matter what role or costume he might be wearing? He's downright archetypal, right?

Now picture an alien.

Moss is that alien. The archetype. You might be picturing some slightly different variations, a different costume if you will, but the conceptual alien at the center is most likely a lot more accurate than you'd think.

I could have just as easily told you to picture something or someone else, by the way, like a pirate or a cowboy. I just chose Danny DeVito because fuck you, I like Danny DeVito.

But it's amazing how much Moss looks like your standard alien from a billion drunken abduction stories. About seven feet tall, gray-ish pale body, huge head, huge eyes.

Whenever some idiot claims he got probed, the sketch artist always ends up with something that looks like Moss.

Except . . .

"WHAT'S THAT on him? On his skin?"

The creature, the pilot, the extraterrestrial we had named Moss, was sitting in a chair in front of a long-dead console that was barely more than a blank monitor and two small trackball-type objects installed into an otherwise empty dashboard made of the same dark, cragged material as the outside of the ship. Everything about the picture seemed of a piece—the alien and the ship clearly tailored for his passage . . . but there was one additional element that was just a little jarring in its unexpectedness.

Moss's namesake: a thin layer of what looked like regular old tree moss covering his skin, from about clavicle to navel (to borrow human terms), and wrapping around the sides of his torso. The green substance was so spread out, so patchy, that it didn't in any way obscure the shape of his body. The milky granite hue of his skin was visible straight through it.

"Is he dead?"

"We don't know how he defines that."

"Has he moved, since . . ."

"Nope."

"Is there a heartbeat, or some kind of equivalent of a—"

"Not for eleven years."

"So that stuff growing on him . . ."

"The moss."

"How is *that* still alive?"

I kept a hand on the gun in my pocket. This is the point where it has been known to start to go wrong.

"Touch him," I said. "Not on the moss part, but anywhere else."

"Really?"

"Really."

You reached out, slow and steady, and touched Moss just above the shoulder, at the crook of his neck. Your hand flinched for the briefest of seconds and then spread over his skin.

"Whoa! He's . . . *warm.*" My heart lifted a little—most people recoiled when they touched him; made a sound, a grunt, a gulp, like they were touching something impure. You sounded like you were receiving a gift. You kept your hand on him and looked back at me. "He hasn't moved in eleven years . . . but he's *warm* . . . ?"

Before I could say anything, the noise began.

"Right on time," I said.

If it's not too fine a point, it was an unearthly hum—or several hums, all at different pitches, as if someone hit a hammer against several strings.

You were understandably concerned.

"Okay—is that—is that—"

The sound began to grow in amplitude.

"It's called the Harp," I said. Another name, another code.

"It's a harp?" Already raising your voice to talk over the noise.

"No. It just looks like one. They think it's the engine, or part of the engine. We're in the cockpit right now—see that door-looking thing over there?"

The noise got louder.

"Yeah."

"Behind that door is the engine room. It's basically a two-chamber ship."

The noise got louder.

"Can I see it?"

"That noise you're hearing? That's Power-Up. You do not wanna be in that room with the Harp when it's powering up. Trust me."

"I do. Why is it powering up?"

"We don't know. About every hundred hours or so, we think it tries to turn on," I explained, my hand in my pocket, wrapped around my sidearm, releasing the safety.

"You think?" you asked.

The noise got louder.

I was practically shouting by this point. And still, not an echo bounced off a wall. "We don't know anything. I've been here eight years. Moss has been here eleven. And it's all still guesses. Better get ready."

The noise got louder.

"Get ready for what?"

"For this."

The Harp reached crescendo and then, as if it breached some unknown barrier, it didn't so much cut out or lower in volume—rather, it *spread* itself evenly across the room. The yellow clip lights blinked out. The heavy air felt somehow even heavier.

We stood there, breathing.

"When the Harp spins all the way up, it kills everything in

Quill Marine for about thirty seconds. Power, surveillance, everything. Right now the entire building's completely dark, except . . ."

The blue-green glow persisted. I could see every contour of your face. Were you always this handsome? And I realized I'd never noticed . . . light and sound in this place were always muted . . . but that smell of you, your scent, intensified.

Ask him, Dak, go ahead. It's time.

"Holy Jesus Christ . . ." you were whispering.

"Just us, and him."

Moss, as always, sat there. Silent. Still.

"You look . . . how can I see you?" You were staring at my face with giddy, glistening eyes.

"We don't know."

"Where does that light come from?" A rhetorical question, asked with awe.

"We don't know."

"There are no shadows."

"I know." *Ask him, Dak. You have to ask.* "So, New Fish. Matt Salem. What are you thinking?"

I remembered shaking your hand and looking into your eyes just a short while ago. Now, in the darkness, I believed I could see every particle of you.

those eyelashes

I thought again of how this moment would define both our lives going forward. I felt a prickling numbness spread across me. *The bad kind of tingly.* Everything depended on how you answered the question. My hand stayed in my pocket. I was suddenly aware that I was holding my breath.

"I'm thinking . . ." you began, then looked into my eyes, "this is the job." You said it with the slightest smile, in that new language I could read. Your voice was clear, your intent even clearer.

And I started breathing again.

thank you

This had been your chance to freak out, to ask one question

too many, to have a panic attack, to throw up, to start to cry, to start to laugh hysterically—any number of disqualifying reactions we've encountered before at this moment. My hand came out of my coveralls, empty of the thing that would have

an image of you hugging your knees, facing the floor, while I stood above you

ended your life and, effectively, ended mine, as well. But that didn't have to happen.

"Guess what," I sighed, inching toward you, with as close to a shrug as I could muster. "You passed."

And then.

I guess we'll never know if it was you who initiated it, or me. It could have been mutual. That's actually a nice idea—especially in light of what happened later.

Whatever it was, our lips were together.

Your tongue insistent against mine.

My hands desperate against the back of your head, running through your hair. Yours on my lower back, pulling me closer.

Like the spaceship had breached and we were in dead space, desperately siphoning oxygen from the other.

Or, no, in the blue-green glow, we were underwater.

Or, no.

Like.

Fuck it. Words fail. The depth of that hunger was beyond words.

It was (*needneedneed*)

It was (*itchitchitch*)

It was (*thankyouthankyouthankyou*)

Oh, you fucking marvelous, horrible asshole.

It was paradise.

IT WAS a huge fucking mistake. Momentous, even. I'd say life-ending but, well, we've already established I was dead by this point. We both were. Seconds into the kiss, we both knew it.

"Oh, fuck," I gasped. "Shit."

"I'm . . ."

"No, I'm . . ."

"Jesus."

"This didn't happen."

"You're right."

"Because . . ."

"This never happened."

"This never happened."

The noise from the Harp was gone. The silence felt lighter. The clip lights all popped back on.

So did a speaker. We'd patched one through into the ship years ago, before my time. Patty's voice came in loud and proud.

"So? What's the verdict? Do we shoot him or not?"

OF COURSE, what happened to me next is what happens to all dead things.

4

THE NEXT step: the great corporeal unknitting. Everything starts falling apart. It might look normal for a little while but under the surface all sorts of little fuckers are at work eating, disassembling, breaking things down. That's how I knew I was dead well before that kiss. Something had already irreparably eroded. It's the only way what happened could have happened. Now everything else was following suit.

The fun thing is that, as the decomposition sets in, all sorts of different versions of the deceased are revealed. A real peeling-of-the-onion thing, with the added joy of each layer being dead or dying aspects of the person you used to be.

The night we kissed I took a scalding hot shower.

I don't believe in cold showers. I like my showers to be hot. I like my food to be spicy. What's the point of showers if they're not hot and food if it's not spicy? Anything good should make you suffer a little bit, right?

I stood in that shower until my skin itched from heat rash. I kept increasing the heat of the water until I couldn't stand it.

I had a plan, though. There was no real reason why we ever needed to interact again. I couldn't really *avoid* you, but I could limit the time I spent with you. I had my job to think about, my place, my lifestyle—hell, I had a literal rulebook to follow. I also knew what happened when we forcibly let employees go. None of this was worth it, not even in the slightest.

Practical Dak had just been revealed by the decomposition process.

PRACTICAL DAK lasted about two weeks before turning completely into mulch. In her defense, shit started to happen really fast to hasten the process. But for a few days, everything seemed perfectly doable.

I'd eat my omelet at the Seaview, alone. I'd show up and clock in, alone. I'd maybe shoot the shit with Patty, do my job, and then leave, alone. All practical. All good.

But, of course, Practical Dak needed rest if she was to operate optimally. So every now and then another Dak would take the wheel. Sometimes it was Drunk Dak, who found herself ordering another round—just one more, to keep her from listening to the songs on the jukebox too closely. Sometimes it was another Dak, an angry, adamant one who found herself staring, glaring at people, hoping they'd start something, hoping they'd give her an excuse. Sometimes it was Endorphin Dak, the one who kept searching for a more sustainable high, straining, exercising, even wearing down the devices she kept by the bedside.

But Practical Dak was in charge for the most part. She was the most resistant to the dissolution tugging at the seams of the Everydak.

Practical Dak was hiding some secrets. Practical Dak was miserable. But you can maintain miserable. Hell, in retrospect, these wound up being the halcyon days.

Then the turbulence started.

WANNA KNOW how much I'd changed already? Halfway through that first week, three days after that kiss, I was sitting through an episode of the Lloyd and Andy Show, which normally would have made me want to gouge out my own eyes and stuff them inside my ears, and instead found myself grateful for the distraction. They were helping me not to think about what I'd done in my car the night before.

We were all inside the front chamber of the ship—the cockpit, which, once you got more than three or four people in there, began to teeter on the edge of uncomfortably cramped.

Guardshift is every thirty minutes. Two sentries at a post. One sentry moves to the next site on the location in the rotation, the other remains. It reduces complacency, raises alertness, and ensures that no two sentries spend too much time together. No one's exempt, not even me. One can expect, over the course of the day, to be stationed everywhere for a little while: up in Bird's Eye, inside Object E, various posts upstairs.

But it's time we talk about Lloyd.

We passed right by him your first day on the floor and I didn't point him out. I figured you'd get to know him all too well soon enough.

As usual, Lloyd had arrived late today. Lloyd tended to be late for things—as well as a cause of lateness in others.

"He is supposed to be here, right?" Andy, one of the youngest members of my security team, all buzz cut, freckles, and enormous ears, kept panting as the two of us stationed ourselves in the cockpit. Andy loved Lloyd. It made them one of my very least favorite combinations of personnel . . . under normal circumstances.

Eventually, we heard the signature call from outside the entry fissure.

"Class is in session!"

Andy practically vibrated as Lloyd squeezed his way into the ship. He had his regular bag, full of measuring devices and doodads . . . and also what looked like a space suit and fishbowl helmet draped over his arms. I was honestly impressed he made himself fit.

"Lloyd, my man!" Andy exclaimed.

"Andy." I had to play my part as the disciplinarian.

"Andy! Dak! Morning to you both!" Lloyd carefully laid the suit and helmet down before pulling out his usual equipment from his shoulder bag. He was a birdlike man with hair the color of television static. That hair always seemed to be in a new position every time you looked at it—it was as amorphous as a lava lamp. His face was composed entirely of sharp angles, and his nose and Adam's apple were locked in an eternal competition between which could jut out more prominently. On first glance, one might mistake his hollow cheeks, his bulging eyes, as signs of sickliness, but there was no mistaking the perpetual sparkle behind his face. This was a guy who got a real kick out of being alive.

"Wait—Lloyd—is that—?" If Andy weren't ex-military like the rest of my team, he would have been hopping up and down.

Lloyd played dumb. "Gosh, this is just my measuring equipment, Andrew, I don't know why you're so excited—"

"No, no! The—" Andy gestured at the suit on the floor.

"Calm down, Andy," I grumbled.

"Is that the *suit*?"

Lloyd gasped. "Oh, this old thing? Could be."

"Holy crap!"

I wished I shared Andy's enthusiasm. "The suit" filled me with dread. Today was my day to practice helping Lloyd into and out of this space suit–looking ensemble and then to see how it maneuvered within the tight accommodations of the ship. Lloyd had made a few new design tweaks—I could already notice a much slimmer overall cut, as well as what appeared to be knobs on the breast, arms, and neck—and he was still insisting that tomorrow the big test could go as planned. Not to put too fine a point on it, I was hoping his little dog-and-pony today would be as unsuccessful as the last time he tried to move around Object E and had gotten so awkwardly tangled up in his own legs he'd fallen right onto his space-suited ass. Then, at the very least, I could convince him not to be the guinea pig when we did it for real. Stern as we tried to be, technically we were outranked by the science personnel and I couldn't just issue the order.

Lloyd brandished his meters. "Moss measurements first, Andy. No dessert before dinner."

"Aw, man, but it's almost Guardshiiiiiift—"

"Lloyd," I nodded to him, firm and even. "Moss measurements."

Lloyd looked at Andy as if to say, "You heard the chief," and set to work.

Every day, with a few exceptions, this was part of Lloyd's two-part routine: he'd come in with his finely calibrated machines—laser levels, microanalytic graphing cameras, a spectrograph, a tablet to document and tabulate—set them up around Moss, and let them run their scans. The second part of his routine was conversation.

"Now, obviously, obviously, there's no reason we can't have a little fun while we work, is there?" he asked as he set everything up.

"Wanna quiz me?" Andy bounced back.

Work here on the security team long enough and you learn the exact interaction setting you wanna hit when you're on Object E detail with one of the various specialists. Some need you to not look at them. Some are blessedly low maintenance. Mostly, though, the rules you start to suss out have to do with how you interact with the scientists, not how the scientists interact with you. The other xenobiologists and xenobotanists and physicists and mathematicians just take our word for it when we say, "Treat us like furniture." But Lloyd . . .

Lloyd wanted to interact.

Lloyd missed the lecture hall.

Lloyd thought the people with the automatic weapons and the stone faces were actually undergrads all lobbying to be his next TA.

He wasn't so wrong about Andy. Andy was one of the youngest members of the security team. He'd been working with us for about five months now. He was good—ex-Marine with crazy fast reflexes and a keen desire to help however he could. When Andy had first met Moss, he had leaned all the way in to smell him. Not in a creepy way (not a *purposefully* creepy way, at least), but he was just so curious he needed all the information he could get. "It looks a little like the kudzu root from back home!" he'd explained. "I just wondered if it smelled the same." I think he fancied himself a scientist in the making, were it not for the fact that he was actually kind of dumb. And I don't mean that as a judgment; he knew he was dumb—dumbness can actually work well in a scientific setting. Gives the not-dumb people someone to effectively bounce off of.

"All right," Lloyd muttered, "measurements running. Let's have a pop quiz!"

"Yes!"

"What is . . . the Harp?" Lloyd gestured at the closed door to the other chamber of the ship.

Andy fired back like a soldier at drill. "The Harp is the power-source of Object E."

Lloyd made a high whining noise. "Not quiiiiiiite—"

"No, no, no, wait!" Andy put a hand to his forehead, summoning the more proper response. "Our, our best *theory* is that the Harp is the power-source of Object E!"

"There you go!" Lloyd clapped.

The thing is, you couldn't just flat out ignore Lloyd. We tried going full Buckingham Palace on him and it creeped him out; he couldn't forget we were there. You had to learn to answer Lloyd's questions once every, let's say, seven minutes. Just often enough to reassure him that he's the kind of stand-up guy who's nice to janitors, but not often enough to be buddies.

"Now," he continued, "we know the Harp isn't connected by any hard cable to Object E's engines—or what we *think* are Object E's engines—so what data is there in support of the idea that the Harp is Object E's power-source?"

"Um. Okay. In support. In *support,* the main thing I'd say is . . . it steals energy from stuff around it to power the engines."

"Well, all right, 'steals' is—obviously I would prefer value-neutral terminology, but—"

"It *draws* energy from stuff around it."

Andy did not have the rules of interacting with Lloyd down at all. Or he didn't care to observe them. Andy answered everything. Andy probably talked to cab drivers the whole way.

Don't think about driving, Dak. Don't think about last night.

I was not thinking about last night. I was listening to the Lloyd and Andy Show.

"Excellent adjustment, Andy." Lloyd sounded like he might even cry with pride. "What stuff?"

Nothing happened last night. I'm not thinking about driving.

"Well, like during Power-Up it drains all the electricity from the whole base for a couple minutes."

"And if it can *draw* energy out without a hard cable . . ."

"Maybe it can, like, *give* energy, too?"

"Precisely! Bravo, Andy!"

I'd talked to Andy about this. Patty'd talked to him about it— at a certain point we knew we might have to have a talk among ourselves. At a certain point, Andy's eagerness to indulge in distracting dialogue might become an actual liability. He was a good kid who just wanted to follow orders, and since, again, at Quill Marine the scientists do outrank us, it was difficult for him to not do whatever they want, but still. For the time being, though, the red flags stayed at about half staff. Just high enough to flick us in the face depending on the breeze.

The pop quiz continued while Lloyd began to smooth out the suit on the floor.

"And Power-Up happens how often?"

Andy had this answer down pat; we all did. "Almost every hundred hours, but not always exactly."

"And *why*?"

Ooo. A curveball. Andy's mouth popped open to answer before his brain realized he had none.

"Um . . . do we know?"

"Good question! See, that's thinking like a scientist, Andrew! No, we do not know. We have no idea! Running theory is the Harp is attempting to restore full capacity, perhaps in preparation for a takeoff, but again: no observable data to support that. Now . . . where else?"

"Where else . . . ?"

"From where else does the Harp draw energy?"

"Oh! Right! From people!"

"From people *how*?"

"I mean, not as long as that door's closed, if the door's closed it just steals—it just *draws* power."

"But if it's open?"

"It . . . draws power from people."

"Draws power from people h—"

He was going to ask "how?" in his professorially prompting way, but then Lloyd's measuring device chimed dully in the thick, sound-deadening atmosphere. It had completed its assessment. Lloyd absently leaned over to check the results and his face fell.

"Oh."

And here was another reason why you shouldn't be friendly with Lloyd: that look on his face right now.

When I first started working here, the moss covering Moss wasn't full and lush by any stretch, but it *was* noticeably denser. It covered roughly the same area of the alien's body but the patchiness was far less apparent. Day to day it wasn't always easy to notice the change, but over any given period of time the conclusion was undeniable: the moss was receding. Since day one, when our study of the big gray guy began. As for what that meant, there was no firm consensus, but we all had a gut instinct. Moss's bizarre body warmth kept us from assuming (and acting like) he was dead, or fully dead if that's a thing with his species, but the thinner and smaller the green coverage on his skin became, the more it began to feel like we were watching something slowly turning off. Decomposing. It was the only change we could register and it was not pointing in a promising direction.

Lloyd measured the moss every day, and every day it got a tiny bit smaller. Every day it made Lloyd flinch in disappointment and fear. He knew: if the moss eventually receded too much, the folks in D.C. who own our fair establishment might give Quill an order Lloyd wouldn't like, be it complete dissection or, worse (and far more likely given Sierra's perpetual profit motives), licensing the rights to showcase Moss to the highest bidder and *then* dissection. And if it seems odd a xenobiologist would be hesitant to roll up his sleeves and really dig into the world's first verified alien carcass, the reason was simple: Lloyd had grown too attached. Quill protocol effectively outlawed in-house love affairs, but somehow Lloyd and Moss's love affair had eluded prohibition. And like any other affair, it was probably going to end messily. At which point my security team would have to compel the issue. Which is a lot harder to do with a "friend."

Don't think about affairs—

I shook the thought. So, apparently, did Lloyd, who turned back to Andy with a mostly sincere smile. The lesson could resume for now.

"Draws power from people how?"

"Um, like their life-force, right?"

Life-force . . .

We'd had our share of accidents regarding the Harp. We'd seen what it did to a person's "life-force" when caught in its ripple. Not many, thankfully, but enough. (Hell, Lloyd's predecessor, Dr. Beritov, had been one of our most unfortunate case studies.) I tried not to think about those, either—and now I was trying not to think of too many things at once.

You haven't done anything wrong. You were just in your car.

Just be practical.

"And what is 'life-force,' exactly?"

"Oh, crap, do you mean like chemically?"

Where's my life-force?

"I do."

You're going through something—a phase—don't make it worse by obsessing over it.

"Aw, maaaaan, I know we talked about this . . . ummmmm—"

"I'm sorry, Andy, I'm afraid it's a B-plus today!'"

And whatever you do

"Dammit! Maaaaaan, I was so close! Well I guess a B-plus is better than any real grade I ever got."

"Okay, then, remember this for *next time*: 'Inconclusive testing'—remember that part—"

"'Inconclusive,' I'm with you."

Don't think about driving.

"'Inconclusive testing' *suggests* the Harp redirects the body's adenosine triphosphate energy production for its own use—" The clarion denoting the great Guardshift do-si-do rang out over the Hangar. Lloyd didn't skip a beat: "—in the process massively inhibiting its ability to generate dopamine, serotonin, and key endorphins."

Tune in next time for the Lloyd and Andy Show.

"Guardshift, guys," I chuffed.

Oh fuck what day is it?

"Okay, hate to say, I am definitely not gonna remember all that."

"I suppose it *is* easier to say 'life-force,'" Lloyd conceded.

"Guys. Guardshift."

Oh fuck

"Aw, man, I'm so bummed I won't see the suit!"

"A week into testing you'll be sick at the sight of it," I heard myself snap. "Now get moving."

"Next time, Lloyd!" He held out a fist for Lloyd to bump.

"Next time indeed!"

Andy squeezed his way out of the ship's fissure. He was to move on to the front of the Hangar. One of the team from the front of the Hangar was to move into the Tent, and one of the guys from in front of the Tent was to join me here.

Don't panic.

And that guy . . .

"Afternoon, guys. Dr. Simon," you said, after squeezing into the ship, already like an expert.

Fuck.

Fuck.

In my not-thinking-of-things I'd managed to forget what day it was. The first day when our rotating schedules finally lined up. A total eclipse of awfulness. You'd had evenings and overnights so far—this would be your last shift for the day and my last one before lunch, both in the same spot. The security staff was just large enough that I was able to avoid you for a couple days, but now . . .

But you didn't really forget, did you, Dak? You don't forget things like that. Just like you can't forget driving to—

You know what? You know what I suddenly realized? This was fucking bullshit.

I'm a grown fucking woman. I have been trained in numerous disciplines. I have been fully capable and independent my entire goddamn life and here I am breaking out into a cold sweat over an idea, a notion, a possibility, a fucking impulse!

I didn't even know this fucking guy.

Guardshift, indeed. Practical Dak took a break and Adamant Dak took over.

I STOOD and stewed. Hating you, hating this, hating everything. Worst of all, hating how the air seemed so much more breathable with you here.

I didn't even know if I should be looking at you. If I looked at you, would I be able to stop? Which was weirder: staring or decidedly not looking? I knew security team member Grant would be up in Bird's Eye now. He was a meddlesome little shit who was always looking for something to complain about—he'd be scrutinizing the closed-circuit video feed of the cockpit looking for any sort of angle, no doubt. I felt even more self-conscious. I felt even more resentful.

Lloyd was beaming. "Good guy, Andy, good guy. Laudable energy. Might make a scientist of him yet, don't you think?" He was still fidgeting with the suit and when he looked up he looked directly at you with hungry eyes.

"Good guy," you agreed, nodding dispassionately, not looking back. Scanning the environment like something could pop out and surprise us at any time.

I had to smile a little at that, despite the belligerency roiling inside me. You nailed it right off the bat: agree with Lloyd, reinforce him, give him positive emotional feedback, but don't give him a conversational hook to grab on to.

But, of course, Lloyd was a curious feller, being a scientist and all. He continued looking at you, his forehead drawn into furrows under his graying hair, and held out a grasping hand.

"Remind me again . . . ?"

"Matt Salem." Even the sound of your name: like a loose tooth my tongue couldn't stop pushing.

"Matt Salem! Thank you. I'm terrible with names the first few times. Maybe because I've maxed out on data?" He tapped his temple indicatively, but there was actually no sense of performance there. It was a legitimate observation to him.

"I'm new, it's only our second shift together."

"Ah! Well. Obviously, clearly, we need to get better acquainted, then! Do you like quizzes?"

Goddammit.

THIS PARTICULAR quiz was, for some reason, about the door to the engine room. Specifically, why should it stay closed? You'd, of course, been briefed on protocol; you knew (at least academically) about the dangers direct exposure to the Harp posed.

After a few leading questions, you finally looked at me. Because I spoke your language, whether I wanted to or not, I knew that exact look meant: "Am I supposed to keep answering these? Please help."

"You know what, Lloyd," I jumped in, "maybe just focus on your suit. We're wasting time here." Suddenly I didn't care how today's practice session went, I didn't care if Lloyd succeeded or failed, and whether or not he decided to actually be the test subject tomorrow. I just wanted to work. Lloyd had been standing over his suit and helmet long enough that I began to wonder if he even remembered it was there.

"But I am focusing on the suit, Dak; that is precisely what I'm doing! Come on, guys: why doesn't the Harp hurt us when the door is closed?"

We both stared blankly at him.

"Insulation!" He clapped. "A finely calibrated chemical insulation that protects our bodies—and obviously more intentionally Moss's body—from the Harp's energy-sapping effects."

We both nodded.

"Now, having said that, what do you extrapolate that this suit is for?"

LLOYD HAD started on the idea of a suit about a year ago. As with all things Lloyd, the relatively simple idea emerged from a hedgemaze of winding digressions and concessions to the ever-winnowing filter that is the scientific method.

Here's part of an early memo from him, just for a taste:

. . . But again, bear in mind, it is entirely possible that intuition loses its value at the biosphere's edge. Our instincts are Earthbound, and very likely nontransferable to extra-solar environments. We take so many ideas for granted, down to the existence of concepts that seem so very fundamental to our physical understanding of the world around us, and forgetting that, as infants, even these concepts were learned, not innate, and thus cannot be assumed to apply to our guest—or, really, guests. Take, as a macro example, the moss's growth on Moss's skin. To us it is a mystery. Perhaps it would strike us in an entirely different way if we grew up on Moss's planet, or a neighboring planet. Being Earthbound myself, of course, I share the following intuition I have heard articulated around our facility: even wearing no garment, Moss gives off a remarkable sense of immaculate self-care and thus the moss itself looks wrong, even invasive. But, here is where I must remind myself: what even is "invasive" if not a concept derived from our own solipsistic perception of self? Would a creature with a more hive-like mind (i.e., a telepathic superstructure such as, for want of a better term, a honeycomb) even understand the concept of "invasion"? We take proprietary ownership of our own corpo-reality as a given. We think of Moss as an alien species, but we would do well to remind ourselves that we, too, are an alien species and our ways might be as wholly unfamiliar and unfathomable as his. Simply factoring in the existence of at least two alien species in one room, ourselves and our Moss, means, to borrow a gross colloquialism, all bets are off. That being said, however, we must begin somewhere and that is why . . .

That was a memorandum just saying he was thinking of making a suit. It was close to five pages long. Ever since that one, Lloyd was required to include a one-sentence summary at the beginning of any written correspondence.

But, so, we began to put his idea into practice. First came the bags of earthworms (unsuccessful). Then birds (unsuccessful, perhaps due to the subjects' stress being in captivity), then some gerbils (unsuccessful, perhaps due to faulty seals). Finally we moved up to larger mammals like dogs.

These sessions made for some of my least favorite experiences here at Quill.

Shit like this is why I'm a vegetarian.

"LET'S JUST get you in the suit, okay, Lloyd? Class dismissed." I needed to do something other than just stand here and watch you two. I needed to move.

You held it up by the midsection and Lloyd stepped into the pants legs one at a time while bracing himself on your shoulder.

"Now, imagine with me, Matt Salem," he said as he worked his way into the suit, "if we determine that the engine room is coated with this protective insulation, what's the smartest next

step to t-aayyyyyy—" He started to topple backward as he lifted
his second leg. I hustled over and caught him. But it's like his
mouth was barely aware of what his body was doing. The nanosecond he was out of any danger his monologue resumed. "Well, we'd
want to make more of it, yes? Which raises the question: how do
we make more of it? Determining the chemical composition of the
insulation is key!"

We worked on getting his arms into the sleeves. Adamant Dak
appeared every now and then, jerking Lloyd around, barking
orders at him, like an unpleasant barber. Once that was done, we
stepped back.

"Okay," you panted, "does it zip up somehow?"

"Great question," I said, examining the suit. The new knobs
placed strategically at the suit's various openings: they must have
been sealing devices. "I'm assuming it's got something to do with
these. Are we good to close you up?"

"Please, be my guest," Lloyd beamed. "Shall I instruct
you?"

But, no, I wanted to figure it out for myself. If this suit wound
up working, I'd have to learn its ways pretty thoroughly.

There were two small knobs and two red buttons, one of each
on both sides of the opening to the suit. I pressed one button and
twisted the knob, then did the same for the other. There was a
strange, almost pneumatic whoosh and buzz and the suit appeared
to seal itself up the center.

Lloyd talked at you over all of it.

"So that's been my little project for the last year. Studying
sample after sample until I could synthesize the N5 insulation
myself."

"N5?"

"Okay!" I yelled. "Before he starts in on explaining the name!
Is that it? Are we sealed?"

"We are sealed! Splendidly done! She's very strict with me."
Lloyd winked at you. You smiled neatly. *What does that smile
mean?* "But she's very good. She's the best."

"Yes, she is, Lloyd," you said. Casually? Sincerely? *What the fuck does that smile mean?*

Fuck.

I hated this. I hated this so much. But there was still work to be done.

"Okay." I cleared my throat. "Salem, you're doing the next one. Here on the arm, see?"

Another seal, another button and knob. You reached your hand out to touch where I was touching. I made sure to pull away.

"All right, I'll spare you the reasoning behind the name, but answer me this: once I've synthesized the N5 insulation, what would the next step be?"

"I guess . . . ," you said as you successfully activated the seal on his sleeve, ". . . you make a space suit out of it." *Whoosh buzz.*

Lloyd looked at the two of us like a pastor overseeing nuptials. "We're going to have so much fun!"

TWENTY MINUTES or so later, after Lloyd had paraded around in his new design without stumbling or falling in the slightest—it was finally time for me to take a break.

The day was far from over, though. Quill's director of operations, Michael R. Harrison, was finally back from a trip to Sierra headquarters in D.C. and needed to be caught up. I had hours more shift to pull. And then I had to go home and be alone with my thoughts. You know: the real work.

At the very least, this was the end of my orbit and yours overlapping.

"It's been real," I said to you, feeling convincingly steely and disinterested, not at all like a petulant twelve-year-old.

Before either of us could say anything further, though, Patty was making a beeline for us, her ponytail bouncing like a standard being borne to battle.

"Done for the day, New Fish?"

"How long do I stay New Fish?" you asked.

"Right, lemme check my calendar," Patty answered, miming

a device in her hand. "Looks like it's just until Go Fuck Yourself."

"Got it," you said. I couldn't tell if you were genuinely stung. You nodded at both of us, and started ambling slowly toward the elevator. Patty and I continued walking leisurely in the same direction.

"All good, Chief?" she asked.

"All good. I got to practice suit-sealing, so I'm gonna train the team on it tomorrow."

"Is Lloyd still planning on—?"

"Yeah, but I'm still gonna try to talk him out of it before EOD today. Who's on the team for the Sierra show again?" With reps from Sierra coming in a couple weeks to see all that we'd managed to do with their money, I wanted to make sure we had a topnotch team on the floor.

"It's gonna be me, Vonn, Shel, Grant, both Davies—" I groaned at the sound of Grant's name. "I know, but he'll be perfect because he wants to kiss up. Oh, and also Chatty Andy."

Great. Must have been my birthday.

"Should we grab lunch?" she asked. "We can prep together before we meet with Harrison?"

My voice rose slightly. "You know what? I actually left mine in the car. Gotta go up and grab it."

I thought I saw your head tilt slightly at that.

"Ugh, if it's that falafel crap you might as well just leave it up there. You can have some of mine."

"Energy bars and beef jerky?"

"All a person needs." She puffed her chest out.

"Listen, Patty . . ." I lowered my voice and stopped walking.

"Oh, shit. What's up?"

"Harrison wants you to sit out this afternoon."

"Okayyyy. Really?"

Usually, whenever I briefed Harrison, Patty was there with me. This morning, for whatever reason, I'd received communication from him on his way back from D.C. that he needed to speak with me, and me only. "You know how this works," I muttered to Patty. "I'll tell you whatever I can tell you. I'm sure he has his reasons."

"Yeah," she muttered back, "and I bet they were on the rocks."

I put my hands on her shoulders. "Someday, my young padawan, you'll have my gig and will be saying the same shit to your deputy."

"Only that's never gonna happen because we're gonna stay chief and deputy forever."

"Right. I forgot." I saw you waiting for the elevator. I had no reason to delay getting on as well. Crap. Let's just get it over with then. I separated from Patty and headed over to the elevator, calling back to her, "Enjoy your dehydrated meat product and compressed carbohydrates."

"Enjoy your mulch balls and hot sauce!" she called back.

THE ELEVATOR was full of scientists. They were chattering about thermal sensors on the hull, how they break down so fast, how they have to replace all of them almost weekly or they get too close to the breakdown point.

The breakdown point. Who says science and poetry don't overlap?

But I was grateful to not be there alone with you.

ONCE OUTSIDE, you walked ahead of me. You handled the maneuver expertly, the training still in your bones. I shouldn't have been impressed—that's par for the course for anyone who ends up working here—but everything you did was somehow managing to confound my expectations.

It was overcast. Rain was probably imminent. We lose all sense of weather down there in the stomach. I was grateful for the chill.

I stopped at my jeep; you stopped in front of the car next to it—just before you'd come out the other side, you bent down to tie your boot. You didn't turn around as I stepped in between the vehicles.

"Figured you said that loud enough for me to hear. Figured it wouldn't hurt for us to talk," you said, your hand moving over your laces.

"I'm gonna make sure we're always on different shifts," I said. "Might take a while. Can't be obvious about it. But I'll make it happen."

"Okay. That seems right."

"It is right."

"It is, yeah. Only . . ." You stopped fiddling with your boots, but you still weren't looking at me. Fat raindrops started to land heavily on the cars around us.

"What?" I asked. My heart was beating about as heavily as those raindrops. "Only what?" No answer. No eyes. "Fuck you, only what?!"

But you knew as well as I did that you'd stopped walking for the absolute longest credible stretch of time. So without any further word, you walked off to your car.

I grabbed my lunch from my passenger seat and then made my way back to the first checkpoint to start the whole process over again.

DIRECTOR HARRISON was already there when I finally got back to Bird's Eye, lunch bag in hand (and Patty was right: falafel with hot sauce, thank you very much). He stood by the desk that held the monitors of the closed circuit feeds to the Hangar.

If I could help it, I always wanted to catch Harrison in the morning. It was a pretty open secret that he did most of his office-drinking in the afternoon. A post-lunch meeting like this was risky.

"Dak, hi." He was wearing chino pants and a polo shirt, neatly tucked in. I'd never seen him in combat fatigues, yet it always seemed out of character to see him in civilian clothes—like looking at a pirate in a basketball jersey or something. He was a fit man in his late fifties, formerly a colonel in the 10th Special Forces, and I always thought his demeanor was a very specific kind of paternal: never patronizing, never dottering. He was like the father who abandoned you and with whom you were reconnecting as an adult who held no grudges. Like I said: a very specific kind of paternal.

I felt my body trying to snap to attention and salute. I settled for raising my lunch bag.

"Welcome back, Director."

"How were things while I was away?" He seemed pretty steady, actually. Distracted, but sober. He wasn't swaying. He wasn't blinking with weights on his eyelids.

"Smooth sailing, most part. Folded in a new guy."

"Any problems?"

"Just the usual Lloyd hazing."

"I, uh . . . I actually asked Lloyd to join us, hopefully he's . . ." He gave a soft snort and his head bobbed.

I stared at him for a second. He'd asked Lloyd to be here but Patty to sit out. What could that mean? Then I shook my head of it; I'd find out soon enough.

"How was D.C.?"

"Good. I think. It's just different, it just . . . takes a lot of getting used to. But I think it's good." He swallowed dryly. "Let's say I'm . . . keeping an open mind."

Quill Marine, like much of Washington, D.C., after the great governmental fire sale of 2019, was owned by the Sierra Corporation, a hefty defense contractor, all hail, long may their bottom line be fruitful. That meant old army cats, like Harrison, like myself, who'd trained themselves, indoctrinated themselves, in service to a country, now found themselves adapting to a far different chain of command. We were servants to a logo now, not a flag.

It was certainly a shift. And, fortunately or unfortunately, the experiment showed no signs of slowing down. What catastrophes you would read in the news about the learning curve sweeping up all sorts of collateral damage didn't seem to really stem the pace of privatization. Things kept getting negotiated and bought out, monopolized and commoditized. If I were young and idealistic I'd say it was spreading like a cancer. But I'm old and I'm wise so I know there are plenty of cancers you can learn to live with.

At that moment, Lloyd came barreling into the room.

"Am I late? I have a problem with being late." A hand went to his temple. "Maybe because my brain gets maxed out—"

"You're fine, Lloyd, have a seat." Harrison waved to the room.

"Um, anywhere, or . . . ?"

We both nodded. Lloyd sat down immediately where he stood.

"So, Dak," Harrison resumed, "after we're done here I'm going to give you authorization to access and erase the security recording of this meeting."

Whoa. "Yes, sir—Director."

Lloyd looked confused, almost like he was about to ask if he should leave the meeting he was personally just asked to attend. He even started to rise, but Harrison dropped the bomb before either of us could get to a safe distance.

"The Sierra visit is going to be a week earlier than we previously expected."

"Wait—are you serious?" I stood up.

"Well, let me just finish what I'm—"

"Respectfully, sir, if that's the case I gotta scramble, I gotta start—"

"Sure, I understand, but don't you think you need to know a bit more in terms of how to scramble?"

He had a point. I sat back down.

"For example you might find it helpful to know that rather than the full executive panel we were expecting . . . it'll just be Trip Haydon and his immediate team."

I was sitting. I wished I could have sunk into the earth, never to be seen again.

"Haydon's coming here?"

Sierra was owned by a Mr. Peter Haydon. He'd always been a bit of a mysterious entity, more of a name on paper and on buildings than an actual human being, but every now and then he would show up places—an event, a gala, a ribbon cutting. Except lately; even what little public appearances Peter Haydon usually made seemed to all be drying up and he was giving his middle son, Trip, way more latitude to ride roughshod. I'd been around for two of Trip's visits, back when I was just a grunt here. They were not fun.

"Apparently he's taken an interest. I'm still trying to get the whole story. But of course one thing we have to consider . . ." He looked at Lloyd. Lloyd looked back at him. Then at me. Then back at Harrison.

"Um . . . obviously, obviously there's a reason you're looking at me like—"

"We have to consider the possibility that Haydon may want to cash out," Harrison said. Another bomb fell on the room.

"Cash out?"

"Lloyd—"

"Waitwaitwait"—another hand to his forehead, this one trembling slightly—"you mean cash out *Moss*?"

"Lloyd, we need to—"

"He can't."

"Well, strictly speaking, he can."

"He can't!"

"You took a moss measurement this morning, correct?"

"Well, obviously, I—"

"And it's still receding?"

"Certainly, certainly the pattern is . . . holding . . ."

Harrison put a tablet on the table.

"Lloyd, this is the image I have of Moss's chest area from eleven months ago. Do you have today's image?"

Lloyd fumbled with his own tablet. "Of course, of course I, it's standard—here."

Harrison took it, looked at it. "All right, well, I'm not a xenobiologist, but I think it's fair to say we're looking at an escalating rate of recession here."

"Yes, clearly, obviously, but, but, but—that doesn't mean anything! That isn't matched by any observable decomposition within Moss's actual body! That whole theory is based on nothing!" Lloyd was starting to sputter. Harrison kept his cool.

"I'm not talking about the science, Lloyd, I'm talking about appearances—what Haydon will see and what he'll infer from what he sees. The very real danger is that he either believes the theory, or doesn't think he can take the risk. In either case he'll cash out."

And by "cash out" he meant, if Moss's perceived value is about to run out, they'll move him to a big city and start selling tickets.

"But . . . but . . ."

"I don't want it either," Harrison said, straight and even. "I don't know what Quill's future is without Moss. A lot of people work here. We work here. Does everyone understand?" Everyone, meaning Lloyd and myself, nodded solemnly. Harrison's voice changed, then, and I understood why I was to delete the security footage of this meeting. "We can't change what Haydon will see when he gets here, of course. But is there any way to . . ."

He trailed off. I needed—we all needed—to hear him say it so I urged him on.

"Sir? Director . . . ?"

"I don't know, *redistribute* the weekly images in such a way that . . . that . . ."

"Will make the rate of moss recession look . . . slower?" Lloyd whispered.

"Is it possible?"

"I . . . I think so . . ." Not committing, just running the hypothesis through his supercomputer head.

"Well, you're as invested as anyone, Lloyd. More so. I suspect you'll find a way. Dak?"

I had my own half-formed thoughts, but they all seemed to contradict each other. So I just shrugged and nodded.

"Well," Harrison slapped his upper thighs like some middle-aged, halfhearted cheerleader. "Co-conspirators, then." He gave a chuckle half good-humored, half poisoned. It was the laugh

I imagined he gave before cracking open a bottle in his dark, lonely office.

"Where are we on the suit?" Harrison asked.

Lloyd was still lost in a thought cloud.

"Um, um . . . the suit . . . is . . ."

"We've now had three dogs in the suits emerge from full-cycle exposure with no deleterious effects, Director."

That seemed to help clear Lloyd up. His eyes widened and he began looking at faces again. "That's right, that's right, three dogs! Flopsy, Mopsy, and, and Queen Buttsniffer. I, uh . . . I didn't name the last one."

"We're ready for human testing," I said, hoping I could gently let Harrison know what Lloyd had been champing at the bit to do. I was already changing my attitude on his plan. Lloyd jumped in before I could finesse it further.

"We're testing me. Tomorrow."

"I'm sorry, what?" Harrison gaped. I tried to intervene and Harrison barreled over me. "Actually *you*?"

"Why not?" Lloyd shrugged, back to full Lloydian confidence.

"In the suit?"

"Why not?"

"With the Harp?"

"Three dogs came out fine!"

"You know we can provide someone, right? You know how many prisons Sierra owns?"

"Ten minutes ago I would've been on your side, Director," I jumped in. He glared at me. I hated to say this. "But if Sierra's coming this Monday, if it's Haydon in person . . . Lloyd's gotta be the one in there running the show."

Harrison turned his attention back to Lloyd.

"We can't lose you," he practically pleaded.

Lloyd held up some fingers. "Three dogs! It'll be fine. I'll be fine."

"Lloyd . . ."

"Look, I promise you! I don't have a death wish!" He looked

at both of us, laughing with a big, wide-open smile. "I definitely, definitely am not planning on dying anytime soon."

Harrison and I exchanged glances and Lloyd let out another laugh.

IT WAS almost dark when Patty and I made our way out to the parking lot—that time where the night sky and the trees below it seem to swap palettes for a little while, rendering the sky brilliant colors and the trees pitch black silhouettes. The smell of a recent rain shower hung in the air as cleansing as bleach.

As per custom, I had hung back, purposefully finding diversions to take up my time finishing up, allowing Patty her privacy while she made her way through the checkpoints. Then she pretended to have a reason to hang around a little while upstairs to wait for me so we could walk to our cars together. All pretense. All ritual. All appreciated.

I told her what I could about the meeting with Harrison—mostly that Trip Haydon was ruining everything by coming personally, and Monday no less. She groaned.

"Well, shit, I'm definitely drinking tonight now."

We exchanged a few verbal jibs and jabs before nonchalantly asking the other what bar she would be patronizing that evening. It was, of course, the opposite of an invitation—a clearing of information in order to avoid company (I was still staying away from the Heron after the Feetbreath incident and bequeathed it to Patty, who gave me the Celtic Yard).

Then, something occurred to Patty, right as I opened the door to my car.

"This is weird, right?"

"What's weird?"

"I mean . . . we like each other, right? We shoot the shit, we work well together, we've got our little rapport down. We were just told we're gonna have a shit week, so this would be when we go get plastered together. Except . . ."

The cool air felt blessedly refreshing—but the edge of frigidness was there, just waiting to take us when we got comfortable.

"Fraternizing," I said.

"Fraternizing," she echoed.

Patty stared off at the inky trees. Against the glowing sky the trees looked as if they'd been cut out of black construction paper. What a weird planet we lived on.

" 'Night, Dak."

" 'Night."

She walked to her car. I watched her go.

Did Patty want to hang out? Did Patty want to compromise the fraternization policy of Quill Marine?

Could Patty hear the static jamming my rational mind?

I'LL GIVE Trip Haydon this much, though: for a little while I'd actually stopped thinking about what I'd done the night before.

Unfortunately, that night, I did it again.

I HAD no reason to be on that road. It wasn't at all between the Celtic Yard and home. Even a cab driver looking to rip me off wouldn't have come this way.

I let myself drink too much. I definitely shouldn't have been driving.

I made dangerous, insistent eye contact with a fisherman about three times my size hoping he'd puff up and start something. Hoping I'd win. Hoping I'd lose.

When I got back into my car, I turned over the engine and the radio was blaring pop music from another era. "You Might Think," by the Cars. Too upbeat. I spun the volume dial to death. This needed to be done in silence.

I felt sick. That kind of sick where you're too sick to get out of bed but also too sick to watch TV, so all you can do is lie there and think, "I'm so, so sick."

The road was my sickbed.

It wasn't a decision to memorize the address in your file. It just happened. I couldn't unknow it.

I pulled to the side of the road, parked on the shoulder. The only sound was the idling of my engine, the occasional other car driving by. And the muffled sound of Practical Dak in my head—bound and gagged, but still shouting, *What are you doing what are you doing*

Your motel room was the second one from the right on the second level. Jesus Christ. Jesus fucking Christ.

The thing is, I didn't even know if I wanted you. That's what made it so unbearable. If I could just say, *I want to go up to that room, peel off his pants, and grind him into paste,* something ugly and animal and purely physical, it'd be so much easier to deal with. It'd be disastrous, but a knowable disaster. It'd be an achievable goal.

But no. It was a compounded fear. It was also the sheer temptation of you, of escorting you past all my defenses. A big red button that says, "Push to Destroy Everything," which for whatever reason I didn't even know if I really itched to push.

But was I actually panicking or was I just panicking over the idea that I'm capable of panicking?

Those eyes

It's nothing

Then the light came on in your room, behind the closed vertical blinds. I couldn't see you, but . . . it was off, and now it was on.

You were awake. Probably getting ready for your shift.

I gunned the engine and drove away.

5

THE NEXT morning, my head thudding dully from another restless night, we cleared out the Hangar. It was just before noon; the Harp was predicted to start up in a little under twenty minutes and we wanted everyone gone.

It wasn't so much that we were worried about introducing a new variable to our Power-Up routine—the plan was to seal Lloyd in the engine room and keep the rest of the base as, to borrow his term, *insulated* from the Harp's effects as usual—it was more that, if this went wrong and the suit wasn't as effective on humans as Lloyd was positing . . . well, we all remembered what happened with his predecessor. Lloyd was a well-known, well-liked figure in Quill Marine. It would not do for morale to have a lot of witnesses around for what we would have to do next.

Once we herded all the stragglers toward the elevators— something Patty did with relish—it was just her and me on the outside of the Tent.

"Okay, so you're in Bird's Eye?" I confirmed with her.

"Unless you wanna switch out. I'm happy to be on Lloyd detail."

"Nah, I wanna close the seals myself. Who's in there with me?"

"Chatty Andy."

Oh, joy. Well, if this went south, Lloyd might as well go out with his favorite student hanging on his every word. Maybe they could get one last pop quiz in.

Patty and I split and headed to our positions.

. . .

ANDY HAD helped Lloyd into the suit and now they were in what, for them, passed as a heated argument. I headed straight to Lloyd.

"Ready for me to seal you up?"

"Please! Seal away."

"But wait—" Andy protested while I worked the seals on Lloyd's chest and wrists.

"Tell me the theory in plain simple language," Lloyd indulged, "as straightforward as you can."

"Okay," Andy buzzed. "So, so, um, so some people think that Moss is warm because he's actually still alive, and that he's actually been dying for the whole time since he crashed, and, and the moss is like . . . like a . . ."

Patty crackled over the communicator. *"How we doing, Chief?"* Boy, this was a bad day to have a headache.

"Almost there." I had one last seal to go: the one at the base of the neck. I plopped the fishbowl-shaped helmet onto Lloyd's head. He kept talking, not missing a beat, and as soon as the helmet went over his face, a microphone inside sent his voice through the speaker on top.

"Like a dependent organism, Andy. Like the bacteria in any human body."

"Right!" Andy exclaimed. "And so like as Moss dies, super slowly, the moss on his chest is shrinking too, because it's dying too. And when it's all gone, that means he's finally dead."

"Last seal, Patty," I radioed as I activated the seal at the neck. It whooshed and buzzed. "Opening the engine room."

"Copy."

"But Andy!" Lloyd exclaimed. "That obviously, clearly, is a *tremendous* amount to rest on just two data points: a warm body and a receding skin-growth! Now, I understand why this theory captures the *imagination,* but that's not the same thing as science!"

Opening the door to the engine room was . . . an interesting process. You had to put your hand inside this kind of nook up to the elbow and squeeze this Play-Doh-feeling apparatus inside that was never quite where you thought it'd be. It was clearly—"obviously," as Lloyd would say—made for Moss's spindly arms. Once I found the mechanism, the door slid open with a sibilant sigh.

"Yeah. Yeah, I guess, Lloyd," Andy was conceding. "I just thought it'd be cool if the moss, like, I dunno. It's stupid."

"No! Andrew! That could not be further from the truth. Only the know-it-alls are truly stupid! I would love to hear your theories about the moss, please!"

"Aw, man. Thanks for that, Lloyd. I—whoa." Andy was looking into the engine room. "I haven't seen in there for a while!"

"Engine room is open," I radioed to Patty. "I am placing Lloyd."

"*You guys still sure about this?*"

"Three dogs come through fine!" Lloyd cried to the heavens.

"*Copy.*"

And Lloyd was probably right—probably—so I put a guiding hand on his back as he made his way over the threshold and into the engine room. There, in the center of the room, was the Harp.

A rusty golden, sloping apparatus with sinewy strands stretched from top to bottom. It stood about three feet high and it sat in a small brown-and-blue base directly off the floor. The edges of the base rose above the tapered bottom of the Harp, cupping it, and two pins passed through holes in both the base and the Harp itself. The pins gave it a sense of almost primitive construction, of something Indiana Jones would slip into a rucksack and kick-start a booby trap, yet the general aura of the thing was appropriately celestial. Unknowable. Dangerous. Thankfully, we weren't in the business of pulling pins here at Quill Marine.

"I feel like an angel should be like—" Andy made a little strumming gesture and laughed to himself. I whipped my head toward him.

"Hit your mark, Andy. Like it's a normal day."

He complied, right away. He stood lateral to the engine-room door, looking in the direction of the cockpit.

"*Power-Up in approximately nine minutes,*" Patty radioed in.

"Want me to seal you in now, Lloyd?" I asked.

"And give up nine whole minutes of chatting with you guys?"

"Well, I'm closing the door in five, either way." I wanted a healthy margin of safety. Looking at Lloyd standing directly next to the Harp—even with him in a suit, everything inside me insisted that this was wrong and needlessly reckless. I thought again of how Dr. Beritov went out, and shuddered. "You sure you want to stand that close to it?"

Lloyd laughed, delighted. "It doesn't matter! The N5 removes distance as a factor, Dak!"

"You *think.*"

Lloyd held up three gloved fingers and started to bark. I rolled my eyes. In that split second of looking away, everything went to shit. I heard Andy laugh with us and then—

"Oh, hey, Lloyd! I almost forgot to tell you my theory about the moss!"

The idiot walked straight past me into the engine room.

Lloyd and I both reacted.

Andy was still talking: "Just real quick, before we close you up. Did you ever wonder if maybe the moss is the—"

And the Harp suddenly roared to life.

I COULDN'T tell if it was because the door was open or because the Harp was somehow aware of us and responding—outraged? hungry?—to our presence, but it sounded louder and faster than ever before.

Patty's voice sprang over the speaker: "*Shit, shit, Dak, it's early, we're live!*"

Andy didn't scream. He didn't spasm. His body didn't seize. But once the Harp began to thrum, he just . . . wilted.

Patty's voice: "*Dak, you gotta close up!*"

"The kid's in the engine room," I reported. The world was slowing down, the way it does in combat situations, everything taking on feverish clarity. But I could also feel the Harp's effect on me immediately. Like I was plummeting from a great height. The Harp sounded like a typhoon, the air became thicker. My mouth dried up and lost all taste. My eyes began to lose focus. My—Jesus, my *will* to do anything began to calcify and crack.

"Dak, it'll eat the whole base for breakfast, you gotta close that fucking door!"

She was right. I had barely a spare few nanoseconds before whatever affected Andy *really* sank its teeth into me, too. And then, if the door was still open when it hit full blast, who knows how far its effects would reach?

Who cares who gives a—

From what seemed like another dimension I felt myself ramming my arm into the nook, squeezing the switch . . .

The last thing I saw before the engine-room door closed was Andy nestled in Lloyd's space-suit arms.

The Harp continued its escalating roar and I dropped to the ground.

I WOKE up to your face staring down at me. Your beautiful face. Those eyelashes. God, how I'd longed to see you like this: intimate, loving, staring down at me. Except . . . Patty's voice . . .

"Chief! Chief, come on, show me something!"

I blinked. Your face disappeared. Patty was leaning over me. I raised myself up onto my elbows—or tried to. Jesus, I felt like I'd just run twenty miles after ten sleepless nights.

"Lemme just . . . ," I managed.

"Oh, for chrissakes, thank God," Patty gasped. "Don't—you don't have to sit up, dummy, lemme bring in a team."

"No, no," I slurred. "I don't need . . . where's—" I blinked again, hoping to find you.

"Everyone's upstairs. I cleared the whole floor, remember? It's just us."

Things came into focus a bit better and I saw the engine-room door was still closed. I sprang to my feet and wobbled my way over to the switch. My muscles barely conceded to the impulses

I was screaming in my brain. Patty was protesting beside me, telling me to sit back down—finally she pushed me gently aside and opened the door herself.

Lloyd was kneeling over Andy, who was sitting on the floor, hands folded over his belly, just . . . staring.

Lloyd saw me. "We need help, Jesus, Dak, get help!"

I could tell by the way Lloyd ran to me and grabbed my shirt: the suit did its job. Lloyd was fine. Freaked out, but physically unaffected. Hell, he had enough strength to almost topple me. Thankfully Patty was there behind me, helping me stay upright.

"Give me your sidearm and get Lloyd out of here," I said to her. I was dimly aware of Lloyd begging us for help.

She looked at me sternly. "Chief, that's crazy, you shouldn't be the one to—"

"It's an order," I shot at her. She gave in and handed me her weapon.

"What are you doing?!" Lloyd gasped. "We need a medical team in here! Now!"

"Get him out, get him checked," I mumbled to Patty. "Top to bottom."

Lloyd was pleading into his bubble helmet, his voice compressed and powerless through its speaker. He knew what had to happen next. Andy had taken a full blast for an entire cycle. No one had ever taken that much. Not since—

"No, wait, wait, listen, we have to—"

"Turndown Service?" Patty asked. I nodded and she led Lloyd out of the ship, soothing him with low tones and platitudes.

"He's just a kid!" he cried . . . and they were gone.

Then it was just me. And Andy.

I checked the sidearm. Loaded. Ready.

Andy just stared straight ahead. He wore the expression of someone who had just received a bit of expected bad news—nothing shocking, just powerfully unhappy. A long-sick loved one had died, perhaps. He blinked. He breathed.

"Can you walk with me, Andy?"

He let out a barely perceptible moan. I don't even think it was in answer to my question.

I carefully negotiated (really, dragged) Andy out of the ship. He came willingly enough, though his motor skills were all but gone. His gaze never veered from its forward, fixed position.

I set him down on the floor outside the ship. I should have brought him to the Slammer, but the trip was too far for me to make. Plus we had the entire Hangar to ourselves for the moment.

"How're you doing, Andy?"

". . . Nothing."

"Say again?" I asked.

"There's nothing," Andy said. His voice was even and sure. Unrushed. Unworried. Unhappy. "There's nothing."

I could have let Patty take this. But it was my fuckup. I deserved it.

I disengaged the safety.

"Andy?" I asked.

"Just nothing." He kept staring straight ahead.

"You understand what's about to . . . ?"

"I don't care," he replied. He didn't look at me, but his head tilted toward me slightly.

I swallowed. My mouth was so dry I heard it click.

"They'll get a letter. Your people. It'll say combat. That this happened in the line of d—"

"Doesn't matter," he said. Not for my benefit. Not for posterity. Just a statement of fact. "There's nothing."

"Okay," I whispered. And I shot Andy in the head.

Then a second time to be sure.

A GUNSHOT in the ship would probably sound very strange. A loud burst with no real reverberation, over as soon as it rang out, almost like a noise balloon in a comic book. Out here in the Hangar it sounded like the introduction of thunder to world. The noise just kept rolling . . . and rolling . . .

A few minutes later and Patty was by my side again. "You . . . ?" she asked. She probably meant, "Are you okay," or "Do you need a moment," or something equally inane. She stopped herself because she knew the answers.

The spatter had extended far across the floor. The blood began a wide, dark pool, hungry and growing. I didn't want to notice those things.

"I guess the suit works," I said.

TURNDOWN WAS the very picture of efficiency. Within ten minutes the blood disappeared and Andy was put in a box. The boxes for these situations are deliberately oversized and colorful so they don't in any way resonate as coffins. It really makes the whole process that much more disquieting.

Then, at my request—my insistence—Patty tipped the box up, I eased a hand-truck underneath, and then brought the box outside myself. Patty insisted on joining me. She could see how unsteady I was on my feet.

Everyone at the checkpoints knows what the big boxes are. What they mean. You still have to go through each station but the clearance process suddenly gets a lot more perfunctory. No one wants to look at them for long. The Gnome doesn't bother stopping the elevator to scrutinize you. Even Rosh becomes a different person: no chit-chat, no script.

The worst for them is it'll be a while before they even know who it is. There's no access to the Hangar security cameras anywhere other than in Bird's Eye downstairs—that way only people who are cleared to go down to Hangar Eleven get to know what's downstairs. Lauren, Rosh, the Gnome, everyone else upstairs just has to watch the big, bright box go by and wonder who we lost.

OUTSIDE, A van with similar garish, harmless coloring (and a big old cartoon fish named Sammy Sculpin on the sides) was waiting at the front gate. The vans were like the boxes: jolly colors, smiling driver, no tinting on the glass. Nothing glum about moving "marine bio-samples" from lab to lab, right? The driver even made a crack about one box meaning it was a slow day, and I was just tired and focused enough to not even fantasize about breaking his nose.

I was already starting to realize what had to happen next. Now that we were down a man.

The box was loaded up, the driver tipped me a wink, and the van pulled away, out of sight.

And thus did it end with Chatty Andy.

HARP CASUALTIES happen; Andy wasn't the first, not by far.

Back when Lloyd was just a junior science grunt here at Quill, Dr. Wendy Beritov, the head of the xenobiological division, had gotten it into her head that the Harp was dangerous because what it emitted affected the alkalinity of the blood of those nearby—that *that* was why there was some sort of hormonal suppressive effect and that it could be easily countermanded. She was convinced if she stood inside the engine room while breathing through a contraption that would essentially provoke acidosis, she'd make it through a Power-Up event intact, with just the symptoms of acidosis to deal with on the other side.

It hadn't worked. When the door had been reopened, she'd been just like Andy: sitting down, staring blankly, utterly disconnected. She'd been brought to the medics, examined thoroughly, and kept under observation for forty-eight hours. She refused to eat or drink the entire time—although perhaps "refused" is too active a word for it. She just . . . wouldn't. And rather than hook her up to drips and tubes and force nutrients into her for God knows how long, keeping her alive without any "life-force," devastating everyone who had worked alongside her, who were trying to continue her work, the decision was made. She was a battlefield casualty. She had to be put out of her misery.

That's when we got a real sense of just how devastating the Harp's effects could be. That's when we made sure we had a policy in place for its victims. A certain amount of Harp exposure and a person could bounce back. But there was a tipping point.

Harp casualties happen. And Quill Marine casualties happen. Some people can't handle Moss, the spaceship, what it all means cosmically. Some people can't handle keeping the secrets. And that's the thing about Quill Marine. You fuck up, you fall apart, whatever it is—we can't just send you back to your life. Not knowing this.

I didn't do the math then, but later I tried to figure it out. Andy was the seventh person I'd had to kill at Quill Marine. The seventh Turndown. The seventh pickup service. I had wheeled each one up myself. Every single time.

Sevens are lucky, right?

You would have been my seventh if your first day had gone poorly.

Lucky you.

BY THE time we made it through the checkpoints the Hangar had mostly filled back up. The thunder had rolled away and was replaced with the gentle murmur of life moving on. But if I really concentrated, I could still hear it reverberating. It clung to the walls like the smell of smoke after a fire.

Straight off the elevator, I headed toward the bathrooms and Patty kept pace as I crossed the wide floor.

"Chief, you look wiped. Maybe—"

I stopped at the door to the bathroom, swaying on my feet just a little and hoping Patty didn't notice. "We need to replace Andy on the special team for Haydon's visit."

"Christ, do you wanna be thinking about that now? You should—"

"It's Monday. There's no time to waste."

"Okay. I can get you a list of candidates pronto. It's gotta be someone smart and reliable, who can stay on fucking script."

There's nothing.

It's nothing.

"You know who keeps cool?" I said.

"Who?"

"The new guy, skinny guy, what's his name."

"You mean New Fish? He's only been here, like, a week."

"He plays it low, keeps his shit together."

"It's just—I mean, Dak—"

"His name's Matt Salem," I said, my head spinning. "I think he can hack it."

She shrugged. "Then we'll rearrange his schedule. Again."

"Great."

And I went to the bathroom and threw up.

6

DID I ever tell you about the time my dad took me fishing when I was ten? I honestly can't remember. It was one of those formative moments when I realized what life and death actually meant.

THE NEXT morning I was feeling mostly recovered. I'd flopped onto my bed that night, still in my clothes, and slept for ten hours on top of the covers. The Harp was a real motherfucker. But as I pulled into my parking space, stopped the car, and began walking toward the building, it hit me: "Matt's already been on four hours. He'll have seen his new orders. He'll know we're back on rotation together." As Practical Dak and Adamant Dak began haggling over how to handle this information, Lloyd fell in step beside me.

"Dak."

Which one do you want?

"Oh—morning, Lloyd."

"Yeah," Lloyd grunted. A bad sign. Shit's bad when Lloyd's monosyllabic.

Then he spoke: "The, uh . . . the young man yesterday . . ."

"Squared away."

"Right, right, um . . . if, um, there's anything with, with his family—"

"Lloyd: end of subject."

We walked.

"I just thought a successful test . . . the suit, the N5 coating . . . would feel different."

SOME THIRTY minutes or so later, Patty assembled everyone on the Hangar floor.

"Security chief on deck!" she called out, silencing the casual chatter. She was leaning on the ship. I came up and stood next to her.

Yesterday damaged me badly—and I'd be hard-pressed to say if the Harp hurt me more than taking care of Andy. I've known people who could have carried out that sort of task with no problem—with glee, even—but I'm not one of them. That being said, if you were to ask me if I'd prefer today's task of addressing the entire goddamn staff about next week's nightmare, I'd probably jump into one of those brightly colored boxes myself. I hate speaking in front of groups like this. But, as with yesterday's duty, I got through this one in the same manner: committing whole fucking hog. Making eye contact with every person in front of me. Not showing a goddamn atom of weakness.

"Okay, everybody. Look. We're all from different corners of the armed forces but we all learned some version of 'Bad situations make good soldiers,' am I right? This is a bad situation. Full stop. We just had to lose a guy in the worst way right on top of finding out that the man who pays all our salaries moved his visit up a week and will now be here in—how many days, Patty?"

"Five."

"And bear in mind, Mr. Haydon and his team—however big or small that team may be—will be trained in exactly *none* of the Moss protocol or Object E protocol or Harp protocol that's standard for anyone else admitted to this Hangar. I'm sure they are all very good at whatever it is they do, but they also do not know shit about shit." That drew some chuckles. Ragging on the elite always works. "Our job is to protect these people from our assets and protect our assets from these people. That's gonna take precision handling, firm but courteous. All of you are here"—that's when my eyes flicked to you. You were listening. Staring—"because you keep cool and you stay on your patch. That's gonna be key to making sure Haydon *and* Moss get through Monday in one piece. Patty and I are gonna get back to you with more targeted assignments by EOD, then Saturday and Sunday we run drills."

No one groaned, no one voiced any displeasure, not a peep. The kind of people who get pissy about losing a weekend don't tend to wash up here. I caught movement behind the group: Harrison signaling me. Lloyd stood right behind him.

"All right," I said to the group, "hit your shifts, but do not leave without picking up your detail in the staff room. We'll reassemble at the time indicated. Now go work for a living."

The staff fanned out to their various positions throughout Hangar Eleven, and inside I breathed a gale's worthy sigh of relief that that was over. Except—

Immediately, the worst case scenario: you were walking straight at me.

Patty was saying something but I couldn't hear her. I was too busy scrambling, wondering which Dak was going to be handling this assault.

"Hey, what, you need something?" I blurted.

"Um . . . I'm . . . on cockpit duty?" you replied. Fuck me sideways, you were just walking past me to your first shift.

"Yeah, okay, fine, do your thing," I mumbled.

"That was the plan," and you slipped past me and into the ship.

"What, is he bugging you now?" Patty snorted. "You asked for him."

Harrison approached, with Lloyd tailing right behind him.

"Bird's Eye, Director?" I asked. "Looks like you've got news."

Harrison grunted and said, "Let's step inside the ship, Dak. We need to look at something together."

"In the ship?"

Harrison nodded and I noticed how pale Lloyd looked. "We just got an interesting call from Sierra," Harrison said. Then looked at me, straight-faced. "You're gonna fucking love this."

THAT NIGHT, I stood in another scalding shower. I was distantly aware my skin was itching from the heat—I wasn't really sure how long I'd been in there—but I had a lot to mull over.

Are we really gonna go through with this?

It appears so.

I thought about how we all stood, crammed in the engine room of the ship, the Harp sitting in the middle of our little circle, staring at Harrison in disbelief as he told us about his conversation with Sierra.

We looked at him like he'd just taken his dick out in church.

"Chief Prentiss," he'd said after a few moments of buffering, "you know, if anyone's been here long enough to say, 'You're kidding me, right?' it's you."

He was inviting my outrage. But I had trouble finding my voice. After a second or two of me shaking my head with my mouth open, Patty offered: "Can I say it?"

Harrison ignored her. "I'm as surprised as any of you. When I made the call to D.C., I fully expected to be talking about Lloyd's successful N5-suit test the whole time. Instead, most of the phone call was about that unfortunate young man."

Now, standing there in the shower, I felt like I could hear the agitated, unfettered roar of the Harp in the pounding water. I shivered and made the water hotter.

"All Haydon wanted to ask about was everything we'd learned about the Harp's effect on unprotected human bodies. And then once he'd squeezed all that out of us . . . Tell them, Lloyd."

"He, ah, ah," Lloyd stammered his way into the conversation, "he asked if the Harp was field-deployable."

Patty's head titled. "As in . . . ?"

"As in 'against hostiles,'" Harrison said. The thought landed like a physical weight.

"Well, clearly, obviously, there's a range of issues to consider," Lloyd began. Harrison cut him off.

"Can we move this thing or not?"

"Can we move it, or can we move it safely?" I muttered, knowing Haydon's only real concern was with the first one.

I knelt at the base of the Harp, examining it, lightly moving my hands across it to see what gave. Lloyd hunkered down with me.

"These pins," he pointed. "Obviously—obviously, these would, uh, have to be pulled out." It looked like the pins, two featureless oblongs made out of some dull, metallic substance, just passed through the Harp and its base. It looked like you could pull them out like the wooden dowels in cheap furniture. "And then, I suppose . . ." Lloyd made a lifting gesture.

"But, we're not—" Patty began and then shut herself up. Her face was sour, perturbed.

"What, Patty?" I asked.

"I just mean . . . this thing literally killed a guy *yesterday*, are we seriously—"

"Yes," Harrison shot back. "A weapon has to be two things: it has to hurt people and it has to be portable. Haydon was very specific on this point: we're under direct orders to showcase the Harp's effects outside this engine room."

Patty was unconvinced, but she held her tongue for the moment. We had more logistical fish to fry. For instance, how heavy the thing was and how many people we'd need to carry it. With the four of us in the room right now we could attest there was no way to really fit more people in, and the surface area of the Harp made it unlikely to accommodate more than a couple pairs of hands. So we decided to start with two.

"But let's make enough for four," I said.

"Four what?" Patty asked.

"Lloyd Suits," I responded absently. Then, immediately upon realizing no one else was calling them that in their heads, "Or whatever they are, N5 suits. We'll try lifting with two people, and we'll keep two other people on backup if that's not enough."

"I do like 'Lloyd Suits,'" Harrison mumbled supportively under his breath.

"How long to make at least three more?"

Lloyd's considerable eyebrows drew down. "Well, obviously—obviously, the seals *alone* take . . . and then you have to run tests . . . We're talking about, conservatively, two weeks? Though, I'd prefer—"

"We need them by Saturday."

He gaped at me like a fish in a tank.

"That's *insane*," he managed to belch once his voice started working again.

"We need at least a day between the test and Haydon's arrival to rework logistics based on what we learn, Lloyd. That's the most wiggle-room I can give you."

His mouth continued opening and closing.

Dead fish and living fish, a small voice intoned somewhere.

"But, Chief," Patty added, "it's not just the suits, it's not just the people carrying the Harp—it's—this room is the only thing protecting the whole base! Shit, maybe all of California! The minute we carry this thing outside—"

Something in Harrison's sagging eyes clicked into focus. "But what is a room? A room is just a big container. Can we treat smaller containers with N5?"

"Right," I nodded, "one to carry it out, one to store it in. That's doable, right, Lloyd?"

Lloyd was still gaping, practically flopping. "What?!"

"But I don't get it," Patty continued. "Who are we even running Haydon's test on? Is someone here supposed to volunteer to get Harp-nuked? Cuz I'd rather—"

"My understanding is that Haydon's team . . . will be bringing a subject with them." Harrison spoke softly, like one ashamed.

"Like . . . a person subject?"

Harrison looked at her as if to say, "You know better than to even ask otherwise."

For a moment, we all became Lloyd: dumbly staring with

mouths propped slightly open. Like we'd forgotten how to breathe.

Finally Patty spoke.

"Okay. So we just need two volunteers to risk their lives moving the Harp and the whole team to be cool with watching a little sanctioned murder."

"Patty." Harrison glared.

Practical Dak took over while the rest of me processed the information. "How can Haydon watch that test without being Harp-nuked himself?"

"I guess . . . we'd need a see-through version of the engine room," Harrison mused.

I looked at Lloyd. "Can we make that happen too?"

Finally, Lloyd's stasis started to splinter. "I—I—I don't understand—what's being asked of me—!"

"This all seems very achievable to me," Harrison stated kindly.

"Achievable?"

Lloyd's splintering could get out of hand. We'd seen it a couple of times before when he gets pushed over an edge. Nothing dangerous, but nothing pleasant. He was already making very small loops with his body, spinning his hips like he was pacing around the room but without moving his feet. This whole time I had been at least vaguely aware that you were here, listening, so I called to the cockpit.

"Salem?"

You came to the doorway. "Yeah, Chief?"

"Can you walk Lloyd? He just needs a little break."

"I—it's—to use the word 'achiev—' "

"May I make a request first?" you asked. I felt my face flush in annoyance.

"No, you can carry out my order."

"You said you need two people carrying the Harp. I'd like to volunteer to be one."

I don't think I realized just how dangerous this mission might be until I noticed the reaction I was having internally. I wanted to lie down and take a deep breath. But, of course, that wasn't gonna happen.

What the fuck are you doing?!

Harrison wasn't having it either. "Well, that seems strange to me, Salem. Why would you do that?"

"Because I don't want to be the New Fish anymore. I want to graduate." You were looking at him straight, standing tall, not giving any airs. I'm not going to lie, either—it was startlingly attractive.

"That's . . . unsettlingly honest. Dak?"

Say no say no you have to say no

I felt a little like Andy, staring off into nowhere, not more than a few feet from where I was standing right now. Right before I put him out of his misery. Only I wasn't staring off into nowhere, I was staring at you.

"Only if I'm the other one."

"What?!" Patty barked. I wondered if this spaceship had ever seen this much human squabbling before.

"Non-negotiable," I said bluntly.

"Well, Dak, I don't know that I concur," Harrison said.

"Not for nothing, I also don't concur!" Patty echoed.

"Due respect to the parties involved," I replied, "but this is bullshit. If Sierra wanted to change the game this much, they should've given us a month. Am I wrong, Lloyd?"

I threw him that question as a tether to start reeling him back into constructive conversation, even while part of my brain was shrieking at me for what I was agreeing to do. "Uh? No, no, you're—! That, that, obviously, is not—"

"But instead it's Monday," I went on. "Fucking *Monday*."

Harrison was staring me down. "That's correct."

"Well, I'm not usually big on 'I wouldn't ask you to do anything I wouldn't do myself,' but every once in a while it's the way to go," I stared back.

"So now I have to choose between 'I disagree' and 'I trust your judgment?'"

"They can't both be true," I shrugged.

"You know damn well they can be." Harrison glared . . . and then something in him broke. The staring contest ended. He sighed and admitted defeat. Once again I realized this was probably how he looked before opening whatever drawer in his office contained . . .

"Who do you want for the backups?" he muttered.

"Anyone but Patty," I said. "If this goes totally south you need someone you can trust at the helm."

I saw something pass under Patty's face at that. Some flicker of gratitude? Of—

"Can you get me names by end of day?" Harrison asked.

I nodded. And inside, Practical Dak was screaming her death throes. She wasn't gone yet, but she'd just been given the news it was terminal.

"Great," Harrison said. He slapped his thighs halfheartedly, his version of banging a gavel. "Then class dismissed." He exited the engine room and squeezed out of the ship.

"I—I guess I've got my work cut out for me," Lloyd intoned. He wasn't looking at us, instead staring somewhere around our feet, whatever whirred around in his brain already sucking up more and more juice. "I'll need to get your, your suit sizes so I can . . ." He chuckled nervously. "It's like we're planning a wedding."

Jesus Christ, Lloyd.

Make us something matching. And if we end up in a jolly colored box we can end up together. Together forever maybe one on top of the other so we melt into each other in one of those boxes after Sammy Sculpin takes us away—

Lloyd made his way out of the ship. I followed quickly thereafter, not wanting to be alone with either of you—one because I sensed she was about to give me an earful, and the other because . . .

I was right. Patty grabbed my arm as soon as I was out of the ship. She'd slipped out right behind me and I didn't even notice. "This is bullshit. You give this to someone else. You're chief."

I looked at her. I didn't want to have this conversation. "Right," I said, "so I get to exempt myself from toilets and third shift and everything where you have to stand up all day. But this . . . is another kind of thing."

That seemed simple enough. Inarguable. Patty knew I wasn't going to have some eleventh-hour conversion to her way of thinking. So she gave up . . . in her own way.

"Look, I'm not gonna start getting all weepy or whatever—"

"Why not? I might die."

She studied me for a moment, suddenly a kind of serious I wasn't used to seeing from her. I wasn't sure what she was going to say next and a wave of anxiety rumbled through me.

"You know," she said, her voice low. "If we were ever like, goddamn, deployed or whatever . . ."

"You imagine? At my age?" I laughed, trying to dispel the sincerity she was conjuring.

". . . I'd follow you anywhere. I'd follow you into anything."

She looked into my eyes for what seemed like five uncomfortable lifetimes.

"And yet," I finally managed, "you won't try my falafel."

"I mean," she said, reading my eyes, her voice still low, "is it a euphemism, or—?" I had to smile.

Oh thank God we're back

"Pick two more names for me," I told her. "Actually three. For all we know it could weigh a literal ton."

"It's gonna be all assholes. If you're all gonna maybe die we might as well make it a good thing. "

"Then definitely put Grant on the list."

"Yeah, well," she chuckled mournfully. "It should be me. It should be you and me."

"Then who'd feed my cat?"

"You have a cat?"

"Maybe?" I shrugged. "I'm not home much."

Patty laughed—hell, maybe she was wondering herself what creatures might be living in her home unnoticed, who knows.

"I'll send you the names," she said after a sigh, and then she walked away. Her ponytail jounced proudly like it had just secured a prom date of its dreams.

I was going to walk away too. I had things to do, and then a night to enjoy—maybe my last real free evening before we went into overdrive to get this nonsense ready. I was going to walk away . . . but I didn't. I just stood there—like I was just standing in the shower now—just stood there until the Guardshift bell rang.

You came out of Object E and saw me standing there. We had maybe two seconds to look at each other. Then:

"Hangar duty," you said. "Northwest quadrant."

"Have fun."

You walked past me and out of the Tent.

I TURNED off the shower. The hot water had run out and my skin was red and patched from the heat. A dark, bumpy rash was forming irregularly over my body . . . like I was covered in something invasive and foreign.

Tonight would be my one night to rest before we go round-the-clock, straight through to Monday. I knew I should sleep. That would be the practical thing to do. Instead I got dressed, went to a bar I'd never gone to before, and hoped someone would start some shit.

7

I'LL SKIP the montage. Suffice it to say, I rode Lloyd's ass until it was raw and it paid off. By Saturday, close to midnight, we had six new Lloyd Suits and what looked like a jumbo duffel bag all treated lovingly with N5. The entire Hangar had been cleared out, too—all the stations of the Bazaar had been either pushed far away or stored in secured rooms upstairs.

You and I stood on the floor, fumbling with our seals. Having only ever sealed someone else it was a bit of a challenge figuring out how to do it to ourselves. It felt like every step we took should have yielded a graceful, gravity-free bounce.

Patty came by to give us shit—"You idiots look like you're on an episode of *Flash Gordon*," to which you replied, "Do you really think there were *space suits* on *Flash Gordon*?" and earned a faceful of middle fingers—and for a few seconds I was actually enjoying myself. Then Harrison and Lloyd trudged over and ruined everything.

Lloyd had two new pairs of gloves in his hands. He held them out to us, which we took . . . in our already gloved hands.

"Lloyd . . . noticed something," Harrison grunted. This led to a typically Lloydian explanation:

"So . . . the basic principle behind N5, as I elucidated to some of you in the past—and which I believe, obviously, has been largely validated—is based on the conjecture that the engine room's shielding effect has nothing to do with the *thickness* of the walls. After all, the Harp does drain the base every time it spins up. But it only drains people who aren't shielded by those walls.

So something in those walls is acting as a kind of filter, blocking the most destructive elements of the Harp, presumably to protect Moss in flight."

"N5, Lloyd, yes, we all know this." Harrison had his arms crossed over his chest, looking very much like a detective studying his last corpse before retirement. "Just tell them—"

Lloyd nodded, then made a gesture that somehow *retracted* the nod. "Well—strictly speaking—N5 is a *synthesized* version of the original substance we sampled from the engine-room walls. There was always the danger that N5 would fail to completely replicate the effect, but of course, three dogs and myself are alive and well, so—"

Patty was in no mood. "What the fuck is up with the extra gloves?"

"Well. Heh. The, uh, the new concern—or, or the X factor, I guess would be equally apt—is"—and here he chose his words carefully and methodically, as if he were posing the question to himself on a blackboard—"what . . . would . . . happen . . . if . . . the N5 solution comes into direct contact with the Harp itself." We all looked at each other. "Have you noticed the base the Harp rests in keeps the Harp from touching the floor? The floor is coated with the same substances that cover the walls and the door."

Oh.

Shit.

You, Patty, and I exchanged understanding looks. If this N5 substance worked as kryptonite to the Harp's potency, then that meant—

"But, of course, I don't *know*! There's no time to develop—much less implement—testing protocols, but we can't at this time rule out the possibility that it might dampen or even . . . nullify the Harp's effects."

"Is that really the priority?" Patty asked.

"Yes," Harrison answered, before Lloyd could even open his mouth.

"Over Dak's safety?"

"Patty: yes." This time I answered.

"The Harp has, overnight, become Haydon's top interest in this facility. I can't risk permanently compromising its functionality." Harrison sounded depleted.

"So," you spoke up, sending the tiniest jolt of electricity through my body, ". . . these new gloves—the new-new ones . . ."

"Yes, they are *not* treated. Well guessed, Mr. Salem," Lloyd nodded.

"But the other gloves you gave us *are*," I added.

Lloyd nodded again, sweating. He dabbed the back of his neck.

"So, we have to get the Harp into the bag wearing these regular gloves." This must have been the same way you laid out a gnarled assignment from superiors during your enlistment. "Which also means not letting it touch the outside of the bag, which has the same stuff on it—"

"Oh my God," Patty sighed.

"And then we switch gloves?" I asked.

"That means unsealing the regular gloves and then sealing the N5 gloves—"

"You've gotta be fucking kidding me . . ." Patty fumed.

"I'm sorry!" Lloyd was tired—I could tell a snap was imminent if we rode him much harder. I suddenly noticed the deep bags under his eyes—deeper than usual. "I'm . . . when there's no lead time, no test trials . . . this is what happens!"

"It's fine," I said, not meaning it.

"It's not fine!" Patty shot back, meaning it.

"The Harp might not even Power-Up while we do this, Patty—it could be a total non-issue."

"Eat my *ass*," Patty roared.

"Maybe I *do* need to institute a more military-style culture here at Quill," Harrison threatened with noticeable impotence.

That's when you jumped into the conversation.

"We can do it." You were nodding, your brows knit seriously, but there was something eager in your eyes.

Patty turned on you. "Not your call!"

"Give us an hour to practice. We'll practice with the glove seals, we'll get it so it's second nature, and we'll make it happen."

I wasn't gaping at you. I'm sure I looked neutral and composed. But it felt like I was gaping.

"Dak?" Harrison asked. Just for my opinion. Not because I was gaping. I wasn't gaping.

"One request, Lloyd," I said.

"Yeah, yeah, certainly, anything within my power to, to—"

"Can the real gloves and the bullshit gloves be, like, different colors?"

His head ticked. He actually looked a little as if the smell of burning metal and black smoke were about to signify mechanical failure. Thankfully, it didn't last more than a heartbeat.

"Diff—*yes*. Yes. That's definitely—that will be done, that will be implemented."

"Great," I said.

"Great," you said.

"Great," Harrison said.

Patty just glared.

A LITTLE while later it was just you and me. Practicing.

We were alone in the Hangar. Lloyd was in the engine room, doing a final once-over. Patty and Harrison were in Bird's Eye with the backups, giving them the need-to-know version of the assignment.

Which just left you and me. Practicing.

It felt wrong, being alone together in this great empty space. It felt wrong being alone with you in general, but like this? The two of us in, effectively, space suits, surrounded by an entire ocean of nothingness—the sort of palpable solitude that only being in a usually bustling place after hours can give you—it felt like a dream. The sort of dream you have right before you wake up to find you're driving on the shoulder.

We practiced. The bullshit gloves, painted in a slapdash coat of red, came off ("Bullshit gloves off," you would echo). The real gloves, a metallic white, would come on ("Real gloves on"). And then we would seal ourselves at the wrists with a weirdly satisfying whoosh and buzz.

Because anything could be treated with N5, the gloves themselves were actually just regular heavy-duty work gloves—the kind you'd use to move lumber with. But the more we worked with the seals the more I had a greater appreciation for the time Lloyd had spent on them.

I could hear him in my head. Obviously, obviously, the seals had to keep whatever the Harp emits out. But quiz time: would that be a particle or a wave? Were layers of seal enough or did it have to be completely airtight? And how do you calibrate a tight enough seal that prevents anything from getting through, but not so tight as to restrict blood flow or movement?

We sealed and unsealed ourselves again and again—enough times until we couldn't keep pretending that we were doing it for any practical reasons anymore. We had it down.

Even though we had the whole world to ourselves, we kept our voices low.

"We doing this or not?" I finally asked. Referring to the Harp, of course.

"I have a thought."

"You have a thought." Again, I felt a faint current run through me.

"Yeah. I had a stretch where I wore suits almost like these over in—"

"No proper names," I prodded. Gently. Quietly. So as to not disturb the nothingness.

"Right. Let's call it an . . . overseas event?"

"Okay, let's."

"They trained us to pair up and . . . seal each other instead of sealing ourselves."

"Because it's faster?"

"Like four seconds faster."

"I respect four seconds."

"It's weird how much it is sometimes, right?"

"It's very, very weird," I said. *Okay, now we have an excuse.* I unsealed my gloves.

"Let's try it. Seal mine."

"Okay . . . and . . . sealed." Whoosh. Buzz. Then you did the same.

"Hold your arms out," I commanded. You did.

"Yep."

"Sealed right . . . sealed left."

"Again?"

"Yeah. Do me first."

"Unsealing left . . . unsealing right."

We kept practicing, our voices hushed and intimate in the cavernous emptiness. Only the sound of our gloves sealing, unsealing—our skins decomposing, recomposing—and I prayed the noise wasn't loud enough to rouse whatever being was dreaming this unspeakably beautiful dream.

NINETY MINUTES later it was go-time. And still that feeling of dreamlike surreality persisted. I knew combat readiness, I knew adrenaline-heightened perception. This was different.

Patty tested our comms and you and I made sure, two times each, that we could get into and out of Object E without abrading the suits.

The Harp wasn't due to power up again until sometime Monday, late afternoon, presumably when Haydon and his goons from Sierra were here to see the show, so this could all conceivably happen without incident. Still, tucked away in Bird's Eye, Lloyd was all nerves, Patty was all teeth, Harrison was all tightly clenched sphincter.

You and I slipped inside the ship one more time. Like we practiced. Like mist.

The otherworldly glow inside felt appropriate to the moment.

"Engine room?" you asked through your helmet's speaker.

I nodded and let you do the honors, opening up the door to the engine room with your long, thin arms. For the first time I wondered if maybe you and Moss weren't secretly the same species.

We walked into the engine room together and made our way to the Harp. It sat in its base, the non-beating heart of the ship, of this mystery.

You and I knelt before it together in sync, our suits making artificial-sounding noises in the echo-resistant air. We gave the pins securing the Harp to its base an exploratory tug. They moved easily enough; they weren't locked down in any way. So we should be able to do this no sweat.

Like a dream.

I had a moment to think how funny it was that such rudimentary technology kept this extraterrestrial marvel together—there didn't *have* to be such similarities between our basic, physical laws of order, but here we were—and Patty's voice came over the comm.

"*What's your status, guys?*" she asked from light years away.

I confirmed we were in place, ready to pull the pins on her go. I confirmed we were wearing our bullshit gloves, with their slapdash red paint across them. I confirmed the giant duffel bag was open and ready to receive its cargo. I confirmed that we were clear on our directives.

We waited for someone to call it all off and no one did.

"*Backup personnel are in their suits and ready if you need them. Handing it over to you, Chief,*" Patty radioed. I'd be calling the shots from here on out. "*Good luck.*"

You stood back up and held the Harp steady with your uninsulated gloves. Two hands on. It might weigh a ton. It might crush me when I pulled the first pin. We just didn't know. But you promised not to let it fall. You promised to keep me safe.

I pulled the first pin.

Nothing happened.

I pulled the second pin.

There was no tilting, no rocking, and no sense of its weight. You held it steady.

I stood up to join you. You grabbed one side, I got the other. I looked at you—into those eyes—and together we took one more breath before lifting. We would lift on three.

You nodded at me: ready?

I nodded back.

You were smiling—a tiny, impish grin. I felt the edges of my lips curl up in kind.

And without further ado, we counted

to

THREE.

IT HAD to have been a dream. All of it.

Hours and hours and hours afterward in my car, driving through the dead of night, I thought: *There's no way that could have happened. And there's no way I'm doing what I'm about to do.*

The night outside was too dark to be real. The headlights showed nothing but the same stretch of road running like a treadmill underneath my wheels. A magician's trick.

It had all just been a dream—from the moment we got onto that elevator your first day and I sensed my life was over, to what we had just done, what we had just gone through. My life had ended, after all, and everything from that moment on had been some fantastic creation conjured up by desiccating brain tissue; one final, beautiful gift before saying goodbye to all that was. It had seemed to go on for days and days, but what is time to the deceased?

The thing nobody tells you about the end of your life is sometimes you have so much damn longer to live afterward.

And now here I was, on this dark, impossibly dark road, on the way to some sort of afterlife.

None of what just happened could have happened. None of what was about to happen could be allowed to happen. All of this was unreal. Illusory.

I drove into that too-black night and replayed what had (*hadn't?*) happened over again in my head. Because dreams are slippery things and can be lost before you know it.

HERE'S HOW it should have happened:

You and I pull on the Harp. It's heavy and awkward, like lifting a large air-conditioning unit, but we manage to get it out of its base and lug it over to the insulated duffel without too much unseemly grunting and puffing. The hardest part is when one of us has to take the weight entirely on their own (the floor is coated in N5, as Lloyd reminded us), while the other grabs the bag and holds it open as wide as possible. Of course, I insist on being the one who holds the Harp, and I bend backward just a bit to accommodate its bulk while you retrieve the duffel. It's a bit harrowing, easing the Harp in—it reminds me of that game as a kid where we had to extract items from some prostrate clown without touching the sides of his open wounds (*is he too young to know what that game is?*)—but we manage. And we carry our booty out of Object E and into the Hangar. The duffel strains at the weight of the object inside—perhaps one of the straps starts to give— and we breathe an immense sigh of relief when we're able to set it down on its designated spot.

Here's what happens instead:

The Harp sails up with our arms like it was made of balsa wood. We both gasp audibly and Patty comes over the comm, demanding to know what's happened. We tell her, laughing.

"It's so light! Patty, it weighs like two pounds, tops!"

We practiced so *seriously* for this and now it appears either one of us could've carried this thing out one-handed. But we have a plan and we are trained to stick to plans, no matter how silly they feel. We go through the motions of bringing this cheap community theater prop over to the staggeringly expensive duffel bag.

We get about five steps when a small, low hum starts to churn inside the Harp. We stop in our tracks.

Lloyd comes on the comm and tells us something is definitely happening—though nothing big yet. Is it something to panic about? He doesn't know. Patty renews her desire to abort. Harrison renews his dismissal of her desire. It all happens over the radio in that dispassionate, eerily calm way you hear sometimes when calamity strikes: a police scanner reporting a shooting, an airplane pilot reporting the plane is going down. Just reportage. The bag is only four feet away. We can do this. You mirror my steps like it's the only way you ever knew how to move.

A light, not altogether unpleasant tingling spreads its way through my body, like I've just taken a shot of liquor on an empty stomach. Only, there's no enjoyable buzz that follows, just the feeling of encroaching anesthesia. I realize: it's like my blood sugar has started to drop.

We're almost to the bag. We're right on top of it. You start to reach down to grab it and we adjust to get ourselves in a good position to lower it

on

three

SHIT

SHIT

What's happening? The voices on the radio are no longer so dispassionate.

The humming gets louder. Is the Harp enacting some sort of countermeasure against being moved? Is it having a bad dream?

We try to report to Bird's Eye but the strain makes it hard to talk while also holding on to this leaden weight, this Buick, this dense collapsing star. It's suddenly so fucking heavy. Except it hasn't taken on any real weight—we're just losing all our strength. It's pouring out through our hands as quickly as if we've slashed our wrists.

We're both of us losing our grips on it, we, it, weighs, can't, FUCK

This is when the dream becomes a nightmare.

We drop it. We miss our target. It lands next to the bag, then pitches forward and leans against the bag. The bag coated in N5.

Meanwhile, we're being blasted with (what?) (space?) (this is just a dream)

It's not a full blast yet—the hum isn't as loud as I know it can get. And also I can still imagine tomorrow. I can still remember omelets and coffee and the smell of trees. But it's getting close. It's not just one shot on an empty stomach, it's an entire bottle being poured down my throat. My eyes are losing focus, my bones are losing solidity. That lack of taste in my mouth I'd experienced when Andy got blasted is back—it is the flavor of absolute nothingness.

Patty's tiny, tinny voice is demanding an update, hurry, we might lose power soon. But the hum is getting louder and the connection with Patty is already starting to get crackly, unintelligible. We're in a car listening to the radio, about to drive through a tunnel. And the tunnel is dark, too dark, and getting darker.

You say my name.

It actually takes a second to realize that's what that sound means—that paltry bark of a noise is my name (nothing), my identity (meaningless)—but the Harp's effects are still not fully realized yet and eventually I understand why you're calling my name. You're pointing to the bag, to the obvious truth.

The Harp is still doing its thing even though it's in contact with the N5.

Only in a dream, I think.

But oh well. My will. My life-force. I'm too drunk on misery, on disinterest, to take advantage of this game-changing observation. I can barely swallow the saliva pooling in my gaping mouth. I realize the engine-room door is still open and I think of what might happen to the base when the Harp reaches full power. We've never experienced that before; the blast very well could hit everyone up in Bird's Eye. I don't care. I'm alone enough in my minimizing world to not—

But, no. I'm not alone. I see you. You. You're trying to crawl toward me.

There's still time.

It's all I need. It takes impossible effort but I get to you—

curl up c'mon nothing matters this is all nothing but NO I pull

*myself toward you. The humming gets even louder but I pull myself
toward you.*

*Our ligaments are coated in lead my eyes are glazed and heavy
but we do it just like we practiced. Just like your idea.*

I unseal your gloves.

Whoosh. Buzz.

You unseal mine.

Whoosh. Buzz.

And the bullshit gloves come off. (Bullshit . . . gloves . . . off.)

I want to stop, to rest, just for a little bit just for—NO

The real gloves go on. (Real gloves . . . on.)

*As soon as I activate the seals on your insulated gloves it's like
you've been injected with life. Your entire demeanor changes behind
your helmet: more alert, more responsive. Everything about you
becomes stronger. As for me, I'm fading fast. The end of the dream.
An icy curtain is descending down over me and on three I'll be gone*

> *one*
>
> *two*

You finish sealing my gloves. I don't get to three. I get to stay
asleep a little while longer and dream this dream with you.

The instant the insulated gloves are on our hands we feel
better. Not 100 percent, but suddenly alive again. We exchange
looks of disbelief. We even laugh.

We get our bodies back under our control and manage to
maneuver the still-humming, really shrieking Harp into the bag.
Once it's in, we activate the seals on the bag, just in time for the
hummingshrieking to culmINATE AND BURST through to its
other sound dimension. We're left in the eerie silence of that
spreading tone of a full spin-up. It's completely off schedule,
there's no telling how long it lasts. It could be days.

But we've come this far. So we pick up the bag.

I squeeze my way out of the ship, then you hand me the bag
(is there anything in this thing? it's so light again) and when you get
out yourself, you try to take it from me but I keep it to myself.
My papoose. I've been looking after it for years.

The dream shifts locations like dreams often do. We're on the other side of the Tent, and in the pitch black, fully offline Hangar beyond. We can't see a thing. It's completely silent and utterly dark.

There was supposed to be some glow tape laid down somewhere—but where? How do we find it? There's just so much ground to cover and not even a horizon on which to orient ourselves. For all we know we could be falling. Floating. It's like that *other* dream, the one we all have after the first time we meet Moss (which I still haven't learned if you had as well): of rushing through incredible nothingness . . . or standing still in wait.

But then I remember. This is my home. This is me. I know where the tape marks are. Social Outcast Dak makes a joke about this being as easy as finding her own asshole in the dark—a piece of cake—and I cringe. I hate her. But she's a part of me, too, and she's in this with us, decomposing, and you don't even seem to mind her at all.

We find the glow-taped X and we set the Harp down, still churning its power-pausing churn. Our job's not done, however. Now it's time to deactivate the seals and remove our baby. The suits want to see "the Harp," not "the Bag," and Lloyd prepared us one more containment apparatus for this moment. One for which we have to wait until the power comes back on, hanging over our heads right now in the darkness.

We pull the Harp out with our insulated, white gloves. I hate that it doesn't glow. It's humming and active, but just as dark as everything else. It feels wrong somehow. But don't question it, none of this is real, it's allowed its own rules. I cradle the Harp in my arms and you're behind me, your arms around me in support, and it's just you and me in the dark again, like we're practicing something (what?). We talk to the Harp, we chastise it for trying to kill us and failing, we make nervous jokes, but mostly we just sit and wait together until

the

Harp

finally

starts

to

fall

asleep. The humming recedes in intensity. Lower . . . lower. All of Hangar Eleven starts coming back online all around us: lights, sounds, refreshed from a siesta and ready to rock. Even Patty's voice, screaming into our comms—she was screaming at us that whole time and we just couldn't hear her. Because we were in space together. Because we were at the bottom of the ocean together.

We tell her to drop it—not just the subject but also Lloyd's final apparatus. She's still screaming at us. This is the first time you and I are seeing each other since we almost died and I pray—I actually pray—that I look as perfect to you as you're looking to me.

I hear your voice now. They say in dreams that you can't actually read things, like newspapers or letters. They say that your brain just provides you with the knowledge of the text you're dream-reading, and that if you're aware enough to pay some attention you'd notice that there are no legible written words before you. Your voice feels like that to me at this moment. I feel like I haven't actually heard it until right now. It hits my ears like a distant alarm and I know this dream is about to end. And because we're not inside the ship, it echoes, it rolls, it reverberates within me.

Like thunder.

"It's coming," you tell me. "We better crawl out of range."

You hold out your hand and I don't even need to think about taking it. It's mine to take. We link up and crawl away as a twelve-by-twelve N5-treated fiberglass cube descends from a winch over the Harp, softly humming its way back to contented sleep.

RUNNING IT all through my head just then, I was impressed I could still remember every moment. That was rare for a dream, wasn't it? Usually they start to discorporate upon any sort of reflection. I could even remember things that happened afterward. I could remember coming back to consciousness several hours later, late Sunday, on a cot by the locker bay. I could remember medics over me, telling me you had already been cleared to go home and now it was my turn. I could remember Harrison even cracking a joke:

"You deserve a year off," he said. "I can give you six hours."

He told me to get some sleep. Tomorrow was Monday. It was going to be the biggest day we've ever had, after all. Even more stressful and insane than Saturday had been.

So why was I in my car, on some road fully and unmitigatedly submerged in nothingness?

The darkness out here was like the darkness inside Object E—light didn't spread, it just punched holes in it. And even though I had my car headlights to help, I also knew this road the way I knew Hangar Eleven. This road was my sickbed, after all. Or perhaps my funeral bier. There was only one way I could go.

There was a cell phone in my hand. A burner phone I'd picked up from a gas station. You wouldn't recognize the number, but I was gambling that you'd understand what it meant.

"Hello?" I heard your voice in my ear. I didn't respond. I just breathed.

"Get here," you said, and for the second time tonight I was reminded of the dream we all seem to have after our first day working at Quill Marine. For years I wondered: are we imagining what it must have been like for Moss, traveling here? Are we imagining ourselves, rushing toward some previously inconceivable truth? Now I had a different understanding. Maybe we're the nothingness. Things might pass through us, but ultimately nothing can change our nature, our hunger—we can't even find the outer edges.

Tonight I intended to ask you about it.

I parked a fifteen-minute walk away from your motel. Part of me was screaming, "You're giving him *so much time* to change his mind!" By the time I was on the second-level walkway of your motel it was like I'd been walking all night.

Oh Jesus. Oh Jesus. There's an easy way to fix this. There's such an easy way to stop everything that's coming. Just . . . don't . . . knock. Wake up wake up wake up

That was Practical Dak, screaming. The way Patty had screamed. I shut that comm link off forever and knocked on your motel room door.

It opened and your hand reached out to grab me and pull me in. I let it, and within seconds you were on me. I was on you. My flesh, my bones, losing all structure and form until they were dust to be inhaled by you. But I refused to let myself worry.

Everything that would happen next would happen fast and relentless. So I deserved this moment. An end to my dream. One last feverish spasm of a dead brain for me to hold on to as consolation as my body dissolved away.

Tomorrow I would wake up and a new life would begin.

PART TWO

AFTERDEATH

INTERLUDE

OKAY, SO. A ten-year-old girl stands next to her father on a pier. It's early, just a couple hours after daybreak, and I guess you could say the same thing about the relationship. They don't know each other very well . . . but they're giving it a try.

They both have lines in the slate-gray water. The father is ambling his way through a monologue about the ins and outs of fishing—why they're here so early, what kind of reels they're using, what sort of fish they might find in these parts. He's talking this way because—even the girl understands this—once he runs out of things to talk about on this subject, he'll have to find something else to talk about with his daughter and he has absolutely no idea how to do that. The two of them have known each other for maybe seven months at this point, and the relationship between them is as mysterious and intimidating as the water into which their lines are sunk.

She's doing her best to listen. She's never gone fishing before.

He's nearing that point, that dreaded point, where he runs out of things to say, when his line jerks and goes taut. They both gasp and he works on reeling in whatever is on the other end. It emerges shortly thereafter: a fat, slick brown fish, twitching and spasming in desperate dialogue for its life. This is not just an expedition for fun, though—this is for food, and so the father is pitiless.

However, the fish is remarkably swollen. Unusually so. Once it has been stilled, he lays the fish down on the pier, slices open the fish's belly and the girl is (*amazed? horrified?*) to see at least half a dozen smaller fish spill out, flopping, onto the ground.

They're not small, either, each one seems about the size of her father's pinky finger.

I thought fish laid eggs, the girl exclaims. Not all of them, the father replies, and begins rattling off a list of names.

This is a miracle, the girl thinks. She thinks this without any reverence—it's as much a statement of fact as her father's listing of the various brands of lines they could have been using. Even at the point of death, new life emerges.

She feels like there's a lesson here, something to help her look at the world with fresh eyes. But as she puzzles this out she also watches as her father tosses the body of the adult fish into their bucket, throws only a few of the newly delivered fish back into the water, and then works on spearing the remaining babies onto the hooks at the end of his and her lines. Only alive for a few heartbeats before being used as bait.

Now we can catch something really big, he's saying. This was lucky.

What remains after death but more life, and what is life if not food for more death? Life and death walk hand in hand. And they're both motherfuckers.

How do I get to be one of the fish he threw back, she wonders.

The water laps against the piles of the pier beneath them as the girl and her father stand in silence. Some ten minutes later, a line goes taut again.

THE RUSTLE of sheets.

It was dark. I don't usually like to fuck in the dark—my mind can wander without direct visual stimulation—but this time it was the furthest thing from an issue. Somewhere internally, I knew that if I allowed myself to have really vibrant memories of this moment, I'd never be able to think about anything else. Better to maintain at least a little obfuscation, if only from myself.

Even so, our eyes had adjusted, like cats', and it felt like I could see every minute detail in the room. It was as if Moss were in here with us, giving us his impossible glow.

We're on the floor of the cockpit during a Power-Up, my mind whispered at one point. *The world belongs to nothingness.*

Now we were talking, our voices as soft as the conversation of bedclothes around us.

"One versus zero?"

"What?"

"What'd they teach you in training? If you're down to the choice, one hour of sleep versus zero, what do you do? What do they say in the SEALs?"

"I guess different people said different things. Most of the field guys said power through. But a couple said grab whatever you can."

I couldn't get over it. How long and thin you were. From your neck, your chest, yours arms, down to your legs, like you'd been stretched as a kid. There was no end to you; I could keep running my hands over your smooth, perfect skin until the world came to a stop. And the thing was, your skin was *far* from smooth and perfect—there were places of roughness, of callus and hair, not to mention the cragged grace notes of scar tissue throughout, mountain ranges on a relief map—but all of it seemed so right, all of it seemed so necessary and perfect and just begging for my hand to find its way over it, continuing down the slender, graceful, never-ending track of your body. There were no impediments; if anything each imperfection propelled my hands further as surely as if you had been made of silk. And if I'd turned the light on, I bet I could have seen your heart beating under your rib cage again. That heart I didn't have to stop. Feeling proprietary already—*my* heart.

"What'd they say in the Rangers?"

"There was like . . . this 'official recommendation' that some is better than none, but . . ."

"Pssh. Official recommendations."

"Exactly. Everybody knows that shit goes out the window when you're In It."

"So, power through?"

"I had this one CSM who was always like singing the gospel of the forty-minute nap. He was obsessed with the forty-minute nap. Like, forty-one minutes, you're a zombie, but forty on the dot, and you wake up like a Terminator."

"Did you try it?"

"Couple times. Never could quite hit whatever forty minutes was for me."

"You know what, I forgot, we had a thing like that but it was different, it was tech."

"Tech?"

"Hooked it up to us. Inside the field apparel. Supposed to wake us up the minute we were at just the right part of the . . . whatever-cycle."

"Did it work?"

"We never really tested it. It was another thing to lug, so . . ."

"I hear that."

"Commander nixed it, we just went back to—"

"Powering through."

"Powering through."

Men talk about running their hands over somebody's curves. I couldn't stop running my hands over your straight lines.

"It's um . . . 4:04."

"We have to be there at oh-six-hundred."

"And the drive from here takes twenty,"

"Big day."

"Yep."

"So . . . ?"

"So . . ."

"You know what else they taught me in training?" Inching in toward my shoulder.

"What's that?"

"They taught me leaders . . ." You leaned even farther in and started kissing my neck. You bastard. You cheat. I don't even know if what you said next was out loud or just the whisper of linen as your hand made its way down past my navel. ". . . have to make judgment calls."

"I'll make a judgment call," I whispered back, turning into you. "We'll power through."

I LEFT with twenty-five to spare.

"Wait the full five minutes before even starting your car," I told you as I finished pulling on my coveralls. "If I see you in my rearview you're a dead man."

As I drove, I watched the sun come up over the treeline. I thought of Patty and the conversation we had in the parking lot what seemed like months ago (*another life*) already. How interchangeable the dawn and dusk can be. Like a word that takes on an entirely different meaning in context. Like the bottom of the ocean and deepest space.

At the front gate, I gave Parker my ID and the life stats of a woman no longer with us.

Date of birth: January 12, 19alonglongtimeago

Middle name: none

Parker handed the ID back and said, "Big day today, huh?"

Parker, you have no fucking idea.

"Catch you on the far side," I said, and drove through the opened gate.

AS I made my way through the security checkpoints, I made sure Rosh and Lauren were both clear on how today would proceed: Haydon and his associates would be skipping all procedures and heading straight through.

Rosh was baffled but accommodating. "He shall be a stranger . . . but not a stranger!" he intoned. And . . . sure, whatever helped.

Lauren took the news about as well as I expected. Which is to say she almost snapped in half from the stress.

"This doesn't—no, this isn't supposed to happen!" She insisted from behind the window of her booth. She looked like someone unjustly imprisoned, begging for help from a visiting relative.

"Lauren. Lauren. You need to understand something." I remained calm and patient. "Haydon might decide to take Moss with him when he goes. Cash in, start a freak show. That's his right, Moss is his property. He might walk up to your station and give you the wrong answer, except with him, there are no wrong answers. Do you understand?" She considered what I was saying. "When they come through here, you let them walk on by. That's a direct order."

She nodded, looking as if she'd aged a decade.

Wonder when was the last time you *got laid, Lauren,* I thought ungenerously. *Might do you some good.* God, I was already doing that thing, that "What the world needs now" shit like so many other giggly, heartsmug fools before me who thought they'd discovered some profound secret to living. I'd have to watch that impulse, I told myself . . . and even then I thought of how you felt against me and had to repress a smile. Repressing that smile took work. Like closing an overstuffed suitcase.

One last person I had to make sure knew the score: the Gnome. True to form, I was eager to get down to the Hangar and start this monster of a day, and halfway down, the elevator jounced to a stop and the red light flicked on.

"I'm only gonna say this once, Gnome," I barked. "Do this again today and I'll make sure Haydon knows who you are. I'll make sure he moves you to the most public post we have to offer, with nothing to fucking hide behind and nowhere to run. Maybe he'll stick you up at reception with Trippi, where you can answer phones every—"

The lights switched back to normal and the elevator resumed its journey.

WHEN I reached the Hangar level, the doors slid open and there was Patty, waiting for me.

"Chief!" she blurted, like a tackle. The team was assembling on the floor and she turned to them. "Okay, people, anyone complaining about losing their weekend, look who's back on the clock thirty hours after taking an ass-whupping from the Harp!"

Everyone within earshot clapped and cheered and I felt myself go red.

The Harp sat right where we'd left it, in the center of the Hangar inside its N5-treated see-through cube. I hadn't even noticed when we'd placed it there that it was lying on its side. It looked as exhausted as the rest of us.

"Did you sleep?" Patty was asking me. I shrugged.

"Yeah, I slept over there." I pointed in the direction of the cots, where the medical team had kept me under observation.

"Okay, but did you sleep *more*?"

"I'm powering through. What's the ETA on our guests?"

"Tower says they're gonna be on time."

"Dicks."

"Right?"

"Any number yet?"

"Yeah. Haydon and 'a handful' of assistants. That's all they'll tell us."

That tracked with the earlier Trip visits I'd staffed back in the day. He liked people uninformed and scrambling. Whether this was a conscious tactic or just another aspect of his well-documented love of endangered big game hunting, I didn't know.

"Plus . . ."

"Oh, God, plus what?"

"The test subject. Also identified on the manifest. As 'X.'"

"Wait—Jesus, he's got the subject on the *plane* with him?"

She nodded deliberately, scandalously. "Supposedly picked out whoever it is himself."

We gave ourselves a collective moment to take that little plot twist in. Then I remembered:

"Oh, shit, how about—?"

"The lunch? Way ahead of you. Had three former marksmen assigned to it like two hours ago and they're probably still muttering curses about me. But it's a spread that would charm the panties off a nun."

"Yeah, word of advice: try not to piss off former marksmen."

"I don't know what Harrison expected—it's not like we coulda just ordered in!"

I had to smile at that thought. "Where are we? Can I get everybody in one place?"

"We're just waiting on one more—oh, there he is."

The elevator opened. There you were.

Good Lord, I would never have guessed the man stepping onto the Hangar floor had been up all night. You looked as neatly put together and ready for action as if it were your first day back after a three-week vacation.

We made eye contact so brief yet so tangible it might as well have been a physical caress, and then you joined the team on the floor.

THE HAYDON team assembled in Hangar Eleven, chatting in low voices. That's the way we operated here at Quill: in teams. The Harp team, the Moss team, the Object E team, and so on. The scientists and researchers were given one specific aspect of our little secret to focus on and start to merge an identity with, but it was unusual for me to have such a specified team—normally we're just "security." But here we were.

Everybody *not* on the Haydon team was given the order to clear upstairs by 1 p.m. and stay there for the rest of the day. Once again, I had the detested assignment of addressing a group, but this time I didn't mind so much—these were my people. I adored everyone who had made it onto this team. Well, almost everybody; there was also Grant. Plus, I was powering through. In fact, powering through was working out great. It reminded me of humping fifty pounds of gear through thirty-hour treks. I almost missed it. There was only one problem . . . and it wasn't fatigue.

"Okay, everybody, stand tall and shut up," Patty told the team as I stepped forward. The chattering ceased and they all looked to me. You were there, toward the front, and I mean, let's have it said outright. The problem was horny. My body wasn't screaming, "Sleep," it was screaming, "There are cots past the lockers." It was screaming, "You gave me a taste of something and I am not remotely done with it."

Power through.

I gave the team a quick rundown of what we were looking at today: a situation, I confessed, with more unknowns than knowns. Hell, if this had been a field op I might have called it off, it was so murky. They kept their reactions private, but we all shared them. We bristled at the fact that we still didn't know how many associates Haydon was bringing along with him. We cringed at the need-to-know nature of X. Most of all, we hoped everything rolled out as smoothly as the itinerary made it sound: guests estimated to arrive at 11, then lunch, followed by Lloyd giving a briefing with holograms in Conference Hall, and then we would gather in front of the large, clear cube in the middle of the Hangar to watch the Power-Up that was estimated to occur at 2:35 p.m.

"Only we're not hoping it goes smoothly, are we, team? Hoping's what you do when you've got no control over a situation. We're going to *make* it happen."

"Ma'am, yes, ma'am!" they barked at me. They were nervous, reverting back to old behaviors. That was okay; I'd let them be soldiers today.

Remember how he felt on top of y—

There were a few more specifics to go over. Lloyd's hologram presentation was sensitive enough that no other security personnel besides myself were to be in the room: the rest of the team would wait outside until it was time to move on. And then there were the logistics of . . . X.

All they needed to know at this point was Haydon's people were to hand X off upon arrival and X would be kept in the Slammer under guard until 2 p.m. At that point, Patty and I would take over.

Once I was done with the rundown, I confirmed with Patty that assignments had been handed out and opened the floor for any final questions.

Two hands went up. One of them was Grant's. Fuck Grant. Let him wait.

"Yeah, Shel," I called on the other raised hand. I liked Shel. Tiny but never intimidated, with jet-black hair bobbed smartly, she somehow came through her service with her smile and her teen acne intact.

"The test subject, X . . . ," she said, choosing her words carefully and darting her eyes to the cube on the floor (*A little sanctioned murder,* I remembered Patty snarling). "Are we allowed to know any basics? Gender? Age? Reason for incarceration?"

"No," I said patiently. "Whatever it's worth, I don't know either."

Another soldier, Vonn, spoke up: "Are we at all concerned about another possible unscheduled Power-Up?"

That was a surprise: Vonn was usually a no-drama order-taker. The kind of guy I could forget was even there sometimes, despite the fact that he was the size and density of a stone statue.

Patty stepped in. "Folks, let's see some hands raised before we shoot off our mouths."

That's not a problem for Grant, who has literally been keeping his hand raised through all of this. Jesus, that guy.

"Vonn. Shel. Guys. You don't have to figure out how to make this okay for yourselves. It's not okay. It's an organizational clusterfuck. Shel, X might be an armadillo for all the advance info we've received. Vonn, Lloyd's analysis of the Power-Up we experienced Saturday night was that it was some sort of reflex or countermeasure against being moved. We won't attempt to put the Harp back until tomorrow, when Haydon's safely on the other side of the continent. That said, Patty is going to be running evac drills with you guys for the next hour. Okay, any other questions? Time's a-wasting."

"My hand is up," Grant said.

"Grant?" I sighed at last, unable to put it off any longer. "I believe you had a question."

He smiled, a prissy, ungrateful smile. The weirdest thing about Grant was that he was actually rather handsome, on paper at least. A proportional, symmetrical face, strong enough features, even a fine head of ash-blond hair. But he had a habit of making the most viscerally unpleasant expressions: sneers, scowls, and most of all, stony, utterly humorless stares. Any attempt over the years to crack a joke or share a laugh with him was met with that goddamn stare, until one just stopped trying. Which was all the same, since when it came down to it, Grant was eminently, effortlessly unlikable.

"Thank you, Chief. Chief, may I speak with you privately following this briefing?"

Also, he was the sort of guy who did things like *that*. He could have just spoken to me privately. Instead he wanted to make sure everyone *knew* he wanted to speak to me privately.

I threw up my hands, maybe a bit more aggressively than I should have. "If you can squeeze it into thirty seconds. We've got shit to do." I turned to the rest of the team. "Okay, everybody hit their marks, we're gonna start running drills in five."

"You heard her, people, fall out!" Patty echoed. They complied.

Meanwhile, there was Grant. I took him aside. "Is there any way this can wait?"

"I want to report an instance of fraternization," he said, squarely.

It was like a Harp blast. I swallowed, hoping the novelty of the accusation covered my shock.

"Excuse me?"

"Fraternization. Among members of this select team."

The panic was like someone switched on a gas burner in my gut.

"Fraternization."

"Of a romantic and sexual nature. I've witnessed it."

This guy—is he—is there any way—could he . . . is he shaking me down?

No. Fuck this. He needs to be put in his place and hard.

"Lemme get this straight," I said through clenched teeth.

"Fraternization is explicitly prohibited by—"

"You come to me just before a critical event, a visit from the people who own your life and the life of every person here, an event I cannot restaff for the simple reason that it's starting in *hours*—"

"I just thought it was appropriate—"

"*Interrupt me again.*" I stared him straight in the eyes, not caring that anyone looking over at us could tell I was a hair's breadth away from tearing off his arms and whipping him with them. I gave him a chance to speak. He appeared to be demurring. "Wanna say something?"

"I'm sorry, Chief."

I brought my voice down to a whisper. "You wanna do this? Come back to me tomorrow. Today? Do your fucking job."

"Yes, Chief."

"Hit your post."

"Yes, Chief."

And he hurried off.

I made a conscious decision not to exhale. I just breathed.

He didn't mean me. He didn't mean you. Jesus Christ, I damn near puked on his shoes.

"I've pulled some people together to be practice VIPs." Patty was suddenly next to me again. I almost jumped.

"Thanks, Patty."

"That Grant thing, is that . . . ?"

"Nah, it's horseshit. Let's roll."

FIVE HOURS later, 11 a.m. on the dot, I was out front trying to look invisible behind Harrison and Lloyd. All things considered it looked like it was going to be a lovely day topside: temperate, breezy, the tang of eucalyptus in the air. Behind the lush treeline, the sky was calm and untroubled.

Down on our level, a convoy of three vehicles had pulled up to the gates and Parker, having been given his own special instructions, was waving them through without any impediment.

"I'm sorry, Dak," Harrison muttered for at least the third time, "just tell me again that Lauren's not going to make a scene . . ." I assured him, again, she'd been spoken to. "And Rosh won't be . . . Rosh?"

"We're good, sir."

Harrison shot a look to Lloyd, who was knitting his hands together, pinching a point between his thumb and forefinger. Lloyd looked up, as if from dozing.

"Yes! Yes, um, short answers, to the point—"

"And we'll be steering clear of the word 'obviously,' yes?" Harrison cocked an eyebrow.

"Obv—uh, indub—uh, yes. Yes." Lloyd pressed harder on the soft spot on his hand.

A tall, red-haired man of about forty got out of a car as black and shiny as a pool of undisturbed ink. All three cars looked that way, in fact—it was a convoy that practically screamed, "Important People Up to Nefarious Things." A bald assistant scurried out behind him.

"That's Haydon?" Lloyd asked. He sounded fascinated, like he'd just witnessed some mythological specimen cross in front of a camera lens. "He's so . . . young and nondescript."

"Right, you never met him, did you?"

"I was, uh, in a junior position last time he came."

From the third car, a security team emerged, two blacksuits chaperoning a person with a dark mesh bag for a head. It appeared to be a woman.

"And," Lloyd gulped, "presumably, presumably that is—"

"Nothing you have to handle, Lloyd," Harrison whispered kindly.

I radioed for Shel and Vonn to report topside so they could receive X from Haydon's people.

"Probably wishing you still were junior man, huh?" Harrison chuckled ruefully to Lloyd, who was practically rubbing his hands into a single glob.

Lloyd gave a weak laugh, then swallowed. "Here they come."

"MIKE," HAYDON cooed, grabbing Harrison by the arms. That's right. Here was the guy who could stroll up to a former colonel and decorated war hero and just say, "Mike."

"Mr. Haydon. It's an honor to welcome you back to—"

Haydon gave me and Lloyd a cursory once-over, as if we were tuxedos he might have to wear later for events he didn't care about. "Okay, I don't know you and I don't know you."

Lloyd began to stammer immediately. I stepped forward, hands at my sides.

"Security Chief Dakota Prentiss, sir."

His eyes narrowed. "Were you here last time?"

"I wasn't chief at the time, sir. You would've dealt with Russell."

"That doesn't sound right."

"Opposite of me, sir. Tall. Blond. Male."

"Oh. Yeah. I remember." He snorted. "Opposite is right."

Meanwhile, Harrison had given up on Lloyd putting together a coherent introduction just yet. He put a hand on Lloyd's shoulder.

"Lloyd Simon is the head of research in our xenobiological division. Also new to the position since last time."

"Christ," Haydon rolled his eyes. "You'd think this is one gig where we could keep people around." I supposed given Sierra's extensive network of prisons, sweatshops, and hazardous clean-up sites, this was one of their cushier locations.

"Lloyd was in the junior position during your previous—"

"Oh!" Haydon turned to Lloyd with a massive smile: all teeth, no eyes. "But now you're Senior Man. Congrats, you're gonna be answering a lot of questions today. Meanwhile standing around outside is getting really goddamn old." He turned back to Harrison.

"Absolutely!" Harrison kowtowed, making my heart ache. "We're ready for you right this way. How many—"

"Just me and this one." He cocked his head at his bald assistant. Harrison's eyes darted to the second, unopened car. "That's just for in case I get bored."

"Very good. And your . . ." Harrison gestured toward Haydon's contingent of scowling, intimidating men in black suits, swarming in and around the cars.

Haydon gave a mock gasp, a hand to his chest. His eyes slid over to me—they were swimming with condescension. "I should hope *your* security's good enough to protect little old me while I'm inside."

"Of course," Harrison sputtered. "Let's get you all inside."
We led them into the mouth.

AS WE approached the first checkpoint, Harrison explained that we had security protocols suspended, but had every person and mechanism still in place so he could see how we'd upgraded the base since his last visit.

"Cooool," Haydon cooed disinterestedly.

We continued walking past Rosh, like he was an exhibit at a museum we'd already patronized for too long. We weren't being swallowed by the Big Bug—Haydon was forcing his way down its throat. Choking it. Rosh had a look on his face very similar to the one he wore when I wheeled out a Turndown box.

"Great mustache," Haydon threw over his shoulder as we passed.

Haydon's assistant fluttered up to Harrison.

"I'd like us to review the itinerary, please," the assistant (who I'd already begun to think of as Needledick for the way he just inserted himself into everything) said. "Mr. Haydon is on a very tight schedule."

"Of course, of course," Harrison agreed. "Lloyd will be making an initial presentation in our conference room in an hour, as we discussed. And I thought we might start off with some lunch."

Haydon stopped in his tracks. "Lunch?" He wore an expression that seemed to suggest Harrison had just suggested we all put potted plants on our heads for good luck.

"We've prepared several menu options that I've been assured are—"

"I'm not gonna spend an entire hour eating. That's bizarre."

"Let's have the food sent to the conference room," Needledick offered. Harrison started to agree and Haydon barreled right over him.

"The presentation's ready, right?" He turned to Lloyd. "You're not buying time to finish it, are you?"

Lloyd went bright red. "No, no! No, it's, no, it's fully, it's unambiguously—"

"Then let's just do it *now*. Jesus, who just *eats*?"

"Of course, we will contact the kitchen—" Harrison stumbled. My stomach burned a little for him. Longtime officers tended to forget what it was like to be down the chain; casual humiliation buckles them. I'd been in the middle long enough that the ability to be humiliated had been sanded off of me.

"Let's keep moving, sir," I said.

Haydon purred. "Terrific."

WHEN WE made our way past Lauren, she stayed in her booth and kept her eyes down, not even watching us pass. It almost looked as if she were praying.

MOSS HOVERED above us, bending, flexing. He was finally free of his mossy covering, which floated a few inches off to the side, and he was lifting his arms, stretching his neck, even doing an incredibly slow and controlled barrel roll in midair while we sat and stared.

We were down in Conference Hall, blinds drawn across the window. Lloyd stood before our tiny group, taking us through a series of holographic images he'd said were culled from eighteen months of footage of Moss.

The hologram projector, a small black box the size of a Rubik's Cube, tossed up high-definition, three-dimensional renderings of Moss. For a better view of the actual body, Lloyd had pressed a button and the moss on Moss's chest had cleanly shifted over to the side. Lloyd was able to rotate both with a tiny remote control, giving us a 360-degree look at points of contact and how the two substances interacted. Lloyd could even change Hologram Moss's positions, show the various ways his alien joints articulated (which, to be honest, were hardly different than our own save for a few fun exceptions: knobby elbows that could hyperextend, wrists that could swivel almost a full 360 degrees, hands with only four spidery fingers, and feet with only two giant thumb-like toes), or zoom in and out to get an unnaturally close look at any area or aspect a person could desire. The images were impressively detailed. They were also, for all intents and purposes, a lie.

It felt awful shutting the door on my whole team, especially Patty . . . but given the misdirection we were trying to pull on Haydon, the fewer eyes the better. Lloyd wasn't *actually* showing eighteen months' worth of images of Moss—more like three. Anyone who worked a daily rotation guarding Moss's body would recognize the discrepancy.

It also felt wrong hearing Lloyd give a lecture so remarkably un-Lloydian. Sure, it was quicker (in fact, he was blasting through his presentation), more concise, but the passion was gone, the fun was gone, the frequent prompts for participation were gone. I gave him immense credit, though: he lied better than I would have imagined.

To cap off the absurdity of it all, on the table, surrounding the hologram projector, and with all the élan of a cold cuts party tray, were various plates of steaks, fish, shrimp cocktail. Exactly the sort of spread you prepare for the exorbitantly rich in an attempt to curry favor. From previous Sierra visits with a larger number of attendees, we'd known that some of the suits had special favorite dishes. Since we hadn't known who to expect this time, those dishes were now scattered across the large conference table. Patty was right—those marksmen probably despised her for making them prepare all that.

"Now," Lloyd whirred, "I do want to stress that while we take regular measurements of the growth on Moss's chest, we don't necessarily extrapolate that—"

Haydon let out a guttural chuckle. "Yeah, I don't know whose genius idea it was to name it Moss and also call that crap on him 'moss.' "

"It is confusing," Needledick concurred constructively.

Lloyd wobbled on his axis a bit. "Well, of course, we've . . . grown . . . accustomed—"

Haydon spun one finger in a circle. "Yeah, keep going."

"While we don't necessarily extrapolate the recession of the growth to any sort of understanding of Moss's life cycle or physical integrity, we do closely monitor—"

"Actually, you know what?" Haydon held up a hand. "Actually, what's even happening right now?"

"Um . . . s-sorry?"

Harrison piped up from where he was sitting. "Lloyd's presentation is specifically geared toward—"

"Yeah, why am I looking at a hologram of Moss instead of the real thing?" Haydon picked a shrimp off of a plate and bit into it. He flicked the tail back onto the plate with a soft *plink*.

Lloyd, Harrison, and I exchanged glances.

"Well." Lloyd gave an anodyne laugh. "Obviously—er, I mean, *actually*, this—"

"How much did this even cost us, making holograms like this?" He picked up another shrimp.

"Lloyd's holograms are really quite remarkable, aren't they?" Harrison chirped. "They're constructed from raw footage taken from several different angles—Lloyd, maybe shuffle through a few more before—?"

Lloyd nodded and Moss began to spin and shift in all sorts of directions. Captions flew in and around the air. *Moss = moss food?* read one. *Space ears!* read another.

Plink. Another shrimp tail landed on the plate. "Right, thanks, but . . . the real thing, the actual alien, it's literally, like, *over there*"—Haydon was gesturing through the wrong wall, but no one was about to correct him—"and I can look at it from any angle I want, right?"

The holograms stopped cycling as Lloyd tried to put on a calm face. "Well, certainly—certainly the footage for the holograms was taken with lighting that—you may find preferential—"

"Lloyd's just trying to say that Object E is rather dimly lit, and these holograms actually—"

Haydon picked up another shrimp. "But it's the actual alien, yes?" The shrimp waggled in his hand as he spoke. "The last time I checked, my phone has a flashlight. Can someone please explain to me why I'm watching *Jurassic Park* when I own a fucking dinosaur *right over there*?" He tossed the uneaten shrimp back onto the plate. It landed with a wet, heavy thud.

"We can . . . certainly . . . relocate," Harrison gulped.

"Great, Mike, then relocate us." Haydon instantly became chip and chipper. It was pure poison. He picked up a napkin and wiped his hands. "The faster you can get us through our itinerary, the faster you can get back to your office for an 'afternoon break.'" He tipped Harrison a knowing wink.

It was a shitty moment. Rather than let it hang in the air, I quickly opened the conference room door and called out to my team:

"We're moving."

SO THERE we were, packed into the dim, glowing cockpit of Object E, as Haydon shined his cell phone flashlight onto Moss's chest. Needledick stood by, an actual paper cup full of coffee in his hand. Needless to say, I wanted this over with as fast as possible.

"God," Needledick whispered. "It's a totally different thing being in the room with it."

"Touch it." Haydon's face was stony, unreadable.

Needledick gaped. "Seriously?"

"Or I wouldn't have said it."

Needledick nodded and slowly reached out a hand.

Lloyd had been holding back, clenching everything to stay silent. He finally let a small protest slip: "It's just, in, in terms of the coffee—" Harrison shut him up with a look.

As soon as Needledick's hand made contact with Moss's shoulder, he jumped back, disgusted. Coffee sloshed over and onto the floor of the spacecraft.

"Oh my God! He's . . . warm!"

"I love that," Haydon smirked.

That made me think of your reaction upon touching Moss—that awed, grateful smile, lighting up your beautiful eyes. Patty had wanted someone stationed in the Tent while our small group "toured" the ship and I'd chosen you. The reason I gave was that you hadn't been around long enough to know, or accidentally spill, how fast the Moss was receding. But the actual reason was simpler: I missed those eyes.

He had that same look when he—

I forced the memories out of my head . . . for just a little while longer.

"But wait," Needledick was saying, wiping his hand on his shirt, ". . . if he's warm . . ."

"So we still don't know if he's alive or dead?" Haydon took the coffee from Needledick and sipped it, but that was a question for us.

"Well, obv—" Lloyd stopped himself. "We, we don't actually know how to approach . . . assessing that."

Haydon handed the coffee back to his assistant, who held it lovingly with both hands. "No heartbeat, no breathing, no blood pumping, no brain activity, correct?"

"If by 'brain activity' you're referring to measurable electro-chemical—"

"The point is there's none, right?"

"No indicator that we would use to define life in a human body is present in Moss's body," Harrison supplied. He looked so tired, especially drained in the surreal glow of the ship.

"Except he's warm."

"Other than the body-temperature factor, correct."

"I gotta tell you, guys, there's a lot less moss here than last time." Haydon tsked. "Even than in the thingies you were just showing me."

This time we all, as a unit, made a conscious decision not to exchange looks.

Lloyd ticked his head to the side as if he were explaining a particularly knotty conclusion. "Yyyes—uh—certainly, we have noted a, a slight decrease—"

"And when all that's dead he's dead too, right?"

"That's, well, that's just one of several possible—"

"Oh, you mean like E.T.'s flower!"

We all turned to Needledick. His face was bright with excitement.

Haydon glared at him. "What are you even—?"

"Like E.T.," he explained. "From the movie. When the flower was dying, he was dying, but then when it came back to life—"

"It's mind-boggling that you're still talking," Haydon said through another poisoned smile. Needledick shut up right quick.

Seizing the opportunity, Harrison took a small step forward. "We don't, as yet, understand the relationship between the moss and the body well enough to answer that question."

"But you understand what I'm looking at. I'm the guy who has to make decisions on resource allocation. Sierra spends a lot of money on Quill Marine. If he starts rotting, if he starts falling apart, then I can't go the freak show route. That means I lose half of the revenue stream I'm ever gonna get outta here."

Harrison looked hard at Lloyd. Lloyd swallowed.

"Yes, yes, of course, and, given that—as you no doubt observed in the chronological hologram display—given that the growth is receding at a rate of five thousand microns per year, given that rate of recession . . ."

"How long before it runs out, Senior Man?"

"I'd estimate at least another two years." It came out of Lloyd's mouth smoothly, unrushed, completely clinically.

Haydon took it as bad news, which made it even better. He sighed with the sense of put-upon-ness that only the disgustingly rich can conjure.

"Shit. All right, we're gonna revisit this in a year, then. If I'm looking at half this amount of moss at that time? I'm cashing him in." And he patted Moss on the skinny sloping shoulder.

I WAS the last one to squeeze back through the fissure and out of the ship. As I passed by, you said:

"How's powering through going?"

"So far so good," I replied.

Instead of running around in circles giggling, I kept walking.

LIKE ALL dreadful things, at last the time arrived.

A row of folding chairs, bookended by klieg lights on black metal stands, had been set up in front of the cube. It was about ten minutes before the Harp was expected to do its thing . . . and so, of course, Trip Haydon was on the phone.

He was yelling at some guy named John. I couldn't make heads or tails of what the argument was about, but I heard the words "ballot measure" and "purchased land" and various other oligarchical dick measurements.

So I stood there, fully ensconced in a sealed Lloyd Suit, sweating (*God, were they this stuffy last time?*), another suit for Haydon under my arm, waiting for him to hang up. Every minute that ticked by, inching closer to the inevitability of a Power-Up, the interior of my suit seemed to go up a degree.

Finally I tapped him on the shoulder.

"I'm sorry—sir?"

He whipped around and promptly laughed in my bubble-helmeted face.

"I'm sorry," he said into the phone, "Neil Armstrong needs me." Then at me: "Why are you standing here?"

I held up the suit in my arms. "Purely a safety issue, sir, I need to help you put on this protective—"

He went back to his phone call. "We're gonna talk again while I'm in flight, John, and I better not hear the word 'referendum' come out of your mouth or I'm opening a window and throwing my phone away." In one fluid motion, he hung up, stuffed his phone back in a pocket, and said to me: "The cube is treated with the same substance on that suit, yes?"

"Yes, sir, it's—"

"Then what do I need that for?"

"Just a redundant measure of—"

"Right: redundant. Can we please just do the thing?"

And the thing was, he wasn't wrong. The cube was thoroughly coated with N5. Hell, I was wearing a Lloyd Suit mostly just so Haydon wouldn't feel self-conscious wearing his. But now it was "Do I insist and lose my job, or do I risk the slightest chance that something goes wrong, Haydon gets hurt, and lose my job?" Over his shoulder I could see Shel and Vonn leading X—whose wrists were bound in front of her with thick black electronic cuffs, and who was now wearing a pinstriped skirt and blouse—to the cube and I figured, if I had to lose my job either way I'd just as soon get a dead or debilitated Trip Haydon out of the deal.

"Yes, sir. We've brought chairs in for you and your—"

"Rock and roll."

He sat. His assistant did the same.

"Okay, Patty," I radioed, "go ahead and winch up the cube, but make it fast; Haydon wouldn't wear the suit." I kept that last part as private as I could.

"*Understood*," she confirmed up in Bird's Eye.

The winch pulled the cube up several feet. I signaled to Shel and Vonn and they gently nudged the still-hooded figure in under the cube's borders, next to the Harp.

"X is in place, Patty, take her back down," I murmured into the comm. Of course, I meant take the cube back down, but given the circumstances it almost sounded like a plea for clemency.

The cube groaned its way back down, trapping the woman named X and the Harp together. I gave the room a quick scan . . . which is when I saw the little look Vonn and Shel were giving each other. It didn't even take a second, and maybe I wouldn't have even spotted it if I weren't so hyperaware of similar matters.

They shared a look like a caress.

Goddammit. This must be what Grant was—

"Chief . . . what was it again?" Now it was Haydon's turn to surprise me. I didn't jump or spin around—I simply smiled tightly and looked him in the eyes. He was still sitting, leaning over his knees like a bored teenager.

"Prentiss, sir."

"Is this thing happening or not?"

"Are you set with how this is going to go down?"

He spun a finger as if he could fast-forward all this. "It gets weird and loud and the power goes out."

"Just to make clear that the power outage is temporary and we don't anticipate any—"

"I'm not scared of a blackout, Chief Prentiss. Can we get started?"

I came over and stood by the tiny little audience seating.

"We're ready for lights, Patty," I radioed. The klieg lights popped on, illuminating the cube with unforgiving harshness. The rest of the lights in the Hangar dimmed.

"I feel like there should be some sort of music or something," Haydon smirked to Needledick. "Something triumphant and fucking—" He made a fist and pumped it.

We sat in silence for a few seconds.

"The Harp is a little unpredictable in terms of exact start time—" I began and Haydon waved me off.

"Yeah, yeah, I get it. Uncuff her."

"Now?"

"I'da said 'later' if that's what I meant."

I radioed to Patty to disengage X's cuffs. She copied and a second later, after a quiet, almost polite, beep, the cuffs—another fine Sierra product, the 2027s, complete with transponder, global positioning, and remote control—clattered to the floor. We had placed microphones inside the cube and when the cuffs landed they sounded like they'd been made of titanium.

With her hands free, X pulled the hood from her head. She noticed she had an audience right away but going from the hood to the lights had momentarily blinded her and she took a second to adjust.

She was a woman in her forties. The light allowed me to see more details of her clothes: they were smart and fashionable but they showed unmistakable signs of distress. I realized: these must have been the clothes she'd been arrested in. Her graying brown hair was pulled back and it frizzed madly at the edges. When she spoke, her voice was amplified by the microphones inside.

"Whoa, that was rough." The amplification and the resonant space accentuated the frantic, brittle edge to her voice. It was palpable—her panic, her rage, and most especially her ruthless desire to hide all of it behind a mask of prim cheeriness—I could feel it in my teeth. "Um, let's see, I'm . . . Is that a *harp*? Okay, weird. Okay." She looked around at the Hangar. "Windowless room, nothing new, but *big* windowless room is new. Actually— shit—really big windowless room. I think this is bigger than the outdoors. I almost wanna run laps or—"

She walked right into the front wall of the cube with a heavy thud.

"Shit! Ow. Shit. All right. All right, lesson learned, I'm not actually in a giant room, I'm in a see-through box *inside* a giant room. Ha. I must look like a really great mime to you guys, like I'm pretending to walk into walls. So is someone gonna tell me what we're doing here, or . . ."

Silence. We all just watched. And waited.

"Or not. You're not going to. So I talk? Is that the idea? I do the talking? It makes sense, that's how I got the gig in the first place. They came to my cell, they're like, 'Do this thing and it's five years shaved off,' get out while I still have some brown hairs, and I'm like, 'Why now? I've been on the waitlist forever. Why am I finally getting a shot?' You know what they said? 'Because you're *chatty*.'"

I heard Harrison murmur under his breath, "Jesus." I could feel his desire for a drink radiating off of him—even my Lloyd Suit didn't block it out.

"Patty, I'm not crazy," I whispered into my comm, "but we *are* at a hundred hours, right?"

"*Past it,*" Patty radioed back, equally quiet, equally perturbed. What the hell was happening, Harp? Performance anxiety?

"First I thought he meant the whole whistle-blowing thing," X was continuing in her sharp, needly voice, "but now I'm thinking he actually just meant my everyday demeanor. I'm chatty. I'm a motormouth. I talk. Don't know why, just always do. Hey, how come there's one person in, like, a space suit and no one else? Where are we?! You really are just gonna stare at me, is that the thing? Maybe I should just stare back, total silence, see who blinks fir—okay let's be honest, I'm not gonna do that, plus someone has to talk about the elephant in the room, right? Did you guys seriously lock me up with a harp?"

She went over to the Harp. Nudged it. Even plucked at its strings, which yielded a flat, muddy, barely audible *twunk*.

God. No one's ever done that *before. It sounded so* wrong.

"Correction: a really shitty harp. Did you want a little concert? Or am I an angel now?"

She was chuckling—close to hysterics—and waving her arms in small, bizarre, snakelike undulations. Her impression of an angel, I guess. But the expression on her face was barely bridled fury.

Meanwhile, the Harp did nothing.

"All right, Mike, this is actually starting to get—" Haydon sighed, still smiling his all-teeth-no-eyes smile.

"I'm sorry, sir, there's no way to control . . . ," Harrison replied.

At the sound of their voices, X had frozen like a deer, eyes wide.

"Control? Control what? Control what, *Mike*?" she snarled. No answer. "You, talking-guy, you sound . . . I know you . . ." After a moment with no answer, she scooped up the Harp and began walking the perimeter of her box, plucking the strings, waving it around, while she spoke. "Yeah. 'Cause see"—*twunk*—"that's the only thing I could think—and I had a *looooot* of time to think in that box—is that if they wanted me for this 'cause I'm chatty . . .'cause I *know* it's not what I'm chatty about." *Twunk*. "None of you want me to keep chatting about the Sierra-designed voting machines, right? Right?!"

"*Chief, should we maybe get her to put that down?*" Patty's nervous, quiet voice in my ear. I had been thinking the same thing . . . but something had occurred to me.

"No," I whispered back. "Let her do her thing."

"So maybe"—*twunk*—"it's not the content, maybe it's just the chattiness, in and of itself, which leads me to think . . ."—*twunk*—"you all wanna try something on me to see if it makes me *stop* being chatty. Is that it? Huh? I mean, you can't have an after without a before."

"This is awful," I heard a voice whisper nearby. I turned to look. It was Shel.

Haydon had also turned to see who'd just made that little editorial, but before he could spit whatever venom I knew was brewing in his throat . . . the Harp began to hum.

"Oh, thank Christ," Harrison actually muttered.

"I figured it out, didn't I?" X was saying. Shouting, really. "Wait. What am I hearing?"

The Harp intensified. It dropped to the ground, the hand holding it suddenly too weak to bear it up. I had a moment of worry—maybe the Harp was as fragile as it was light—but it seemed undaunted by the fall. X began to sag. She dropped onto her knees.

"Is, is this normal?" Needledick gulped.

"Hey." The groggy, amplified voice from inside the cube began to fade in and out, a radio station in the mountains. ". . . Is that . . . lemme guess: this isn't a real har—"

The Harp reached its culminating, penetrative peak. All the power in Quill Marine cut off. Just as the klieg lights went out, I saw her fall. Wilt.

Total darkness. Total silence, except for the Harp coming down from its crescendo.

"I'm sorry, are the lights gonna come on, or—" Needledick sounded positively terrified.

"Yes, sir, momentarily," I said, gamely concealing my disgust.

"I want total fucking silence in this room right now," Haydon said. The sound of his voice in the complete darkness was like a hand under the bed gripping your ankle.

"Hear that?" he asked.

What we heard was X not talking.

The sound from the Harp began to recede. The power and lights began to come back on. Needledick ululated with relief.

She was lying on her side, eyes open, staring . . . Except—no, that sounds too active, like it was something she was doing for a purpose. More like her eyes were just open and we happened to be in the direction they were facing.

"Okay, so—" Harrison began.

Haydon was already up on his feet. "Wait."

He walked over to the glass cube and knelt down as close to X as he could get across the barrier. Then, softly, gently rapped on the glass with a knuckle.

"Hey," he whispered. "What do you want to say?"

Her voice came over the amplification, flat and robotic—although the dejection it conveyed was nothing if not human, the sound of giving up. "Nothing."

"Are you sure?" Haydon asked. I expected devilish glee, but his brow was knit. Serious. Sympathetic. This was all just another puzzle.

"Yeah," X sighed.

"But you're a whistle-blower. You made important secrets public. Don't you want—"

"Pointless."

"Pointless?"

"Worthless."

"You have a lover. You and your lover have a child. Are they—?"

"Worthless."

"Your family is worthless?"

"No point."

The assistant gasped. "Wowww . . ."

"No point to what?" Haydon demanded—still gentle.

"Anything," X said quietly, assuredly. "They always win. You always win."

"Sure, but . . . you know, I'm in charge. I could release you. Right now, if I wanted to. Do you want me to?"

"No."

"What do you want?"

"To lie here."

"What else?"

"To lie here."

Haydon rose from where he was kneeling. He looked at me.

"This happens every hundred hours?"

"Well, not always exactly—"

"Or if you move it, right?"

"That's only happened the once so far, but—"

"What was it just now? Was it the timing or because she was screwing with it?"

Actually, that's a good question.

"I'm, I'm sure the Harp Team will provide a detailed—"

Haydon called out. "Mike!"

Harrison rose.

"I'll be in touch," Trip Haydon said, buttoning his jacket. "Very, very soon. Thanks for a great lunch. Who can show me out?"

SHEL ESCORTED them back up and out. As soon as Parker confirmed their cars were gone, I ordered Patty to raise the cube again and to call for Turndown Service. Once I could, I walked over to the woman whose only name I knew was X.

"Ma'am," I said.

"Mm."

"Do you wanna say anything?"

"No," she said.

"Okay," I said as I dragged her out of the perimeter of the cube and then put two bullets in her head.

Thunder, rolling across the world. But more distant than before.

This time there was no need, no impulse, for reflection. This was a job, not an accident. This was as it should be—and we still had more work to do.

I looked at the Harp. No blood had sprayed in that direction so Patty was able to lower the cube back over it right away. We still had to put the fucker back where it belonged, but for the time being it was fine where it was. We all deserved a break—and besides, Turndown Service would be here any minute. I called out to whomever was nearby:

"Who wants to help me get out of this fucking suit?"

And there you were, hands already undoing the seals. You looked at me, so close, with the most beautiful smile I think I'd ever seen. A living snapshot of a moment I wasn't expecting to be so perfect.

"Oh, I love you," I sighed, grateful, utterly sincere . . . totally fucking out loud.

Uh . . .

I had just a moment to contemplate my chosen form of suicide before everyone in the room burst out in long, ragging laughter.

"Smooth, man. James Bond!" Vonn clapped.

"*Right?*" Patty cackled over the comm. "*That's the kinda man I want, where I'm like, 'Do this thing!' and he's like, 'I'm already doing it,* ma'am.' "

You shrugged, blushing. "What can I say? I aim to please."

And, for not the first time, you helped me out of what I was wearing.

10

I HATE parties. I mean, I get their purpose, I don't deny that they can be good for morale or whatever, but, goddamn do I ever feel like they're a drag. To attend, to sit through, to wait for them to be over. And it always seems like things find a way to take a turn for the worst whenever everyone's gathered together during moments of unabashed mirth—like the universe looks at every party as a dare.

Given what ended up happening, I took no delight in being proven right this time around.

But Harrison's logic was sound: it had been a long fucking week and the team needed this. Also, three aggrieved marksmen had made some crazy good food and desserts that had to get eaten somehow. No alcohol was allowed—making it something more like an elementary school dance than a real grown-up party—but given the relief, given the sleep deprivation, we were all basically hammered anyway.

Music was blaring from the speakers around the Hangar. It was probably even patched in and pouring through the comm speakers we'd installed in Object E. That meant Moss was sitting there at his forever station, slowly rotting away, to a playlist chock full of some of twentieth- and twenty-first-century Earth's grooviest goddamn pop music.

A few of the bravest among us had turned Hangar Eleven into a dance floor. Lloyd was one of them, although you couldn't really call what he was doing dancing: he was miming, probably with freakish accuracy, every instrument featured in every track, putting on a private little air concert for anyone who wanted to watch. Patty, meanwhile, had her full body invested in some sort of gyrating mosh pit of her very own. She was like what I'd imagine a washing machine looks like if you could remove its chassis while it was in the middle of operating. Her ponytail seemed to be in four different places at once. It was hypnotic.

The Harp remained on the floor, safely inside the cube. They danced around it. I thought of old black-and-white movies set on mystical islands where the natives performed dances in front of some totem before enacting some sacrifice.

That's when Grant crept up to me, a tiny plate of food untouched in his hand.

"I wonder if now might be a good time to speak with you regarding—"

"Jesus fuck, Grant. Tomorrow, okay? Tomorrow, tomorrow, tomorrow."

He looked at me for a moment, then acquiesced. "Yes, ma'am." He drifted away as silently as he'd approached.

Fuck that guy.

And, look, I got it. He was probably a little jealous. Maybe he was harboring something for Shel (or Vonn, who cares) and wanted to get one of them in trouble for a little on-the-job flirtation. Also he *was* just following the rules, after all. But I guess it should be pretty understandable why I wasn't especially sympathetic to anyone wanting to snitch on anyone else's happiness. As long as I could avoid knowing about it, I could avoid acting on it. And as long as I avoided that, I could fantasize about my own happiness's invulnerability.

Speaking. Of.

You'd disappeared on me. I had been tracking you throughout the evening but you shook me. That was okay—I let you do it. I could have found you if I'd really tried, but I thought it'd be fun to remember what the world was like without you for a little while. Let you remember, too, that I could cope just fine if you didn't exist. But then you crossed into my field of vision again. Across the "dance floor."

Our eyes met and there was zero doubt what was on both of our minds. The look ran a hand down my cheek, my neck . . .

"NOW HERE'S WHAT I DO WHEN I REALLY WANNA BRING ALL THE BOYS TO THE YARD," Patty screamed as the song changed and her dance moves evolved. Yells of admiration and derision met her advanced techniques.

Where? Everyone was milling around, everyone was getting silly. We could do it, if we were fast and discreet. It was insane—*insane*—but doable. And totally worth it. But where? The cots by the showers? Too risky. What if someone decided they needed to lie down for a while, or rinse off some dance sweat. In fact, any sort of common area was risky—this little party was essentially a rare moment of sanctioned fraternization, sure, but given every employee's cultivated sense of social discomfort, there were bound to be waves of wallflowers ebbing and flowing into the action.

Then I realized: the place where nobody would think to drop by during a good time.

The Slammer.

I flicked my eyes in that direction and gave you a look I prayed you understood meant "Hold off a minute, let me go first." I made my way toward the corner of the Hangar where the door to the Slammer, Quill Marine's detention hall and island for misfit toys, was kept.

Felt kinda appropriate, not gonna lie.

THE SLAMMER was not actually one individual room but a door opening onto a short corridor offering a number of options on either side: first interrogation rooms, then holding tanks and solitary cells. No windows for any of them, save for the Plexi slits around eye level looking into the tanks and cells.

I popped in and out of the Slammer every now and then between shifts, just to make sure nothing was out of the ordinary, so it shouldn't seem too strange if I were noticed slipping in now. One of the perks of being security chief was I could practically show up anywhere under the guise of "Just makin' sure." But the Slammer was also far enough away from the action and so poorly lit that I had reasonably high confidence pretty much everybody forgot this corner existed. And it was just vaguely enough in the direction of the lockers that it shouldn't even seem abnormal when you started gravitating that way on the floor. Frankly, it was so ideal for a quick-fuck-rendezvous I was almost kicking myself for not thinking of it until now.

I did have one pretty major concern, though: I'd been riding adrenaline for like fifty hours straight and there was a real danger I might experience a complete postcoital crash. A person can't power through forever. I considered briefly the idea of just focusing on you, but then pretty much every nonrational part of my body howled *fuck that very much*. I'd just have to remember everything got pulled up and zipped right away after—

Wait.

I cocked my head to the side and realized I was hearing something. Breathing. Moaning.

Is that me, my brain, like . . . sneak-previewing somehow? That doesn't . . .

It was coming from one of the interrogation rooms; the one nearest to me, in fact. The door wasn't shut and I pushed it farther open. It swung silently. The lights were off inside but it certainly wasn't empty. Dismay dumped into my guts and I realized almost instantly what was happening.

Those fucking idiots.

The noises hadn't stopped yet—they weren't seeing me, standing there in the doorway, but I had no doubt in a second they would. And then a second after that they'd see you, meeting me here. Could I think of an excuse fast enough? Some shit about needing to talk in private? But why here? If we needed privacy it was a secret, if it was a secret it would put us in the position of four people trying to keep it—that's a lot of variables. That's a lot of potentially destructive leverage. No, I couldn't let them even suspect I was as vulnerable as they were. Somewhere down the line they could get desperate. They could try anything, say anything. If there was anything I was already learning it was that having a secret like this did feverish things to the brain. So I had to move first and fast.

I flicked on the lights. Huge, quiet Vonn was taking tiny, acne-faced Shel from behind, as she leaned over the table. They stared at me wide-eyed, in complete, horrible horror.

"You stay right there," I said through gritted teeth, and moved toward the door to the Hangar. I made sure they could tell I was poking my head out, not talking to someone with me.

"Hey! You. Salem!" I barked.

You were almost at the door—I was louder than I needed to be for you to hear me, but they didn't know that. Thank fucking God you were quick. You picked up on the tone of my voice right away.

"Chief?" you responded, as if you'd been plucked out of the blue to assist your commanding officer.

Vonn and Shel were already righting themselves, begging desperately for my attention, my understanding. Apologizing, equivocating, explaining. It'll never happen again. They got swept up because of all the stress. And so on.

"Get in here, Salem, I need your assistance!" I called over my shoulder.

"Right away, ma'am!"

"Best way to help yourselves is to shut up right now," I shot back to Vonn and Shel. Tears were streaking both of their faces already. They knew how bad this was.

You came in and joined me. You saw them.

"What do you need, Chief?" you asked, stern and at attention.

"I'm going to need your assistance detaining Lansing and Michaels here."

". . . Detaining," Shel whispered. It wasn't a question. It was a resignation.

I radioed to Patty. "Patty? Yeah, I'm sorry to call you right now. I need you to meet me in the Slammer. We've gotta prepare a room."

"Matt . . . man . . . ," Vonn was pleading, but the energy in his voice betrayed any optimism he might have had.

You and I hadn't entered the room. We were still standing in the hallway. You took the doorknob to the room in your hand and said, "You guys should say your piece to each other now. You've got two minutes."

And you pulled the door shut.

11

I SAT across from Shel, looking into my reflection. It was younger and pockmarked, but it was me all the same. The same stupid ideas, the same risks. The same potential fate.

Patty had never run an interrogation like this before, so I let her run Vonn's first. I sat in only in case she absolutely needed me, but men tended to be easier—they go stony, hurl a little obviously defensive abuse, and just overall make for a less personally painful dynamic.

Vonn was no different. He snarled. He scoffed. He rightly guessed there was no real room for leniency—he'd signed contracts, he knew the score—and used that as his excuse to respond to every question with bitter cynicism. Hell, he even refused his right to an advocate. It would have been a Sierra-employed advocate, he explained, so what's the fucking point?

When Patty read to him the relevant section from the rulebook covering punishment for failing to comply with the fraternization policy—*Violations of this prohibition carry an automatic penalty of six years' incarceration at a Seirra-owned-and-operated penal facility, followed by reassignment to a different Sierra program to be determined at that time*—he got even hotter. He knew what "reassignment to a different Sierra program" most likely meant. One of the Zones. Hazard suits every day. Shortened life expectancies, some rumored as low as five years. His time in jail would probably be the high point of the rest of his life.

But soon he got quiet.

"I did good work for you," he spat. "And before that, I served this country with distinction. I should be getting a fucking parade and a . . . a medal."

The problem with handling the situation like he was—as most men invariably learn—is it's like lugging a bag full of iron. You tire yourself out. You have to take breaks. Vonn's energy was fading fast, although he had one more offensive maneuver up his sleeve. He leaned forward, as far as the restraints holding him to his chair would allow, and looked Patty right in the eye.

"I just want you to say something. While we're still on the record. I want you to look me in the eyes and tell me you think this is right. I want you to do that."

I looked at Patty with interest. Vonn was far from the first person to use this tactic in his position, but I was curious to see how Patty would respond.

"This is right, Vonn," Patty replied squarely, holding and matching his icy stare throughout. "It's one hundred percent right. If I didn't believe that, I wouldn't have signed the exact same contracts you did."

With that, the rest of Vonn's reserves were up. He sagged back in his chair, spent. Patty continued.

"You'll remain in the brig here two nights. Transport'll pick you up Thursday morning."

"I can't leave tomorrow?" he asked weakly.

"Tomorrow's when they'll move Shel."

"Right. To a different facility."

Patty nodded. "Very far away." Then she looked at the guard standing in the room with us. "You can take him to the brig now."

The guard approached Vonn, detached him from the chair, and then, with an absurdly (given the situation) respectful "sir?" lifted Vonn up.

"You know my name," Vonn said to the guard.

The guard only nodded, put a hand on Vonn's lower back, and said "sir" one more time as he led him out.

Patty had done well—really well. She even offered to handle Shel next. I refused her. I'd never done two interrogations like this in a day—no one had. Ending peoples' lives administratively was hard enough. When it was people you'd worked alongside . . . ?

Also I deserved this. But I didn't tell Patty that.

We had Shel brought in next and, for a few moments, I just looked at her.

SHE ONLY sobbed once, quickly, as I read her the code. It was a tiny gulp, barely more than a crack in her otherwise collected demeanor. But I knew a stress fracture when I saw one—it was going to get messy.

EXCERPT OF INTERROGATION TRANSCRIPT,
August 12, 2029

SEC. CHIEF PRENTISS: Now, Shel, you understand this is the portion of the code you violated?

MS. LANSING: Yes, Chief.

SEC. CHIEF PRENTISS: And that this code was included, verbatim, in your contract, over your signature, a copy of which we have here?

MS. LANSING: Yes, Chief.

SEC. CHIEF PRENTISS: Do you have anything to say on the record before we conclude this session?

MS. LANSING: No, Chief, I fully . . . just so, just so I know—

SEC. CHIEF PRENTISS: If you have something to say, that's one thing; but this isn't where you ask questions.

MS. LANSING: But just so I know, Vonn's—

SEC. CHIEF PRENTISS: Vonn is outside your purview. Permanently. You knew that before you asked.

MS. LANSING: I did, I knew, I just— (unintelligible)

SEC. CHIEF PRENTISS: Okay—

MS. LANSING: I just had to— (unintelligible)

SEC. CHIEF PRENTISS: Is crying really how you want to go out, Shel? Come on. Stop.

MS. LANSING: I don't even know if it's Vonn, you know, that I love, or if—

(CROSSTALK)

SEC. CHIEF PRENTISS: All of this, everything you're saying right now, is being documented and added to your record—

MS. LANSING: —Or if I just had all this love and I just had to—

DEPUTY SEC. CHIEF GARBER: You were horny, soldier. Own that.

SEC. CHIEF PRENTISS: Patty.

MS. LANSING: No! No! It was more than that—you don't know!

SEC. CHIEF PRENTISS: This isn't the venue for any of this, Shel—

MS. LANSING: And now no one's gonna touch me for six years! At least six years! Probably forever if you send me to a—

SEC. CHIEF PRENTISS: No one in this room's sending you anywhere but the brig. Everything else is decided up the chain.

MS. LANSING: Is this just how we're supposed to live? Until we die?

SEC. CHIEF PRENTISS: You could have gone buck-wild off base, but we have rules—

MS. LANSING: Do you? Do you date off base? Do you, Patty?

SEC. CHIEF PRENTISS: This is your last chance to make a proper statement—

MS. LANSING: I'll tell you why not, I'll tell you why not! 'Cause what do you even say? To a person who's not in here? They don't live in the same universe! What do you even say?

SEC. CHIEF PRENTISS: Okay, you're done—

MS. LANSING: Look at my face. Look at my face. I got this acne when I was eleven, this bad, and it never went away. Two tours in Zones didn't make it go away! Men don't see me. Men don't even . . . but he did. I don't know if it's him or just . . . the feeling that happened when he saw me.

SEC. CHIEF PRENTISS: Jesus, kid . . .

MS. LANSING: Six years. Maybe the rest of my life.

SEC. CHIEF PRENTISS: You shouldn't . . . you shouldn't think that . . .

MS. LANSING: Why?

SEC. CHIEF PRENTISS: You gotta stop crying, Shel.

MS. LANSING: Why shouldn't I think that? I'm fucking disgusting and— (unintelligible)

SEC. CHIEF PRENTISS: You're not . . . come on, you're not . . . You deserve love, Shel. For fuck's sake, of course you do! You deserve love. That's not—you just— Fuck! Stop crying. STOP—

MS. LANSING: Are you—

(CROSSTALK)

DEPUTY SEC. CHIEF GARBER: Dak! Whoa! Okay!

SEC. CHIEF PRENTISS: Stop it!

MS. LANSING: I'm sorry, I'm sorry, please, don't hit me again.

DEPUTY SEC. CHIEF GARBER: Come on over here, Dak, cool down. Are you okay, Lansing?

MS. LANSING: My jaw . . .

SEC. CHIEF PRENTISS: Lansing, you stow that shit right fucking now. You'll remain in the brig tonight. Transport'll pick you up tomorrow morning.

DEPUTY SEC. CHIEF GARBER: Dak—

SEC. CHIEF PRENTISS: This session is concluded.

Shel was led out of the room. After she was gone, Patty looked at me. She looked at me for a long time. My hand tingled and throbbed from where I'd struck Shel. My cheeks burned. That had been a massive fuck-up, on camera no less. Still, part of me felt relieved. Or maybe just momentarily exhausted.

"Dak—"

"I have to go put the Harp back," I said to nobody, and my chair scraped hard against the floor as I stood.

I WALKED quickly across the Hangar, which suddenly felt like a goddamn tomb. Not that it was empty, or even that quiet—Guardshift was back in swing, the still-reconfigured Bazaar was murmuring, and there were already three crews hard at work applying N5 solution to the walls and ceiling of the Hangar to keep people safe topside now that the Harp was out of the engine room. But everybody liked Vonn and Shel. The jubilant, relieved atmosphere of earlier had been sucked out of the room as sure as smoke through a ventilation fan and what was left was funereal.

I stood in the center of the room by the Harp.

"Okay, people?" My voice pinged off the walls. "I want everyone to take ten! We're putting the Harp back in place and we're assuming it's gonna get cranky!"

Everyone began packing up. They'd gotten good at it over the past few days. You were standing nearby, on quadrant shift out on the main floor. I called to you without looking in your direction.

"Salem."

"Lloyd Suits?" you asked, already moving.

"Fast as you can."

I'd started crying. Jesus fucking Christ. Right before I smacked her, I started—

"Chief?"

FUCKING GRANT.

"Not now," I seethed, wishing I had somewhere to walk to quickly.

"Chief, I just wanted to make sure it was on the record that I raised the original objection to Lansing and Michaels's conduct—"

"Are you fucking kidding me right now?"

Grant swallowed. "That the moment I became aware of such conduct I unhesitatingly—"

I wanted to grab him by the shirt and headbutt him in the fucking mouth. I wanted to feel his teeth fold in against my skull and watch as his mouth filled up with blood. I settled for taking a step into his personal space. "Okay, do you wanna let me protect you and everyone else in this base by moving an unstable extraterrestrial object or do you wanna stand around polishing your dick?"

Grant stiffened.

"Chief," he said. He turned and walked off, his head high.

I radioed to Bird's Eye. "Nagouchi, you there?"

Nagouchi responded: *"Yes, Chief."*

"You know how to work the winch?"

"I . . . I can figure it out."

"Great. Pull the cube up."

"*Copy that. Director Harrison is here, Chief. He says he wants a debrief as soon as you're done.*"

Great. "Will do. Gimme fifteen."

A few minutes later, the winch growled to life and the cube lifted.

You and I were getting good at suiting up. Efficient. Only this time there was no sense of flirtation, no sense of enjoyment—it was purely utilitarian. I sealed you perfunctorily, not making eye contact. You caught my vibe and did the same.

Then we lifted the Harp into the N5-bag and began carrying it toward the tent like pallbearers. It was amazing—now that we knew we could wear the insulating gloves, there was almost no sense of dread. The Harp began to Power-Up in protest after we'd walked a few feet, but it already felt more like an annoyance than the apocalypse it had been before.

"Keep walking," I said to you. "Let's just—" And I stopped talking before the words "power through" could come out of my mouth.

The Harp had almost reached full Power-Up as we lowered it back into its base inside the engine room. I grabbed the pins, which had been laid neatly to the side of the base, and slid them in. Just like that, the Harp was where it had always been. Like nothing, like X, like everything before and after, had never occurred.

It's going to be exactly like that.

I waited until the Harp hit its peak and the whole station went dead. Then I finally looked at you.

"Don't contact me. Don't speak to me outside Quill Marine. It's over."

You blinked. Then nodded. "Yeah."

WHAT DO you do when all you wanna do is break things? If you're an adult, you decidedly don't break things. You simply hope the breaking-things-energy doesn't reroute somewhere where it will cause permanent damage.

I remembered my deliciously half-formed fantasies of you and I, together on the floor of the cockpit during a Power-Up while the station, the world, belonged to nothingness. Even then my mind had wandered, as it often did, to darker things: what if we opened the engine-room door during the blast? What if we took it, entirely unprotected?

I bet it feels something like this, I thought, as I squeezed out of the ship and prepared to unseal myself.

THE WHOLE process of putting the Harp back had gone almost absurdly quick. I'd told Harrison I'd be up in fifteen and I could have made it in ten. Instead I purposefully took my time in the bathroom and arrived five minutes late. I knew walking in late was going to raise eyebrows—I'm never late—but it put off any chance of my having to be alone with Patty.

When I stepped off the elevator leading into Bird's Eye, Harrison was there, looking mildly bewildered.

"Sorry, Director," I said, and took a seat in front of him.

"Well, you don't have to be sorry because I know it won't happen again for the rest of time itself, correct?"

"Correct, Director."

Patty sat nearby, munching on an energy bar.

The debrief wound up being pretty perfunctory. Harrison was, if not half-lidded, then maybe a quarter. Not so bad that you could smell anything on him, but just far gone enough that, if you knew him at his full working capacity, you'd notice something was off. Dampened.

But, at least this time, I couldn't say I blamed him for needing a drink.

The ostensible reason Harrison hadn't joined us for the interrogations was a conference call with D.C. He wouldn't tell us what was said beyond an ominous, "Something's brewing there. New orders are coming, I'm just not sure what they are yet." But he seemed as shaken up by the call as he'd been by the events of the past couple days.

I made sure to say, in my recap, that Patty had done an exemplary job handling her first interrogation. I meant it sincerely. I was also giving her the opportunity to say that I had not fared so well but she took the compliment with characteristic Pattyness and shrugged before opening a sprig of beef jerky.

"No one ever promised me a rose garden. I understand what's incumbent on a leadership position."

It's just, while she said it she looked at me with concern.

Harrison didn't notice, though; he was too busy staring off into the middle distance.

"Jesus," Harrison sighed. "This week, huh? Even by this place's standards." A thought occurred to him. "How short does this leave us?"

That was an excellent goddamn question.

"We can keep Guardshift rolling, hit our daily marks," I mused. "Just not always with top people."

"Yeah. Well, I guess we're not looking at a Special Guest situation like that for a while. If there are B-teamers in the mix no one higher than me'll notice."

"We should still put in a request to look around," I grumbled. "Now the precedent's set where we're getting forty-eight hours' notice for things."

"Fair point. I'll put in a request." He didn't sound too confident, though.

"Would it help to include a request to knock off the forty-eight hours' notice crap?" Patty grumbled.

"I suspect," Harrison replied, sucking on his teeth, ". . . it would not."

"Even for the crazy-dangerous things like removing a fucking alien death engine?"

Harrison sighed. "You guys have only seen Haydon here," he

said. "I see him every time I go to D.C. Chaos is his comfort zone. Natural habitat. Meetings rescheduled an hour before. One vendor dumped in favor of another, no reason. He likes people off balance. Uncertain, ready to fight each other for a good spot in his sight. If we're in his crosshairs now . . ."

He trailed off, but we got the gist. Haydon could come back any time now. He had the taste for it.

"Still," he said finally. "I'll put in the request. Anything else?"

"Main takeaways, I'd say: the suits work. Even partial insulation's better than none, the whole bullshit glove thing proves that. But total insulation works across the board."

"And based on that power outage we just enjoyed . . . ?"

"Looks like it's safe to say if we move the Harp, we should expect it to go off."

He grunted. "Then we should prep for that. I suspect we'll be moving it quite a lot." He stood up after a smart slap of his thighs. So did we. "Thank you both. Dak. This has all been a lot—are you getting rest?"

"Grabbed a forty-minute power nap," I lied. "I swear by 'em."

"I've heard that too," he said absently. "Forget where." He headed toward the elevator.

Then it was just me and Patty. I kinda wished I was one of those animals with the defense mechanisms like soiling themselves or vomiting on command. Something to make this moment even less palatable and give me an excuse to leave. Instead, I sat back down, feeling heavy and dreadful.

Maybe Patty wouldn't say anyth—

"So, Chief . . ."

"First things first," I ventured, a preemptive change of subject, "we need to put together a whole new set of drills." I could feel her trying to interject so I steamrolled. "And I'm talking base-wide drills. Based on scenarios where the Harp is on the move—"

"What if we picked a few days?"

"For what? For drills?"

Patty surprised me by sitting down next to me. It was an intimate move, one I was very much not expecting nor excited about.

"For you."

"What?"

"I'd never float this to Harrison without running it by you first . . ."

"Float what?"

Patty seemed suddenly fascinated with the chair on which she was sitting: how did it feel under her fingertips, how strong were its joints. "Like. If we identified a few days in a row that we knew for a fact would be completely routine . . ."

"Uh-huh . . . ?"

She gave up the coy business and looked at me. ". . . Maybe you could, like . . . chill somewhere?"

There was a pause.

"Patty . . . ," I warned.

"Not like—this isn't like—I'm talking a few boring-ass, by-the-numbers days where we don't expect—"

There was my anger again. Hello, friend. "What the fuck are you talking about?"

"I'm just saying, the way things went in the room with Shel—and I'm not, I'm not—I only know how you told me to be, but—"

"Right."

"I'm not gunning for your spot, Chief! If that's what—I would never." She was looking as deeply into my eyes as she could, really trying to convince me. "I mean that. There's nobody like you, you were born for this, I'm just saying . . . just to watch some TV, get hammered, get some surfer to eat you out like twelve times. After the shit you've done, in, what, the last hundred hours?"

I had another urge to do something violent—only this time it was more than an urge, it was a certifiable spasm. I saw myself doing it like it was a memory that hadn't happened yet. I could feel the sensations, I could hear the sounds, I could clearly summon the sensation of self-control evaporating and yielding to action. I had to stand up and take a step back, just to prevent myself from doing something incredibly stupid.

"Do you have anything else—anything else—you wanna say about my conduct in the position of Security Chief of Quill Marine, a division of Sierra Industries?" I asked, calmer than I felt.

She seemed suitably chastened, but it wasn't enough for me. "No, Chief. I'm sorry."

"When are you off?"

"Nine."

"I'm off seven. Do we need to go over anything or are you on it?" Deep, degrading poison in my voice.

"I'm on it."

"I'm in the cockpit for thirty. You need me, I'm there."

I left her to think and made my way to the Hangar, to the Tent, to Object E, to the cockpit, without managing to look at or talk to anybody.

IT WAS a relief to get thirty minutes without Patty, without Lloyd, without Harrison, without you. I could just look at Moss's black eyes in his gray-white skin and think about what, if anything, was there. A younger guard I hadn't seen in a while was there too. His name was Slade.

"I haven't been on days in a long time," he said, after reminding me of his name. And I grunted.

The moss on Moss seemed to have receded another millimeter. It could have just been my imagination, but if I could have placed a wager, I'd put fifty on Lloyd's next measurement resulting in a mumbled, "Receded another millimeter."

I wondered what Slade would think if I said, "Hey so Moss, are you dying? Like dying, present tense, not a foregone conclusion? If I were a decent person, would I be hitting you with defibs every hour to try to make you gasp and wake up?"

. . .

THAT NIGHT, you called me.

I HAD finally gotten comfortable. Sitting on my bed, on top of the covers. The news was babbling unobtrusively in the background—another senator being pressured to recuse himself due to the amount of campaign donations he'd received from Sierra—and I was drinking a glass and a half of water for every whiskey, hoping somehow I'd manage to both fall asleep and avoid a hangover.

When I heard the phone ring, I didn't even have to look at the screen. There was no question. It was my burner phone. The one I got for exactly one reason.

It continued ringing.

Now, the dilemma couldn't have been simpler. All I had to do—the only thing I had to do in the entire world for the next six hours—was just . . . not . . . answer that phone.

But I did. Of course I did.

We breathed together. Out of one, into the other. Out of the other, into one.

Finally, I said, "Get here," and hung up.

IT WAS dark where I told you to jump the back fence. You could only see someone there if you knew to look.

I knew to look so I watched. The way you moved—the speed, the quiet—I knew two things: one, you were beautiful, and two, you were sent on some bad runs. A person who moved the way you moved was used. A person who moved the way you moved was sent to do things.

When I opened the door and pulled you in, you were whispering, "Just to talk, okay, I promise, it's just to talk—" But I silenced that bullshit with my mouth, hungry and furious on yours, as we crashed into my kitchen.

"Get me on the counter," I ordered, I pleaded. "And get these off. Come on. Come on."

Your pants clattered to the floor. Mine were thrown off

somewhere. You lifted me up like I was made of breath and were inside me before I even knew where I was.

"Oh . . ."

"Fuck . . ."

"Please let me say a stupid thing that doesn't mean anything," I whispered into your hair as you buried your face into my neck.

"Say it," you begged.

You continued thrusting into me and I cried out in a voice so small and desperate I barely recognized it as my own.

"I'm home, I'm home, I'm home."

FORTY-FIVE MINUTES later I was on the floor, naked, rooting through a backpack.

I kept a desk, full of bills and other grown-up crap, but the most important stuff in my life was stashed in the pack. It was the pack I lugged around on my last two tours. It was a stupid superstition, I know, but I never lost anything I put in there. It was better than a lockbox or a filing cabinet any day of the week.

It's where I kept my contracts.

My mind was on fire. *Oh my* God, *this is so stupid, so stupid, like this is the most pathetic thing I've ever done in my life, nothing's ever been this bad—*

"Hey." Your voice, behind me. I jumped. "Sorry," you said.

"I thought you were—"

"I was. Then I heard you wake up."

"Go back to sleep, I'm just . . . I don't know, figuring something out."

"Well . . . I don't think I can go back to sleep, but I can get back in bed."

"Okay."

"Or . . . I don't know . . . I can also leave, if that's the . . . right thing to do here."

"I don't know what's right here," I said, not looking at you anymore.

What did I want to tell you in this moment?

That this was a slow-motion disaster somehow moving too quickly?

That I was furious with you for coming over?

That this was all so pathetically obvious as to be suspect on both our parts? It was no small thing—this all fell way too neatly into a pathological, observable narrative. You knew that I was older, that I was in charge; you probably recognized, maybe consciously, maybe not, that I was like a mommy for you. One look at you and I could see your life: you were a fucking faun, you showed up places gorgeous and helpless, and everybody tripped over themselves to take care of you. That's something you got used to. So, *of course*: you wanted me. And *of course*: I wanted you. Not only did you catch me on a bad day the day we met, when I was feeling guilt and shame, but . . . your want fueled mine. To *be wanted* by you? Jesus, usually only big guys went for me—big husky guys with beards, looking for a hearty gal with birthing hips to split logs with. And that was fine, it was always enough to hold me over, but I'd always wanted to try a long thin boy, some long thin boy like you, my opposite, who could make me feel like a different person for a little while. You were a carnival oddity, a freak show, an escape. And that I could perform this analysis in a split second, looking at the two of us? That's how clear it was. It was fine, it was obvious, it was novel, and it was precisely why we shouldn't believe *any* of this!

Yes, all of that! I wanted to say all of that.

But I just stared at you, trying to put it all into words, and you went and fucking said, "You're looking at your contract, aren't you?" and something in me snapped.

"Get the fuck out of my house," the words out of my mouth before I even thought to say them, bubbling with rage. "What the fuck is wrong with you?"

"Okay," you said. "I just need to get my . . . where did I . . . ?"

I was suddenly filled with sulfurous hate. I was very aware of being naked, vulnerable, and wanting to hurt you twice as bad as you could ever hurt me.

"Kitchen. Your pants are in the kitchen," I snapped as you went to find them. "Jesus. You must've been a real prize on incursions with a memory like that."

"Never took off my pants on incursions," you said from the other room.

"Put them on and leave!"

When you came back in, you were holding the pants in your hand.

"You . . . were looking at your contract," you said, even and direct. "With Sierra. To see if there was any kind of—"

"Put your fucking pants on and get out of my house." I was starting to feel frantic. Ready to do anything to change this situation—for better, for worse, didn't matter, so long as it changed.

You didn't put your pants on. You pulled out a stack of papers stashed in a pack looped into your belt. I knew what it was before your pants fell back to the floor and the papers were presented to me.

"Here's how I know," you were saying, your voice cracking with sincerity. You held your own contract, the one you must have also been poring over, out to me. "Here's how I know."

But I had already grabbed your contract and thrown it behind me, so you could put both of your hands on me where I wanted them to go.

THIRTY MINUTES after that we were back in bed, in my softly glowing bedroom, flipping through each other's contract. God, divorce that image from its context and we were a normal couple, reading in bed before turning in for the night—not two desperate fools pathetically scouring for a loophole somewhere within the life-binding contracts in which they'd hastily signed their freedom away.

You sounded lost. "I mean, it's . . ."

"Yeah."

"There's no leeway of any kind. I mean, I'm not a lawyer, but—"

"Did they let you have a lawyer? To review it?"

". . . No. That was pretty stupid, right?"

"Yeah, it was. For me, too."

Finally, you put the pages you were reading down with a frustrated rustle.

"Why would we . . . my God, why would we—"

"They want lifers," I said dully. I don't think I'd ever really appreciated how much advantage they'd taken over vets before. "They want people who already don't want to go back. Only one way to control secrets in this world: keep the circle small. Ideally we'd be on Moss 'til pasture time."

"What happens then?"

"I hear about these homes they run," I said. "Word is they're nice. Good food. Movie nights."

"Jesus Christ."

"Yeah."

I wanted to cry. I wanted you to cry. I wanted something . . . Instead what I was getting was a tide of numbness washing in over me.

"You know, I thought about quitting," I reported from that numbness. "Very seriously. Your first day."

"Really?"

"I mean, if you had fucked up at any point, I was going to have to . . . well, you know."

"Yeah . . . shit . . ."

"But for some reason, for whatever reason . . . the thought of doing that to this, this kid, this person I didn't even know . . ."

"Would you have?"

"Without a doubt. But I don't think I would have gone on afterward. It would have broken me. So I had pretty much decided that would be it for me, I'd quit right then and there afterward. Maybe even before Turndown arrived."

"What would have happened to you then?"

"I have no fucking idea," I said, in slow, measured tones, as if I were describing a suicide attempt. I guess, in a lot of ways,

I was. "Transfer, maybe? Or . . ." I pictured two bodies occupying one brightly colored box and felt nothing. The tide kept rolling in. "My whole life, I never called a shot. First I was a kid, then I enlisted—seventeen—then they just kept bumping me up. Fancier division every time, and every time I was running things in like eighteen months. But it was always their things. Never mine."

"You run the units but you don't get to decide what they're for in the first place." You nodded, taking one of my hands in yours and kissing it. Not with lust, with sympathy.

"Best way to trick a person into thinking they have choices: keep putting them in charge of things." I was staring at how our hands looked together, trying to put any real thoughts into words and finding my mind was just . . . white.

After a few moments of silence together, you said it. "It could just be sex."

I nodded. "It could."

"It gets stale in a month or two and we're like, 'Jesus, were we actually looking at each other's contracts?'"

I chuckled. "That could definitely happen. If I was laying money, that's where I'd put it."

"So if it's just sex it's logical: we stop."

"Absolutely. Fuck around with townies, work it out, see what the world looks like with empty balls."

"See each other at work, smile in that kind of embarrassed way . . ."

"And then time goes by and we forget what we were even embarrassed about."

"That is, no doubt, a hundred percent the right thing to do."

"All you gotta do is put your pants on."

"Oh, so it's all on me?"

"Shoulda brought this up when we were at your place. Rookie mistake."

"Rookie mistake."

"So do it."

"I will."

"Put your pants on."

"I will."

Neither one of us had looked at the other during the entire exchange. Neither one had let go of the other's hand. Neither one of us moved. We just stared straight ahead. *Like Andy,* I thought fleetingly.

Finally I let go and smoothed out the blanket covering my legs. The numbness left my palms feeling clammy and cold.

"Jesus Christ." I chuffed. "I feel like, I feel like . . ."

"What?"

"Like . . . 'You hang up first.' "

" 'No, *you* hang up first,' " you responded in a mocking, thick voice.

I finally looked at you, legitimately surprised.

"God, they still have that? Your generation still knows what that—"

"Oh my God, 'my generation'?"

We were looking at each other, wide-eyed.

"See? *See?*" My voice was rising, not in anger but in a desperation half-sincere, half for show: like that play where the guy tries to trap his stepfather with some obviously hoary melodrama. "*You should leave.*"

You played along. I wonder how sincere. "*I should leave.*"

"YOU SHOULD LEAVE."

"SO TELL ME TO LEAVE. KICK ME TO THE CURB."

"I WILL. I DID."

"SO DO IT AGAIN."

"Stay. Please stay." I began kissing your neck. Your shoulder. Your chest. The numbness was still there, but, fuck it all, I could at least build a home there. With you. "Please stay."

We rolled into each other, kissing, groping, like we were falling down some dark tunnel and grasping blindly for purchase. I heard our voices, interchangeable.

"Oh no. Oh no no no no no. What're we gonna do?"

"They'll catch us."

"They definitely will."

"Unless we run."

"They'll catch us if we run."

"You're right."

"Unless . . ."

"We run to one of those places where they can't catch us."

You pulled away, just a little, for breath. You had been hearing our voices too. You looked into my eyes. *Those lashes,* I thought again.

"But . . . we can't," you whispered, and kissed me.

"Why not?" I whispered, kissing you.

"Money. It's more money than . . ."

"Yeah." Quiet. Soft. We were back in space, with not enough oxygen for thought or voice.

That glow.

No. We weren't in space. And the soft glow that had been subtly illuminating the room wasn't the mysterious ambient luminescence of the inside of some alien spacecraft. It was the TV I'd completely forgotten was still on, muted. We had grown so used to seeing each other in such low light, I don't think it crossed either of our minds that the thing was on. A reporter was blathering away, oblivious to this audience's complete disinterest in anything she was saying. For all we knew she was talking about Sierra. An image floated in the air next to her head on the screen . . . like a hologram . . .

"It's more money than even both of us would ever . . ."

It was out of my mouth before any thought could intervene. I was a witness to it as much as you were. "We'd have to sell something."

You kept kissing my lips. It took you a moment to understand what had just changed.

"What?" you asked, kissing. "Sell what?" You kissed again.

But I'd stopped kissing back. That veil of numbness had been ripped away and what was left exposed was raw and pulsating . . . maybe even alive.

"Matt," I said, no longer whispering, feeling as loud and resonant as a gun blast. You looked at me, curious, vulnerable, not understanding but receptive—like the day we met. "The footage. We'll sell Lloyd's footage of Moss."

PART THREE

CONCEPTION

12

JUST AS we'd hoped: a couple days later, with the memory of Haydon and the Sierra situation fading, Lloyd was getting his groove back.

"Mr. Matthew, would you mind, ah, holding the instrument just like this while I make some notations?" His entire demeanor was springy and jovial, ready to bounce into the magic of scientific discovery at a moment's notice. Exactly what we needed.

You and I were both on duty in the cockpit, on sentry duty while Lloyd set up his measuring devices. You moved closer to help, as requested, and Lloyd's eyes flicked rapidly back and forth between the tablet and the instrument you held against Moss's forearm.

"Nine hundred . . . and . . . actually two microns," he mumbled, writing. "Nine hundred and two microns of recession since derma-survey of August eleventh."

Almost a millimeter; I was right. Well, almost right. Close enough for a layman. I look at you too much, Moss.

"Here's where I chime in and remind you for the nine trillionth time that you need an assistant, Lloyd," I cracked.

I was in high spirits. No, more than that. I felt incredible. Not incredible in an exemplary way, but in a perfectly mundane, baseline way. The sort of incredible you only appreciate on, say, your first day of full health after being ill. *This is what normal feels like,* your body sings, *and it's . . . incredible.*

Because I had an assignment. We had a plan. A mission. Oxygen.

"I don't want an assistant," Lloyd whined. "I'd have to talk to them. I wanna talk to you guys!"

"Sierra pays for them, you should use them," I said.

"Sierra pays for you, too!" Lloyd smiled.

"I don't mind," you added, looking very much like the new boyfriend meeting the parents for the first time and being put to work on some chores around the house.

"I mind," I said, sternly. "You *have* a job you're supposed to be doing right now."

But I didn't mind. Not one bit. This, all of this, including my disapproval, was all part of the plan.

WE'D GONE over it the night before in our motel room. More specifically, in the shower.

I'd picked this motel for three equally important reasons: there was no unpleasant smell, they didn't require ID, and there were places nearby where we could both inconspicuously park our cars overnight. That being said, old habits die hard and old instincts die harder, so we slid the dresser in front of the door before we put ourselves in the loud, isolating shower.

"It has to be you on intel," I said, while my hands ran over your slick body.

"Don't you know the base a million times better than I do?"

"At least. But ninety-nine times out of a hundred, intel isn't about maps, it's about the mark. Lloyd's our mark. And Lloyd loves shooting his mouth off to awestruck new guys. He'll be careful with me. Not with you."

You were getting hard in my hand. You spun me around.

"Okay," you said, kissing the back of my neck, pressing up behind me, "but I can't just say, 'Where on the base do you keep the footage for your holograms?'"

"You're absolutely right," I moaned.

"The water's getting too cold," you said as you positioned yourself. "Make it hotter."

"WELL, LUCKILY for you, Chief, I am almost done with him." Lloyd finished some notations. "Thank you, Salem, you're very patient."

"I don't know how you can work in here without frying your eyes, Lloyd. You can barely *see* Moss."

Something in Lloyd lit up. He smiled, almost as if he had a particularly juicy bit of gossip to pass on. "One of the ongoing mysteries of Object E, isn't it? Is this the ideal full in-flight lighting? Is this reserve power? Are the lights broken?"

"I can't even tell exactly what the lights could be," you said, with just enough aw-shucks-gee-whiz wonder that I wanted to high-five you. That was catnip for Lloyd—and he started rubbing on it immediately.

"Mmhmm! And of course, obviously, it stands to reason that answering that question would not only tell us more about the ship itself, but alsooo . . . ?" He looked at you with giddy anticipation.

"What—me?" You pointed to yourself with incredulity.

"Well, what follows naturally?"

". . . Wwwould it also tell us about Moss?" you hazarded, then made a show of looking at me for support. I shrugged, as if to say, "You asked for this, Fish."

Lloyd pumped his fists in victory. "Precisely! Precisely! See?! This is why I prefer your guys' company to the assistants'. This stuff is old hat for them, but with security staff, I have the pleasure of watching you experience discovery for the first time! It takes me back to that feeling; it's rejuvenating!"

You nodded slowly, seriously. "I get it, so like, you're saying, how much light does Moss need to—or *did* Moss need to—"

"Exactly! Perhaps this is an overabundance of light for his species. For all we know this could be *blinding*!"

"He does have really big eyes, maybe that's—"

Lloyd waved his hands. "Well, well, well, of course obviously ocular cavity capacity doesn't necessarily indicate—"

"How did you get him so easy to see for the thing?" you asked abruptly, as if the thought had just bumped into you. It was awkward and ill stated and perfect. I wanted to kiss you. No, fuck that, that was the least I wanted to do to you.

"I'm sorry?" Lloyd was puzzled.

"I mean—shit—lemme say it right—how did you get him so brightly lit for the hologram? For when the suits were here?"

Your Andy impression was so good it was kind of unnerving, I thought. So good Lloyd didn't even realize that you wouldn't have seen the holograms from the Haydon visit.

"Ah. Well," Lloyd chuckled, devilishly. "Just between you and me?"

"Oh, yeah, totally." God, you were so *sincere*!

Lloyd looked at me, then with a stage whisper, back to you: "I fibbed a bit. Not a lie, precisely, more adjusting the truth."

I shrugged—*don't hang yourself, Lloyd*, the shrug said.

"Adjusting how?" you asked.

"We took all the footage out on the main Hangar floor. I had to make a judgment call, you see. Which is more damaging: to temporarily move Moss out of the environment of the ship? or to bring several pieces of lighting equipment and a complex camera rig onto the ship? These are the judgment calls, my friend, every single day."

"Wow. That must have been—"

The Guardshift tone rang out. It was time for me to move on—you still had another shift inside the ship. More time to work Lloyd. All moving precisely as we wanted it to.

"Slade should be on his way in," I said to you both. "Hey, Lloyd? Don't talk Salem's head off, all right? He needs it for his job."

"I think this is valuable!" Lloyd protested, like I told him to go to bed.

You and I risked a look: "It's all you now," mine said. You nodded, using fewer microns than the receding moss to do so.

AFTER ONE shift on the Hangar floor I got three shifts up in Bird's Eye, where I was able to start on my end of the intel gathering. System access was always monitored, and I never knew exactly what might raise a red flag, so today I was very much rolling the dice. But I felt lucky.

Until Patty walked in.

Fuck me with hedge clippers. I forgot.

Now was when we usually had our daily brief with Harrison. I'd been so excited when Harrison told me he would have to miss today's brief, giving me so much time by myself, I completely forgot to let Patty know.

Rookie movie, Dak. More disturbingly, the thought came in your voice.

Patty noticed Harrison's absence right away. "Oh—hey—are we not . . . ?"

"Shit, Patty, that's my bad, I should've messaged you. Harrison's stuck on a conference call with D.C. It's some late-breaking crap so . . ."

"Uh-oh . . ."

"I know. But, say a little prayer, it might not involve us." My weak laugh died on delivery.

Patty had her lunch in her hand: a plastic shopping bag full of jerky and energy bars. She sighed and swirled into a chair dramatically, then began pulling out food. *Godfuckingdammit! How could I forget to message her?!*

With no Harrison to distract us, the chances of her not addressing our fight the other day seemed remote. The best case scenario was if we just marinated in lukewarm, leftover piss.

"You think they'd come back?" Patty asked about Sierra, unwrapping a bar. "This soon?"

"Who, Sierra?"

"Mmhmm."

"Harrison thinks so." I shrugged, trying not to look too intently at what I was doing, but also trying not to look away.

"Yeah, but how good is his read on the D.C. people?"

"Well . . . that's always the thing, isn't it . . . ?"

The thought hung there, long enough for us both to know we knew what we were talking about. How clear was Harrison's mind at a given time? Whatever call he was on right now, was he on it by himself, or had he snuck the friend he keeps in his desk drawer in to join him?

"Do you ever miss the field?" Patty asked out of fucking nowhere, before taking another bite of her brick-shaped food replacement.

"Do I . . . what?"

When she finished chewing: "I mean, not the bullets or the blood or the Zones, but like . . . the clarity? Like, 'This is the objective. It'll keep being the objective 'til we get it or die.' It's easy to miss that these days, right?" She stood up and started pacing around the room. Not aimlessly—no one with her kind of training moved aimlessly—but with no discernible stopping point. She was curious about what I was doing, but didn't want to make a big deal out of it.

I sighed. I didn't like where this topic could go. "I mainly just don't miss the bullets and blood." I turned my attention back to my screen.

It was silent for a few minutes, when she asked: "Are you looking up journalists?" I'd been getting ready for that question ever since she stood up. The computer I was on was pretty much right out in the open, and to attempt to hide what I was doing would have looked suspicious as fuck. There was no real way to conceal the browser tabs and internal files I was scrolling through.

"Yup," I said, distantly. "Just in our opposition files. Something I do every time we boot people. Total overkill, I know, I just like to, you know—"

"Do opp research on the media?"

"It's stupid, it's not even like Shel or Vonn are getting shipped to *The New York Times* or whatever, it's just, whenever there's people with a grudge out there I always wanna remind myself who they might talk to. So I'm just scrolling through . . ."

You're disclaiming it too much, Dak, your voice said between my ears. *You're putting ideas in her mind.*

Stuff it, Salem—it's not a good answer but it's the best one I've got.

Patty was sucking on some particularly tough jerky now. Playing it cool, making it hard to read any skepticism. Or maybe she was just genuinely curious. "Okay . . . I mean, we don't disclose personnel movements; hell, they can't even have visitors in Sierra facilities—their families think they're on missions, so . . ."

"I know," I said, getting irritated. "I didn't get where I am by leaving stones where they were, though."

"Okay."

While we were talking, I kept scrolling through the windows open on the screen.

There it is.

The name I was looking for revealed itself. *Rachel Lesser, 9Source.* Flagged numerous times in our internal media coverage rosters as a sensationalist reporter with a raging hard-on for Sierra and its suspected development of weaponry. Bingo. I kept scrolling so there was no record I'd stopped there.

"Have there been any new stories on Quill Marine in a while?" Patty asked, like she was suddenly curious about the topic.

I went back to a window with search engine results, my stomach crinkling in annoyance. "Uh, latest is . . . about seven months back."

"That's what I was thinking." She was upbeat, impressed. "It seems like we've gotten really good at squashing shit."

I had one last thing I needed to check. I shifted in my seat so Patty couldn't see the screen, trying not to look obvious about it.

"Yeah," I mumbled, slowly, as I worked, "the sense I get is even if it's an outlet we don't own, or one of our affiliates doesn't own, there's usually at least one person in the newsroom we've got a lever on."

Last week, Harrison had granted me clearance to delete security footage for our little cover-up with Lloyd and the moss. But did he remember to rescind the clearance afterward?

I double-clicked on a secured file that should've told me "access denied" . . . and it didn't. Harrison had forgotten.

We were in business.

That done, I turned in my seat to look at Patty, hoping my look read as "We done?" without any unnecessary alacrity or ill will. She stared back . . . lifted the piece of jerky to her mouth to attempt another bite . . . then brought her hand down. It was a weirdly weary, sad move.

"Look, review whatever you want," she said, her voice casual. "Just . . . if we were gonna rank the shit we're worried about . . ."

"Like I said, Patty. There is a reason I am where I am." Shorter than I meant to be.

"Okay," she said. "You do you. I'm gonna stroll around downstairs."

The victory felt hollow and awful. I hoped Patty was able to translate the tension into having something to do with the extra-stressful week, the Harp, the near-death experience. Anything was a billion times better than her knowing the actual source.

TWO HOURS later, all senior employees received the dreaded memo from Harrison: "**Emergency Update, Conference Hall, 4:30 p.m. TODAY.**"

We all filed into a room and took our seats at the conference table. It was a lot more people than I expected. Because the universe has an insatiable appetite for coincidence (and the gnashing of teeth), you just happened to be taking post on the meeting. I shot you a look on the way to my chair and you gave me another of your amazing micro-nods. Lloyd must have talked. I could have kissed you right there in front of everyone.

"Okay, folks, everyone settle in, we've got a lot to get through,"

Harrison said wearily, leaning his knuckles against the lacquered walnut of the conference table.

"Fun call today, sir?" Patty asked. The room chuckled. Harrison did not.

"Lloyd, I'm gonna put you in the hot seat first," he said, "and then we're gonna talk about that."

OF ALL the dedicated teams—the Moss team, the moss team, the Harp team, the Object E team, et cetera—Lloyd was a team unto his own. He bounced around all of them. Since, for all we knew, even the ship might be a biological organism, as chief xenobiologist ("Senior Man," to quote Trip Haydon) he needed to be comfortable with every aspect of our assets here.

Still, whenever you put people on teams, rivalries are gonna be inescapable. It's a good thing—it lends a healthy sense of competition to inform analysis and speculation. When Harrison asked Lloyd what he asked him, it normally would have sent bristles up and down the hides of all the other senior scientific staff. In an ordinary situation, someone on the dedicated Moss team would have piped up angrily and cried they knew this specific biology better than Lloyd, that Lloyd shouldn't be the only one making such declarative statements, that's why we have teams to begin with!

Except Harrison also used the "A" word. So nobody wanted to touch this. They were more than happy to watch Lloyd squirm.

"So, look," Harrison began. "I'm just going to say this outright. Some of the people on the call I just took were from Allocations." Everyone clenched. Allocations meant money. Money meant Trip Haydon. "They're expecting me to follow up with a recommendation. So the question I have for you, Lloyd, is: has your assessment of Moss changed in any way?"

Harrison edged away from the floor—Lloyd was still sitting, but now seemed very much alone. Tactical cruelty.

"I . . . regarding . . . ?"

"Regarding being able to save Moss's life."

Lloyd certainly felt the radioactivity and squirmed. He wanted to have a different answer, but, "I . . . don't see how it can have changed, sir."

"Explain."

"Well . . . clearly, clearly, as long as we maintain the overall parameter, the overall mandate to not, of course, *dissect*—or vivisect, as the case may be—which obviously would defeat the purpose . . . it's impossible for us to know enough about Moss's biological processes to effect any kind of medical treatment I can imagine. And of course that's still operating from the unproven assumption . . ."

"That he's still alive."

"Well, yes, as, as I'm sure the Moss Team can expound upon in some detail . . ." Lloyd looked to the room. No one took him up on it. He swallowed. "Um, but, well, very simply, nothing is . . . moving inside Moss's body. Nothing that looks like a heartbeat, nothing that looks like circulation, nothing that looks like a cerebro-chemical process, nothing. The moss is our strongest observable data point to, to, to suggest dormant life. Beyond that we'd have to rely solely on the, the inexplicable body temperature and, heh, the fact that he hasn't turned to dust. But, I mean, really, let's be honest, we're just looking at the outside of a house to, to try to diagnose what might be wrong with the plumbing."

Harrison was rubbing the bridge of his nose. "So the only way to know enough about him to treat him is to cut him into small pieces."

"Yes, obviously that's the um . . . the pertinent dilemma."

"Right." Harrison sighed. He unexpectedly pointed to another scientist at the table, Dr. Ronz, an officious little mouse with thick brown bangs and even thicker glasses. She headed up the Object E team.

"Susan."

She was so caught off guard it looked as if she'd forgotten the sound of her own first name. She looked about ready to point to herself and say, "Who, me?" But she didn't, she just blinked extra hard behind her massive glasses as if to make sure she was still awake, and said, "Yes, Director?"

"I read your reports every week. Some of them could easily be copied and pasted from the one the week before."

The mood in the room was changing palpably. Was this going to be some sort of grill session?

"Oh—sir—I—"

Harrison waved her off. "I know you don't do that. I know it's just the same data coming back week over week. I just want it on the record for this meeting. Do you believe your team has made any significant progress toward making Object E flight-worthy in, let's just say, the last year?"

"Well, we certainly know a great deal more about the composition of the outer—"

"Can you make it fly, Susan?"

She gave a hard blink again. "No, Director."

"Thank you, Susan." He sighed, more to himself than to the room. Harrison sat back down. We were all watching him intently. "Then I really have no counterargument to take back to Allocations," he was saying. His voice was loud and present, but again it seemed more like he was talking to himself.

After a few beats of silence, Lloyd piped up. "Counterargument to . . . ?"

I shut him up with a look. Harrison clearly needed a second with this one, whatever it was.

Uncomfortable silence swathed the room. As is so often the case with a silence like that, once the thing was said that broke that silence, we all wished we were back in it.

"I've been informed that we're going to be implementing a restructuring process," Harrison said at last. Chairs creaked, breaths were held. "Going forward, we won't be maintaining a dedicated Moss Team or a dedicated Object E Team." Gasps rippled through the room. "We're not dropping anyone—I want to make that clear, no one's losing a job today—but the Moss and

Object E Teams will now be folded into the Harp Team, with an eye toward a new mandate."

The faces around the table—everyone was perhaps 3 percent more terrified than they were furious. Susan was the first to speak.

"Respectfully—Director—" Her voice was breathy with the forced laughter of the incredulous.

"Before anyone says anything else"—Harrison held up a hand—"there is no point in arguing this with me. I don't like passing the buck. I signed on to Sierra with open eyes, just like we all did. I'll give my input, sure, but when a decision is made, I'll back it. And this one comes direct from Trip Haydon."

As a nonscientist, I had the smallest dog in this, so it was easiest for me to ask the most important question.

"What's the new mandate, sir?"

He looked at me, grateful to have been given the go-ahead to vomit up whatever poison he was carrying in his system.

"To create a prototype clone of the Harp. With an eventual eye toward mass production."

The room was no longer silent. Lloyd in particular started sputtering all sorts of vowel sounds. I had to wonder, which part of Lloyd was stronger, his ego or his fear?

"It just doesn't make sense!" Lloyd finally managed to blurt. Harrison began trotting out all sorts of calming platitudes, none of which proved effective. "Moss is a verified, a, a *verified extraterrestrial being*!"

Finally, Harrison turned to the room, wincing. "Okay. Can someone—?"

"*Object E is a verified extraterrestrial transport!*"

Harrison noticed you. "Salem?" You nodded, approaching Lloyd with caution, as if he were an IED left on the side of the road. The rest of the scientists in the room were looking away, trying not to catch what Lloyd was afflicted with, I imagined.

"Hey—"

"*Am I crazy? Am I crazy? These are, are the most important discoveries of all time!*" He was pounding on the table now. "*It doesn't even—it—we're not even trained to—they want us to, to just* make another Harp*?!*"

"Lloyd? Lemme give you a hand," you offered. Lloyd's volume was coming down but he was still seething, spinning. "Let's go grab some water, huh?"

He looked at you with a sincerity that would have been heart-breaking if we weren't all so shaken. "We're xenobiologists," he pleaded, "we're—forget science, just organizationally, it makes no sense! *'Folded into the Harp team'*?"

"I know, it's—" Trying to get him to the door.

"*Somebody say something!*" He started up again. "*Am I out of my mind?*"

"LLOYD. SHUT UP AND TAKE A BREAK." I used the voice I save for only the most out-of-control situations. My copvoice, my slapvoice. It worked. Lloyd stopped and gaped at me. "It's okay," I continued, once I was sure he was hearing me. "It's okay. We're gonna figure it out."

"I feel like—"

"We're gonna figure it out. Take a walk with Matt, give your-self a break."

"Everybody needs a break, man," you concurred. "Let's just hang out."

He gave in and you led him out. He kept muttering—sentence fragments mostly—but the gasoline had burned off and soon he was out of sight and sound. Harrison, meanwhile, was address-ing the rest of the table—who might have been quieter than Lloyd but were no less appalled and concerned.

"Lloyd's wound up, but he's not all wrong. This is going to be a challenge. But it's a challenge we're going to meet. Okay? Let's talk about how."

For a split second I caught Patty looking at me.

Have I called him "Matt" in front of her before? I wondered.

13

I TRIED the new toy that night while we were in bed. I waited until we'd done it twice and you were in a doze. It was cruel of me and I didn't regret it for a second.

"I WANT YOU TO EAT ME, MATT SALEM."

You woke up like you'd been electrocuted. "Oh my God, what the fuck?!" Your hands had come up, ready to swat at whatever was making that godawful robotic noise.

"I WANT YOU TO LICK ME LIKE AN ICE CREAM CONE." Beginning to lose my composure with giggles. Between that and you noticing I was sitting there with a black mask covering the bottom half of my face, the jig was up.

"Okay, that is . . . holy shit."

"PLEASE TEABAG ME, MATT SALEM, IT IS ON MY BUCKET LIST."

"I think that scared me more than, like, most incursions." You lobbed a knuckle-punch into my arm. It stung like a bitch and I loved it.

"SCARED? IT'S JUST LI'L OL' MEEEEEEEEEEEEEEEeee eeeee."

"Is that for tomorrow?"

Okay. No fun anymore. I took the voicebox off of my face. It was like a heavy-duty surgical mask, only black, with thick straps that wrapped all the way around the back of the head. The front of it bulged out with a filter-type apparatus that covered the mouth.

"Yeah, see?" I said, making a show of how it obscured my face. "It also works like a mask."

"Two birds with one stone. Nice."

"I thought so."

I'd picked the thing up at a damn toy store earlier in the day. Hypervigilance was kicking in; I was maybe 70 percent sure I could've safely done a search online at home for voice modulators—maybe even gotten a drone to drop it off right at my doorstep next day. Conceivably, our employers *shouldn't* have any sort of access to my personal internet account, my browsing history, my online shopping . . . but even a 30 percent chance that I was wrong seemed astronomically reckless. I paid with cash.

"God, you look sexy with your hair like that," you chuckled. Taking off the mask had tousled up my hair in the back something fierce.

"I meant every word, you know."

You kissed me for an exquisite moment. But now that you were somewhat awake you had questions; now that I had the mask the plan was definitely going forward.

"So we actually have this lady's parking space on file?" you asked. I forgot sometimes that you were still new to Sierra and its insidious ways.

"Any reporter who even glances at Quill Marine, we get their *shoe size*."

"Makes sense, I guess." And then, oh God, you actually started rubbing your eyes. It was like two in the morning.

"I'm sorry, I'm sorry, you can go back to sleep! That was mean of me."

"Right, fuck you." You pushed me with your shoulder. "Like I'm ever gonna be able to sleep again now."

"Christ, you baby, aren't you a decorated combat veteran?"

"Or something."

I put the mask back up to my mouth. **"WANT ME TO TALK DIRTY TO YOU? A NAUGHTY BEDTIME STORY?"**

"Yeah, metallic shouting, that's what gets me hard. Put it down, Chief."

I obliged, then tried to burrow. "C'mere. Cuddle with me if you're not gonna sleep." We arranged ourselves into some sort of knot, secure and blissful and contented. "We definitely shouldn't meet here tomorrow. We both need a full night's sleep."

You chuckled softly. "Cool, I'll see you here." I bit your exposed skin. After (what I thought was) a warm moment, you said, "Is it weird, like . . ." And then trailed off.

"What?" No answer. I untied myself from our knot to get a better look at you. You didn't look particularly pensive, more bemused. "Jesus, what? Don't start a sentence like that."

". . . That we haven't . . . with all the other secrets between us . . . that we haven't talked about . . . ?"

"Talked about what?" My momentary panic was ebbing, leaving a metallic taste in my mouth.

"Our stuff. Our service. Just . . . whenever I've been with people in the life before . . ."

I dropped my head back onto you, relieved and exhausted, though I'd have been at a loss to describe precisely why. "Christ, you mean swapped stories?"

"I mean . . . yeah."

"Okay, I . . . look, you're younger than me." Trying to find my way back into a comfortable position, that sweet spot we had found so naturally, so quickly.

"Do you think I have a problem with that?"

"Not what I'm talking about."

"Okay."

"It's like . . . did your generation have Mad Libs?"

"Jesus, my 'generation.'"

"Like where you filled in the blanks in the sentences and—"

"*Yes.* I know what Mad Libs are! It was one of the first apps I can remember getting on my—"

I groaned like an air raid siren. "Oh my *God*! Yours was an app?"

"What was yours, on paper?" you asked, like it was the weirdest thing.

"Yes, it was on paper! Jesus! Does it even let you put dirty words on the app version?"

"I don't remember. I think we might've just put silly stuff."

"Ugh. If you never put 'cockfart' in a Mad Libs you haven't lived a life."

"I don't know what to tell you."

I'd almost found it: a position as natural and knotty as the one I had a minute ago.

"What I'm saying is: do I have stories? Yeah. Do you have stories? I'm sure you do." I kept my voice low. "I bet we even have the same stories even though we were in different parts of the world. We just put different words in the blanks. 'One second *blank* was there, and then *blank* was gone.' 'I kept looking at *blank* for like thirty seconds after *blank* got hit, 'cause my brain couldn't figure out why *blank* looked different.' 'The IED went off and *blank* kept walking around even though *blank* didn't have a stomach anymore because *blank* hadn't figured out that he was dead yet.' 'Actually, we killed *blank* before we were even in hostile territory, we accidentally *blanked* over him with the *blank* when the driver wasn't looking.' '*Blank* killed herself with a *blank*. The whole day leading up to it she was fine.' 'We were in one of the Zones, and *blank* made one mistake, literally one, one tiny mistake, like anybody could've made, and twenty seconds later her whole face was running sores.'" Although our bodies pressed together, I suddenly felt very cold. I shivered.

"Jesus," you whispered. Out of disgust? Out of commiseration? I wasn't sure.

"How many does that cover?" I asked, trying to warm myself up again.

"It covers a lot," you replied and kissed my shoulder. "It covers a lot."

"I have at least two of each," I said distantly. "More of some."

"I have at least one." Kissing my shoulder again. "But are you saying . . . because they keep happening the same way they don't matter?"

They all mattered. But what the fuck can be done with that? What can be done with everything mattering? It just turns into some giant pulsing cloud of mattering. It's too much, you can't react, there's no next thing to do. At a certain point you just have to decide only *something* matters. If just something matters . . . then you know what to do next.

I let the question hang there for a minute, for a day, for a year. I was suddenly aware of the scars all over both our bodies. My own felt as if they'd taken on weight—each one laid heavily, tightly against my bones. Then I said, "Let's get some sleep. Tomorrow I gotta talk to Rachel Lesser."

SAY WHAT you want about Quill Marine, at least they don't make us rent our parking spots by the month. 9Source does that to its employees and that's a real dick move, if you ask me. It's basically just another chunk of change out of every damn paycheck—not only that, should an industrious person come along and try to find out which specific parking spot is yours and where they can find your car, that info is just *there*, waiting to be plucked off the tree of knowledge like a juicy little apple.

It was a silver Honda Civic sedan, practically anonymous, close to a decade old already, but in respectable shape. Roomy in back, decent upholstery, all of which was appreciated since I'd been hiding there for about ninety minutes before she clip-clopped her way to her car. I could hear her approach from what felt like miles away. I mean, seriously, she was a reporter, a glorified blogger, why the hell did she need to wear *heels* to her office (an office that didn't value her enough to even treat her to a tiny square of concrete)? Yet another question about civilian life I was glad to leave unanswered.

She unlocked her car remotely—the beep echoed through the lot with a plaintive loneliness—and in a few minutes she was inside. As soon as she pulled her door shut, I pressed the muzzle of my automatic against her ear.

"IF YOU TURN AROUND I'LL KILL YOU."

"Jesus Christ!" she gulped in a terrified whisper.

"SHUT THE FUCK UP. DO YOU FEEL THIS?"

She whimpered, but that wasn't an answer. I pressed the muzzle harder against her skull. **"ANSWER ME: DO YOU FEEL THIS?"**

"Y-yes."

I had a hoodie pulled up over my head, so, along with the mask (and, hell, my stockier build) she most likely didn't know if I was a man or a woman. I must have seemed, well, not to put too fine a point on it, rather alien. I didn't want her doing anything stupid or potentially destructive. This was meant purely to be a recon-type mission. She'd know why soon enough.

I pressed my weapon against her skull just a tiny bit harder. A micro-nod.

"WHAT THIS MEANS IS: DON'T SAY ANYTHING UNTIL I SAY YOU CAN. NOW TAKE A REAL DEEP BREATH. DO IT." I tried as best as I could to make my voice sound patient and accommodating—no small task given how inhuman the filter made it sound. I waited until she breathed, ragged and staccato, and I felt her head move against the barrel of the gun. **"NOW ANOTHER."** She breathed, a little more confidently this time. **"NOW ANOTHER."** I let her breathe two more times, deep, cleansing breaths. While she did so, I studied her—really studied her—in the rearview mirror.

Something was amiss.

"NOW HERE'S SOMETHING TO KNOW. THE GUN ISN'T LOADED."

I could have said it three more times in the moment it took her to compute what had just been said.

"W-what?"

"I CAN STILL KILL YOU, I CAN KILL YOU WITH YOUR OWN SEATBELT IF I NEED TO, BUT THAT'S NOT MY GOAL HERE. THE GUN WAS TO KEEP YOU FROM LEAVING THE CAR UNTIL YOU WERE CURIOUS ENOUGH TO TALK TO ME."

"Curious about what?"

I took the automatic away from her skull.

"WELL, HERE'S THE PROBLEM. I WAS EXPECTING RACHEL LESSER TO GET IN THIS CAR. YOU'RE NOT RACHEL LESSER."

"S-SHE DOESN'T work here anymore, she . . ." The woman trailed off, swallowed.

"AND YOU'RE JUST NOW REALIZING YOU SHOULD'VE SAID 'I CAN GO GET HER FOR YOU,' RIGHT?" I gave a short, dry chuckle. It sounded like a computer trying to learn how to hiccup. **"WHY DOESN'T SHE WORK HERE ANYMORE?"**

"She had an affair. With her editor. They're both gone."

I computer-hiccupped again. **"HA."** It figures they'd use something like that.

"What?"

"WHO ARE YOU?"

She didn't respond—not fast enough for my liking, at least. **"IT WOULD BE NOTHING FOR ME TO GET YOUR ID OUT OF YOUR BAG. YOUR NAME *AND* ADDRESS. OR WE COULD JUST TALK."** The threat came out in a low, inhuman monotone. I liked it. She didn't.

"M-Monica Sears."

"YOU TOOK RACHEL'S OLD JOB?"

"More like her parking space."

"WHAT DOES THAT MEAN?"

"Her job doesn't really exist anymore. We're not doing long-form deep-dive stuff anymore. I'm more in the 'GIF-after-every-paragraph' business."

"AND YOU WORK BY THE POST, RIGHT? 1099, NO BENEFITS?"

"I mean, that's pretty much any job in the field. To get on a masthead these days you have to—"

"DELIVER SOMETHING HUGE, RIGHT?"

It really is amazing how, when you give someone the opportunity to first complain about their job and then dangle a promotion in front of their eyes, you could literally be a hooded monotone space assassin who just held a gun to the back of their head but still the mood will thaw just a little bit.

"You wanted Rachel, not me. It's something on one of her stories, right?"

"BIG FAT HINT: A FACILITY SHE THOUGHT WAS A COVER FOR DEVELOPING ILLEGAL WEAPONS."

The journalist gasped, not as privately as she probably hoped. "She was right?"

"I CAN'T FIND YOUR AD RATES ONLINE."

"It's a whole customized scale, based on a consolidated score, targeted across platforms—"

"LET'S PRETEND IT'S A DOLLAR PER UNIQUE VIEW."

"Okay . . ."

"HOW MUCH WOULD A HUNDRED MILLION UNIQUE VIEWS BE WORTH TO YOU?"

"Um . . ."

"SAY, TEN MILLION? LIKE A TEN PERCENT COMMISSION?"

"It doesn't exactly work like 'commission'—"

"WOULD YOU PAY OR NOT?"

"For something that would get those numbers? Yeah, I bet they would. But nothing would get those numbers. The president screwing a cat wouldn't get those numbers."

"TALK TO YOUR PEOPLE. CONFIRM THEY'D PAY. THEN—"

"You want me to have a completely hypothetical conversation?!"

"*THEN.* IF YOU WANT TO SEE INDISPUTABLE PROOF OF THE EXISTENCE OF EXTRATERRESTRIAL LIFE, PARK THIS CAR . . ." I passed her a tiny slip of paper over the seat. She took it. Her hands weren't shaking. I took that as an excellent sign. " . . . **HERE. ON THIS DATE.**"

"Proof of extrat—?"

"**IF YOUR INSTINCTS ARE WORTH ANYTHING, ASK YOURSELF IF I'M A CRANK.**" I let that sink in. "**IF IT'S NOT PROOF, YOU DON'T PAY. GOT THE ADDRESS MEMORIZED?**"

"Um . . . yeah."

"**BE VERY SURE.**"

"Yes."

"**THEN GIVE IT BACK.**"

She did. I tore it up and put the pieces into my pocket to be burned later.

"**MONICA.**"

"Yes?"

"**NOT TO BE TOO PRECIOUS ABOUT IT? BUT YOU BETTER COME ALONE. BECAUSE I DEFINITELY WON'T BE.**"

I slipped out of the car and disappeared into the parking garage.

14

WE DIDN'T talk as we hurried down the hallway. We were entering an incredibly reckless phase of the plan and any unnecessary talking might make either one of us realize just how insane we were being.

But it turned out Haydon had given us a small gift, in his own, shitty, indirect way. Since the announcement of our new mandate, Lloyd had been spending every chance he had in Object E, like it was a relative in hospice or something. Which meant we had a pretty clear shot to do what we had to do.

"Which one's his?" you whispered.

"End of the hall."

In between Lauren's security station and the freight-elevator doors that took you down the long tracheal tract of the Big Bug, the walkway actually split off into two directions, which led to other areas aboveground in Quill.

There were all sorts of high-tech goodies to be found. Sound labs, isolation booths, rooms full of different light sensors and spectra—as expansive a playground as a person could wish to run any and all sorts of tests on the various data collected from Object E.

The senior scientific staff also all had their own private, windowless offices.

At some point between my leaving you alone with Lloyd and us all gathering in Conference Hall for Harrison's rather devastating news, you'd managed to get from Lloyd that he kept the raw footage used for making his holograms on a green laptop somewhere in his private office. I could only imagine what the inside of that office looked like: I pictured cascades of paper and boxes and toys, his own mad scientist filing system making it impossible to find anything. I dreaded it. But with Lloyd currently indisposed in Object E, this was our only real option. The footage was certainly also on the company-wide server, but how would I ever explain why I was making a copy? We were being insane. We weren't being stupid.

We had to move fast. Not so much because of the cameras (thanks to Harrison I could screw with the footage later), but because neither of us had a really good reason to be here. And if we were caught here together? Curtains.

At last, we reached it: a flat metal door with the nameplate "DR. LLOYD SIMON, *Director of Marine Biology.*" To the very end, aboveground, we kept up appearances. But there was no way to look into or out of these offices—to either the outside or to the hallways. Maximum security, maximum isolation.

"Okay," you said as you settled yourself by the door.

"You remember your line?"

" 'I'm just waiting for Lloyd,' " you said innocently. "You got the drive?"

I nodded, held my breath, and slipped in.

LLOYD'S OFFICE was almost completely sterile and pristine. A few random grace notes on a bookshelf here and there—a troll doll on his desk, a coffee mug that said, "[Ah!] The Element of Surprise" on a bookshelf—but no sense of this being the office of some great eccentric genius.

Lloyd lives more in his head than in the world around him, I realized.

We kept the door cracked open so I could hear what was happening in the corridor. I began opening drawers and doors at random, looking for the green laptop.

A few breathless seconds later I heard someone walk by and offer you a greeting.

"Everything okay?" the voice asked.

I held my breath and my position.

"Yeah, just meeting Lloyd," you replied.

The voice laughed. "Yikes. Better you than me."

Then footsteps walking jauntily away.

Within a few heartbeats I'd found stacks of paper, a vast array of drives and discs, a framed photo of a golden retriever, and more than a few tattered paperback novels with all sorts of aliens and weirdos on their covers. Lloyd liked his sci-fi, it seemed. I'd found at least three laptops, as well, but none of them were green. I was preparing myself to scroll through each of them when I looked up and noticed one last place to check: a container unit hanging on the wall. A small plastic alien figurine that looked surprisingly like a baby Moss sat on top.

I pulled out the drawer of the unit and inside was a green laptop.

I quickly, quietly removed the laptop (careful not to disturb baby Moss from its place of honor), put it on Lloyd's desk, booted it up, and hooked up the drive I'd carried in.

Our computers at Quill were top of the line, powered for unimpeachable efficiency . . . yet even then the amount of time it took to recognize the drive, read the drive, open up windows for their exploration . . . it felt like trying to make a getaway riding on a tortoise.

I watched the progress bar move across the window and thought:

I bet if he were here right now Lloyd would be explaining to me the theory of relativity and how it applied to how slow time felt right n—

Another voice from the hallway:

"New Fish?"

"Oh," you said. ". . . Hey, Patty."

Holy Christ.

Can stomachs perform a belly flop? Mine did.

"Just . . . hangin' out?" Patty asked.

"Yeah, uh—"

"Just hangin' out . . . in the Moss Team wing . . . nowhere near the Hangar."

I inched my way closer to the door so I could hear better, so I could react to whatever I was going to need to react to.

"Yeah," you were saying in your best casual voice. "Chief was like, as long as I'm not on rotation, could I go be nice to Lloyd for a couple minutes."

"Be nice? Isn't he in Object E right now?"

You dropped your volume a little: a secret. "I guess she's a little worried about where he is . . . y'know, mentally?"

Inside the room, the computer gave a (blessedly tiny) beep. Copying was done. I went over, ejected the drives, and re-filed the green laptop back in its drawer as quietly as could be.

But fucking now what? It's not like I can just stroll out while—

"Okay, so," Patty was intoning. "Dak's worried about Lloyd's mental state . . . which somehow puts you in the Moss Team wing . . . standing in front of a door."

"Oh—I'm not—sorry, I'm not trying to like stand in front of it, I was just watching for Lloyd. Do you need to get in?"

Fuck what are you doing be careful with her.

"I kinda think I do wanna go in, actually," she challenged.

"Go for it," you shrugged. I began assessing my options—*do I hide do I try to knock Patty out do I come out first and make something up*—but then I heard you ask, "Do you mind if I say something first?"

Patty chuffed. "I don't have to wait 'til you're done before I do things."

"Of course you don't," you replied, casually, dangerously unimpressed. "You way outrank me. That's why I said, 'Do you mind.'"

Holy Hell, you're playing with fire here.

But Patty considered. I could practically hear her crossing her arms in front of her chest and cocking her head. Her ponytail would be bobbing like the pendulum of a doomclock.

"Okay. What?"

"Dak's your friend," you said. Another lower-toned secret. "I'm not trying to take her from you."

Are you out of your goddamn mind?! I screamed internally.

"Are you out of your goddamn mind?" Patty asked.

"It's weird. It's weird for me to say it," you conceded.

Patty's fangs were coming out. "Yeah, I'd say it is."

"Things are different with me and her since the Harp thing. Like they would be with anybody. It's like a tour, it's like a fire-fight, like any of the Things. So sometimes she drops me a quiet little line, like, 'Go look after Lloyd,' but that's all it is. I'm not, like, after your spot. No one but you should have that spot. You and Dak are more than tight, you guys are partners."

I could hear Patty sucking on her teeth, trying to figure out if she was being played. "That was some awful shit with the Harp."

"Yeah."

"Decent outfit woulda sent her on a six-week leave."

"Right?"

"Messed up thing is: I don't even know if she'd have accepted it," Patty snorted, a weirdly sentimental sound. "But they should at least give her the fuckin' . . ."

"I'm with you, I agree."

" 'Cause I feel like it's . . . I feel like she's . . ."

"Look," you said to her, "do I have a field crush on the chief? Of course I do—who doesn't?" I could picture the smile you were wearing: deprecating, remorseful, charming. *We all fuck up sometimes,* that smile said. *Who am I to judge?* As if you weren't perfect.

"Fuck is a 'field crush'?"

"I heard it in my unit sometimes. Like someone who's so shit-hot at the maneuvers you'd follow them anywhere. How many of those do you get in a career?"

"Not a lot."

"But, I mean, there's a big difference between a field chief and the real thing. I know when people work together. You guys work. I wanna serve under both of you. I don't want to fuck that up."

Somewhere deep in the center of me, in the awful, awfulest part, I felt a thought crawl out: *He sounds exactly that sincere when he's talking to me. Doesn't he?*

I tried to stuff that thought back down from where it came. I also slipped behind the door just in time for him to crack it open.

"Anyway," you apologized. "If you wanna head in I'm just gonna wait out here for Lloyd."

Silence. I held my breath. Maybe Patty was taking your measure. Maybe she simply glanced through the open door—I had no idea. But she didn't enter the office. And the next thing I heard her say was, "When are you back on rotation?"

"Half an hour. Less, actually."

She grunted. "Then don't let Lloyd get going; it's your ass if you're late."

"Understood."

And Patty walked away. I heard her footsteps get fainter . . . and fainter . . . until, from the other side of the door:

"All clear."

I hurried out into the hallway.

"Holy shit," I managed.

"Yeah." You were smiling your small, private smile, contradicted by your furrowed brow.

"How did you know to work her like that?"

You shrugged. "I just watch people. Don't you?" I narrowed my eyes, trying to read you. "Is that—did I—?"

"No. You were great," I said, mostly meaning it. "You were perfect."

We were just standing around. We were being stupid.

"Okay, get this into your car before rotation," I said, handing him the drive. "I've got to go erase some surveillance."

"When's the meet with the reporter?"

"Four days."

"So we just have to make it four days."

Before I turned, I risked looking into your eyes. "Pretend I'm kissing you so hard it hurts."

"Pretend I'm kissing you so hard it hurts," you replied.

"Now move."

We peeled off in two different directions.

15

ONE OF the things you learn in an active combat situation is that the most dangerous time is often the period after the trauma. If you come through an attack, a firefight, a sudden explosion alive and mostly intact, it may feel like the worst part is over, but that's when you've really got to keep an eye out for the shit. That's when the adrenaline ebbs and you realize that trauma doesn't actually *go away,* it shrinks down to the size of a pinball and starts ricocheting inside everyone involved, looking to chip away at things almost at random.

The previous week was all trauma. Andy dying was a trauma. Losing Vonn and Shel was a trauma. Harrison's announcement of our change of focus was a fucking trauma. The first sign things were about to fall apart was Lloyd.

Lloyd, Lloyd, eminently Lloydian Lloyd. It was easy to forget there was a human being there sometimes, not just a collection of quirks coiled around some unfathomably, unrelatably brilliant mind. Easy to remember him freaking out in the conference room, him monologuing in broken and excitable fragments about whatever he was working on in the cockpit, and to look at him as more of an obstacle than anything else. Hell, we didn't even think twice about using his flightiness as an excuse for your loitering outside his office—nor did anyone passing by think twice about making fun of him, however lovingly, behind his back.

You and I were on shift inside the cockpit. And Lloyd was late.

Of course, Lloyd was almost always late. But given his new obsession with spending all his time in Object E, his absence

felt like some sudden, ominous silence after a continued bar-
rage of noise. It felt like breath being held before letting out a
scream.

I mean, it went without saying, you and I were already on edge.
It was the day after our successful boost of the copied footage. I
had built in four days before we met with the reporter again, in
case we needed a few more cracks at procuring everything, but
now we were ahead of schedule . . . and the waiting was murder.
The footage was just sitting there under my bed like an un-
exploded mine.

Our already complicated relationship with small talk felt especially strained now. Knowing there was someone up in Bird's
Eye able to overhear our every word, we covered the weather,
what kind of cars we like to drive, and whether either of us had
ever owned a dog. I was about ready to ask you your opinions on
the goddamn Kennedy assassination when, finally, we heard the
scream it seemed like the world had drawn in breath to make.

"EVERYTHING MUST GOOOOOO!" Outside the ship and
getting closer. It was Lloyd.

You and I looked at each other, nervous, as Lloyd squeezed and
stumbled into the cockpit. He was babbling and cooing, laughing and whirling. It seemed like he was drunk off his ass,
except . . . neither one of us could smell anything on him.

"Everything must go!" he kept cackling. "Final closeout sale!
Put a tag on that!"

We managed to sit him down onto the stool we kept in here
for him, and he clocked who was in here with him.

"Matt and the chief! Matt and the chief! Just who I wanted!
Matt and the chief!" he sang. Then, "Wait, no! Did I bring
my—?!" He started patting himself down.

"Your measuring thing? It's in your bag," you said. The tool
was poking out, perfectly visible.

"Oh! Obviously, obviously—good, excellent—although—
although—"

"Lloyd, did you get a good night's sleep last night?" I tried to ask, but his train of thought was already shoveling rocket fuel in its engine room.

"Although how great would it be—how wonderful and ironic and timely would it be if *this* week we measured the *opposite* of a regression? Huh?"

"A . . . progression?" you asked. "More moss?"

Lloyd touched his own nose and started making beeping noises.

"Sleep, Lloyd. Have you had any?" I demanded.

He rolled his head over to me. "Well, of course, clearly, clearly I did at some point."

"How recent—"

"You know how you can tell? I'm not psychotic!"

"Okay—"

"I'm not dead!" He stood, beat his chest, to prove his point.

"Hey, hey, why don't you stay sitting down, Lloyd?"

"Oops, did I bring my device to—oh, you already told me."

"Yeah, Lloyd, it's right here in your bag by your tablet, want me to—"

"*Tablet!*" he shouted, a "Eureka!" dampened by the weird acoustics of the ship. "Thank you for reminding me!"

"How 'bout this, Lloyd." I tried to soothe him down while he went tearing through his bag. "How 'bout we help you do the measurements, then me and Matt'll back off and let you have some quality time with—"

"It's on my tablet! What I wanted to show you! Both of you. That's, that's why I timed it out to arrive now, right after Guardshift. So I'd have time to talk to you guys. *Specifically* to you guys."

Our eyes met each other, instantly: what the hell could that mean? There's no way he—

But he was presenting us with his tablet, trying to press it into either's hands so he could pace.

"Can, can one of you hold—"

You took the tablet and held it in both hands. It might have felt like we were about to look at vacation photos or a particularly funny viral video . . . were it not for the mania in Lloyd's voice and eyes. It wasn't the mania of excited discovery. It was the mania of a late-night phone call begging for one last chance before trying something stupid.

Meanwhile, Lloyd hurriedly pulled out his measuring devices. "Just gonna get this under way and then, then, then . . . ," he muttered.

"Why don't we do the measurements for you, Lloyd," I tried, "and you can just sit and breathe?"

He looked at me with desperate eyes. "No." He almost whispered. "No. This might be the last time."

" 'The last time'? Come on, you don't—"

But the look on his face shut me up. The look said I knew better. And I did. Every time now could be the last time.

"Let me have this," he pleaded softly.

I nodded. He set up his devices on and around Moss, initiated them, then whirled around for his tablet before remembering you were standing there holding it in your hands.

"There it is! Good man! Right. We'll see our, heh, progress in a moment!" He held up crossed fingers for luck, then took the tablet from you. "So, I'm sorry, we'll have to crowd around me, no big screen in here. Wouldn't want this on a big screen anyway."

"Um, what exactly are you about to show us, Lloyd?" I wanted to put him in some sort of hold, swaddle him until he calmed down.

"Not porn!" He laughed shrilly. You and I exchanged worried glances. "I can promise it's not porn! Here. Here."

He pulled up a video and, with a trembling hand, pressed play.

Distant sirens.

Choppers in the background.

People yelling indecipherably into walkie-talkies.

The sound of ocean.

"Okay, helmet-cam is live, and we are effecting entry." A voice, seemingly directly under the images.

Directly ahead, captured by a camera teetering on some constantly unsteady y-axis, incongruous amid the broken trees and trampled grass near the border between woods and beach, growing larger as the camera approached, perfectly lit by an irrepressibly bright moon yet still somehow an inscrutable shadow . . . a giant walnut.

No. Fucking. Way.

"You can see there's a . . . I guess sort of a fissure in the side of the object, and we are going to attempt to enter via that aperture," the too-close voice says, then sighs. "Jesus Christ, I guess we're doing this."

Squeezing, jostling through tight, oppressive darkness . . . then emerging on the other side in a diffuse, bluish glow. Indecipherable shapes, low-light camera noise.

"Okay, I had to drop most of my equipment to squeeze through but I am inside the object now . . . there's some kind of lighting, but it's very . . . I'm gonna switch to night vision, and my camera should do the same—" The picture goes from color to a grainy green-and-black. "Okay, we're definitely looking at some kind of—oh my God. Oh my GOD. Oh my GOD, Staging, please tell me you're seeing this too."

Another voice, from far away, compressed twice over by distance and alien acoustics. "We're seeing it, Sergeant."

Sitting in front of what appeared to be an astonishingly simple control console. Tall. Thin. Utterly motionless. Shaggy with growth.

The pilot.

Moss.

Unsteady swaying. A torturously slow spin in a circle. "I'm just gonna get some footage. I'm just gonna get some footage. I don't know what else to do."

"Okay, but stay sharp, Sergeant, we don't know what its . . . status is."

The controlled, whistling breathing of a person confronted with the end of comprehension.

Inside the ship now, our own voices were tumbling, awed. We'd all seen footage of the impact, of the ship burning through our atmosphere and thudding gracelessly down, captured by various third parties from various distances. But this footage—

"Okay, is this actually—?"

"The initial entry? Object E woulda been on the ground, what—?"

"Three hours and three minutes," Lloyd provided absently. My voice and your voice continued tumbling over each other.

"We're looking at the first time a human ever saw an alien!"

"I mean, at least that *we* know of."

"Look how much moss there was on him then!"

"So much more," Lloyd sighed. Just like that, Manic Lloyd had vanished. This new Lloyd, sober and somber, looked like he had just taken a full blast from the Harp.

Decomposition, I thought.

"Now . . . Matt . . . Chief . . . what do you notice?" Sober Lloyd said, nodding toward the footage.

I gasped in understanding almost immediately. You were still peering, trying to suss it out.

"What would you notice if this was you walking into Object E on a normal day?" I asked you.

"On a normal day?" Your brow was knit, seeing it but not seeing it. "I'd freak out."

"Why?"

"The engine-room door's open. You can even kinda see the Harp."

"You didn't know about this, Dak?" Sober Lloyd asked me, legitimately surprised in a muted, fuzzy kind of way.

I shrugged, shaking my head. I had never seen this footage, nor had I ever seen an initial entry report. "Guess they didn't figure it for need-to-know."

"The speculation entered into the official report . . . obviously one of those offhand things someone randomly posits that becomes gospel over time . . . is that the door was forced open by the crash landing."

"But . . . ," you started, seeing the flaw in that already. I was right there with you.

"Doesn't sound right to you, does it?" Lloyd led.

"I mean, you have to stick half your body up that thing to reach the switch."

Lloyd was nodding. "An effect so difficult to achieve on purpose that it's impossible to imagine it happening by accident."

Now it was my turn to see it without seeing it. "But that's stupid, why would Moss want the door open? The Harp would fry him."

Lloyd gave me the saddest smile I think I've ever seen. Warm with understanding and frigid with loneliness. "You know . . . I envy how easily you ask that question, Dak."

I was ready to protest—the fuck did he mean, "easy question"— but then you spoke up and I understood.

"You think it was open on purpose. That he was trying to . . . fry himself." You met Lloyd's gaze. Empathetic. Commiserating.

Lloyd nodded. "What's the biggest problem this vessel would have with long-distance travel? And I mean long-distance travel. Light-years."

"It's small . . . ," I reasoned. "No equipment, no food . . ."

"More than both of those: there's only one occupant. Dak, what kind of mission could you imagine deploying with a personnel roster of one?"

That was an excellent point. "No mission," I said. "Ever."

Lloyd rewound the footage to the first moment the unnamed sergeant really saw him twenty-five years ago. A lone, lanky, knuckle-jointed creature sitting in front of a minimalistic console that appeared to consist of only a dead monitor and a steering apparatus. Hell, there didn't even seem to be a way to communicate now that I really took it in.

"Look at him. Look at Moss. Imagine. He took off from some unknown point of origin, alone and without supplies, in a ship about the size of two rooms in a house. And then he removed the one barrier protecting him from an engine that would leech the life-force right out of his body."

I found myself missing Manic Lloyd. This new Lloyd filled me with chilling unease. I wanted to put a hand on his shoulder, but I was scared to even touch him, as if whatever he had was catching. It made me think of the way the scientists at the conference table broke all eye contact with him when he began ranting about the new Harp mandate. *This has always been within him,* I realized, and a part of my heart broke.

"Lloyd, have you . . . ever put this in a report, or . . . ?"

"No."

"Ever told anyone?"

"No."

"Why?" you asked.

"Best way to make a colossal mistake in science? Project yourself onto the work." Lloyd took the tablet away, looked at the image still frozen on screen for a moment before turning it off. "There are so many ways to read the pertinent facts of the crash landing of Object E. Why am I speculating on just one? Because I'm simply projecting my struggles onto an entity that may share no cultural or biochemical context with me at all. I don't have a fraction of the data I'd need to back up what I just proposed. I just believe . . . in the region we call 'the heart' as a useful shorthand . . . that it's true. Just like I believe that even if we could? Even if we knew how? I wouldn't want to save Moss. Because I don't believe that's what he wants." He had calmly put the tablet back into his bag. He was no longer looking at either of us, so we were free to exchange concerned glances. "You're my best listener, Matt. And, Dak, you've always watched out for me. Just . . . if I fall apart over all this—"

"No one's falling apart," I offered, impotently.

"I just wanted someone to know the truth. My truth." He smiled, and his measuring devices beeped, having completed their analysis.

Two thousand four hundred twelve microns of recession this time.

So much for progress.

A FEW hours later, I found myself up in Bird's Eye eating lunch next to Patty for the first time since I overheard your conversation outside of Lloyd's office. I felt a little like I was seeing someone after having just caught them unclothed and unawares.

Even so, the atmosphere from both of us was clinical and self-aware. Unnecessarily polite. As if we'd had no interactions up until this point. It was a real Exhibit A in why I'd always tried to avoid any sort of relationship with another person whenever I could. Still. I was only able to eat quietly for a few minutes before giving in to the urge to say something.

"Have you . . . noticed anything off about Lloyd lately?"

She chuffed. "Have I noticed anything on about him ever?"

I tried to laugh, failed. I didn't have the heart for ragging on him. "Just . . . keep an eye on him. If you can. I'm worried about all the shit in the air taking its toll."

"Okay," she said. Looking at me a little too long before going back to unwrapping a second sprig of dried beef. "Yeah, you got it." I knew she was good for it, I knew she wouldn't take my observation lightly. But I also knew that dragging tone in her voice meant she was fighting the urge to say more. Maybe I was still shaken by Lloyd. Maybe I was totally projecting (*Best way to make a colossal mistake in science*). Maybe the tofu satay in my mouth was tasting like dirt no matter how much sriracha I poured over it so I needed to distract myself by talking more.

"You know I'm all good, right?"

I regretted saying it immediately. It was precisely the sort of thing someone only says when it's the opposite of true.

Patty gave me another quick look. Playing casual surprise. "Say what?"

In for a penny. I kept going. "My head's in this. I'll take a break sometime, sure, but . . . y'know. I'm good."

"Okay," she nodded. "Great."

Still, that dragging undertone. We ate in silence for another few moments, leaving me to ponder over how broken the ice I was standing on might be. Then she threw me for a loop.

"I think I'm gonna let New Fish graduate."

"Oh, yeah?" She answered me with a nod. "Wow."

"We, uh." She bit into her beef with gusto. "We did a little mano a mano a couple days back and I think—"

"You guys hanging out now?"

"Ha. Nah. But . . . he's all right. Matt. Matt is all right." She said your name like it was some foreign concept she was just starting to wrap her mind around.

"Well," I chuckled. "Good. Good to have *all right* guys on the team. I mean, when you have my spot, you're gonna need guys like—"

"Dak, I'm gonna stop you right there."

The worst part of keeping secrets: you're always on edge, even when you've forgotten you're keeping secrets. A flash of heat rippled through me as I tried to prepare for her to say . . .

"You're staying forever. Remember?"

. . . something other than that. It was such a go-to standard in our usual repartee that hearing it now in the context of so much change and anxiety was like a drink of cool water.

"Right," I managed.

"I thought we'd covered this: they offer to kick you up? You say nuh-uh. No way."

"It'd be good for you, though," I found myself laughing. A genuine, surprised, breathy laugh.

Patty kept a straight face. She finished up her jerky and moved on to one of her energy bars, this one slathered in chocolate. "No," she said, quiet and straight. "It wouldn't."

I felt a wave of . . . God, what do you even call it? Gratitude? Détente? Relief? Maybe there's no real word for it. She was my deputy and I knew my back was secure on more fronts than perhaps I was aware. It was a good feeling.

I went back to my food, which had somehow found its flavors again.

"Joke about your stupid veggie lunch," Patty muttered.

"Joke about your stupid meat lunch," I muttered back.

"Taking your meat-lunch joke and making it dirty."

"Taking your dirty joke and making it dirtier."

THAT NIGHT I watched you sleep, feeling my own pinballs ricocheting. It was our first night together we didn't fuck—I didn't lie outright, I told you I was too distracted about Lloyd, about the plan, to really be in the mood, and that was true to an extent . . . but it did mark the first time I felt like I was keeping something from you. The first little betrayal that all relationships have to walk over like cobblestones.

A relationship? What is this? Who am I?

I did make sure to warn you that Patty would start calling you "Matt" from here on. I couldn't tell if you were glad or a little sad to be growing up—you received the news in an oddly distracted manner. Maybe you were feeling the edge of your own secrets underfoot.

Eventually we fell asleep in each other's arms. I managed to stay asleep for an hour or so. Now here I was, awake and staring.

Am I the mark?

What an absurd, idiotic question.

Then why are you thinking it?

Because I'm an absurd idiot. I wanted to shake you awake, interrogate you for—what? For being so good at lying to her, for sounding so sincere while spouting insincerities?

Ping, my thoughts bouncing, ricocheting, chipping away.

Was this . . . all some sort of con?

Yes, I could hear your voice, *here I am helping you engineer the theft of something epically classified in the hopes that some shitty click-trawler gives us enough money to run away from the punishment I wouldn't even be facing if I hadn't agreed to do this in the first place as a* con.

Good point, smartass.

Ping. Ping. Like shrapnel.

What was this feeling, then? Suspicion? Jealousy? Did I think you were lying to me like you lied to Patty? No. Not even in the slightest. Yet, still, I didn't trust . . . anything about this. It wasn't a "who." It wasn't even a "what." It was all of this—a late-night, half-asleep amplification of all the insecurities I'd voiced that night we pored over our contracts. If my uncomfortable silence with Patty was Exhibit A for why I gladly signed away my fraternization rights, this, this stew, this swamp, this volcano of fear and worry inside my chest was Exhibits B–Z.

Ping.

I thought of the word "love" and all its infinite groanings. Wondered if I could actually say the word to you, on purpose, with all the intent it demanded. I had seen so many things in my life, but with this I was a baby.

The room started to feel very hot.

That's why I can't sleep. The room is just hot.

Ping.

And I'm just stressed and anxious.

That was all this was. Just a physical response to emotional overload. There was nothing to really worry about. Just needed to tire myself out a little. So I got up and paced. Thinking you were asleep, but never truly sure if you weren't watching me through barely slitted eyes.

16

THE DIFFERENCE between a soldier and a civilian is when the internal question *Are we really doing this?* arises, the soldier simply answers, *Yes.* It's not that the doubt isn't there. It's that the doubt has learned its place: as an observer with no veto power. Orders are followed, missions are kept, no matter how doubtful they might feel.

Two days later, finally, at the prescribed time, I waited in the parking lot of an abandoned car wash. It was two towns over, a location I'd just happened to have noticed once when I was on a meditative drive, headed nowhere in particular. When I passed the place I remembered thinking, *That looks like where a doomed deal would go down in like a Tom Waits song or something.* How quickly our jokes become prophesies when the chips are down, huh?

The sky was slate gray and heavy with an impending downpour. One of those days where you want to curl up next to a sunlamp and . . . well, listen to Tom Waits sing about doomed deals in abandoned car washes.

Are we really doing this?

Yes.

I was standing outside, under the awning for what used to be the waiting room, wearing my mask and hood. Next to me was the cavernous mouth leading into what used to be the conveyor-belt carnival ride of the car wash proper. We'd gotten here early just to scope out the place, make sure there were no possums or derelicts using the place as real estate. All was clear. You were standing off to the side, just around the corner of the entrance to the parking lot, in jeans and a ratty T-shirt, a nondescript baseball cap pulled over your head. I looked at you with two pairs of eyes: an objective pair that was impressed at how seamlessly you were able to blend into the surroundings, as inconspicuous as a road sign. Even if anyone *did* notice you, you looked exactly like the kind of person who might be seen around a place like this: rooting through weeds, barely more than set dressing, there but for the grace of God go I.

And I had another pair of eyes too: a pair that knew you, knew what you were up to, and thought they'd never seen anything as gorgeous before in all their years of seeing.

The reporter didn't appear to notice you as she drove past you and into the lot. I could tell by the hesitant way she was driving that she wasn't quite sure she'd remembered the address right. But she made her way to the parking spot farthest from the road and her car gave the tiniest of lurches as she put it in park. You gave me the all-clear from your position and I walked straight up to the car, ready to slide into the backseat.

The fucking back door was locked. I knocked on the window, keeping an eye out for any unlucky passersby who might see me while I was stuck standing there like an asshole.

"UNLOCK IT NOW!"

The driver's side window scooted down a crack. Her voice, nervously from within:

"A-are you—?"

"NO, I'M THE OTHER PERSON YOU KNOW WHO SOUNDS LIKE THIS. DO IT NOW."

The door unlocked and I got in, pulling it shut behind me.

"SEE THAT STALL OVER THERE? TAKE US THERE."

She drove us to the stall where they used to towel dry cars after they'd made it through the Tunnel of Love, then put the car in park. "I'm assuming they don't still wash cars here," she muttered. Trying to find her sea legs, unsure of just how nervous she should be.

"NO. CLOSED FOR YEARS. TURN OFF THE CAR."

She did.

"NOW TAKE OUT YOUR PHONE AND TURN THE FLASHLIGHT FUNCTION ON."

"Flashlight? It's not that dark, just a little cloudy—"

"IT'S GONNA BE DARK IN LESS THAN A MINUTE."

"But it's only like—"

And there you were, right on time. You walked to the car with unbroken purpose and threw the tarp over us in a motion so smooth it was like the world's fastest total eclipse.

She screamed.

"I TOLD YOU TO TURN YOUR FLASHLIGHT ON."

"This is too—this is too much—I'm getting out!" I heard her scrambling for her seatbelt, for the door.

"DO YOU KNOW WHAT'S ON THE OTHER SIDE OF THAT TARP NOW?"

Silence. "N-no."

"DO YOU REALLY WANT TO FIND OUT?"

Also, I didn't say it but thought wryly, if you've ever tried to get out from under a tarp while stressed, any illusions of a quick and easy getaway are dispelled pretty damn quick.

She stayed where she was. Smart.

"TURN YOUR PHONE FLASHLIGHT ON."

"Gimme a second, I'm . . ." I heard her fishing around. Then the glaring white spray of her phone's light burst through the darkness. ". . . Okay."

"BETTER, RIGHT?"

"I feel like this is unnecessarily frightening."

It was a really old tarp. From the street it should give the impression it was just covering an abandoned shit-heap. But she didn't need to know that. I wanted her a little scared.

"JUST PRETEND WE'RE AT THE MOVIES. THIS IS BETTER WITHOUT A GLARE."

"What is?"

I hit play on the tablet she didn't even realize I was holding.

IT TOOK close to half an hour to get through the first several angles. We watched in silence—the video itself had no sound and Monica was rapt.

While she watched I sent you a quick text: *All clear?*

You responded: *Ghost town.*

I found myself wondering if Monica would have the same dream the rest of us did after our first day at Quill. It was one of the rare bits of empathetic small talk we'd all allowed ourselves while conscientiously trying to avoid becoming friends. Obviously, we didn't want to get to know each other too well, but we could talk about shared experiences on the job and this was one of the weirder ones: that dream of hurtling through space, not knowing who or what you were, right after learning, conclusively, that aliens existed. Anyone I'd ever spoken to about it at Quill had admitted to having that same dream. Although, I realized suddenly . . . in the rush of all that had happened, I'd never asked you.

I'll ask him about it tonight. When we're celebrating.

I smiled a little bit behind my mask.

"This footage," Monica finally spoke up, her throat sounding very dry. "Why is there so . . . much?"

"**THIS IS ALL RAW FOOTAGE USED TO CREATE HOLOGRAMS FOR BRIEFINGS.**"

"Holograms? Why—?"

"'CAUSE . . ." That was actually a decent question. "**WHO CARES?**"

"Seems expensive." Jesus Christ, reporters . . .

"**IT'S NOT TAXPAYER MONEY.**"

"Well, a lot of taxpayer money does get funneled into Sierra, th—"

"**STOP. I DON'T CARE.**" I really, really didn't.

She kept watching, rewinding, pausing. After a few more minutes of total silence:

"I mean, this is . . . I mean, this is obviously . . . I . . ."

"YOU'VE NEVER FELT SMALLER IN THE UNIVERSE, I KNOW—WILL YOUR PEOPLE PAY THE TEN MILLION OR NOT?"

I expected "Of course," or "Are you kidding?" or, at the very least, "Five million, final offer." What I got was . . . nothing.

"OKAY, YES AND NO ARE BOTH PRETTY EASY WORDS."

She put the tablet down and picked up her phone/flashlight.

"So . . . here's the thing—"

"DON'T POINT THAT IN MY FACE."

"Sorry." She moved the stark circular glow away from me. Everything in the car took on an almost black-and-white vibe. Like one of those films where things discussed in the shadows start going disastrously wrong.

"WHAT COULD BE 'THE THING'? THAT'S AN ALIEN."

"It definitely looks like an alien. I'm inclined to believe it's an alien."

"YOU THINK *ALL OF THAT* WAS A GUY IN A SUIT?"

"No," she considered. "No, one thing it clearly isn't is a guy in a suit. And it's not a mannequin, or a, I don't know, like a sculpture, or, what do they call them, a maquette."

"YOU'RE RIGHT. IT'S NOT THOSE THINGS. I WOULD KNOW BECAUSE I WORK WITH IT EVERY DAY."

"Okay, okay, but back off for a second while I tell you what I'm dealing with here."

I wasn't here to talk about feelings or dilemmas. **"WILL YOUR PEOPLE PAY OR NOT."**

"My 'people' have in fact said they would meet your price, no questions asked. For indisputable proof," she said. She was finding her sea legs, all right. "In fact they agreed so fast it made me think you should've asked for more."

"I DON'T NEED MORE, I JUST NEED WHAT I NEED."

"But here's what's gonna happen when I go back to them

with this." She put her phone/light on the passenger seat, facing up toward the ceiling, and picked up the tablet again to cycle through the footage. "There's gonna be a whole conversation about the ramifications of releasing this, what'll happen after it's out. 'Cause a company like Sierra is like—I mean, they're an octopus, you know that, right?"

Of course I fucking knew that.

"What I'm saying is, when a company like that does damage control, they do damage control. You must've seen this in action. They don't just rebut the story, they obliterate the story.

They demolish its credibility from every conceivable angle. My editors, my publishers, they're gonna have a long speculative conversation about all the ways Sierra might respond. 'Cause if you've brought me a fake, they'll laugh it off, at most give a few curated tours of Quill Marine to prove it isn't there."

I felt rage boiling. "**YOU SERIOUSLY THINK I FAKED THIS?**"

"To fake this, you would need the most expensive CGI or prosthetic people in the business."

"**RIGHT, AND GUESS WHAT, I DON'T HAVE THAT KIND OF MONEY.**"

"But Sierra does." I started to protest and the bitch had gotten confident enough to talk right over me. "*If this is fake,* that's one thing. If it's *real,* that's when they'll really go to war. They'll attack everyone at 9Source, which, whatever, that's just the game, but—where they'll really focus their effort is on making this story totally worthless to us. Here's what I think they'd do: I said CGI and makeup, right? Sierra will do one of each. They'll hire a top CGI team to *make* an alien, and they'll hire a top Hollywood practical effects team to make *another* alien, and I guarantee you they'll both look as good as the one in this video. You know them better than I do: does what I'm saying sound like a reach?" She gave me a moment to respond. I let it pass. "I'm guessing that's a no. At which point we've paid ten million for the cover of the *Weekly World News.*"

Finally, I gathered whatever reserves I had to not explode.

"DO YOU . . . DO YOU HAVE ANY GODDAMN IDEA WHAT WE'VE RISKED TO—"

"I'm sure it's awful," and holy fuck it sounded like she really sympathized.

"YOU SAT RIGHT THERE AND MADE A DEAL WITH ME—"

"The deal was for indisputable proof. That's not what this is," she said. She passed the tablet back to me over the seats. "This is what life is like now: if it's on tape, it's fake until proven real. You should know that."

"WHAT THE HELL ELSE DO YOU EXPECT FROM ME." I hated how weak, how desperate I sounded, even amid the dehumanizing buzz of the face mask.

She turned around to face me, propping both arms over the inside shoulders of the front seats. In the demented, campfire glow of the upturned flashlight I could see that she was smiling.

"Is there any way you can bring us the, uh, the specimen? The alien? Or, or, even part of it?"

You must be out of your goddam mind, I thought. Somehow she heard me.

"Here's the thing: I believe you. I believe I'm looking at the biggest story since there have ever been stories. I'm not asking, 'Would it be difficult?' I'm asking . . . is there any way at all? Because it would be worth it."

I hated the look on her face. It was so conspiratorial, so cheap. But I also couldn't think of any arguments against what she was proposing—besides the obvious, of course.

"THE PLACE IS LIKE . . . I'D HAVE TO BE ABLE TO WALK THROUGH WALLS AND THAT STILL WOULDN'T BE GOOD ENOUGH."

"I'm sorry," she said. "I really am. Maybe you can take it somewhere else and get a different answer. But I really, really don't think you will. And who knows, it's probably for the best.

Sierra's an octopus, right? I don't even know where a person could run."

AFTER SHE drove away, you and I folded up the tarp together. Like the world's biggest, dirtiest American flag being presented at a funeral. I had given you the rundown as best as I could. I conveyed the facts; I don't know if I did justice to the humiliation.

From that point on we worked in silence.

I dropped you off six blocks away from your place. It went without saying.

OF COURSE, bad days often love to get worse. I know the feeling of a doomed mission when I encounter it. A doomed mission is rarely the result of one shitty turn of fortune. It's a shitty chain of shitty dominoes.

As I approached my place, I saw an unfamiliar car parked out front.

Wait. No. Not unfamiliar. I've seen it in the Quill Marine parking lot. Jesus, have they already—?

But they wouldn't have sent just one car.

I pulled into my driveway . . . and Grant got out. Fucking. Grant.

There was no need for niceties. If he was here, I could already intuit why. I rolled down my window. "What the fuck do you want, Grant?"

"I wonder if I could speak to you inside," he said in his prim, eminently hateable way.

"Speak to me about what?" The foregone conclusions were thick in my throat.

"I think you'd prefer it if I said the rest inside."

"No, you can tell me right here, Grant. Actually what you can do is drive straight to base and submit yourself for disciplinary—"

He leaned in toward the open window—wisely not far enough

for me to trap his head if I rolled it up. "I know you and Matt Salem are currently in contravention of both Quill Marine's and Sierra's policies regarding personnel fraternization."

There it was. And there Grant was. A little piece of shit who couldn't even bring himself to say the word "fucking."

"Perhaps now you'd like to speak inside?" he invited.

I rolled up my window, turned off my car, and got out.

Are we really doing this? The voice in my head asked.

Yes, the soldier replied.

WE SPOKE in the kitchen. The same kitchen where you'd fucked me on the counter what seemed like decades ago. I leaned against that counter, hoping it might lend me strength.

"Talk," I said.

"Do you want to offer me a glass of water? I'm thirsty," Grant swallowed hard for show. "I've been waiting all day—"

"You've got two hands; there's the sink." I imagined slamming his head into the stainless steel, running the garbage disposal on his tongue, filling the basin around his face with boiling hot water.

"You shouldn't be treating me like this. I could ruin you."

"What do you want?"

"What do I want?"

"You haven't turned me in yet, what do you want?"

"So you admit it." He folded his arms in front of his chest. "That you and Matt Salem are in contravention—"

"I don't remember admitting shit."

"I was right about Lansing and Michaels. I was right and you wouldn't give me *five minutes*." He punctuated his last two words by tapping a finger onto the kitchen table he stood next to. I could have snapped that finger like a green bean. "So I started thinking: why does it make her so angry? What I was doing was right. I learned the regulations in detail, I follow them, and I expect my colleagues to do so as well. You should've been thanking me. You should've been *praising* me. Instead you were angry. Why would that be?"

"You ever heard of the concept of 'no one likes a snitch,' Grant?"

His face peeled into a venomous snarl. "I've heard that my whole life. It makes no sense! Why do we have regulations at all if it's bad to snitch? Hmm? Those two things don't make sense in the same world!" He was starting to get shrill. I didn't know how much more of this I could take.

"Okay, Grant, you need to—"

"You should've said, 'Thank you for snitching, Grant. I should've listened to you!' Instead you snapped at me like I did something wrong, and I did nothing wrong! I double-checked, and I did nothing wrong!"

"You 'double-checked'?"

"So I thought: there's a reason. There's always a reason. So I'm going to find out what. And I bet you're thinking, 'Nobody followed me. I could see if someone followed me.' Right? Aren't you thinking that?" I *was* thinking that. "Except we work in the same place. And we park in the same parking lot. And it only takes a minute to place a magnetized tracker under a car. And it only takes a night to follow that tracker to a hotel. And it only takes an hour to record two people entering the same hotel room—taking care, of course, to clearly capture their faces." He stood there, breathing heavily. I was breathing slowly, evenly. "If you're thinking of hurting me, taking my phone, you should think about what arrangements I might've made if something happens to me."

I've been thinking of hurting you this whole time, I wanted to say, *but I figured as much.*

"Doesn't following regulations mean you should've turned me in already?"

His mouth tightened. "Nobody likes a snitch," he hissed. "Following regulations means everyone hates you. Following regulations means you never get anywhere because all the people who cut corners are fun and cool so they're the ones who move up. Hard work doesn't matter. Regulations don't matter. Only 'fun and cool' matters. I wish someone had told me that. I could've been that instead."

"Yeah, that's easy to picture," I snarled.

"You shouldn't talk to me like that!" he roared. "Your life is in my hands! His life is in my hands! Pretty boy Matt, I could send him to prison and then a Zone. That's forever!"

For a moment, I was right back there with Feetbreath, hearing his petulant, outraged whines to his wife. Not killing him was like deadlifting three hundred pounds. I was practically buckling under the effort. I wasn't normally a violent person, I remembered thinking—*but that Dak died a while ago*.

"What do you want?" I repeated.

"Deputy. Security. Chief."

His answer was so unexpected, so staccato, that it forced a laugh out of me.

"But that's Patty."

"WELL, NOW IT'S NOT!" He punched his fist into my table. It jumped slightly. "Now it's not Patty! 'Oh, Patty's so fun and cool'—well, now you're gonna find some pretext to demote her and put me in as deputy so when they move you up then I run security and it will finally, finally be run right!"

"Don't punch my table, Grant." I kept my calm but I spoke through gritted teeth.

"I'm—sorry—" He was rubbing his fist, red faced.

"I can't do what you're asking."

"You have to."

"Patty's earned her position. She's worked hard for—"

"Right," he scoffed. "By being fun to joke with at lunch. Find something she's doing wrong and replace her with me. Or you and Salem go to separate prisons, and then separate re-deployments, most likely at chem-zones, until your teeth and your fingernails fall out. Whichever one of those you prefer."

We stared at each other for a moment. Then he approached me. I readied myself for violence . . . but he reached over and started opening cabinets.

"Now," he was saying, seething, "where do you keep your—ah!"

He pulled out a glass. Then he turned on the sink and filled the glass with water. All the while, he kept his eyes on me, his thin lips curled in a smug sneer.

"Think you can snap at me like I'm a child," he hissed. "I'm not a child now, am I?"

He brought the glass to his lips and drank its contents slowly, still looking at me. When he was finished, he held the glass out. "If I don't hear from you by Friday, I go to Harrison."

I took the glass from him and he showed himself out.

I PACED for a few minutes. I heard his car driving away and seriously considered throwing the glass I was still holding—against the wall, against the floor, against my face, it didn't matter, I just wanted it broken—but in a supreme test of will, I placed it in the sink and began walking in and out of every room of my house.

I thought of my options.

I thought of our options.

I thought of Patty and losing her.

I thought of Grant and trying to work alongside him.

I thought of you and me, attempting some sort of prohibition, never making eye contact again, as forcibly separated as Shel and Vonn in our own private prisons.

I thought of Moss, dying quietly and persistently, the slowest kamikaze suicide dive in Earth's history.

I thought of the reporter from 9Source and her advice. Her request.

I thought of jail cells and tortures and dead ends and darkness. Of campfire stories and tarps and funerals. Of broken collarbones and gunshots and the entire Mad-Libbed tragedy unspooling before us.

I thought of being buried alive with you. A mass grave for two.

And I thought of a fish being gutted on a pier as its babies squirmed and leapt out of her. Death leading to life. To freedom if you could squirm away fast enough.

My face felt flushed and wet and I might have been crying.

Packages. Containment. Smuggling.

"Is there any way you can bring us the, uh, the specimen? The alien?" the reporter had asked.

Holy shit.

Yes, there is.

I thought. I thought.

Are we really doing this?

PART FOUR

GESTATION

17

YOU MIGHT think flying domestic seems like some sort of step backward after spending years guarding an alien spacecraft, but you'd be wrong. The comfort, the room, the beverages, the upholstery, the very existence of toilets? It all felt positively futuristic compared to the cramped and cragged walnut I knew had crossed cold black space to get here.

I'm sitting inside an airplane, leaving the lab, the state, the job, making my way to a haunted house.

This was three days after my car wash confrontation with Monica, my kitchen conversation with Grant, my continuing confrontation with the eminent shittiness of everything.

Two days ago, I'd tied up what I could.

ONE OF the reasons I never really believed in a Hell is that even the hardest things, with some repetition, can become routine. Granted, eternity's a long time and too much repetition can drive you crazy, but it's all a cycle—and is it really punishment if you at least have regular intervals of not giving a shit? Once Sisyphus knows that rock's gonna roll, it's really gotta be more tedious than tormenting. His mind probably gets to wander—shit, he might even get to enjoy it sometimes and *then* where's your punishment? I had friends on bomb squads who would tell me, after long enough, the only bombs they remembered were the bad ones . . . which meant you could even *diffuse bombs* and forget about it afterward. Knowing what you're in for can be one hell of a calmative.

So can, if I'm being totally honest, a light sprinkling of sui-cidal mania.

We had just been asked to move the Harp out again, in light of our new directive, so that the Harp Team could study it under full light without having to make repeated trips into Object E. I felt no dread this time. In fact, it felt like a lucky break—it fi-nally gave me the excuse to talk to Harrison afterward and set things in motion.

PATTY, ON the other hand, was less than thrilled. Mostly she was pissy she wouldn't actively be involved with moving the Harp. She'd had her own suit made up by now and was stuck wearing it in Bird's Eye away from the action. She still had her concerns about my general aptitude, too, I'm sure—although she'd never admit to that playing a role in her belligerence—but I insisted: this was to be myself and Salem one more time. It would be our third time moving the Harp together, once with incident and once without, and we needed to break the tie. We also knew we worked well as a team, and it was a good idea to eliminate as many vari-ables as we could before the Harp Team's refocused efforts began in full.

These were all true and valid points, but really I just had some-thing to tell you when the moment was right.

The process went painlessly. We suited up and went through all the motions, edging into the ship carefully to protect the suits, pulling the pins at the base inside the engine room, bracing the Harp even though we knew it weighed about as much as a card-board cutout. Once it was unpinned, we got on either side and lifted it together. It felt as ridiculous as ever, two people carrying something this weirdly light, but the Harp had sprung into action each time it had been carried a little so we knew what was coming. Especially now that we knew we could wear our insu-lated gloves, there was fear and focus, but a distinctly narrower kind of both.

The two of us working together. It's going to be a long week away from him.

We'd gotten a few steps from the engine room when the Harp started to spin up. The lights were dimming as we eased our way out of the ship, the Tent, but I could still make out the whole "new and improved" Hangar Eleven. All of the Bazaar had been reconfigured to prioritize study and replication of the Harp for field deployment. All that was missing was the final, humming puzzle piece currently trying to pull its ass out of our grips.

"We're gonna be moving in the dark soon," I reported.

You were wearing a helmet but I could still make out the look in your eye: "We're good at moving in the dark," the look said.

An entire week. How am I going to—

And then a new internal voice I didn't quite recognize: *You should tell him soon. Now.*

The Harp grew louder.

"Okay, assholes," Patty's voice came crackling over the comm. "I'm probably seconds from losing you. How do you feel?"

I felt good, no tiredness, no depression. The suits worked. The procedure felt comfortable. I reported as much to Patty, and you did the same.

All the while, the Harp was getting louder.

"See you on the other si—" Patty began. Then all the power went out.

We were back in darkest space, in deepest ocean, alone together.

We whispered through our paces out of Object E, out of the Tent, and into the Hangar proper, viscerally aware of the fragility of that blissful peace around us. When we reached the designated area:

"Aaand . . . down." Like I was trying not to wake a sleeping infant.

"Down," you confirmed, squatting along with me.

Once it was placed, while the world was still ours, I walked straight to you and leaned my helmet against yours. If I could have I would have nuzzled straight into your suit.

"I'll be gone for a week," I said. Yours eyes must have widened in the pitch blackness. "Just trust me. Trust me. And wait for me."

"What are you—"

"Don't talk. Just wait for me. Trust me and wait."

It killed me not to tell you everything. But you had lie detectors to pass while I'd be away.

The Harp began to quiet, whirring down. I hurried back to the other side of the Harp as the lights blinked themselves back on. You kept staring at me. I knew how badly you wanted to ask me for more information, for anything—but you were also like me: bred for the rituals of need-to-know.

You should say it. Say it to him, Dak. Say it while you

"Guys? Guys?" Patty's voice over the comm.

"Still here," you reported, eyes locked on mine. "All good."

"All good," I repeated. "I think we've got this shit down."

"Yeah, yeah, kid. Don't get cocky," Patty radioed back. "I want that thing silent for ten full minutes before you take off so much as a shoe."

"Understood. We've got it on the mark, so you can bring down the cube now. And, uh, can we chat in Bird's Eye in a couple minutes?" You and I were still staring at each other. All the lights were back on now so I could see your face, your look of restrained curiosity.

Patty wasn't expecting my request. Her tone brightened with curiosity. "Lowering now. Am I in trouble?"

"Nah," I said. "*I* am." You gave the tiniest of tilts, an immensely subtle version of a dog hearing a strange noise and cocking its head.

The sound of the winch lowering the familiar transparent cube over the Harp filled the Hangar as the very last of the Harp's whir died away, making me think momentarily of those red plastic whistles I had as a kid.

Playtime was drawing to an end, I thought, as I finally broke eye contact.

SHE WAS waiting for me, as requested, up in Bird's Eye.

"Hey," I greeted, stepping off the elevator.

"Everything okay?" She was harried, practically talking over me.

"Yeah, yeah, suit works like a charm." I lowered myself into a seat. She came over immediately and stood in front of me.

"No, I mean, you said—"

"Yeah. That's why I'm here."

"Talk to me," she said, crossing her arms over her chest.

I took a deep, long breath, then said it all with as little drama as I could muster. "You're right. You've been right. I'm fried. I've pushed way too hard the last couple weeks. Particularly with this Harp shit. I'm going to ask Harrison for time."

She blinked, like she'd just been spritzed with something. Her ponytail flinched with her. Then she yelled.

"THANK BABY CHRIST. Jesus, this is why you think you're in trouble with me?" She laughed. "I've been praying to hear this!"

"Okay, but hold off: I mean I'm gonna ask him right after I walk out of this room," I said. "Like starting tomorrow."

"Even better! Come on!"

"Which, which—listen—puts you in the hot seat for establishing security protocols for the new Hangar Eleven. It's a whole new layout. That means new rotations, new Guardshift, new everything."

"Fine, whatever." She shrugged.

"It's gonna be nonstop trial and error figuring out where everybody goes. Like, just off the top of my head, we're gonna want a rack of emergency Lloyd Suits out on the floor, which means you can expect major whining from Harp Team people whose workstations you have to move. Plus, the Moss and Object E Teams are already walking around, pissed off. You're

gonna be baby-wiping asses and doing nineteen-hour days."
None of this was inaccurate.

"I mean . . . actually, yeah, that does sound shitty."

"Really shitty."

"But the worst'll just be us not getting to bitch about it over
lunch." She beamed at me.

Fuck. There it was again. That wave of (*what?*) affection, of
gratitude, of—

"Yeah." I nodded.

She sat down next to me.

"Dak . . . you need this. I mean you're gonna do it right, right?"

"It's gonna be Jack for breakfast and banging stupid dudes for
lunch and dinner."

She slugged me in the arm. Hard. "Exactly!" I took a moment
to rub the pain away.

"But, you know, it's more than just the week. If you knock this
out of the park, which I know you will—"

She saw where I was going with that thought. "No, no, no, you
shut the fuck up with that—"

"—Harrison will notice. You'll be next on the list for security
chief with like an asterisk and a heart and a smiley face by your
name."

"Except for the part where you're never, ever leaving." She
threatened to punch me again. I threw up my hands and smiled—a
smile that said, *I'm humoring you,* but she dropped her fist, all the
same. Okay, this step was accomplished.

"You feel good?" I asked, slapping her knee.

"I feel good. Real good. Only one condition."

"Hit me."

"Come back with stories."

Oh, I will, I thought. *Just not ones I'd ever tell you.*

NEXT STOP was Harrison's office. It was tucked away above
Hangar Eleven—some peripheral organ located laterally from
the digestive tract, forgettable but vital all the same. It was a

notably sterile office, but unlike Lloyd's office, which felt neat and tidy more due to neglect, this felt purposeful. There were no medals on display (though we all knew he'd received more than his fair share), there were no pictures of his family (the kids he had, the wife he no longer had). Of course there were no windows. There were only two things adorning the room. One was the medium-sized print of a painting—I think it was a Hopper—of a small catboat staffed with four or five people, none of whom you could really get a great look at. It seemed like a serene, generic little scene, but the darkening of the waters in the distance, the way the clouds were gathering, the swell beneath the boat . . . The more you looked at it the more you realized some shit was on its way.

The other framed item was a newspaper clipping, gone sepia with age. It was a small, vertical article, only two paragraphs long. The entire thing was neatly redacted line by line with a black marker, except for the headline ("LOCAL BOY CATCHES BIG ONE") and one quote near the bottom: "He's going to be all right!"

"And it really has to start tomorrow?" Harrison was asking me. He was sitting behind his neatly compartmentalized desk while I stood before him.

The timing had worked just as I was hoping. Harrison was so damn grateful I kept the Harp issue out of his life one more time he couldn't bring himself to be as grumpy as he wanted to be. He was annoyed, but he also knew he was talking to a four-time Harp survivor just in the last two weeks.

"If it's possible, Director," I said, doing my best to not stand at full attention. "It's become clear to me that I'm overextended. Frankly, I'm concerned I'll reach a point of endangering ongoing operations without rest."

He leaned back, regarding me. He rubbed the area just above his chin with a thumb and forefinger. "It certainly has been . . . quite a while since you asked for time."

"I can't even remember." I shrugged, trying on a polite chuckle.

"And this whole Harp fiasco on top of it . . . ," he was muttering, not even for my benefit. Hell, he might have finally been articulating for the first time just how truly fucked things had been lately. His eyes snapped back to me, though. "I assume your recommendation is for Patty to—"

"If I had anything less than full confidence in Patty, I wouldn't be asking now."

"She would be overseeing a crucial transitional period. One with no margin for error."

"I agree completely. And she'll step up." I would have sworn it in court.

He unfolded his hands and began drumming his fingers lightly on his desktop. "Well . . . if anyone's earned the right to make an assessment like that it's you."

I kept myself rooted, silent, awaiting judgment.

"One week, lost time," he nodded, pronouncing. "You're back here a week from today."

I couldn't help it—my spine stiffened, my chest raised, my arms went straight to my sides. Full attention. "Thank you, Director."

He waved me off. Then, almost as an afterthought: "It's funny."

"Sir?"

"You're the only one here even close to me in age, or . . . maybe temperament? I don't know what word I'm looking for . . ." He sighed, suddenly seeming unbearably worn down. "Do you have plans?"

"Nothing I hope to remember," I said, and made my way to the door.

If I ever hoped to make it past Lauren's security checkpoint again, that was.

ONE LAST stop on Dak's (Temporary) Farewell Tour. The worst one. I knew where he was posted and I headed straight for it.

All around me on the Hangar Eleven floor, the flow seemed

jagged and unfamiliar. The victorious Harp Team was moving their toys into place. Farther out, the vanquished Moss and Object E Teams were sitting at their relocated workstations and waiting for new orders. The pulse of the place was still pounding, the river of scientific murmurs was still flowing, but there was no denying it all just felt . . . different.

But Grant, of course, was exactly on his mark, probably to within the millimeter. As constant as the tides and as incurable as cancer.

"You're on dinner after Guardshift, right?" I growled at him, walking up close, offering no salutation.

"Why?"

"Meet me by the cots." And I walked away.

TO THINK this was where I once fantasized about fucking your brains out while we put the world on hold. Now it was where I was about to fingerbang the driest pussy in the Western Hemisphere.

At least when he came to meet me he had the decency to look scared.

"I will remind you," he began, before I could say a word, "that I have copies of the video ready to go out if anything should happen to me." His voice was trying *so hard* not to tremble.

"I'm sure you do."

"One to Harrison. One to Central. One addressed directly to Trip Haydon."

"I'm sure they'll put that right on his desk."

"Have you reached a decision?"

"I'm going away for a week. Leave. Lost time."

He started to grow red. "That doesn't change your deadline. You owe me an answer by—"

I barreled over him. "I've left Patty in charge of reconfiguring security for the new Harp mandate. When I come back in a week, I'm going to 'realize' that Patty's done an unsatisfactory job. In light of this, I'll be going to Harrison and recommending that she be removed from the deputy position. He'll accept my recommendation, and ask me for a short list of replacements. When I give it to him, it'll be one name long."

You and I never got to make good on our urge to screw illicitly somewhere in the Hangar. The feeling I had now, a visceral need coupled with dread at the thought of someone walking in and catching us, was like that impulse's evil twin.

Grant was nodding, his face stony. A genuine smile on that face would seem, well, alien.

"Excellent," he proclaimed. "That . . . that will work."

I got up close, wishing I had that glass from my kitchen in my hands again. "Now listen to me, Grant. Are you listening?"

"What?" He matched my tone, challengingly.

"This only works if you play it cool. For the next week, you hit all your marks, you leave Patty and Matt alone, and do everything normal. You fuck that up and you can still ruin me, but I promise you, it would be the easiest thing in the world to take you down with me. You wanna be chief in two years? Hold your fucking water."

I started to walk away. His voice stopped me.

"That's what I've always done, *Dak*." He spat my name out like a stone. "Only now I'm finally being rewarded for it. Have a nice vacation."

I got out of there, like I was running from a bad dream.

NOW THAT I'd secured leave time, I needed to travel. The people I'd need to talk to in order to make this slowly baking plan a reality were conveniently all in one place—Washington, D.C.— but my going there wouldn't make sense. I wasn't expecting Sierra to follow me, not exactly, but they would likely keep a vaguely interested eye on my transactions. What reasons could I possibly have to cross the entire country for a relaxing vacation when the West Coast of America stretched languidly at my feet? Also, who goes to fucking Washington, D.C., to unwind? So where could I go that would get me as close to my actual destination as I could get, with an obvious enough narrative to keep the hounds from sniffing too hard?

About a decade ago I had been stationed for a year in South Carolina. People went to Myrtle Beach all the time. Maybe a sentimental old soldier would too—rent a beach house, drink at some favorite bars, probably see some old boyfriends. And if she happened to rent a car while she was out there, what of that?

SO HERE I am, *flying the friendliest skies Earth has to offer. No walnuts for earthlings.*

I settled in as the flight crew went through its tiny Busby Berkeley routine of life vests and face masks and tried to get some rest. Once we landed, I'd still have a load of traveling ahead of me, so I could certainly use it.

I closed my eyes and tried to picture all I had to accomplish. The plan was half-formed at best. A collection of ingredients for no exact recipe. I had notions; I was running on instinct, down a dark hallway with a small flashlight. I'd just need to focus on each step as I discovered it. I trusted the process.

First I'd do a little recon. Then I'd need to visit my old friend, Lisa: she of the haunted house. Would she be excited to see me? Would I ruin her life again? I'd find out soon enough.

Most of all, I thought of you. Wishing you were there next to me, holding my hand.

I never quite fell completely asleep. And in my half-immersed state I imagined I was covered in a pulsing, rolling tide of some bluish-green rash. It expanded and contracted almost with every breath. It gave me comfort, knowing it was there under my clothes, my little secret.

ONCE I landed in South Carolina, the hot sun hanging languidly in the late afternoon sky, I went through the requisite steps of renting a car for the week, of paying for a cottage a stone's throw from the water (it was August; I actually had to call several places before I could find an available rental—I'd started sweating a bit until finally I was able to pay way too much for a bungalow courtesy of Lena's Low Tide Leases), and then one last step: I pulled a shit ton of cash out of an ATM so I wouldn't have to use a card at all from this point on.

I got into my rented gray hatchback, turned up the radio (the Cars' "You Might Think" blared—what were the fucking odds?) and I reached D.C. about seven hours later.

THROUGH MY night-vision scope I was able to see Sierra's Arlington headquarters, a half-hour drive from the Pentagon. I knew two things from Harrison shooting his mouth off over the years: Trip Haydon always works late, and his car's the only one allowed to drive right up to the front doors to pick him up. Lo and behold, there he was: talking to both his phone and that poor bastard Needledick at the same time. Oh, to be a sniper.

It was 8:13 p.m. eastern time.

By 8:28, Haydon's car let him out at a hotel I'd be able to stay in for one night if I mortgaged my entire life's assets away. Curious— he lived in Arlington, with his wife and his three children, another ten minutes away.

By 8:30 I was inside, watching him join a young woman in a booth. He sat with his back to the room so I was able to stay a little longer to just observe. The girl looked maybe old enough to have graduated college, if she'd studied extra hard and if I'd squinted.

By 8:39, they'd finished talking and were heading for the elevators together. I almost made my move then . . . but, no. Not ready yet. Wait until the plan comes together more surely.

By 8:45 p.m., I was back in my car, ready to drive the twenty minutes to Georgetown . . . and to Lisa.

LIKE EVERYTHING else these days it seemed, visiting Lisa was a risk—on a number of levels. But the primary level was that this was Saturday night and this was Lisa Fang. She was probably out at a Thing. Lisa was born and bred for Things. She needed them, and they needed her. When I was with her years ago, she went out almost every single evening, so there was a very, *very* good chance I would be spending the first night of my "vacation" in my car, waiting for her to come home until . . . God, *dawn* was like the median choice. It was a risk I was willing to take, though. Without her help, nothing could go forward.

I walked up the red brick steps of her building and rang her apartment.

"Yes?" Almost right away. Holy shit, she was home.

"Dak for Dakota," I said into the intercom.

A momentary eternity later, she buzzed me into the building.

I took a breath. How was she going to receive me? How was this going to go down? Was I walking into a trap?

I pushed the door and walked inside.

"OH MY God. Oh my God. *Oh. My. God.*"

She was standing in her apartment doorway, wearing a blue silk robe over black pants, hair clipped up with indifference, practically peeing with joy as she watched me walk down the hall toward her. I wasn't sure if I should hug her, shake her hand, honk her boobs. I settled for shrugging and saying, "Maybe I should come on in and we'll get this door closed, huh?"

"Yes—*yes*. Please."

She ushered me in and closed the door behind me. And there we were. Dakota and Lisa, together again.

"Did you know," she was saying, shaking her head and looking me up and down, "about once a year—actually maybe more, maybe once every nine months, ten months—I think, 'Will I ever see Dakota again?'"

I smiled for the first time in what felt like years. Fuck that, I even blushed.

"I'm surprised you're not at a Thing."

"I had my pick of four Things tonight. Even thought of trying to make all of them."

"No shit?" I laughed. "And yet—?"

"It felt like a night for being alone."

I really clocked the robe, the un-made-up face, the hair.

"Shit. Lisa. My bad, if you don't want—"

She grabbed me by the arm, gently. There were not a lot of people on this planet my reflexes allowed to do that, gently or otherwise. "No, no, *no*. This is actually so much better. Dakota. Fucking. Prentiss," she rhapsodized.

We stared at each other, awkward and overwhelmed, for a few moments. Then she said the thing that tends to be said during reunions like these: "Do you still drink?"

"It's been known to happen." I grinned, and she spun on her heels and began to pad toward the kitchen. I followed.

"In that case, what would you say"—she reached her kitchen, gorgeous and intimidating in that way only a large kitchen full of spotless new appliances can be—"to some good tequila mixed with really gross margarita mix?"

"I would say, 'Get that inside me, stranger.'"

It wasn't too swampy that night so we decided to sit on the back balcony, overlooking her building's garden. Unsaid, by both of us: *our old spot.*

I let myself smile a little more because it was a damned nice night for some nostalgic balcony riding. And also with relief, because Lisa's apartment was haunted, so I would take my pleasantries where I could get them.

I WASN'T expecting my plan to move forward much tomorrow, so I let myself indulge—in a lot of margaritas and in a little truth.

"Jeeeeeesus," Lisa gasped, delighted and appalled, "for *real*?"

"Honestly, I haven't fucked this much since . . . okay, when was I in Dubai?"

"How in the hell would I know when you were in Dubai? It was probably quadruple-classified." She chuckled, licking salt off the rim of her glass. I was lost in a small squall of nostalgia.

"I think that was ten years ago . . . maybe more . . . fuck."

"We're so old," she shrugged, half kidding.

"Anyway, it's like . . . it's like if you don't have meat for a while and then you have a little and suddenly you've gone crazy."

"Only now it's man-meat."

"MAN-MEAT." I roared. We clinked glasses.

"Oh—sorry, it *is* still men, right? Look at me, assuming."

"Still men," I said. "Still women?"

"Still women." She sipped at her margarita. "Well—one man at one point, which was . . . fine? He was like a movie you see when you're bored and just want to enjoy some air-conditioning for a little while. You know a lotta work went into it, but it was all pretty forgettable."

"Fair's fair, then." I lifted my glass again. "WOMAN-MEAT." Clink.

"I'm so glad we're still assholes." I sighed, contented. A moment of anxiety shivered through me: *This is so nice, are you really going to upend everything?* I took another, deeper sip of my margarita.

Lisa's smile curled her upper lip—she was having her own private reaction too. In fact, it told me all I needed to know about her current relationship with woman-meat. Something had ended recently, and not well. Something that kept her from attending Things and even encouraged her to welcome people from her past, people so filled with painful memories it hung upon them like a stench, into her home for margaritas.

"I'm gonna guess . . . I'm not the only asshole in your life right now," I hazarded.

"Everyone has assholes." She tried to shrug.

"Yeah. They shit all over everything," I commiserated.

"It's boring."

"So I'll yawn."

"Love just . . . always ends up making you ask yourself if it's worth it, doesn't it? I guess it's like any other drug. You get the high, you get the crash."

"Was it worth it?"

She took a sip of her margarita and smiled ruefully. "She had a British accent, so . . ."

"Oof. Well. You know I kill people, right? If you wanna give me her name . . ."

I regretted the joke immediately. Not just because it's a truth I genuinely don't enjoy, but because the silence that followed was her way of saying, "I remember." That silence draped over us. It lasted long enough for me to consider excusing myself for the night and trying again tomorrow.

"God," she said finally. "Wouldn't it be great if we could, you know, *actually* catch up on things? Like, I could tell you what was going on in my life and you could tell me what was going on in yours?"

"Well, I told you about the fucking—"

"Sex gossip is fine, Dak, but it's also kid shit." *Kid shit I could lose my life over,* I thought, but I followed her. "You and I both know we have plenty of other things we could talk about. The things going on at your"—she swallowed, chose her words carefully—"place of employ? The speed at which things are changing in this town? It's getting bad, Dakota. I mean, it's getting not-funny-bad. And now here you are . . ." *Working for them,* she didn't say.

There was poison in her voice. I know she'd made an effort to keep it from seeping in, but poison doesn't discriminate.

Eleven years ago (around the same time Moss landed, actually), Lisa had been a low-level diplomat and Mandarin translator. This would have been a stressful enough job given the relationship between the US and China at the time—a trade war looming over the horizon, disagreements over certain irradiated peninsulas. But then Lisa had agreed to hand off a tablet with what she thought was minor stuff on it to a Chinese intel guy to get herself out of a bind. The next thing she knew, her life was over, though her body didn't get the memo. Her tiny act of indiscretion kickstarted a clusterfuck among United States intelligence agencies: one wanted to flip her, another one wanted to kill her. Neither wanted to communicate with the other. Unfortunately for the agents assigned to take Lisa out, my team of rangers had been hired to keep her safe. For about six months she and I were practically roommates. Only instead of arguing over dishes, I was fighting off assailants until the situation was finally reassessed. One of the many side effects of our increasingly privatized world: governmental oversight positions went purposefully understaffed. It takes a long time for shit to get straightened out. It's by design.

Sierra's design.

"Look," I tried to explain, "I didn't know where else to go after—"

"I'm not saying I blame you, Dak—"

"Everyone who ends up with them is wrecked, it's—"

"It's what they *do*, I know, it's—"

It all tumbled out like snatches of old melodies. So many things having to stay unsaid. So many redactions out of our mouths. How do you explain to someone you used to protect that now you work for the bad guys?

"There's so few safe conversations we can have," she said, reading my mind.

I nodded. "Even so. Night like this? Girls' night? It's sorta like the sex. Had no idea I needed it so bad."

She gave me a wry half smile. "You don't have a, like, a 'best girlfriend' back in . . . whatever sort of facility they have you in?"

I thought of Patty. Wondered how her first day running solo went. Maybe Moss had woken up and flown everybody to a distant planet and out of my hair. "I do, kinda, but this . . . not possible with her."

"Those Sierra contracts are the stuff of legend."

"That, yeah, plus . . . we're both kinda broken in the same way? So . . . I think we'd just make each other bored and sad." The margarita in my hand was melting, sweating, and starting to taste cloying. Judging by Lisa's expression, she was starting to feel the same way about hers. We still drank, though. We knew a thing or two about mission commitment.

"So I haven't made you bored and sad?" she asked with a rueful grin.

I shrugged. "I mean, this margarita mix is making me sad."

"Give a girl a warning next time. You're getting the emergency cache."

I stood up, stepping in place. "Actually, there's an emergency cache about to happen in my drawers. This is, like, all water now."

"I'd tell you where it is, but there's no way you don't still have this layout memorized, is there?"

"It's like I never left," I said. "Be right back."

I PISSED for like a century. It gave me plenty of time to look around the bathroom and remember.

That's where I stood guard while she showered.

Over there's where I put the guy's face into the floor enough times that "face" stopped being the right word.

I washed my hands and tried to avoid looking at myself too closely in the mirror.

WHEN I stepped back onto the balcony I knew even with her back to me that the party was over.

"Lemme guess." I joined her looking out over the garden below. "Me plus this apartment equals every corner filled with memories. It's sure happening for me."

She took another sip from her glass and grimaced at the taste. The neon drink wasn't a treat anymore, it was a tool. "How many people did you have to kill to keep me alive?" she asked flatly.

"You want a number?" She nodded. "Four."

"Four," she repeated. "All Americans?"

My turn to nod. "It was a pissing match. It should have all been reined in by people at the top, and it wasn't, and there we go."

"There we go."

"It was my job to protect you, Lisa. And it was their job to kill you. I was just better. We don't need to—"

"No, I know. I know." I could tell she had more to say, so I let her think. "That feeling never goes away, though," she said at last. "Of being hunted. Of . . . pursuit. Even when you know it's over, it's never really over."

I guess I'll find out soon enough. "But they lost interest. It happens," I offered. And it was true. It *was* true. "It wasn't personal, it was just a job—for everyone. The people assigned to you have probably all been transferred two or three times by now and I guarantee you none of them are bored with where they're at now. They've moved on."

She was nodding. "That makes sense. Turnover is the order of the day. Sierra's the only constant."

"Exactly. All hail the lifesaving cracks in the bureaucracy."

"But you haven't forgotten. And I haven't forgotten," she said.

"That's true."

"In fact," she went on, "I think the reason you're here tonight is because you were counting on it not being forgotten. I owe you a debt."

I prepared myself for what I was about to ask. "One thing would square the books for me."

"One thing . . . but you've needed all night to work up to it. Do you want another drink?"

"Shit, no," I said.

She put her glass on the ledge of the balcony and turned to face me.

"Then I think it's time you tell me what you need."

IT WAS the kind of drunk that worked on a slow release. When I left Lisa's apartment I could have passed a competency exam with flying colors . . . but by the time I was halfway back walking to my car I felt like I was a UHF channel barely coming in. My ligaments began to waver, desolidify, melt—

I'm underwater
Blue and green

I could have risked driving to a hotel—even trashed I had confidence in my motor skills, if you can pardon the pun—but the infinitesimal chance of being pulled over, my name being run through a computer that would then be intercepted by someone at Sierra, contradicting everything I'd told them, made the whole idea distinctly not worth it. I poured my liquefying self into the driver's seat of my parked car.

I'll sleep for a little bit, until I'm solid matter again, and then drive my hungover ass to a room somewhere
First I gotta think
Did I really say what I think I said
I did. I know I did.
But I didn't use the word. That's a victory.

"I need a sit-down," I'd told her, the two of us standing on the balcony with the muggy, warm air suddenly feeling very heavy around us. "With whoever the guy is."

"The guy for what?" she asked, even though she might have known.

I told her. Crossovers, the lingo had dubbed it.

"Oh," she exhaled. "Dak." It sounded like a eulogy.

"For two people," I added.

"Two people," she repeated, awash in piteous understanding.

"Yes. Give whoever handles that my name and tell him to contact me." I was writing the number to my burner phone on a slip of paper.

She was nodding, but not in agreement. In comprehension. In sympathy. "So all the sex you've been having . . ."

"Give him my *real* name," I continued.

". . . is not just sex." She sounded like she was repeating a bad diagnosis she'd just received from the oncologist. I kept talking, before I lost my nerve.

"Let him look me up. Won't be much there, but enough to take an interest. Let him know I can pay my way with Premium Content. Let him know I don't just say things."

"Dak, my God, please." She wasn't even talking to me. It was a prayer to the universe.

"I go back Tuesday," I pressed on. "The meeting will need to happen in the next three days."

After a moment, she set her jaw and looked at me. "It would be irreversible. You know that, right?" I stared back at her: yes, I knew it. She sank into herself a little. "I believe you know yourself." She sighed. "I've always thought that about you. So just . . . answer me and that will be enough. Do you love him this much?"

"More," I said. And again, so I could hear it: "More."

She nodded, sadly. "Then I'll make it happen. I'll get you in a room with the guy. You'll have to do the rest."

But I didn't really say the word, I thought, as I melted away.

18

I WOKE up in my car about five and a half hours later. I was slimy with sweat and as cramped and knotted as a broken fist. The inside of my mouth felt like stale bread and tasted like staler shit and the world looked like it'd had a transparent copy of itself laid over incorrectly, an image double-exposed.

I'm going to puke my fucking tits off.

Fucking margaritas.

I gotta get to a hotel.

I ran a quick mental check to make sure I was functional enough to drive the streets of D.C. (counting backward from seventeen, an old trick from the service), tried to crack the stiffness out of my back and neck, then started the car.

THE CHIRPY chicken behind the front desk of the first cheap-looking hotel I found was doing a C-plus job of masking her dismay at my raggedy-assness as I approached her. I'm sure she had a mental Rolodex of platitudes to say to someone checking in under all sorts of circumstances but she probably couldn't tell quite what I was. Hungover? Beaten up? Just naturally disgusting? So she lifted her upper lip in an attempt to smile politely as I told her I needed a room.

"I'm afraid check-in's not for another three hours, though," she clucked.

"Then point me in the direction of your nearest diner."

. . .

PREPARING FOR a battle means two major considerations: tactics and logistics. Tactics are the fun part—the on-the-ground, semi-improvisatory call-and-response between expectation and reality. Logistics are the nuts and bolts. The inventory. I was still fuzzy on the former (hell, with this hangover I was fuzzy on everything), but I sat in a booth as far away from the door as I could get and tried to nail down the latter.

The diner was busier than I would have expected this early, probably full of staffers and interns and all sorts of other Washington busybodies fueling up for their various exploits of good and evil. The noise was just below unbearable. The coffee and veggie omelet were dissolving into a poisonous stew in my gut.

Logistics: I knew I needed to finish up with Lisa—that was most important; nothing could go forward without that. I knew I needed to find time to meet with Nikki. And then . . . one last meeting, the one I went to that hotel for . . .

It's really fucking risky, Dak.

But is it too risky?

What does "too risky" look like if it doesn't look like that?

Sometimes you have to run the Charge. Be a madman.

But it never works.

That's why you do it. That's why it could *work.*

That doesn't make s—

Okay. I stuffed all the debating voices down. The floor was closed. The plan was forming. The "what"s were falling into place. I just had to figure out all the "how"s.

"Anything else?" the waiter asked, driving by to refill my coffee.

I ordered a bearclaw. It sounded disgusting but I still had time to kill. Assuming time didn't kill me first.

I looked at all the bodies coming in and out of the diner and wondered if one day you and I would ever get to enjoy a meal together, in a booth, in public, without one or both of us constantly looking over our shoulders.

A few minutes later, the poisonous humming in my guts, like the Harp, reached a crescendo. I made my way to the bathroom and laid waste to everything.

I'll leave them a good tip, I thought.

FINALLY I was able to drop myself onto the tightly made bed of my cheap hotel room. I felt shellacked with grime and sweat. It was hot and stagnant enough that I was even willing to give a cold shower a try.

I DIDN'T hear back from Lisa until Monday morning, the day before I had to leave, but I was fine with that; it gave me two whole days of rest. I stayed in my hotel room—no sightseeing, no potentially visible trips outside unless absolutely necessary. This was a utilitarian adventure, but I might as well try to get *some* rest.

Of course, it did mean a lot of things had to go down in one day.

An hour or so after daybreak, as I finished a particularly strenuous set of crunches on the dingy carpeted floor of my room, my burner phone chimed in my bag. For the briefest of moments my heart lurched at the thought that maybe it was you. But of course it wasn't you. You knew better than that. And anyway, someone else had this number now.

A text message from an unknown caller. A single numeral: "9."

So that meant 9 a.m., I would meet with Lisa's contact. There was no location given so that would mean it was back at Lisa's haunted house.

Perfect. I'd been planning on meeting Nikki at some point today, so I might as well see if I could squeeze her in first.

I USED the hotel phone to give Nikki a call. It was early, but she'd be up—she was a runner and a churchgoer, both of which meant she rose traumatically early. When she answered the phone, I chirped, "What's up, Q?"

She knew right away who I was—she even knew not to use my name just in case anyone was listening. We set up a meet right away, timing it out for the end of morning rush hour. At L'Enfant Plaza, I transferred to the Orange line, squeezing through the crowds until I could find a comfortable place to stand. She spotted me across the car, but we rode a few more stops so she could make her way to me naturally, without pushing.

When she finally made her way to me:

"God bless everything: Dak." She said it quietly enough that I wasn't sure if it meant "It's good to see you," or "I thought I was done with your ass." But her eyes were bright and excited.

"Fuck you for not looking a day older," I muttered back.

"I don't get a lot of sun," she shrugged.

She asked if I was back with the Seventy-Fifth and I shook my head. My new squad was a more informal one, I told her.

"As long as it's for the real stuff," she intoned.

To Nikki, "real stuff" meant America, civilians, people who can't protect themselves. Nikki was the sort of patriotic do-gooder who was really rather pathological about it. Like, she probably drank out of a mug with a flag on it. She cried when she heard the national anthem. I don't wanna begrudge anyone their crushes, but frankly the amount of goodness in her heart, particularly for the downtrodden and helpless, always made Nikki and America seem like a strange couple.

I would have preferred not to straight-up lie, but she'd boxed me in a bit. So I set my brow and nodded, looking as serious as I could.

"Always the real stuff, if I can help it."

Neither of us looked at each other while we spoke, only quick glimpses while the other was speaking.

"Tell me," she said.

"Hallucinogenic. Reasonably fast acting. Discreetly applicable."

"Would topical work?"

"Whoa, is that a thing now?" Fuck, I could talk to Nikki all day about the gadgets and toys she had access to as a researcher and developer in the Quartermaster Corps. She actually worked for the same outfit that brought me and my team in to guard Lisa. Whenever we'd needed toys, Nikki was the person to see.

The loudspeaker interrupted us, though. Next stop was Potomac Avenue. Once we got past the Armory the crowds were gonna thin out.

"There's another rush hour at the end of the day," Nikki said. "Let's do this again going the other way."

"Hotness."

The train stopped and she became an entirely different person.

"Getting out, people! Getting out!" She marauded her way through the walls of people—the real stuff—and I thought, *You and me both, sister.*

I BUZZED Lisa's apartment and made my way to her door, where I found a man waiting for me. The no-nonsense way he frisked me and took my bag suggested training; probably PLA Special Forces. When he was done he pointed me to the living room, where Lisa and another man, handsome and tall, were waiting.

"Dakota Prentiss," the man said.

Lisa made the introductions. "Dak, meet Zhang Liu."

"Zhang's fine," he said. "Hi."

"You don't have an accent." It was out of my mouth before I realized what I was saying.

He looked at Lisa, his lips curling into a devilishly tiny smile, then said, "What kind of accent did you have in mind?"

I felt my face redden. Of course he didn't have an accent—or, to be more precise, he sounded like he could have been from Long Beach. A big part of his job was putting Americans at ease. The current placement of my own foot inside my mouth was proof positive alone of how we tended to act if we thought someone was from Somewhere.

"Why don't we just forget I said anything?" I tried to chuckle.

With introductions out of the way, Lisa gave me one last inscrutable look—sadness? fear? resignation? all of the above?—and left the room. A few moments later, I heard her leave the apartment. A good idea, that. When your friends are engaging in illicit conspiracies, it's usually a good idea to remember errands to run. Zhang and I had one last moment to size each other up, then we both sat down: me on the plush, white sofa, Zhang on a plush, white armchair.

"So, obviously I've read everything we have on you," he said. I nodded. "It's not much—you're not in espionage, but you've intersected with that world a bit."

"Everybody needs a door kicked in sometimes," I shrugged.

He gave me another devilishly tiny smile. "We have similar collaborations on our end." Damn, I was starting to like him immensely already.

"So what was in my file?" I asked.

"Enough for me to conclude two things. One, it's awfully late in your career to suddenly groom you as a double agent. If you're reaching out, it's likely in earnest." I could have kissed him. "And two, you probably don't begin your meetings with a cocktail and ten minutes of small talk."

"You got me on both counts," I said. "I'm ready to work."

"Then work," he sat back in his chair, ready to hear my pitch. Except:

"Your guy at the door took my bag. There's a laptop in it that contains footage I need to show you."

He gave me the sassiest head tilt I could ever imagine witnessing in a clandestine meeting about life-and-death matters. "You can't just tell me in words?"

My turn to be devilish. "Okay, let's try that first." I sat back too, crossing my legs and clasping my hands primly in my lap. "If I give you the body of an alien from outer space, will you give me and my boyfriend fifty million dollars and asylum in your country for life?"

He blinked. Then cleared his throat and nodded. "You're right, let's get your computer."

WHEN HE was done watching the footage, he looked at me, squarely and for a good amount of time.

"I can't think of a single reason why you'd come to me with falsified footage of an extraterrestrial," he said. His voice was soft, musing.

I played along. "If I'm a spy I'd come to you with a credible story. If I'm a nutcase my footage wouldn't look this good. If I'm not a nutcase, I'd know you'd insist on verification before payment. And if that verification were to fail—"

He put a finger-gun to his temple and said, "Oops."

"Oops," I nodded.

"A lot of countries don't extradite. Why us?"

"It's not about extradition. I'm not stealing this from the US government."

He chuckled at that. I knew why: the difference between the US government and Sierra was nominal at best these days.

"From your particular vantage point, Ms. Prentiss," Zhang smirked, "just how aware are you of what's happening in your country?"

I didn't want to argue the point. "It's none of my business. I'm done."

"I find it hard to believe a former soldier has no feelings whatsoever regarding her—"

"I've done my part, all right? More than my part. I've kicked in, no one can say I haven't." I was getting agitated. "No one can say I haven't given my—"

Zhang put his hands up, apologetically. "You're right, you're right."

I was on a roll, though, and I had to get this out, for myself as much as for him. "I've earned not thinking about it anymore. I've earned a life. God knows I've earned a fucking life. And the only way I can have one is to go somewhere they can't follow."

"Which, given Sierra's numerous Russian ventures . . ." He began.

"Pretty much leaves you," I completed.

He gave me a nod. Fair enough.

"Here's a question. The body's not dissected." He settled back into his chair, getting comfortable. "You've had him, what, ten years? Why isn't he . . . ?" He made gestures, lopping off various parts of his body.

"Mostly it's that Sierra wants to keep an option to cash out."

"Cash out?"

"Put Moss on display for money."

"Ah. But that's only mostly? He's not *alive*, is he?" I think he was kidding, there, but when he saw my face any humor in his fell. "Is he—?"

"There are . . . theories," I said. His eyes widened.

"Does he breathe, does he have a heartbeat?"

I almost wished Lloyd were here to stammer through something more unnecessarily descriptive. I felt like he and Zhang would get along.

"No. Nothing like that. Well, except that he's warm."

"He's . . . warm? You mean, he's—"

"His skin is warm. To the touch. But look, he's a fucking alien, we don't *know* anything. And once he's yours, you can handle him however you want."

"Once he's ours."

"Right."

"Which would transpire how, exactly?"

I stiffened. "None of your fucking business."

He chuckled. "Apologies, you're right, that was amateur." Yeah, it was. Also, I still wasn't completely sure. "You've likely anticipated that I'll ask to keep the laptop, correct?"

"It's yours."

He closed it, put it in his lap like a sleeping pet.

"Obviously I'm going to make inquiries on my end. I'll be candid . . . I'm not optimistic, but I will certainly—"

"Wait. What does that mean, you're not optimistic?"

"But I will try."

Whoa, whoa, whoa.

"How can you not be optimistic? What is everybody's deal—it's a fucking alien!" I no longer wished Lloyd were here; instead, I felt in danger of becoming him, storming and raging during the meeting where Quill Marine received its new mandate. I needed you here to calm me down, take me for a glass of water. "It's *the* discovery of all time! You're telling me your scientists wouldn't be—"

"Oh, they'd be overjoyed," Zhang smiled, holding the laptop to his chest. "I have no doubt. But when I leave this apartment and start making calls, I won't be talking to scientists. I'll be talking to, for lack of a better term, risk assessors. And they're going to tell me that the risk of meeting you in a North American location; verifying the item; and then transporting it, you, and one other American safely back to home soil is more than is justifiable given that the item—remarkable as it is—is entirely without strategic value."

"Jesus Goddamn Christ!" Flashes of Monica, of the humiliating rendezvous in the car wash the week before, whizzed at me like strobe lights.

"Speaking for myself? As a patriot? I want it," Zhang conceded. "And your price is reasonable. I mean, I have very little faith that you can actually acquire the item—I honestly don't expect to ever see you alive again—but if you somehow managed to do it? I want it. But it's not up to me."

I was well aware that any second now, he was going to stand up. As soon as he did, everything was over. As soon as he stood, he would be asking me politely to leave and if I fought that, there went my credibility. I became the frazzled crazy woman digging her heels in and needing to be removed no matter how well the meeting had gone initially.

I wasn't thinking. Or I was thinking too hard. I don't know. I leaned forward, speaking slowly. Deliberately. So he knew I was serious.

"What if . . . I could sweeten it?" I could hear his voice in my head: *strategic value, strategic value . . .*

"Sweeten how?" He looked at me, that devilishly tiny smile beginning one more time.

And here's where I made everything a thousand times worse.

"What if," I said, choosing my words carefully, "there was also a weapon?"

He considered. Then crossed one leg over the other, settling farther into his chair, ready to hear what I had to say.

OKAY, SO now I had to move an alien *and* an unpredictable death machine. Aces.

Why didn't you plan for that? Why didn't you prep better? You didn't even have a clear idea of how everything was going to go down without *throwing the Harp into the mix and now—*

I miss Matt.

It was true. I felt frazzled, overwhelmed, nervous, angry . . . but underscoring every emotion was the aching need for you. It wasn't even a distraction or an inhibitor. I didn't blame it for my shoddiness. It was just there, a constant underscore. Which meant maybe I could use it to refocus my efforts.

So that's what I did. I set to work unknotting the situation in my head, using the knowledge that the sooner it was all over, the sooner you and I could live our lives in peace. I had lived far too long without you; I'd be damned if I was going to let any more time go by.

In fact I was concentrating so damn hard I almost didn't see Nikki approaching. I was standing in a clump of commuters, back on the Orange line, a few hours later. Before I knew it she was standing next to me. I almost yelped—thank God I noticed her right before she started speaking or I would have killed myself in embarrassment.

She pressed a small baggie containing what felt like a small vial into the hand hanging by my side.

"It's a powder," she murmured. "Don't open it until you need to use it. Regular latex gloves will protect you. Put them on, then dust the outside. Let the visible powder fall away. It'll look like it's all gone, but it's not. Then: any exposed skin you touch will be affected. Be very careful taking the gloves off."

"How long?" I murmured back.

"Still in test trials. We're seeing between ten and twenty minutes."

"What do I owe you? No friends-and-family bullshit; you're sticking your neck out."

I wasn't looking at her, but I could practically hear her nodding stoically. "If it's for the real stuff? Nothing."

I could have wept with gratitude. I was suddenly overcome with an absurd and fierce jealousy for her faith, her unerring belief that, even though this country went back and forth, it was always hers, and nothing she would do would not be in service of it. I didn't have that. I was selling something potentially devastating to a foreign power for a little selfish chicken scratch and all I felt was anxious to get it over with. Hell, I was even making her a party to something she might have literally killed me for if she'd have known. The gratitude I felt burned with white-hot irony—the kind you feel when sending someone off to die on a battlefield as a sacrifice to some larger tactical maneuver.

I'm sorry, Nikki, I wanted to want to say.

We reached the next stop and she was gone.

Which meant my vacation was almost over. Just one last thing left to do.

IN COMBAT training, it was a longstanding joke that, no matter how out of options you felt, no matter how pinned down and ready for surrender you might be, there was always one last card to play. You could run the Charge.

It's exactly what you think it is. It's messy. It's unwise. It's a glorified suicide mission. You run straight into the fray and, if you do it exactly right and are astronomically lucky, you're suddenly inside the enemy's defenses before they understand what's happening. For a moment, they become vulnerable and maybe you can turn the tides. It almost never, ever, ever works. It's a horrible idea.

But it's always an option. There's always a chance. That's why they call it gambling.

So I was about to run the Charge.

WHY IS it that the people with the clout to work a four-hour day never seem to do it? That night Haydon decided to put an epic shift in. I hunkered in my car for hours, peering out through night-vision specs, and it was close to 10 p.m. when he finally came out of Sierra Headquarters and got into his shiny black car. If he didn't see his little sidepiece tonight, I'd be screwed. I'd have to tail him through the city or, worse, I might even have to follow him home, which was forty different bad ideas rolled into one.

But I was lucky. I kept a discreet distance in my car and when I saw him turn into the parking lot of the Redwood Hotel, I let out a verifiable sigh of relief.

I let him have a few more minutes of head start. I wanted to be sure I caught him at the bar.

The room stank of overpriced drinks and soft piano. It was all browns and golds, low lights and gleaming, reflective surfaces.

When I walked in, I immediately clocked that his guards were giving him a wide perimeter. Trip Haydon must have wanted a little privacy with College Girl—they were just far enough away to not feel invasive, but of course still close enough to jump into an incident should one arise.

An incident like me.

Haydon was currently at the bar alone. Waiting. Now was my chance. All I had to do was do it. That's the whole point of the Charge, right? Blast right past the defensive line like you belonged inside?

So I strode past the goons with purpose and was slapping my Sierra ID badge on the bar next to Haydon before I could even sit down.

He looked at it, then at me, with the look of weary smugness that's the exclusive domain of the mega-rich.

"Well, this is weird," he said.

His guards were already on their way. I had about three seconds before they were over here and, best case scenario, hauling me back out onto the street. So I wasted no time.

"You're being lied to, Mr. Haydon. Moss is dying fast and I have proof in my bag."

Charge.

19

HE BLINKED. "All right: wow."

He waved at his bodyguards. They stopped in their tracks and he signaled for them to beat a retreat. So far so good.

"Say that again: I'm—?"

"Being lied to. Specifically by Harrison. If you want to cash Moss in, it's gotta be now. Would you like to see?"

I gestured to my bag. He made a movement that seemed enough like a nod that I went ahead and pulled my tablet out.

"Call me a micro-manager," he said while I did so, "but aren't you on the wrong side of the continent right now?"

"Officially I'm in Myrtle Beach, South Carolina. On vacation."

"Officially?" He snorted in that smug way of his again. He looked over at the bartender and gave a little wave. The bartender set to working on a specific, though unmentioned, order. Haydon looked back at me. "Drink?"

"No, thank you, sir."

He tsked. "Right. I forgot. Lot of you Friends-of-Bill types wash up with us."

"I'm not in AA, sir. It's just, I'm talking to you. That means I'm on the clock."

He continued to eye me suspiciously. His drink arrived, clear and potent-looking in a tall martini glass. He took a sip. "Someone's not very good at vacationing."

He was fucking with me. He'd use up all my time with him just fucking with me. I had to drive the conversation. "I can do this fast, sir. No reason to hold up your evening." I pulled up

Lloyd's raw footage of Moss—the real footage, filmed recently and showing the true recession of the moss on his gray, thin body. "The images you were shown on your visit were presented as if they showed a year's worth of moss recession. They actually only showed a few months. This is what the past year's recession really looked like."

He studied the images for a few moments, then turned off the tablet, handing it back to me. He reached for his drink and brought it slowly, carefully to his lips. "I'm feeling a lot of things right now," he said. "Mostly, like, blinding rage that you're flashing these images out in public like this. But also—" He did sound angry *but also* curious. Here was where I could find out if his contempt for Harrison was as deep as it had looked last week.

"I'm here to undermine my boss, sir. And to kiss up to you. I didn't want to be subtle."

He took another ginger sip and mused. "I don't think I've ever heard anyone actually say all that with words before." Sip. "You're telling me you want Harrison's job?"

I nodded. "At the current rate of recession, the moss on Moss's skin has months—maybe even weeks—left. We need to shit or get off the pot."

He grunted. "Huh. So if 'shit' equals 'dissect him' . . ."

" 'Get off the pot' equals 'cash-in,' " I finished for him. "Go Bearded Lady with him or lose the chance forever."

"And you came all the way to Arlington, Virginia, to—"

"If I'd emailed or called, sir, when would that have actually gotten to you?"

Peripherally, I saw College Girl trot in, fashionable and mysterious under all that youth. She stopped and noticed her date speaking with short, stocky, serious-looking me and appeared puzzled. Haydon signaled to one of his guys to keep her on deck. "Also," he bellowed. "Walker, put in an order of mozzarella sticks." Another one of his guys peeled off to make the order.

Either you're surprised a bajillionaire scion eats mozzarella sticks at a posh hotel or you've met a bajillionaire scion before.

"I'd ask you if you like mozzarella sticks, Prentiss, but you're going to be gone before they arrive."

"That's fine."

"Meantime, while we're 'undermining your boss,' who all was in on this?"

"Just Harrison, as far as I could tell."

"Not the science guy who was *actually* lying to me?"

"He was lying under duress. That's why he was such a nervous wreck."

Haydon grunted, reviewing his memories.

"Look"—I pitched my voice low—"I respect Harrison. I've been happy to serve under him. Until recently."

"Recently."

"I understand the mentality. You look at Moss and you see the next frontier, the future, whatever. It's hard to say, 'It's cash-in time.' Maybe you even start hoping—"

"He'll wake up."

"Yes, sir."

"But you don't think that."

"It's not that I don't think that. It's that I don't care."

"Well, that's interesting." Another delicate sip.

"We're not the Moss Base anymore, we're the Harp Base. Two weeks ago we were a novelty. Now we're *strategic*. Our work-product will see field deployment. We're not tucked away anymore, we're on the board. That's a house worth running."

"Worth running . . . by you."

"Yes, sir. Worth running right."

"As long as we're talking hypotheticals, then . . . How would it work? How would you see this little transition going down?"

This I'd certainly thought about. "You generate an order on Sierra executive stationery, over your signature, granting me the position of interim director at Quill Marine, effective immediately. This letter would further empower me to implement the transfer of Moss's body to the location of your choice."

"Maybe I'll bring him here, sit his rotting ass right up in the Smithsonian."

I ignored that and went on. "You'd e-fax the letter to me, then send the original—witnessed by an attorney and couriered under official seal—directly to Harrison's desk."

He laughed, shaking his head and leaning back on his bar stool. "Jesus Christ. You're a hungry little beaver, aren't you?"

Hercules himself saluted from the Underworld at the effort it took for me to stuff my suddenly ballooning rage at that little comment. Haydon was trying to ruffle me. I had expected this.

Enemy territory. Keep charging.

"I'll do an extraordinary job, sir. I'll run Quill like a machine. It'll be one less thing you have to worry about."

"See, that's funny. I kinda think the exact opposite."

"Sir?"

He picked up his drink again, but he didn't sip. He just eyed me over the glass.

"How long you been a vegetarian, Prentiss?"

I stared back at him. I wasn't going to let him rile me up or knock me off my foundations. This was me, well rested and

And being absolutely insane.

"I actually know a fair amount about you," he continued. "It's all trivia until the rubber meets the road, but . . . I wouldn't have suspected you were someone so, to use your word, undermining."

And he was right. Harrison didn't deserve this. But there was also already no way this could all go down without dragging him along. So.

Charge.

"I would have preferred not to be here, sir."

"And yet." He gestured: here we are. "I hadn't pegged you as a climber. I look at you and I think: she wants to nest. She's solid. I'm not usually wrong about these things. And being wrong doesn't sit well with me. 'Cause the thing about climbers is, they always tell themselves, 'Oh, yes, this is my branch, I'm happy here.' But then . . . time goes by. They start looking up."

"Respectfully, sir, who could I could sell you out to? I can't see that working with your father." The upper echelons of Sierra management were, like the most dangerous of conditions, congenital.

"My father said maybe three things to me before I was twenty. And one of them was: always watch out for people who give a lot of thought to their *position*." He let that hang for a moment. Then, at last, he took a sip. He sighed as he put the glass back down. "When are you back at Quill?"

"Wednesday, day after tomorrow."

"Meaning you'd need the letter and the e-fax to go out tomorrow?"

"Ideally at end-of-day. I want him to know what it says but not have time to react."

"Jesus," he chuckled. "You really are going to be a problem." But there was something in his voice. I think it might have been respect.

A waitress was suddenly by me, laying down a plate of steaming hot mozzarella sticks and marinara sauce on the bar. She did it consciously, as if she'd been yelled at or worse for putting food down incorrectly before. Once she placed the plate she disappeared.

Haydon looked at the food, then at me. He was grinning. It looked positively malevolent in the dim light.

"Look at that, Prentiss. You done surprised me again. That's the last time you're allowed to do that in this lifetime. Next time I'll have to get stern. Now, if you'll excuse me. I'm planning on fucking somebody tonight and Christ knows it's not gonna be you."

I stood up. "Goodnight, sir."

As I passed College Girl on the way out, her eyes met mine. They were shining and intelligent and completely without illusion. We're just two flies feasting on the same carcass, those eyes said.

.   .   .

THE NEXT morning, I texted Lisa, *I'm here,* and my phone chirruped with a response from her number: *u-n-l.* I took it to mean her apartment door was unlocked. I was right. The lights were all off, and while I could see for the sunlight coming through and around the closed drapes, the gloom was palpable. It was the opposite of the glow inside Moss's ship: rather than a mysteriously omnipresent light source, a strange, diffuse darkness saturated everything.

I headed straight for her bedroom before checking anywhere else. Sure enough, she was there, lying down, facing away from me, on top of the covers. I remembered this. This is how it ended with us the last time.

Lisa's apartment was haunted—this room most of all.

"I'm gonna get up," she sighed. "I just need a minute." She sounded . . . well, "exhausted" is too quaint a word. She sounded like she'd been bled.

"Or sleep a little," I said softly. I got in bed with her, laying my back against hers, letting her feel at least part of me there. "I'll sleep too. I'm wiped."

"No, you won't." Her voice, hollow and bruised. "When I get up I'm going to give you a piece of paper with coordinates, a date, and a time. Usual procedure: memorize and shred."

"Sure."

"They said, 'Bring both items or no deal.' The rendezvous is a stretch of desert. Near the Tex-Mex border but on our side. The Coyotes don't use it, neither do the ICE hunters. The driver will be Mexican. The van will be a rusty, old fruit van that goes back and forth so often the border personnel treat it like it's a running joke. Plus, you're crossing in the easy direction, so." She swallowed. Her throat clicked. "He'll wait for half an hour."

"That's tight," I said, as if I could somehow bargain, as if this all weren't already set in stone, take or leave it. She went on.

"He'll drive you, the items, and your . . . partner to a mobile lab Zhang's colleagues control outside Juarez. One team to examine and confirm the one item, another team—and Zhang didn't explain what he meant by this—with a disposable subject to test the other item."

"Okay." Another X. My stomach cramped momentarily at the thought.

"I suppose you won't tell me what any of this means?"

"Sure—what do you want to know?" I chuckled ruefully.

She gave the tiniest of laughs—but genuine. "Okay. Bluff called."

At one point in time I could always make her laugh. And there had been situations where she had really needed to. Unfortunately, laughing together in the face of near disaster after near disaster . . . led to complications. Laughing is a lot like cumming: in the right light it can look like something else.

But there was a very real chance that right now she was just sad about her recent breakup, nothing more. I clung to that.

"If both tests conclude satisfactorily," she went on, "payment and papers will be presented for your review. If those are satisfactory, the next stop will be an airfield, then Managua, then Helsinki, then Beijing."

"Understood. All of it."

"That's all I have to say," she sighed. "I guess I should get up now."

She didn't move. A thousand variations of what I could say, what I felt like I should say, fluttered through my mind like a startled flock of birds, each one effectively blotting out the other. *Are you okay can I help is there something you need to say something you don't want to say,* and so on, taking flight in a deafening disarray. So I stayed silent. I didn't have to wait too long before she let me in, anyway.

"You're changing your life, Dak," she said, her voice pitched high. She was trying to sound positive, excited even, and it took the effort of someone bending rebar. "I've never changed my life."

"That's fucking crazy talk; you're drama city." I hoped that made her laugh. It didn't.

"My drama never came from me. I was in it; I didn't write it. I just did whatever was on the pages they handed me."

"You know I know what that's like. That's been my whole life too. Following orders."

"Except not anymore. Even if you die halfway . . . and let's be honest, you are going to die halfway . . . you're changing your life. You're taking charge. A better friend would be happy for you."

Ha—I took the Charge, all right.

It's the recent breakup talking, that's all. She's just in a shitty place right now.

"Come out some time when we're settled. Meet him," I offered.

A flash of a night many years ago. In this very room. Cheeks sore from laughing. Her mistaking the signals. My rebuff, harder than it needed to be. We'd spent too much time together, too many extreme situations; we were drunk on each other's company and I could be a nasty drunk. A night of painful confrontation—not too dissimilar from yours and mine, actually, when I squatted naked over my backpack, what I'd already begun to think of as the Night of the Contracts. Only in this case, the night ended with an unexpected break-in, an attempted assassination, and my overzealous commitment to my job.

No, that's not where the night ended. It ended with the horrified look on her face after I reduced a man's skull to compote on her bathroom floor.

"I don't think I want to," she said at last. "As long as I don't meet him I can keep thinking he's good enough."

"He's good enough," I replied, and I was surprised by the broken desperation in my own voice.

We stayed in silence for a while longer, and when she finally spoke, her voice was as flat and dull as an old knife . . . but goddammit there was still steel there.

"I really am going to get up."

"I know."

"I just need one more minute."

And just like that I realized something. The rest of my plan had fallen in place with horrible, thudding clarity. I saw it all, every step. In fact, I had known what to do all along. It was simple. It was cruel. And it would work.

I COULD have driven straight from D.C. to the Myrtle Beach airport but I figured, what the hell, there was time. I made a detour to the beach. The sun was setting and the world seemed queerly empty. Everyone had gone in for dinner or to get plastered, I imagined. Or maybe they'd all been erased by some great Etch A Sketch shake-up and I was left all alone on this strange and breathable planet. Just me and the birds. Had you survived? I would walk across the country to find out if I had to.

I stood looking out at the water for maybe ten minutes—my actual vacation—and tried to empty my mind.

I BOUGHT a ticket for the last flight out of Myrtle Beach. I grabbed some snacks, sipped some seltzers at an airport bar, and then purchased a change of clothes for both of us at a souvenir shop called Life's a Beach.

I touched down in California well after dark, lingered a little longer in the food court picking at some soggy, sodium-enriched food until everything began to close, then headed to the long-term airport parking lot to steal the most nondescript van I could find. It was old and a little shabby—it might have once been white but now I'd have said it could only be called the color of neglect—and the empty space behind the front seats, caged off by a sheet of mesh, looked exactly big enough.

First I drove to your hotel. I pulled over and looked up at your window. The tiny room was as monumental to me as any ocean and so I sat and paid homage like some silent and awed tourist. I needed to be there so bad. I needed to be wrapped around you, swimming in you. But if I did that I'd tell you everything. And you had a lie detector to beat tomorrow morning.

One last time.

I forced myself to drive away.

I parked the van under a bridge about a mile from Quill Marine. Hiding it only made it more conspicuous, but I only needed it to stay there another twelve hours. I stashed our change of clothes under the passenger seat and then all that remained for me now was the hour-long walk home. I was grateful for it. It might make me tired enough to sleep a few hours. With the day I had coming tomorrow I needed all the rest I could get.

You're still running the Charge, Dak. This is why it's so dangerous. Everyone thinks the initial assault is the risk, but you've done that and now you're looking at the actual hard part. Everywhere you look is enemy territory now.

Not for long. This time tomorrow either I would be driving that van to Mexico or I'd be dead.

One or the other.

I started walking.

PART FIVE

LIVING FISH AND DEAD FISH

20

I HAD roughly ninety seconds of feeling like maybe things would go okay, and then:

"Well, it's not off to a great start!"

Parker had just handed me back my ID at the front gate. He'd made some anodyne statement about how good it was to have me back, and I'd responded with an equally trite "Let's see how it goes." That's when he hit me with that first of what would soon be a marauding army of red flags.

"What? What are you talking about?" I did my best to keep any actual alarm out of my voice. I aimed for bemused—an "Uh-oh, this monkey house again" sorta vibe.

"Harrison," Parker responded, and the winch holding my stomach went slack for a second. "Showed up a little after oh-six-hundred looking cornholed. Suddenly he's Mr. Mornings."

"Harrison's . . . here?" He would have received his termination early yesterday evening (though I couldn't predict who else would know that). I supposed it wasn't abnormal that he'd need a little more time to clear out—it wasn't as if he were being spirited off to prison or anything—but still, I'd wanted him removed as a variable.

"Sort of," Parker snorted. "He doesn't look *all* here, if you know what I mean."

"Huh." Red flag, flapping in the cool summer breeze. "I guess I'll find out."

"Want me to let Patty know you're here?"

"Nah, I'll see her downstairs. Thanks, though." The last

fucking thing I wanted was Patty anywhere near me while I went through the lie detector. While I did what I had to do to Lauren.

Parker opened the gate and I drove through. Your car was where it should be, two lanes down from mine. I let that steady me. If you'd flunked the lie detector, they would have been stripping your car down already, making it disappear. But it was there. You were safely inside.

Time for me to attempt the same. I opened the door to Quill Marine and fed myself to the Great Bug.

"MY—MY GOD . . . My God, what is this? What is this I see?" Rosh's voice echoed as I walked toward his station. "Yet another total stranger approaching my humble booth?"

"You know what, Rosh, I think I was gone just long enough to miss these jokes."

"DAMN YOU, HOW DO YOU KNOW MY NAME?" he cried, his hands curling into fists that shook impotently at the heavens. "Place your chin here and slowly exhale without blinking."

I did as he asked, smirking in spite of everything.

I hoped he got out of today okay. I hoped he'd go and find himself a Renaissance Faire or something to live out the rest of his days in hammy, prescribed bliss. I hoped—

"It's . . . it's like a miracle," he stage-whispered. "I was blind and now: vision! It's Security Chief Dakota Prentiss!" I stood up, ready to move on, but Rosh was just taking a nice, meaty pause before: "Or should I say: *Acting Director* Dakota Prentiss."

That stopped me.

He was still going. "I MUST NEEDS get my eyes checked one of these days, what with all these people I keep not recognizing—"

"No—Rosh—what did you just say?"

He sputtered. We were going off script, right as he was finding his groove.

"W-what?"

"'Acting Director'? What—"

"Oh. Um—a, just a joke. That's me: jokes. Bad ones, usually." He gave a thin, reedy laugh. I stared at him, unblinking. He caved right away. "I don't know, Dak! Something Harrison was saying when he came through. He was laughing, so, so I assumed . . . Is, is that bad?"

It wasn't bad, per se. But it was more attention than I wanted. Another red flag. I turned and walked off to the next station without giving him an answer.

NATURALLY, IT was Lauren's checkpoint I was dreading the most. The Rhinestone Cowboy was draped over its chair, as always, and I approached it as I would a lion I had been ordered to tame. No fear. Let it maul me if it must. I had a whip, at least, to protect me: I was just gonna tell the truth.

Cccrackle. "Please put on the apparatus and apply the electrodes to the appropriate areas."

"Okay, Lauren? We gotta talk." I sat down, cradling the Cowboy in my hands.

Cccrackle. "I'm sorry but there is a mandated order of events. First you put on the apparatus and apply the electrodes to the appropriate areas—"

"And I'm doing that, I'm doing it right now, Lauren, but we need to be clear about something ahead of time. There's gonna be a change in protocol."

Cccrackle. "Chief." She sounded panicked already, her rushed monotone picking up irregular bursts of speed. "I . . . don't know why you're doing this." Like Rosh, any deviation from the regularly scheduled program threw her. Unlike Rosh, it made her wobble, spin out. I wished, not for the first time, that Quill Marine was staffed with more socialized creatures.

"It's all right, Lauren. It's a little weird, but it's all fine."

Cccrackle. "Please finish applying the electrodes. Following that—"

But I had already obliged her. I was wired and jellied and ready to go, putting on the device with hands that didn't need eyes to do so. A magician's trick I would only need to pull one more time.

Cccrackle. "Thank you. Now I am going to a—"

"I have something you need to look at, Lauren." I pulled out a folded letter from my uniform and held it up so she could see it. Trip Haydon's letter had been waiting in my e-fax queue as promised. I printed it out first thing this morning.

Silence. A very long silence.

Cccrackle. "My training is very clear."

"I know it is, Lauren."

Cccrackle. "My standing orders are very clear."

"Your standing orders are changing."

Cccrackle. "If any party—any party—entering or exiting Quill Marine attempts to forestall the questioning process three times, I am to alert security."

"What is your protocol supposed to defend, Lauren?"

Cccrackle. "I'm supposed to alert security right now. If it was anyone else I would have already."

In the back of my mind I wondered if I was causing a bottle-neck for the other check-in stations. Rosh might be spinning like a top. But this was going to take a while.

"It's a two-word answer, Lauren: what is your protocol supposed to defend?"

Cccrackle. "Quill Marine."

"And Quill Marine is owned by . . . ?"

Cccrackle. "Sierra Solutions." I could hear hatred gleaming off her voice like sunlight off a blade. She was supposed to ask the questions.

"And who is the COO of Sierra Solutions?"

Cccrackle. "Trip Haydon."

"And whose signature is on this document here?"

Another breathless silence. And then the unthinkable: Lauren came out of her booth.

She walked with a limp—a surprisingly inconspicuous one

given she was missing her left leg from about the middle of her shin down. Thanks to her training in amphibious recon, she had been hired as an on-site analyst for one of our many lakeside war zones about five years ago. Rumor was, friendly fire had chewed off her leg and that was why she was so skittish and weird around people now. I had a feeling she was always like that. After all, she was an analyst.

I could smell the sweat and dismay coming off of her. She plucked the letter out of my hand quickly and cautiously, like she was expecting some sort of booby trap—when she did so, I noticed the tattoo on her hand and thought of your first day. In a few hours our time at Quill was all going to be a memory.

Lauren looked over the page.

"I don't understand this," she muttered as she read.

"Sure you do."

"I don't understand this."

"What it means is: I'm gonna respect protocol. I'm gonna answer the standard questions, and I'm gonna answer them truthfully. But you're not gonna like my answers. And you have to let me through anyway."

"I don't understand what's happening." She wasn't even looking at the page now, but slightly above it, staring off into nowhere. Her voice had lost its metallic tang—not just because she was no longer behind a speaker, but something in her had been made fleshy and vulnerable for the moment.

"Harrison's already here, right?"

That brought her back for a moment. Something to be officious about. "I am prohibited from commenting on who has or has not—"

"You're right, you're right, I apologize." I waved her off. We needed to get this over with—I could just imagine crowds of people waiting at the previous checkpoint, wondering what the hell was going on. "Why don't you just call his office, and he'll either answer or he won't. If he does answer, say, 'Dak just gave me a paper and I don't understand it.'"

She nodded, still a little dazed, and limped back to her booth to use her station phone. She didn't even remember to close the door behind her.

"This is very unusual," she mumbled like a litany. "This is just very unusual." Someone on the other end of her phone picked up. "Yes—Director? Yes, this is Sentry Lauren Hayes. Security Chief Prentiss has just given me . . ." And she went quiet.

She stayed quiet for a very long time.

Finally: "Thank you, Director." She hung up her phone. Looked at me with an inscrutable expression. Closed the door to her booth.

"All good?" I asked.

Cccrackle. "Please ensure the electrodes are still in place."

I did. They were. I slid the plate down over my face. Just me and my truth.

Cccrackle. "Are you here at this facility with the intent of sabotaging or removing any materials or personnel on site?"

Deep breath. Tell her.

"Yes," I stated. "Removing."

Cccrackle. "There are only *two* acceptable answers—" The hatred I heard from her . . .

"Yes."

Cccrackle. "Are you here at this facility with the intent of damaging, removing, or otherwise interfering with Moss, the Harp, or Object E?"

"Yes."

Cccrackle. "One moment, please."

When her voice came back over the speaker, I could hear she was fighting tears. The break was subtle, but unmistakable, like *the smell of salt water close to the beach.*

Cccrackle. "Thank you, Security Chief Prentiss, you are cleared to descend to Hangar Eleven."

"I'm sorry, Lauren." I started to remove the Rhinestone Cowboy.

There was another long pause. I thought she'd let me go without further word, but then.

Cccrackle. "I just think protocol is important. That's just what I think."

I nodded at her through the glass. She was speaking the truth.

FIFTEEN SECONDS into my ride down to the Hangar, the elevator stopped.

"Thanks, Gnome . . . ," I grumbled.

Don't talk.

(I have got to get down there and find out what's going—)

Just wait.

(I need to talk to Matt and let him—)

Keep breathing. Focus.

I swear to Christ they kept me in that elevator for at least fifteen minutes. Time dilation is a real thing when you're isolated and on edge. I remember a particular night in [**REDACTED**] when I had to wait for a pickup in the middle of the night. I sat alone, in the dark, in the silence, for I would have sworn four hours. My convoy tried to convince me it was more like twenty minutes. Honestly, we were both right.

One of Matt's legs is a little bit longer than the other. You have to make him lie down and hold still and push his feet together to see it.

(What is Harrison doing here?)

Matt has a couple gray hairs, but they're only behind his ears. It's like his hair is vain.

(How am I going to live with myself after I do what I need to d—)

The elevator started moving again.

"One of these days you'll have to watch me pee," I said at last to the empty car.

IT WAS the most disorienting egress outta that elevator since my very first one. As soon as I walked onto the floor, volleys of

"Dak!" and "We missed you!" and "Hey, why aren't you tan?" and one particular genius's "Oh, hey, were you away for a little while?" flew at me like dodge balls. It was a scene out of a god-damn sitcom. I played it off as being overwhelming for only good reasons as well as I could.

I guess they missed me.

Despite that, one thing I saw immediately was that Patty was running things as great as I'd expected. Good overall use of space in the Hangar, the sentries were well-placed, the geeks didn't look crowded, and the Harp was well lit with a decent perimeter around it.

Okay. Step one.

I flagged down the nearest security team member, a guy named Harley, who wore a silver beard as cultivated as topiary. "We should probably have emergency Lloyd Suits out on the floor, right?"

Harley chuckled and pointed. "Patty set them up over there." Off in the distance: a rolling wardrobe rack with white suits hanging from it. Helmets were stacked neatly on top and below the rack.

"Sure came in handy on Sunday, I'll tell you what," he chuffed.

"Sunday? What was Sunday?"

"Power-Up."

"Wait—*Sunday*? Did somebody move the H—"

"Nope. Definitely caught us by surprise. Working theory from the nerds is every time it goes off it, like, resets the clock for its hundred-hour thing."

Huh, I mused. We'd set it off when we'd moved it onto the floor the day before I left. That would have been about a hundred hours before Sunday. *Shit. Guess I need to reset the schedule I've had in my head for the last eight years.*

Not for long, though. Soon it wouldn't be my problem anymore.

I quickly made my way over and grabbed two suits, one helmet. Next, I had to find—

"You . . . need those right now?" Fucking Harley had followed me over.

"Don't ask," I said to him, looking harried and busy. "Long story."

"Oh. Yeah. I heard some shit's going down."

He "heard" from whom? What kind of shit? Jesus, Harrison's got the whole base talking. Another red flag raised high. I hurried away from him and scanned the room for—

Oh.

There you were.

Placed near the Tent. My entire chest lit up like the Fourth of July.

Oh.

Where did you earn the right to look so good? I didn't realize I had been holding my breath for seven entire days. This was my first gulp of oxygen.

You caught my stare and our eyes met for the briefest of moments. I gave you a flash and a micro-nod before moving myself over to the north supply storage closet. I slipped inside and waited for you to join me.

EVERYTHING THAT followed—every horrible moment—felt at once too quick and interminable. Caught within a single heartbeat yet monstrously slow.

THUD.

You joined me inside the closet. I'm sure it was a perfectly considered amount of time, whatever it was. There were no cameras in the supply closet, and thank God for that, nobody but you would be able to witness my trembling. It wasn't from fear. It wasn't adrenaline. It was the trembling of something wet and wretched pulled from a near-death and dizzy with the rush of survival. I missed you so much.

No cameras, but it would be noticed fast if either one of us went missing. We had to move quickly. So I didn't dare kiss you. I might never have stopped.

But, oh, the smell of your skin. Lock the door from the outside and starve us to death. I could die happily in here.

That wasn't the plan, though. "You'll be in Bird's Eye a little later," I whispered. I gestured to one of the suits I was holding. "This will be up there too. As soon as you're alone, put it on."

"But I'm not on Bird's Eye today—wait—"

"You will be. Watch me. When I signal, winch up the box around the Harp. But—wait to put on your helmet. People might see you from the floor, start wondering."

"Wait for what?"

"For me to pick up the Harp."

"Holy shit." You were getting the picture. "What are you planning on doing, D—"

"We're gonna be free. We're gonna be together. That's what I'm planning. Winch up the box when I signal. Put on your helmet when I pick up the Harp. Okay?"

You nodded, troubled but willing, and before you could say anything further I slipped out of the closet.

Thud thud.

I WAS upstairs, rummaging through the storage lockers in Bird's Eye, looking for Lloyd's insulated duffel bag. I'd stashed one of the suits and the helmet under the monitor console, out of sight but where I knew you'd check. The other was thrown over a chair.

I'd finally found the bag when a voice came from behind me.

"Whatcha need that for?"

I whirled around, the bag in my hand.

"Holy shit," I gulped, already pivoting, "Patty! Good to see you."

"Where's the tan?" she chuckled. *Was that suspicion in her eyes, though?*

"I'll show you later. Man, the Hangar setup looks fucking phenomenal."

"Aw, shucks."

"No, I mean, you actually screwed yourself—it's so good I'm gonna stop coming in to work. It's all yours now."

"Can I have your paycheck?"

"Just leave me something for booze."

She nodded. "Sounds like Harrison's retirement plan." There was no comforting, joking rhythm to her words. Her tone was cold, uninsulated and steely.

I swallowed. This was not where or how I wanted to have this conversation, but time was running out. The blood pounding in my ears sounded remarkably like red flags in the high wind.

"So you talked to Harrison, huh?"

"Oh, yeah."

"Today?"

"He basically kept laughing and congratulating me."

"Congratulating you?"

"Calling me Security Chief Patty."

"Huh."

"I mean"—she dropped her volume—"he drinks in the afternoon. Everybody knows it. But this . . . today feels different."

"A lot of things are . . ." I so didn't want to show her the letter from Haydon. I wanted that to be something she learned about long after the threat of seeing her disappointed face was behind me. "Transitions are rough, right?"

"Transitions."

"Yeah, like if—"

"Were you on vacation or not?"

I stared at her.

"Look. I get that you can't tell me everything, just . . . at this point, I would think there'd have to be a really good reason for you to not tell me something."

"There is."

"So there's a really good reason you're walking out of this room with a suit and Lloyd's insulated duffel bag." She didn't ask it—she stated it in a tone so challenging, it stopped me in my tracks.

I kept my cool as I reached into my pocket. I didn't want to show her the letter . . . but I pulled it out, unfolded it, and held it out to her. She took it. After a few moments:

"Okay . . ." She kept staring at the paper.

"Now, I'm gonna give you a bunch of orders and when I do? You're going to carry them out because you're the deputy and I'm the security chief."

"*Are* you the chief? Or are you the acting director?" She kept staring at the letter, waiting for it to make sense.

"What difference does it make when I'm giving you an order?" I asked and plucked the letter out of her hands. I felt myself starting to get pissed and, on some level, I was grateful. It was the only way I could do what I had to do. *She's relied on me too long,* I found myself seething. *I don't have to save this fucking friendship. It's not like I'm coming back to clean things up.* "I'm taking the bag. I can't tell you why." And while I was pissed, I might as well storm into the very last thing I needed to tell her. It would upset her. Lord knows it would upset me in her position. "Now, I need you to make some changes to Guardshift."

"Guardshift? What, tomorrow's Guardshift?"

"Today's. Fifth Rotation." I'd checked the assignments before coming in this morning, not just my own but everyone's. "You've got me in the cockpit with Matt Salem and you've got Grant up here in Bird's Eye."

"So?"

"I need you to swap them. Salem goes up here, Grant down with me."

She blinked, color swirling beneath her cheeks.

"Why?" Her own anger was playing tug-of-war with the sort

of vulnerable confusion that comes from a superior you trust maybe fucking with you. But I wasn't fucking with her.

"Wanna read the letter again?" She stared at me. "Who else did you have with Grant up here in Bird's Eye?"

"Me." And the thing was, I couldn't remember if that was true or if she was issuing one final challenge. Either way I could trump it.

"I want you on the floor."

"You want Salem working all the security screens by himself. He's barely been here a month and—"

But she cut herself off, already seeing my answer. Matt would be in charge of the only surveillance feed of Hangar Eleven and I was going to insist on it. We stared at each other.

"It's just one shift," I offered finally.

"I don't . . . Dak, Fifth Rotation is like twenty minutes from now . . . what the hell is happening?"

The bag felt wrong in my hands somehow. I realized why. As a soldier—even as a manager—you tried to avoid thinking of the macro narrative as best you could. Focus on the mission at hand and let the higher paygrades worry about the sweep of history. Only now, I could see clearly what was happening. I was stepping into the role of villain.

It is what it is, I thought. *It was only an adjustment. Better get used to it if I'm going to do what needs to be done today.*

"Look in my fuckin' eyes, Patty." She did. "If you ever believed me before, believe this: by the end of today—by the end of this shift—this'll all make sense."

"But—"

"I just issued direct and specific orders. You can either carry them out or we can move on to disciplinary review. There is no Option C."

She deflated. "I worked hard figuring out the rotation. I wanted it perfect by the time you got back." Her voice was small and hurt and such a juxtaposition from her normal self that I hated her for it.

"Grant with me in Object E. Salem in Bird's Eye. You on the floor."

"I'll make it happen." She turned on her heels and retreated. It was like she was never here—the entire encounter, caught inside a heartbeat and over before I knew it.

You should have told her first thing. You put it off until it was almost too late and made it harder on her than it needs to be.

Yeah, well, some other voice, cold and merciless. *Somehow I don't think that's what she'll be upset about by the end of today.*

When she disappeared into the elevator, I stashed my Lloyd Suit into the duffel. Then I slid under the security camera and pulled on a latex glove. I took out the vial Nikki gave me on the train, and unscrewed the top.

Thud thud.

MOSS DIDN'T care about any of this. Any changes going on around him, any tension, any upset: he just sat there. His big black eyes, dry yet reflective, made me wonder what they'd look like when they actually focused on something. Would it be even discernible? Eleven years of minimally invasive biological examination hadn't revealed pupils, or even eyelids. Would his eyes be this bottomless and inscrutable even if he were alive (which, of course, we had no way of proving he wasn't)?

"Your shag's looking a little light," I said to him. The moss on his chest had receded noticeably while I was away. Noticeably to me, at least.

I was sorry for this. I knew he couldn't know that—for all I knew, being sorry was a state of mind he couldn't even comprehend—but for whatever might happen to him after all this was said and done, I was sorry. Of all my coworkers, Moss had never once given me shit.

The Guardshift bell rang throughout the Hangar and the Fifth Rotation made its way into place. Grant squeezed himself through the ship's fissure, punctual as expected. Here was a coworker for whom I would not feel sorry.

The N5 duffel bag containing my Lloyd Suit was at my feet. No helmet; I'd deal with that later.

"Chief Prentiss." Grant's voice sounded even more snide and intrusive in the ship's bizarre acoustics. "Nice vacation?" He took his place in the ship, clasping his hands in front of him, looking directly ahead. He was upset.

"You've probably been hearing a lot of shit going around." Given how gossip was already floating around like so much pollen in the air, none of it presumably mentioning his name, Grant would be feeling his patented mixture of excluded and personally slighted.

"There've been rumblings," he said. He wasn't just not looking at me to play it cool, the motherfucker was giving me the cold shoulder like we were a high school couple learning how to fight.

" 'Rumblings.' "

"But I prefer not to dignify rumors."

I sighed. "Let's just say, there's gonna be an announcement today." I stuck out my hand. "Congratulations."

I expected a little more resistance, but I guess he really wanted good news. His stony butthole of a face broke into a smile, a goddamn genuine smile that cleared away years of scowling—instantly negated when he looked at my hand and the scowl returned.

"Why are you wearing a glove?"

"Picked up a nail fungus on the beach," I said. "Don't wanna contaminate the site." He hesitated, staring at my hand like I was holding out some rotting horse dick, a spasm of hesitant disgust curling his upper lip ever so slightly. *Shake it, you contemptuous prick.* "I'm taking shit for it, asshole, you're fine," I hissed.

He reached out and shook my hand. Once we made contact something in him became resolute.

"It's about time." He jutted his chin out. "I want a meeting. First thing tomorrow. I have a number of ideas I want to put into play."

"Looking forward to it."

"We're going to have discipline here at Quill Marine. You'll see."

"Let's just get through today."

He let go. We went back to our posts and I waited for him to learn a thing or two about being undisciplined.

Thud thud.

EXCEPT, NO. Fifteen minutes later, there had been no change whatsoever. Not a twitch, not a sniff. Grant seemed downright chill. My heart felt stalled in my chest.

Nikki wouldn't let me down, I tried to remind myself. *Nikki wouldn't let me down.*

Eventually I had to say something. Observe him.

"How they hanging, Grant?"

He shrugged, contentedly. "I'm just thinking."

"Thinking?"

"Making plans."

Other than seeming the closest to happy I'd ever seen the petty little prick, there was nothing abnormal.

Fuck.

My mind was swirling. Maybe I'd applied it wrong? Maybe it actually had all been left on the floor up in Bird's Eye, or in a trail behind me as I walked to the ship trying to keep my hand inconspicuous? This was supposed to be fast-acting and here we were, a lifetime later, with nothing to show for it.

I had to busy myself. I clicked on my communicator.

"Salem, confirm position," I radioed.

Your voice came back right away like a strong, encouraging hand against my back.

"Up in Bird's Eye, all good, all quiet."

To keep up appearances:

"Patty, confirm position."

"Seriously?" Her voice, less like a comforting palm, more like a middle finger.

"Deputy, confirm position."

Rather than answer me, there was a tiny chime in my ear—Patty had opened our private comm channel.

"*Since when do you 'confirm positions'?*" she sniped at me. "*Dak, what the hell is going on?*"

"I'm asking you to confirm p—"

"*On the floor, Jesus, like you said.*"

I was about to come back with something equally snotty—I was still the fucking security chief, wasn't I, I should be allowed to confirm positions without my deputy acting like I'd called for Jell-O shots and group sex—when I noticed Grant out of the corner of my eye. He was blinking heavily, trying to clear his vision, rubbing his face . . . and staring at Moss.

"What is he doing?" he whispered.

"You okay, Grant?"

"What is he doing, look at him, what is he doing?" His voice was low and private, but in the deader-than-dead acoustics of Object E, there was no problem hearing him.

"What's who doing?"

"You didn't see that? YOU DIDN'T SEE THAT?!" Now he was shouting.

"*See what, Grant?*" Patty's voice came over the comm. We were still on our private channel.

"Switch off, Patty," I ordered.

"HE JUST MOVED! HE JUST MOVED!" Grant was bouncing up and down in position, pointing at Moss.

Even now he's a fucking tattletale, I thought distantly.

"Who moved? Nobody's here, Grant." I eased my way toward him—not too close, in case he did anything stupid. But there was also no such thing as "far away" in this ship.

Grant was jabbing his finger toward Moss. His lips were stretching across his face in an aggressive, actually painful-looking scowl. It looked almost like the two ends of his mouth were trying to wrap themselves around his head and meet on the other side.

"*Dak?!*" Patty was still on the channel. "*Dak, is he talking about Moss? Is he telling the truth?!*"

"No."

"YES!" Grant shouted. "YES! IT'S TRUE! HE MADE THE GESTURE!"

The gesture.

"*Dak, do you need assistance?*"

"Lemme suss it. Switch off!"

"YOU . . . you didn't see the gesture?!" Grant turned his wild and staring eyes to me, his face still frozen in that horrid scowl-mask.

"What gesture, buddy?"

"The-the-the-that-the-one-that-means he CHOSE ME!" His hands had found the zipper to his uniform. He pulled it down erratically, trying to strip off his clothes but having difficulty getting his motor skills to cooperate. "The one that means he's inside me!"

"*I'm getting people in there now.*"

"Wait. Wait, I don't know if that'll—"

"THE ONE THAT MEANS HE'S IN MY BLOOD." Grant was shouting again. He finally emerged from the top part of his coveralls and began to rip his undershirt off his body. "I'LL PROVE IT! WATCH!"

"Grant. Buddy—"

He started to claw at his exposed skin.

No, not claw at. Dig into. Like there was no pain, like his skin was mud and he could just furrow his fingers through with minimal effort. Dark red pools began first to form then spill out in his fingers' wakes. The amplifying ambience of the ship let me hear the wetness of his ragged flesh, smell the coppery tang of blood. I saw with horrifying clarity the front of his shorts were beginning to tent out. He was relishing this.

I didn't think it would be this bad.

Yes, you did. This was exactly what you wanted.

I knew Nikki wouldn't let me down.

I didn't want to try to restrain him while my hand was still wearing the doped glove—what if I made it worse (*how?!*). I carefully peeled the glove off, conscious in my harried state to not make any contact with the powdered side. The process felt unbearably slow. Grant, meanwhile, was continuing to dig into himself, a man trying to peel a layer of paint off a wall. At last the glove was off. Given what was about to happen in a few minutes the time for caring about evidence and shit was over so I threw the glove to the ground, kicked it out of sight, and hoped whoever found it and picked it up one day later had a nice trip.

"Okay, okay, Grant," I cooed, "Can't you see you're hurting yourself?" I held my now-bare hands out and inched toward him.

"Take it back!" He was grunting. "Take the gesture back I don't want it get it out of me."

"Shhhhh."

I managed to pull his right arm away from his chest. I was so distracted by the bloody ruin of his skin that I didn't even notice him pulling his gun out of his holster.

THE SHOT did not ring out. It *burst*. As quickly as it occurred it was over, no rolling thunder, no echo. Just an unbelievably loud bark and then a chunk of the console to the left of where Moss sat compressed into itself. The ship took the bullet the way a body would. No detritus. No explosion.

I'm sure this all happened very fast. But, time dilation: still a hell of a thing. It felt like we danced with the gun forever.

I heard panicked voices—I wasn't sure if it was over the comm or outside the ship, I was focused on getting the weapon out of Grant's hand. I yelled to whoever might hear me, "Stay back, there's a gun out!"

I was about to kick Grant's legs out from under him—not my first choice given how uncontrolled it could get—when Grant just . . . let go. I stumbled forward into the wall of the ship while he ran at Moss.

"WHY ME?!" he was screaming. "YOU DIDN'T HAVE TO PICK ME!"

In another eternal nanosecond, I watched in dumb amazement as Grant wrapped his hands around Moss's slender throat and squeezed. He was trying to strangle the (dead?) alien.

"Dak!" I heard Patty shout—she was standing just outside the fissure of the ship. "We clear?"

"I CAN'T LIVE LIKE THIS!" Grant continued throttling Moss. It was almost funny, he might as well have been strangling a broom, except for the rabid, merciless look on Grant's face. "I CAN'T LIVE KNOWING YOU'RE IN MY BLOOD!"

"I'm calling it, Patty," I yelled back to her.

"You're—?" I wasn't sure if she didn't hear me, or if she wasn't clear on what I meant. It didn't matter. I had Grant's weapon in my hand. I walked up next to him, taking care to not accidentally hit Moss or spray him with much blood and brain, and shot Grant through the head.

Grant's hands were still fiercely clasped around Moss's neck. They didn't unknit even after his brains burst out, so when he crumpled to the ground, he took Moss down with him. Moss slid out of his seat and they both thumped pathetically onto the ship's deck.

"All clear," I heard myself call out. Patty squeezed her way inside in an instant.

"Are—" she began. Then broke off and stared at Grant and Moss. "Jesus."

"Yeah," I muttered to her. I radioed up to Bird's Eye. "Salem, you still on?"

"*Chief, I saw that all go down on the feed. Are you—?*"

"I'm fine. I need Turndown Service."

"*On it.*"

Patty was still gaping. "Shit." She swallowed. "He just—" She gave some weak gesture approximating Grant taking Moss down with him.

I knelt down next to the knot of bodies. "Help me get them separated."

She joined me, tentative.

"Should we . . . check him? Moss, I mean? In case—"

"I didn't hit him. And Lloyd should be here in thirty or so. Let him do it."

My knees were starting to hurt. Grant's blood pooled across the floor.

We pried Grant's fingers off, careful not to touch the moss. I could feel Patty's eyes slide to me every few moments, suspicious, confused.

Once Moss was free, Patty and I got on either side and lifted him back into his chair, a little sneak preview of what I hoped to be doing with you about ten minutes from now. Moss was heavy, but not as heavy as one might think, considering how tall he was.

There was some blood on him. It pearled on his strange, gray skin. I wondered if Turndown had any idea what they were in for and whether or not they'd handled something remotely like this mess before. The fuck do you use to get blood out of a space-walnut?

"I wish you hadn't pulled Salem out, Chief." Patty pulled me out of my reverie. "You could've used somebody just now. It was a lot of risk."

"I was supposed to anticipate this?"

Her look said: *well actually yes.* Or maybe it asked: *did you anticipate this?* Either way she held her tongue. For now.

I realized that my heart hadn't been beating for what felt like hours. But now it was going, no longer impossibly slow but at a frenzied trot. Combat speed.

Thud thud

Thud thud

Thud thud

Are we really doing this?

Thud thud

Yes, we fucking are.

Everything else today had felt like it was moving underwater; now it felt like we'd hit hyperdrive.

"If you have questions for me, Patty, you can ask me in my office later."

"Which office?"

"Go get me something to wipe this blood off Moss. Now."

She stiffened, gave me a half salute, and left.

As soon as she was out of the fissure, I started putting on the Lloyd Suit.

The time had come for step two.

WHEN I came out of the Tent, Turndown was already wheeling an oversized, colorful coffin our way. Damn, they worked fast.

I ordered the sentry to roll the box right up to the opening of the Tent and sent them back to wherever they came from.

I think someone was talking to me, but I wasn't listening. I was looking around at the Hangar, my home, one hand on the box that was to be my way out of here, trying my best to savor this final moment. I was failing. I felt no nostalgia, no whimsy. Just an urge to get everything over and done with.

I looked up at Bird's Eye. You were there, watching. I couldn't quite see from this angle, but I had to assume you were wearing your suit. I gave you a thumbs up and boosted my hand up and down. Within a minute, the winch started up, raising the giant class cube up and away from the Harp. The murmur on the floor ceased. Everyone, including Patty, stopped to watch what was happening. When they turned to see me, it was like I'd stepped out of the ship naked. Or like I was a goddess emerging from flames unscathed. They didn't know what to make of it. In one smooth motion, I walked over to the rack where the other Lloyd Suits hung and grabbed a treated helmet and pair of gloves.

Patty was shouting at you over the comm, demanding to know what in the hell was going on, ordering you to reverse the winch. From where I could see, you were following my motions, putting on the helmet and gloves.

The roar of the winch was practically prehistoric. A very different, very alive kind of thunder rolling through the echo chamber that was Hangar Eleven.

"Jesus, Salem! Fish!" Patty was screaming. "You're uncovering the fucking Harp!"

Peters, another security team member assigned to this area of the floor on Fifth Rotation, was watching me. "Wait. Chief," he was asking, "should the rest of us be suiting up too?"

Patty turned from where she was glaring up at your position in the tower and saw what I was doing. The look on her face—it was the look I had tried my best to avoid throughout this entire endeavor, but here we were at the end. There was no avoiding it now.

"Dak," she gulped, astonished, betrayed.

Fully sealed and suited, I walked over to the Harp, picked it up, and began walking in a large circle.

21

THE PLAN had finally fallen into place that final morning with Lisa.

I'd already figured I could take Moss out in a Turndown box. I'd already figured it would be a box meant for a doped Grant. I just hadn't quite figured out how to make certain no one else in Quill could stop us.

Lisa had been curled up on the bed, pithed by depression and I had known I actually had the power to take some of that despair away, even for the moment. But I didn't. Either she'd get better or she wouldn't—I had my own journey to make and I didn't need her getting in the way. So I let it consume her.

PATTY WAS screaming at me, pleading with me. She had drawn her sidearm, as had most of the rest of the security team, but between the general standing mandate to not harm the Harp and the paralyzing confusion of just what the hell I was doing, no one risked a shot.

Patty's voice cracked on the brittle edge of tears. "Dak! For fucking God's sake, what do you want me to do?"

Other guards were yelling at her—should they take the shot, what was the order?—but no one seemed to be able to quite commit to any one idea, one emotion, and that's what I was about to take advantage of.

They didn't know the Harp like I did.

I had been in its blast. I knew firsthand its levels of dosage and what they did to a person. I had felt it for about ten unprotected seconds right before I sealed Chatty Andy into the engine room and I stayed icy and numb for about an hour. I had felt it for about thirty seconds, the day you and I tested the suits, and felt its effects lingering overnight. I had seen what had happened to those who had taken a full dose for over a minute and had been reduced to apathetic zombies who would lie on the ground until starving to death. I knew the Harp, I carried a visceral understanding of it in my body, the body it had passed through, the way a tree must understand the wind.

I also knew that it went off when you carried it.

If they knew the Harp as I did, they would already be running.

It was taking its time to prove me right, though. I'd made it almost a quarter of the way through my giant circuit when Patty's paralysis broke.

"Next person that has a clear shot—take it! But don't hit the Harp!"

Come on come on come on

Someone called out, "I've got it!" Patty bellowed, "Take it!" and I turned to try to face the voice. As if it sensed the imminent potential threat, finally the Harp began to hum in my hands.

"Shit—everybody grab a suit!" Patty screamed. "Wait—no—fall back! FALL BACK!"

"Fall back where?!" Another guard, I couldn't tell who. I knew everyone on this team backward and forward, yet in their fear and panic they were becoming anonymous.

The Harp grew louder.

"*Object E!*" Patty waved them toward the ship. "*Get to the engine room!*"

The scientists and crew all broke in that direction. I felt a flash of pride for her—of love. I can admit that now. Patty thought fast. She didn't tell them to hide behind something, or run to the elevator. She figured out right away the safest place to be—the only safe place, really. It was a damn good idea and it would have fucked us over completely if it had been carried through. But the Harp grew louder and everyone scrambling for the ship began to sag, like their joints had all been coated with lead.

A spasm of fear suddenly crossed my mind: *Had Matt thought to hop onto the elevator right away? He only has a few more seconds to get down here—*

But there you were, sealed in your suit, the insulated duffel in your hand, by my side just in time to watch them all start dropping like bowling pins.

You held the bag low and open and I heaved the device inside.

"Close it, close it, or they'll all die," I breathed, but you were already on it.

The Harp grew louder, close to its climax, as you sealed it inside the bag. Every person in the Hangar had been blasted, completely unshielded, for about thirty-five seconds. They lay scattered across the floor, still and silent.

"Hi," I said to you. "It's about to go dark. Hold on to me."

The Harp whirred to its highest point and the lights went out.

WE MADE our way through the dark, careful, feeling for bodies with our feet. They seemed everywhere, an impenetrably dark battlefield carpeted with casualties. I led the way forward, testing with my foot, through the Tent, to the ship, where I edged our way around its perimeter until we reached the entryway. Someone had almost made it inside—I rolled the body to one side, gently, and then we eased our way in.

It was a relief to be on the ship, where the omnipresent glow somehow made the world make sense again.

Grant was still face down in his slowly congealing pool of blood. Moss sat stately by, in his chair.

We carried Moss to the fissure and then you mindfully made your way outside the ship so I could pass him off to you. Moss was so tall, almost foreboding when he wasn't in a seated position, that the thought of him passing through that slim crack in the ship's wall seemed like an impossibility—but of course the ship was made for him. Creatures of his kind who were lanky and imposing, yet when they turned to the side they almost disappeared.

"Careful not to scrape any of his moss off," I called to you as I fed Moss through the fissure. "They might want to study that, too."

"Who's *they*?" you asked, the tiniest hint of frustration already in your voice. "Can you tell me the plan now?"

All this, what already felt like a full day's worth of work, while the Harp was still humming. As I made my way out of the ship, the hum began to whir down, the lights began to flicker back on. You stood there in the strobe, cradling the tall creature like a drunk, amid a field of bodies. I can't lie—the image was almost erotic.

"Dak?" you asked again.

But the power was almost fully restored. I held up a finger: one sec. "I gotta make some calls."

"Calls?!"

"Get Moss in the box." I switched on my comm and let the necessary people upstairs know that, yes, that had just been an unscheduled Power-Up, that everything was okay down here, that we didn't need assistance, and that, unfortunately, we were coming up with a Turndown box. I made one unusual request:

"Is the Turndown van here already?"

"*Confirmed*," the voice of one of our topside security staff radioed back. "*In the parking lot, like normal.*"

"Have them meet us outside the front gate."

"*You . . . want them to drive back out?*"

"Yeah. Just outside the gate. I'll explain why when I'm up top."

"*Uh. Copy.*"

So far so good, but our already short window was closing fast.

"How's it going over here?" I asked you. You had the box open and were carefully trying to negotiate Moss inside. I hustled over to help you. "Thank God they make these so big, huh? We'd never get him into a real coffin." I made a noise that, under normal circumstances, might have resembled a laugh.

We gently laid Moss to rest inside, bending his stiff joints with care, tucking him in as securely as possible. The way his abdomen curved within the box made a natural cradle into which we were able to place the Harp next.

"How are we gonna wheel this through with all the . . ." You didn't want to say "bodies," but there they were. A certifiable obstacle course.

"We made it in the dark, we can make it with the box." I began to push the garish coffin forward.

I remembered a time in [**REDACTED**] when I had to throw a newly legless ranger into a wheelbarrow and maneuver him through the aftermath of a mortar shell hitting a tent full of people. This was somehow better and worse. Better because there was no stench of death, no smoke, no need to keep one ear open for another round whistling toward us. Worse because the box was way more unwieldy, there was a clock ticking against us . . . and all the bodies on the ground were awake and blinking. The scientists and guards—my team, my charges, my colleagues— were, for all intents and purposes, corpses, except I could hear the collective sound of their breathing over the sound of the casters underneath our Turndown box.

Making our way through was torturous. For every stretch of open floor there was another knot of human cordwood. And then I saw Patty.

"What's wrong?" you asked, as I let go of the box and knelt down.

She had fallen forward when the Harp finally got her. She was lying on her stomach, her face squished against the floor. She could breathe but it looked unbearably uncomfortable. Still, she didn't make the slightest effort to adjust herself. I rolled her over. Her ponytail flopped down first and was crushed under the weight of her listless head.

"Patty, I . . ." I swallowed. "Look. The ship's still here, okay? There's still the ship, so they won't close this place down. And they'll give you my spot. The way you ran things while I was gone? They'll give it to you. You're gonna be great. I know you are."

Her eyes stared straight ahead. Not unlike Moss's dull, black, inscrutable pools. She said one word, barely audible.

"No."

THE ELEVATOR stopped a few seconds into its journey up. Then I realized:

"Lose the helmets. Gnome needs to see who we are."

We unsealed ourselves at the neck, removed the helmets . . . and then waited.

And waited.

I wondered if you'd been through this enough times to understand how the Gnome liked to operate. He always kept us stopped for just a little longer than you'd expect. Just long enough for any guilty questions to start bubbling up to the surface. You have a little countdown in your head: "If everything's okay, they'll restart . . . now." And then it's always a minute longer.

"Jesus, Gnomie," I sighed at last. "In the middle of my second Turndown Service in two weeks?"

I looked over at you. It was getting to you. Your eyes were beginning to bug. Your skin was getting slick with sweat and—

"We should open our chest seals," I said casually. You looked at me, not understanding.

"So we can put Lauren's electrodes on in a minute."

"Oh. I—"

I unsealed my suit and a moment later you followed my example. Whoosh. Buzz.

We stared straight ahead.

We waited.

And waited.

"Feels better," you said, putting on a cheeriness that maybe read as false, maybe as noble.

"These suits are stuffy," I agreed.

"Yeah. I was . . . I was just thinking that."

What would we do if they came on and said, "We caught you. We'll have a team waiting topside to take you to prison"? Would you look at me like, "At least we tried"? Or would you look at me like, "You ruined my life"?

We should be moving . . . now, I thought.

(*What the fuck was the Gnome doing?*)

Now.

(*Were we unconsciously giving off the wrong kind of stress vibes?*)

Now.

(*Were you going to hate me for the rest of—*)

The elevator started moving again.

DOWN THE hall from the elevator, I could see Lauren looking miserable as we approached her station. Between what had happened earlier and now a Turndown container, this had to have been her worst day since active duty.

You stopped abruptly and bent over the box, inspecting one of the wheels below.

"Answers?" you asked through clenched teeth.

I knelt down next to you to see if I could help with that darn stubborn wheel.

"Say 'Yes' to both of them. Don't say anything else you don't have to."

You had your back to Lauren, so she was directly in my line of sight. She wasn't looking our way, though. She moved over a bit in her booth and I could see someone was standing behind her.

It was Harrison.

Goddammit.

"'Yes' to both of them," you repeated, "okay."

"I'll do the rest." I stood up and resumed pushing the box toward Lauren. At first she didn't even look up when she sensed us coming.

Cccrackle. "Please put on the apparatus and apply the elec—"

That's when she decided to see who was coming: a giant colorful coffin flanked by two people in half-open space suits. "O-oh."

In the booth, leaning against one of the walls, Harrison looked up at that. I could see him sway the tiniest bit on his feet.

"You understand the same protocol statement is in effect as last time, right, Lauren?" I'd placed my helmet on the coffin and was already sitting down, picking up the Cowboy and looking to you. "Salem, you good to go next?" You nodded, tight-lipped.

Cccrackle. "Okay. Please put on the apparatus and apply the electrodes to the appropriate areas—"

"Hello, Director Prentiss."

Harrison was leaning over Lauren, speaking into her mic.

"Director Harrison," I responded coolly. "I'm in the middle of a Turndown S—"

"I thought, 'She pretty much has to come this way,' so—"

Lauren, ruffled and slightly off mic: "I need to complete this process before any unrelated convers—"

"Lotta excitement for your first day on the new job." He was holding down the mic button, amplifying everything in the booth: his breathing, the slight slurring of his words.

"Yep. That's why we're dressed like this." I tried to sound dis-interested, distracted, while I applied the electrodes. One last time performing this trick. "Grant snapped. Started messing with the Harp. Had to put him down. When we tried to put the Harp back—"

"Blackout!" He practically belched into the mic.

"I'll do a proper report shortly. I'm ready, Lauren."

Lauren commandeered the mic. "All right, I'm sorry, I'm sorry, I know I don't understand things now, but it's supposed to be questions first, before anything else!"

"Oh, shut up, Lauren," Harrison snapped.

And she did shut up. For just a moment. She stared at her (now former) boss with big, wounded, furious eyes. Her hand still held the mic switch open. Harrison continued:

"Things change, Lauren. Get that through your head. Everyone thinks, 'Someday I'll hit a certain age when I just *get* it'"—he tapped his temple—"'and when that day comes I can just kick back and enjoy my little rut like it's a hammock—'"

"Just ask the questions, Lauren," I told her. She looked at me with those same furious, confounded eyes. Harrison was still monologuing.

"But what actually happens is you never *get* anything—because things never stop changing! And the energy you need to deal with that change just gets less and less and less. That's all the Harp does, it just fast-forwards you to where you're going anyway: flat on your back, too numb to—"

Lauren finally switched off the mic and turned to say something to Harrison. I gave you a quick look. I had given the folks downstairs a Harp blast potent enough to keep them down for something like a few hours. But what if the math was wrong? What if Patty's crawling for the emergency phone right now? What if someone shows up early for the next shift?

"Lauren," I barked, more annoyed than I would have liked.

Cccrackle. Lauren back on the mic. "Yes, Director."

Harrison laughed in the background. "Which one?"

"Go ahead, Lauren." I slid the plate down over my face.

Cccrackle. "Are you here at this facility with the intent of sabotaging or removing any materials or personnel on site?"

"Yes."

I could hear Harrison laugh. I could imagine him shaking his head, saying something I couldn't quite hear.

Cccrackle. "Are you here at this facility with the intent of damaging, removing, or otherwise interfering with Moss, the Harp, or Object E?"

"Yes."

Lauren kept shutting the mic off after every time she spoke—honestly, I think that was always part of the reason she wanted this position and why she kept her station so technologically anachronistic: so she could shut the world off at her command.

Cccrackle. "Thank you. Assessing now."

At the same time, Harrison was laughing, "—even gave you the whole week to make it happen—"

The mic switched off as the machine ran its course and analyzed my responses.

"Director? Director?" I couldn't see him but Harrison could hear me. I knew he would have stopped his muted mumbling and would be listening. "Once I've completed Turndown, you and I can have an in-depth conversation in your office. Okay? Right now I'm carrying out the most solemn duty a soldier ever enacts and I'm asking you, respectfully, not to impede in me doing so." I stared into the darkness of the plate in front of my eyes.

Cccrackle. "Director Dak Prentiss, you are cleared to depart Quill Marine."

"Great." I slid off the face plate, ripped off the electrodes, and turned to you. You were already sitting down.

I watched you apply the electrodes to your exposed skin (*remember that heartbeat*). You'd gotten almost as fast as me. I didn't notice the sound of Lauren's booth opening and closing—I only noticed Harrison was heading toward the elevator when he crossed my peripheral vision. I sprang to action, leaving you and getting in Harrison's path, barely covering my panic.

"What are you doing?!"

"You know what, Dak?" he wavered in front of me. "Take your time. Finish your Turndown. Enjoy the sunshine. I'm going down to the Hangar."

"What? Why?" The edge in my voice was brittle and unpleasant. He looked at me with half-focused eyes.

"They've just had Turndown and an unscheduled Power-Up. They need leadership down there. In your temporary absence, I'll provide it."

You started to rise, voicing protest. Lauren barked at you to remain still, that her questions took priority. Everything was getting out of hand far too quickly.

"Okay, everybody, chill the fuck out for a second!" I ordered.

Harrison kept his steely, rheumy eyes on me. "It's all right,

Dak," he said, calmly, patronizingly. "You've got your solemn duty; I've got mine."

Distantly, I could hear Lauren asking you your first prompt. Harrison and I stared each other down while you waffled your first response.

"No—YES. Yes. The answer's yes."

Cccrackle. "Single-world answers, please!"

"Sorry, I'm just not used to saying . . ."

That made me blink and look back at you. Harrison took his opening and left for the elevator. He'd already pressed the button by the time I sprinted over to him.

"I do not want you down there, Director."

He leaned himself against the wall as he waited.

"S'lemme—so let me ask you, then. You think I'm gonna spend my last day up in my office doing . . . what? Packing a box? Wouldn't take me very long."

"Not this."

"I wanna be with my colleagues. I wanna say goodbye to my people."

"This isn't your retirement party, that's not how this works."

"You know how long I've been here?" He was getting too close to me. I could smell the booze on his breath. This felt all too familiar—the subconscious tug of a past life. "Tomorrow morning, who the fuck am I? Who do I talk to—?"

I could hear the elevator approaching.

"Then I will take you down to say goodbye after—"

"I want to be useful, Dak! It's my last day, my *last day*!" Tears threatened to spill out over his bottom lids. "I want to do something that at least resembles doing my duty!"

DING! The doors to the elevator slid open.

We stared at each other for several beats, before he said, proudly and almost soberly, "You can find me downstairs." He began to sidle his way into the car. I grabbed him by the arm and held him in the car's threshold.

"You know what, *Mike*?" I wanted to squeeze his arm until it burst. I wanted my voice to give him secondhand steam burns. "You failed to do your duty back when you decided to drink at work." I'd never called him by his first name before. I've never called him on his drinking habits before. I've never even shown him much anger before. "So what you're gonna do right now, Mike, is get back to your office and start prepping for top-to-bottom debrief. What you're *not* gonna do is get in the way of professionals in a crisis situation because you're looking for some half-assed victory lap. Step back from that elevator. Go to your office, look at that painting on your wall, and realize: you're not some sailor bravely facing down a storm. Now you're a man who owns a picture."

As I loosened my grip he pulled his arm away petulantly. He stumbled on his feet.

"Dakota." He mumbled, unsure of just how to respond.

"I will see you there in about half an hour, all right?"

"Yeah." He broke eye contact, looked down. I began to relax. He seemed chastened enough. "Yeah."

I took just a fucking moment to exhale. Just a moment to stretch away the unbearable tension that had gripped the back of my neck, to turn and look at you and Lauren. Harrison slipped into the elevator, stabbed the button, and the doors closed. The last thing I saw were his eyes, glinting with an almost gleeful rage, staring back at me.

Holy living *Christ*.

As soon as my brain could process sight again, I saw that you were standing by the box, which you'd already begun to push down the hall. You'd passed.

The short way back to you I was screaming in my head: *don't run, don't run, don't run.*

"We've got to hustle," I said to you, low.

I'D NEVER in my life been more grateful for how the Turndown box killed Rosh's sense of humor. He saw the box, sensed our harried energy immediately, and, without a word, gestured to the seat in front of his scan. After the first glance, it seemed like he was doing his best to not even look in the box's direction.

I sat down, calculating. The Gnome would hold the elevator; Harrison looked sketchy as hell right now. That would give us, what, five minutes to—

"I'm very disappointed in you, Dak."

Rosh's voice hit me like a slap.

"What? What are you—"

"You blinked," he said, kind but firm. Apologetic. "I have to run it again."

"ARE YOU FUCKING KIDDING ME?!" The shout was out of my mouth before I even knew it was coming. Rosh jumped and flinched. He started to stammer.

"I-I-I—"

I tried to fight it, but the anger was boiling over. I did not have time to babysit this fucking—

You hopped in. "Sorry, Rosh, hey, it's all good, you're doing your job, it's just, you know, second Turndown Service in a month—"

"Yeah, yeah, that's—" Rosh's face was growing a shade of red that seemed to indicate he might physically explode.

I managed to keep a lid on whatever the hell was happening inside me. I wasn't calm, but I started to at least remember what it felt like. I bit down and kept my jaw closed. "Just . . . run it again, Rosh. I'm . . . all set."

"I didn't mean to, to—"

"I know. Come on. I'm a crazy person you don't recognize, right? Rosh? How did I get in?"

He laughed weakly, something more like an exhale than an expression of mirth. "Hah, yes. Yes. A, a person I don't recognize! Right. Identify thyself!"

He ran the scan. I kept my eyes open.

"Did I say I didn't recognize you? Well, shut my mouth, for thou art—"

I stood up and waved at you to sit.

"I'm a stranger, Rosh, what're you gonna do about it?" You settled your chin and stared into the machine.

"Truly, it is a banner day for strangers!" Rosh exclaimed as he ran the scan, still pointedly not looking near the box.

I WAS so clammy, so close to overheating from the nerves and the not-very-breathable suit, that hitting the fresh air was like diving into cool water. Not just a temperature change but the very texture of the air felt like a different substance than whatever the hell we'd been trudging through indoors.

I could see the garish Turndown van trundling up ahead outside the front gate.

Was it always this far away? Was the parking lot always so long?

"Why did you make them park outside?" you asked.

"Because we wanna be on the other side of that gate when they see us throw the Turndown guys out of the van."

We pushed the box toward Parker's booth at the gate. I radioed him as we moved.

"Parker, you there?"

"*Chief,*" he responded.

"Get the gates open. We got Turndown. Hurry."

"*Hurry? Everything okay—*"

"I'LL EXPLAIN LATER." I was starting to panic. Not good. We were so close. We were so fucking close.

"*Copy. Hey, was there an unscheduled Power-Up?*"

"Open the goddamn gate, Parker!"

"*Okay. Sorry,*" he chuffed and the gate began to creak and squeal open.

"Can we go faster," you asked me out of the side of your mouth, "or will that get the Harp—"

"Yeah, faster." I nodded. "Faster."

We broke into a trot, pushing the container down the parking lot toward the excruciatingly slowly opening gate. I could see the

dickhead driver they always sent, opening the side door and probably thinking of a shitty joke. Another fifty yards and—

We're gonna make it

We're—

A klaxon began blaring, compound-wide, like an air-raid drill,
like the bellow of some angry god poised to stomp out existence.
It tore through our heads.

The gate paused, then started to close itself back up.

"PARKER. WHY IS THE GATE CLOSING?"

"Sorry, Dak!" I heard Parker shouting over the noise. "It's
lockdown!"

"KEEP THE FUCKING GATE OPEN!" I screamed.

And just like that, just like they were trained, a whole squad
of my perimeter guards fanned out between the Turndown
van and the road. I saw the driver jump at the sight of all the
rifles.

The klaxon continued winding, shrieking, tearing the world
to shreds. But there was another noise, too. Coming from inside the box.

The Harp was powering up again.

"Open it up," I heard myself yelling to you.

"WHAT?"

"PUT YOUR HELMET ON AND OPEN THE BOX UP."

The guards were shouting orders too—lie down, hands over
your head, step away—we had a scant few seconds before they
disintegrated us with bullets. Parker kicked open the door
to his booth and sprinted for cover. As Parker ran, I noticed
with absurd clarity that Lloyd was driving up the road. He
pulled his car over behind the van and got out to see what was
happening.

"Seal me," I called to you.

"Stop what you are doing or we will open fire!" one of the
guards intoned over a bullhorn. The klaxon continued blaring.
The Harp noise got louder. "Take off your helmets and look at
me so I know you hear me!"

Your hands flew over me—we knew this protocol almost as surely as we knew the map of each other's bodies.

"Please, Dak!" the guard begged over his bullhorn. His name was Erikson. He was a good guy. Fought with mobile infantry. I trained him about three years ago. These were all my people. Their trust in me was about to be their downfall. If I'd been anyone else they would have ripped us to shreds already. "You have five fucking seconds!"

"Sealed . . . sealed . . . sealed," you itemized.

"FIVE!"

"Arms up." You complied.

"FOUR!"

Sealed . . . sealed . . .

"THREE!"

. . . and sealed.

"TWO!"

The nanosecond I knew you were safe, I reached down and unzipped the bag. I had the briefest moment to see Lloyd, standing at the gate (which had already frozen in place), realizing what was inside our container, before I held up the Harp and ducked down behind the crate.

The Harp's hum grew insistent, the klaxon continued blaring, and I braced myself for a few rounds to head our way . . . but there were no gunshots. Only the clatter of dozens of human bodies and automatic weapons dropping to the hard ground, unmistakable even under all the din.

I stood up to confirm. Not a man standing.

"Close it, they're down!" I heard you say. I waited. I wanted to make sure everybody stayed down for a while. "Dak! We don't wanna kill—"

"I know what I'm doing!" I snapped. After another beat, I quickly dropped the Harp back into the bag and zipped it up. A few moments later, the sound of the Harp reached its peak. The alarm cut off. The world was quiet beyond the baseline post-climactic hum of the Harp. Not even a bird.

We pushed the crate forward and through the gate. Thankfully it had stopped just wide enough to let us through. Finally a lucky break.

The driver of the van and his partner were both slumped inside. We tipped them unceremoniously out onto the asphalt, then lifted the container into the van and closed the door. Still operating against the clock, we ran to both sides of the cab. I let you take the driver's seat.

"Keys still in?"

"Yeah, but, I just realized—"

"Fucking drive!"

"Dak—"

"GO! Please!" I almost choked on the desperation in my voice. We were there now, right at the threshold of getting away. You put a hand on my leg.

"The Harp, Dak. Cars use electricity. We have to wait for it to power down."

I could have screamed. Maybe I did, I don't know.

"Everybody's down," you said. "Everybody's down. We can wait."

"I—"

"We can wait."

I tried to match my breath to the rhythm of your hand on my thigh. I tried to still my heart—it had been beating so slowly before, now it felt like it was going to mimic the Harp: ramp up to a climax and burst through. *Thudthudthudthudthud—*

Outside the passenger-side window, I noticed Lloyd. He was crumpled on the ground, just like everybody else.

I've hurt everyone I've ever remotely cared about today.

No. Not everyone.

I opened the door and got out. You cried my name in surprise but, like you said, we could wait.

Lloyd was trying to say something but his throat didn't want to comply. I put my ear close to his lips.

". . . me . . . with . . . you." I think he was begging.

"I'm sorry, Lloyd," I whispered back to him. I stood up and looked at him with what I now understood to be love. How easy a concept that was to grapple with on this side of inflicting trauma. "I'm sorry."

I ran back to the van and slammed the door. As soon as we were able to, we got the fuck out of there.

22

WE'D MADE it about ten minutes—thankfully all we needed to reach the van I'd stashed under the bridge—when the Harp started to go off again.

Some realizations are a fist: different aspects of the problem curl in like fingers until the unit is complete and ready to sock you right in the fucking gut.

Because, *of course*:

Keep moving the Harp and it goes off.

If it keeps going off we can only drive so far at a time.

If we can only drive so far at a time they'll catch up with us.

Even if they don't catch us right away we'll leave them a trail of blackouts.

If that weren't enough, if we wanted to at least keep using it as a weapon, we'd have to stay in our Lloyd Suits and stick out like fucking spacemen.

Wham. All the air rushed out of me.

I hadn't thought of this.

Of course, if we kept the Harp in its bag no one was in any direct danger. But until we figured this shit out, the danger *we* were in was clear and present. To put it another way: we were completely, utterly, resolutely, mercilessly fucked.

I'm not someone prone to hyperventilating. But this blow was too sharp, too unexpected. I couldn't catch my breath. We transferred our cargo from one useless van to the other, and then I sank to the ground.

"Can we dump it?" You put your hand on my back. The Harp hummed insistently inside the duffel.

"No." My voice was a husk, a whistle, a death rattle. "I promised them."

"Promised who? You still haven't told me—"

"I don't know what we're going to do." I had to think. Every time I tried, wham, there was that fist.

"Okay," you said. "Okay. Where's the nearest hardware store? I have an idea."

WE'D JUST made it to the closest Home Depot when the Harp spun up again. The van sputtered and stopped dead right as we pulled into the parking lot.

"Let's wait until everything comes back on. It'll be a tomb in there."

I pulled out the bag of clothes I got from the airport. "I guess we should change before we go in."

You looked at the options I handed you—something close to distaste crossed your face.

"Trust me," I muttered, sliding out of my suit, "there wasn't much to choose from."

"Right . . . ," you said. I suppose I should have recognized there was something more going on than your unenthusiasm at wearing board shorts and a Myrtle Beach T-shirt, but I was too busy trying to rub away the stress headache grinding under my skull.

"We're giving Sierra a map right to us."

"How big's the radius of the Harp's blast, you think?"

"Against tech? At least the distance from Object E to the perimeter of Quill Marine. But the effect never reached anything in town, so . . ."

"And against people?"

"I mean, once we got it out of the engine room, we insulated the Hangar, remember? So we never really got to find out. I guess let's try to keep it that way." I looked at my watch. "We gotta be fast. I figure we've got about an hour or two before they're more or less able to eat us alive again."

THE STORE was full of nervous chatter—people's voices leapfrogging over each other to see who could express the greatest surprise over the blackout. They weren't even actively shopping anymore, just babbling wide-eyed with their hands on their chests, like they'd just seen Godzilla tramp through the city in a wedding dress.

"We should split up so we can get stuff faster," you said. "Can you get the bungee cords?"

I sighed, nodding, looking around. "We don't even know if this'll work."

"We definitely can't dump the Harp?"

"They won't take us without it."

"You still haven't told me who."

I opened my mouth to respond, but before I could say anything a giant in an orange apron approached us. The kid was well over 6′5″ and head-to-toe red: a red, curly mop of hair, a red beard, skin pixelated with red freckles.

"Can I help you guys find anything?"

Of course, we both knew not to leave behind a trail of "seemed-like-they-were-in-a-hurry" eyewitnesses. We switched over to a casual, suburban frequency like two synchronized swimmers.

"Oh, hey, thanks. We're looking for towel racks. Like, really quality ones. Stainless steel, maybe. And they've gotta have the bar that goes through."

He pointed us to aisle fifteen. "Did you guys miss the excitement?"

You and I turned to each other, dumb and innocent.

"This weird power outage," he filled us in, "freaked everybody out. Flashlights, lanterns, even emergency lights didn't work. Crazy."

"Wow."

You turned to me. "Maybe that's what made our car konk out,

too!" You turned to the kid. "All of a sudden, our car's battery just *ttbbplt*. We figured it was just us!"

"Nobody got hurt?" I gasped.

"You'd think, right?" the kid laughed. "Total darkness plus power saws. But it was only for a minute. Still." He shuddered.

"Speaking of sharp stuff: drills."

"Aha! Follow me!" Like some great, easily sunburned wizard about to lead you on an epic adventure. I had a moment to think of Rosh—then immediately shook him from my head.

You turned to me. "Catch you up front, babe."

"But don't forget—" I gestured to my wrist. Tick tick.

"I know, I know." You rolled your eyes and gave me a quick peck on the lips, then we headed in opposite directions.

It was our first kiss in a week, and without a doubt the lightest and driest of our entire career, but it was like looking into the future: you and me, together for years, for decades, just going to the store.

I hustled to aisle fifteen, feeling in my pocket to make sure we could pay in cash, somehow smiling to myself.

AFTER FORTY agonizing minutes of waiting in the sweltering van for you to charge the cordless drill's battery at a coffee shop, we went about implementing your scheme. It was dark and hot and the prospect of Sierra's inevitable approach seemed to be squeezing the air out of everything millimeter by millimeter.

We were crouched in back. There was barely any light—and certainly none of that otherworldly glow we'd become so used to—but we didn't dare open the doors of the van. Both Moss and the Harp had to come out of the Turndown box.

We leaned Moss against the wall. He watched, unimpressed, while we worked.

"Okay, so, I'm trying to think like Lloyd, right? Hold it steady." I held the rim of the now-empty Turndown box as you climbed inside it. "Thanks. You can unseal the Harp bag, too. So. We know if we pick up and carry the Harp, it flips out. We now know if we put it in a vehicle and drive with it, it flips out. So it's almost like you just can't move it at all. Except . . ."

"It crossed a gajillion light-years of space." The whoosh-buzz of the bag seal punctuated that conclusion.

"Right. If it got all the way to Earth, why can't we drive it down the street? Maybe start opening up the towel racks next." We'd gotten several different kinds—this was going to take some experimenting.

"Right."

"Plus, it's light, like balsa wood. And I know this isn't scientific—Lloyd would give me so much shit—but what if it's also delicate like balsa wood? And that got me thinking about babies."

A laugh burst out of me. I couldn't help it.

"So babies," you went on, and somehow I could hear you blushing, "human babies, right, not like a lot of kinds of animals, but human babies are born not ready to live yet. They can't walk, they're defenseless, they're fragile. They're balsa wood."

"Okay." I was still laughing.

"Shut up and hand me the drill." I did. You gave it two quick test whirs. "So we swaddle them. So they can't move too much. Makes them steady and safe."

"So you think the Harp—"

"Is dangerous and fragile. So maybe they made it like a baby, like it freaks out of it doesn't feel safe, if it's bouncing around. Remember the pins locking it into the base in the engine room?"

Holy shit. "I do."

"So hand me the paper-towel rods and then climb in here with the Harp."

THE WHOLE process took another forty excruciating minutes. We crouched in the sweltering darkness, the only real light coming from my crappy burner cell phone. I held the Harp upright while you fed towel rods through the holes at its base and drilled them into the floor of the box. We'd purchased a variety of rods and the thickest wooden ones seemed to work the best: once they were secured to the floor, the Harp barely even wiggled.

Next, we bungeed the Turndown box to the walls of the back of the van to keep it from sliding around. And since Moss looked comfortable enough where he was, we bungeed him to the wall too.

The ordeal was long and uncomfortable and involved enough that I didn't realize until it was almost time to crawl out: we'd just been in a coffin together. That vision I'd had the night Grant lit a fuse under our asses, of you and I snuggled together in a death embrace, had come true. And yet somehow we'd escaped. Somehow we'd been sliced out of the darkness. It remained to be seen whether we'd be allowed to flop away to safety or speared as bait . . . but I felt a glimmer of hope.

My eyes had adjusted to the dark, and God, you looked amazing. The urge to devour you was countermanded by the urge to collapse weeping and relieved into your arms. I settled for neither.

"Let's give it a try," I said. "If you can stop thinking about babies for a few minutes."

FIRST WE drove around the parking lot, like a preteen practicing behind the wheel for the very first time, like we had priceless crystalware balancing on the roof. It seemed steady enough. But the real test was distance. It was time to hit the road again—and fast. For two people on the run, we were almost exactly where we'd started.

There was only one problem.

"Matt?" I said as I eased us toward the parking lot exit. "Just realized something."

"What?"

"If we're wrong and the Harp starts going again . . . ?"

"Yeah?"

"It's not in the bag now."

"Oh."

"Yeah."

"Oh. Fuck. Can we put the bag, like, over it?"

"Won't work. We can't seal it."

"Okayyyy . . ."

"Here goes nothing." I gulped and pointed us toward a freeway. I saw out of the corner of my eye that you were clutching your knees like we were making a particularly hairy turn. "Good news is, at least, we won't have to worry about the hundred-hour thingie again."

"What do you mean?"

I reminded you about what had been learned while I'd been away: that the Harp's internal clock seemed to reset itself after every Power-Up. Since we'd just used it (*on Patty on Lloyd on everyone we'd ever*—), we'd have four entire days before having to worry about it acting up again. Assuming there's no Power-Up now as we're driving, we'll have handed the damned thing over and be home free by then.

"But Dak?"

"Yeah?"

"Who are we handing it off to? I don't have to beat any more lie detectors, so I think it's time you actually told me what the plan is."

You had me there. I took a deep breath.

"We're hitting a spot on the US side of the Tex-Mex border, about two hundred clicks south of El Paso. Someone will be waiting there in a beat-up-looking fruit van. We load Moss and the Harp into that, cross into Mexico; they'll take us to a mobile lab."

"Whose mobile lab?"

"The Chinese." I let that sit for a moment. "They'll check out Moss and the Harp. If they're happy, we get fifty million US and asylum for life."

"We're . . . wait . . ."

"We'll be rich, we'll be safe, and we'll be together."

"We're giving Moss to the Chinese? We're giving the Harp to the Chinese?"

"As opposed to who? The totally awesome and responsible people we just stole it from?" I took a breath. "Drive time should be about eighteen hours, so we'll probably need to break for the night. We should be prepared to move the box with your whole Harp setup to another van. Probably smart to switch up vehicles a few times."

"Um . . . yeah, I guess, probably . . ." You sounded dazed. You'd just been hit with a fist of your own.

"Of course, we gotta see if it works first, so—"

"And we can't . . . like we can't . . . No, of course we can't . . ."

"What?"

"Like, go by my house or—?"

"Your house."

"Right, no, I know it's stupid, obviously we're not—"

"You know how many people they'll have camped outside your—"

"I know we're not going to my house!"

"Yeah, we're not."

We should have driven in silence. That's where it should've ended, with an awkward, hurt silence that was apologized for later. But I couldn't let it go. I was suddenly furious.

"I mean, what the fuck, Matt, why—you know how this— you're in the game, you're trained, you're—"

"Right, except, in the game, you get the briefing before the thing, not in the middle!"

"This was the only way it would work! This was the only way you could beat the—"

"I get all that. I'm not stupid."

"Then why are you talking about—"

"I have shit there, Dak! I have stuff, pictures, memories, family things, I'm a fucking human being with a past, okay? I don't know about you!"

I don't know about you.

Okay. That hurt. "We agreed. We had a plan."

"The last time I knew the plan we were selling Moss to 9Source and going to Costa Rica or whatever—"

"They can get us in Costa Rica! Sierra can get us in Costa Rica, they can get us in Switzerland, they can get us in . . . think of a place, they can get to us there. But they can't get to us in China."

"Right, and that too, that too. This is all old news to you, you've been setting it up for days, but I'm in the first five minutes of knowing I'll be living in China for the rest of my life."

"Right, with me—together!"

"I mean, do you know anything about China? Do you know any Chinese, beyond tactical shit we all got in training?" It was spilling out, all of it, realizations pummeling the both of us, fist after fist. "Do you know how to live in China, do you know how to go to the store?"

"I know how to live anywhere with fifty million dollars! Do you know what I had to do to put all this together—"

"I'm not shitting on your plan, Dak, I just need a minute to— I'm leaving everything, like everything, and I'm—what if someone woke you up this morning and said, 'Put a shirt on, put some shoes on, we're going to China forever,' what would you do?"

"If it was you? If it was you saying this? I'd put my fucking shirt and shoes on!"

"Fine. You know what, let's just drive and I'll—"

"I'm sorry my plan to make us rich and happy forever didn't include stopping off to get all your lacrosse trophies and letters from ex-girlfriends!"

"I'm done talking, Dak. You're right. I'm wrong. So just . . ."

"I'm sorry I didn't think of every single thing!" The fight had gone out of me. I must have sounded more desperate than angry. I must have sounded like I meant it.

The thing was, I did mean it. He wasn't wrong. Tactically, it was a horrible idea, but of course a person wants to take their stuff when they go. *Why didn't you think of that, you stupid bitch?* Another, colder voice answered: *But you did think of that. You decided to forget. So he'd have nothing to cling to but you.*

I shuddered, despite the heat.

We didn't speak again for close to four hours. Too many questions, too many doubts swirling around, curling into one final realization, one final punch aimed right at my heart. The blow made a specific sound upon contact. It sounded like your voice, echoing between my ears: *I don't know about you!*

Once again you were right. We don't know each other at all.

When you broke the silence, the sun was hanging low in the sky, slapping a coat of yellow and blue paint across the darkening clouds.

"Dak."

"What."

"It hasn't made a peep."

The Harp had been silent this entire time.

We weren't dead. We weren't screwed. At least on this front, we weren't screwed.

"That was a really great idea, Salem," I said. "I never would have thought of it. You saved our lives."

"Guess we're both good planners." And was that the faintest hint of smile on your lips?

"Guess so."

"Find somewhere safe."

"What?"

"Find somewhere safe."

I FOUND some crap-ass little town where almost everything was closed and boarded up and I parked behind some store-shaped fossil with broken windows. Not the most romantic of locations, but whatever. I would've parked in hell for this.

When I came, I cried so loudly and hoarsely I thought my throat was going to turn inside out. It was the sort of noise a person makes trying to lift up the car that had just pinned down their child.

"Damn." Now it was your turn to catch your breath.

"Sorry."

"Hey, I'm not complaining, just . . . I mean it was just a week, you didn't get out of prison."

"Felt like a month. Thought about it like twenty times a day. Like I'm a goddamn high school sophomore or something."

"Like I said, not complaining, just . . . don't be disappointed if that's all I can do for the night."

"What, the whole hot-windowless-van-with-dead-alien-watching thing doesn't turn you on?"

You turned around. There was Moss, disinterested as ever. I'd forgotten about him for a while too. But there he'd been.

"I'm sorry I didn't tell you everything," I whispered. You turned back to me.

"It's . . ." It wasn't fine. None of this was fine. But it was forgiven, I could see that much.

"It's a lot."

"Yeah. But here we are."

You took my hand in yours. I kissed it. And then I told you everything.

I started from the moment Grant left my apartment, and the jolt of despair that switched my whole brain on to fight back. Then Myrtle Beach, D.C., Lisa, Zhang, Nikki, Haydon, the letter, Lauren, shaking Grant's hand. In some ways it was weird filling you in—you had been so on my mind it felt like you had always been right there with me the entire time. I told you that, too. And though his back was to us through the mesh partition, it was as if Moss were listening with you. Like I was explaining myself to both of you.

When I finished, you squeezed my hand.

"Miles to go," you whispered, with a distant, unreadable smile.

WE PULLED over again as the sun was setting a few hours later. We hadn't quite crossed over into full desert . . . but almost.

The clouds trundled thick and pendulous across the Technicolor sky. They rolled toward us with the promise of ill fortune, but with no judgment that comes with otherwise ominous things. "This is ours," they seemed to say, overtaking everything above the sloping, mountainous horizon. They were a tiger's roiling lip, a snake's upraised head, a churning ocean—any number of things that could be our doom or pass us by unscathed. They owed us no warning. Theirs was a language unconcerned with foreshadows or narrative promises. They simply took ownership of all that our eyes could see and what was theirs had no choice but to bow in supplication.

And behind that sky was blackness, emptiness, punched through with jagged holes of tiny light. It was always there, that blackness, waiting for us, no matter how bright the day might be.

I wanted to continue justifying myself to you. I wanted to say, "This is what they did to us, they hammered into us that not only should we be willing to die for the objective, we should be willing to make others die too; and so, they have this coming." I wanted to assure you that I was using all my instincts, all my skills, just this one more time, then never again, then I'd be off the clock for good. I'm not a warrior anymore. My tour's over. It's just life now. It's just life until it isn't anymore, for as long as that takes. I've earned that, you've earned that.

But I didn't speak. And the sky didn't care.

We are inheritors of a grand lineage of fruitlessness. Our entire species, toiling under this very sky. Since our first days, we unrolled doomed and laughable plans: stealing a sheep, robbing a bank, confessing a love, raising a family. The sky rumbled on, full of ruination and havoc, but honest and pure in its ambivalence. I felt small and comforted by my smallness. I had made myself at least somewhat bigger by joining with you. As long as I had your hand to hold on to.

You had about forty-eight hours left to live. And if I'd know that in this moment I would've thought: of course.

23

"STUPID QUESTION: you can steal a car, right?"

"Of course. Another van, right?"

We'd driven all night, napping in shifts. Now, the next morning, we were pulling into a small desert town—not as small and dead as the one we'd pulled into the day before. Everything seemed to be made out of dust and clay.

I nodded. "Or a truck, as long as it's not with, like, a big company. I'm gonna grab us a new burner in case we need it to make contact." I'd ditched the last one as we pulled out of the previous town. "Plus," I couldn't help but grin ever so slightly, "I wanna take a look-see."

"At what?"

"At whether or not Sierra's made us famous."

And I threw my arms around you and kissed you—blissfully not caring if anyone could see.

THERE WAS a gas station at the edge of town, the ghost of a tiger or a lion on the sign. I tried to remember what the name for that brand of gas was—it had been long enough since the oil reserves had been consolidated under one corporate identity that the brands I'd grown up with had all started to fade from memory just as effectively as they had from signage.

The phones were kept behind the counter with the headache medicine and condoms and lottery tickets. While the clerk rang me up, I scanned the racks next to the counter. A few shitty magazines, a couple paperback books, and a few self-published pamphlets. *Ghost Tours!* one of them shouted. *Murder Maps: Trace the Path of the Copycat Killer of Arroyo!* read another one, under a hand-drawn image of a person wearing a blood-soaked pillowcase. Jesus. What a delightful place to live.

"Hold on a sec," I told the guy after he read me what I owed for the phone. I grabbed some waters and then quickly gathered up a load of snacks off the shelves. Energy bars. A few sprigs of beef jerky in case you liked that.

Patty's okay, I found myself thinking. *I'm sure of it. Hell, I could even imagine her being the only person tough enough to take a full blast and shake it—*

No one could do that and you know it.

I did.

I tried to force the thought of her out of my mind and settled up in cash.

Outside, I worked on getting the phone out of its clear plastic shell—those things are a nightmare even for someone with combat training. Then I stuffed the phone in my pocket.

Next up I found the local FedEx Post—the sort of place I could imagine for a town like this was the hub for information. I was right. They had computer bays at the front for the public.

"Can I pay for computer time in cash?" I asked the dazed employee at the front desk.

He told me there was a thing to put my card into by the computer. I showed him a wad of cash and asked him if there were any other methods of logging on.

ROLLING BROWN OUTS CONFUSE
HUMBOLDT COUNTY RESIDENTS
Bizarre Series of Power Outages
Temporarily Shut Down All Devices
By Jenna Bix

BEATRICE—Walton Riggins has dealt with power outages before. Ever since Johnston-Stearns took over the power supply to this area, he says, service has been spotty. "But I've never seen something like this: my flashlights, my watch, even the dang phone my daughter bought me for my birthday! All of it, dead! And not just me!"

Mr. Riggins's neighbors reportedly experienced a similar phenomenon, as well. Service restored itself within about ten minutes, they say, but until that time, "It was like living in the Stone Age again!"

When asked if this phenomenon was perhaps the result of the rising temperatures, a representative from Johnston-Stearns declined to comment.

We met back up by our van just outside of town. Something about the dry, warm air, the gravel crunching under my feet, made me feel like maybe we'd actually get through this. Like we were already on another planet.

"All good?" You were wiping down the van, erasing our prints and making sure we'd left no other identifiable marks. Another van, a beaten-up old VW Transporter, was parked almost ass-to-ass with ours.

"So far. No wanted posters yet."

"Maybe all is forgiven."

"They're burning the earth to find us. They just don't want to put our faces out there and risk some local idiot nabbing us *and* meeting Moss."

You grunted in mock disappointment. "What do you want to move first, Moss or the Harp?

"Harp last. They'll be looking for freak power outages. I want us almost ready to go if that happens."

The vans were physically close enough that it probably wouldn't be an issue. But when you're this close to achieving something, it's usually the tiniest of things that can really fuck you over, so my stomach knotted all the same.

You got into the old van and pushed Moss out to me. I took

his legs and helped guide him out. The sun was directly above us.

"Shit . . ."

"What?" You tried to prepare yourself for some new calamity.

"Seeing him in the sunlight like this . . . the moss is a *lot* less, isn't it? On his chest?"

You peered out of the van to see. "Um . . . yeah, I guess."

It was, though. Significantly less. We weren't dealing with microns anymore. Moss was going through some sort of reverse puberty, losing his bluish green chest hair by the day.

"Just, if it happens this fast, he'll be dead in, like—"

"Dak," you said from your shady metal alcove.

"What?"

You stared at me for a good, long, patronizing moment. "He's already dead. Probably."

Seeing the alien in the sunlight, though, I was torn between two realities. He'd never felt so distinctly *real* before. As real as the rocks beneath us, the cactus to the left of us. And the warmth radiating from inside him was notable even in the hot summer sun. But also, here he was, catatonic as always, with not even a drop of shade to hide the fact that there was no reaction from him whatsoever . . . besides the shrinking of this mysterious growth on his skin. He was like that old cat in a box: dead and not dead at the same time.

"Right." I tried to sound convincing.

"Besides, even if it was true, and we knew it was true . . ."

"We couldn't do anything about it." The Chinese didn't need him to be alive. Just to be real. Still. "I'll just tell them to put him on ice or whatever."

There had been a shift in my feelings toward Moss and I hadn't registered it until right now. Back at Quill I'd never really felt this way—he was the objective, literally the object—but now out here in the cruel alien world, I was realizing he felt more like . . . my responsibility. My charge. A soldier under my command whose body had to be brought home.

We finished loading up the new van and got back on the road.

IT WAS your turn to drive. We were making good time now—a full day's drive from the rendezvous. I knew we couldn't avoid them forever . . . but we didn't need forever.

"What do you think is, like, the nice part of China?" you asked from behind the wheel.

We'd had to turn the radio off—too much Bible and static.

I shrugged. "I mean, China's huge, I'm sure there's all kinds of nice places."

"Wow. Can't believe you haven't figured that part out."

"We'll have a lot of time on our hands. What's the rush? We can look around."

"You think they've got good Mexican food there?"

I'd opened my mouth to call you out on that stinker of a joke when the phone in my pocket chimed.

"Jesus," you gasped. "Was that your burner?"

"Sounds like a text." I shrugged. Even before it was out of my mouth, though, I realized the problem.

"Dak—"

"I know."

No one should have this number.

There came that numbness—that combat-readying wash of adrenaline that turned my body into a willing pin cushion. I pulled the phone out. There was a text message waiting for me. From an unknown number:

When I call, put it on speaker.

"But it's a . . . that was the new phone, right? It's impossible." You were having a hard time focusing on the road and looking back at me. "What's it say?"

I told you. "It's either Sierra or . . . is anyone following us?"

"Not that I've spotted." Same for me. I'd kept looking for any vehicles riding behind us for more than a few minutes. There'd been nothing.

The phone started to ring. A nauseatingly chirpy chime. An unknown caller.

"We don't answer, right?" You were gripping the wheel with knuckles turned ghost white. It suddenly felt very hot in the van, despite the air-conditioning.

"Maybe it's Zhang?" I knew it was a stupid question even as I asked it. "Maybe our contact?"

"How would he have your new number?"

"I don't know, I don't know how anyone has it!"

The ringing stopped. We held our breath.

"Okay, look," you said. "I guess there's nothing to do but keep making time until—"

The phone chimed again. Another text.

I read it silently. My stomach curled in on itself.

"Jesus, tell me," you whispered.

I read you the message:

Put it on speaker or Patty suffers.

The phone began to ring again.

"Okay." I swallowed. "Don't say anything."

"Wait, wait, are you seriously—"

I accepted the call and you shut up.

Haydon's voice cooed over the other end.

"*So, you're gonna want to hang up. Don't. Put it on speaker. I wasn't kidding.*"

I gave you another look, one that said stay quiet, and I put the phone on speaker.

"*Now here's what you're gonna do next: you're gonna confirm we are, in fact, on speaker by saying, 'Yes,' each of you, in turn. Think*" *we can handle that?"* The cheap device made Haydon sound even more inhuman than normal. *"Again, lovebirds, that's 'yes.' First one, then the other."* Neither of us said a word. *"Come on, I know who's in the car! You're not keeping anything secret from me. Handsome Dak and Young Matt! Now. Say. 'Yes.'"*

"Yes," I croaked.

"Yes," you echoed.

"Thank you! You'll want to hang up fast, so I'm gonna say it all in a row. Sierra has a reciprocal relationship with the Bureau to use their updated facial recognition system. We got a hit near the store where you bought the burner and we leaned on the owner for this number. Take a second to think about what that means. How close we must be."

I checked the rearview mirror again: different cars from last time, no repeaters.

"Want another piece of interesting trivia? Everyone in law enforcement contracts with Sierra! At this moment we are rapidly and exhaustively reviewing reports of stolen vehicles large enough for what you're carrying. We're onto traffic cams, toll cams, everything with a lens between that store and Mexico. And every vehicle that could possibly contain my property will be searched comprehensively at the border. You're cooked. It just hasn't happened yet."

I hovered my thumb on the button to hang up. He cleared his throat.

"But this is weird for me, guys, 'cause the thing is: I'm not really a manhunter by nature. I mean, I have to be right now because you guys have sorta made my whole fucking reputation dependent on mopping up this little spill of yours, but what I really am is a **dealmaker.** *And a dealmaker never comes to the table without an offer. So here it is: stop, call in your location, and wait for us there. You'll get a year each. Then you'll be released to separate locations, unburdened from your contracts. You won't do more tours, you won't go to Zones. You'll have nothing, but you'll be free. This offer expires when we find you first. All right? All right. And, really"*—his voice dropped

low, an absurd secret—"*congratulations, Handsome Dak. I've never called anyone as wrong as I called you.*"

The call disconnected. Haydon had hung up first. I couldn't think of what else to do so I snapped the phone in half and threw it out the window.

We continued driving in silence. Neither of us wanted to be the first person to say it. We were fucked. Again.

But we'd been fucked before. Finally I spoke.

"There's a solution."

"What solution?" Your voice sounded dried and cracked.

"I don't know." I dug my fingers into my legs. "But you've lived the same life as me; how many times did it look like there was nothing until there was something?"

"Lots of times," you whispered. "And lots of times there was just nothing."

"Okay. Okay. Keep driving."

"Driving to *what*?"

There was no way they could check every large vehicle at every crossing-point. That was insane.

But also, so was Haydon. He would do anything. This was personal. He and his quadrillionaire father might be searching cars on the border themselves.

"We need . . . we need . . . okay, first we need another van."

"Which'll get reported as stolen and then Sierra will have the description—that won't make a difference!" I didn't like the panic that had crept into your voice. It sounded like giving up. "Dak . . . seriously . . . I don't see any—"

"Jesus, you know what we actually need?"

"What?"

"We need another person who no one's looking for, with a big-enough vehicle that isn't stolen to drive us to the rendezvous. I mean, we need . . . we need a fucking friend!"

We thought on that in silence for a while. There was still no one following us that I could see.

Where are they?

I felt like I could chart the sun's progress above us, time slipping away, as surely as I could chart the almost microscopic regression of Moss's moss back in the lab. I was about ready to burst out in apology for being so fucking stupid, for being so utterly useless, when you spoke.

"There might be someone."

"What?"

You wouldn't look at me.

"There might be someone."

WE FOUND a dead-end exit, bought another burner phone at a gas station with our heads down like two children buying something forbidden and embarrassing. Now I was watching you pace in the sand, talking to someone. It was taking forever so I tried to distract myself by opening up the back doors and taking another look at our silent companion.

The moss is definitely receding.

"I'm sorry," I whispered to Moss. "I didn't know what else to do."

At last you hung up and came back to me, wiping your sweat off the phone with your shirt.

"I don't know about a vehicle or anything, but I at least know where we can get off the road for the night."

I'd had plenty of time to pick apart this little plan, though. "Matt, we have to assume they're camped outside all our known associates—"

"I never put her down. On any of the vetting forms."

Uh . . . "Who?"

"Some of the stuff she does . . . I wanted to protect her. If they investigated her . . ."

"*Who?*"

"Her name's Teresa."

"Teresa." I didn't know what the fuck I was feeling anymore.

"It's four hours out of our way. In Odessa. Means we'd have to double-back to make our rendezvous tomorrow night."

"And Teresa is . . . ?"

"Someone I trust."

I nodded, trying to process.

"Wait—'if they investigated her'? What kinda stuff is she into?"

24

TWO PEOPLE, on the run from an insidious global corporation that owns much of the privatized world, after stealing one of its most prized possessions . . .

So what the fuck were we doing eating pasta and drinking wine on a screened porch during a beautifully cool summer night?

Well, I was biting my tongue hard enough to worry about bisecting the thing accidentally, while kneading my hands under the table.

A couple hours earlier, we'd made the mostly silent four-hour detour to Odessa. It was a risk (what wasn't these days?), but we decided not to steal another van—no point in gifting them another potential hit on their radar. Thank goodness for small favors: at least my nerves quieted down for the trip. We had a plan, and, just maybe, heading in the opposite direction would throw them off a bit more.

However, pulling up to a beautiful ranch home, miles away from anything other than flat Texas plains, the nerves returned. They just had one question: *Who the fuck is Teresa?*

"She said the driveway goes around back. She said pull all the way in; she'll see me and come out."

"This is where she lives?"

"No," you said absently as we pulled up behind the house.

The moment we stepped out of the van, several bright yellow lights clicked on, stabbing through the darkness and casting long, alien shadows behind us. I jumped.

"Shit!"

"It's just motion lights," you said. "Just a sensor."

That's when we heard her voice from just inside.

"Matt?"

"Yeah!" you answered, a little too excitedly for my taste.

The lights were bright and in my face, so at first all I could see was her silhouette. I watched it bound out the back door, babbling, "Oh my God, oh my God," and when my eyes fully adjusted, I could more clearly see the goddamn absolutely gorgeous woman throwing her arms around your neck, pressing her hips toward yours, and kissing you firmly on the mouth.

When she finally detached herself, she sighed. "You came back. Oh my God, you came back." Then she kissed you again.

I stood frozen. I was never the type to freeze, yet here I was: overloaded. I could only . . . watch.

You moved her gently back, about half an arm's length. My rational mind knew this was all right—this was somebody we needed, somebody who could help us—but, holy hell, the baser part of me wanted you to fling her away like a spider on your hand, for me to stamp in the dust.

"T . . . T . . . ," you stammered. "I'm sorry, can you—"

Her eyes went wide as if she'd just realized something. "No! I'm sorry! God, I'm so—that was totally wrong of me!"

"It's okay."

It was?!

"No, it's not, you don't just *kiss* people. It's just—your call brought me right back to . . ." She shook her head, smiling. *To what?* "That's no excuse. I didn't even ask; I'm so—"

Your call brought her right back to what*?!*

You smiled and told her it was okay. Again. And that's when she noticed me.

The way she looked at me, I knew instantly you hadn't told her to expect two people.

"Oh," she sputtered. "Hi! Sorry, you're catching me in the middle of melting, apparently I don't even have basic manners—hi! Teresa Pérez."

She stuck out a hand. I took it. It wasn't petite or delicate—much worse, it was firm and capable and calloused and still somehow fucking glamorous. It was the hand of someone with a bone structure they could've coasted on their entire life, but who also clearly lacked the temperament to know how to coast.

What am I, twelve? Why am I freaking out like this? Who am I—

"Dak," I said, suddenly aware of how leaden and graceless my name fell out of a mouth. It was short and clumsy. In fact, Teresa even looked at me, confused—warm, charming, embarrassed, but confused. "Short for Dakota," I clarified.

"What did you mean," I heard myself asking, "that his call 'brought you back'?"

"Dak," you warned. I wanted to glare at you. I stared at Teresa.

She smiled. It was a warm smile—humble, charming. "Sorry. It was a stupid thing from when we were—"

"From when you were—" I began.

"Together," she said with a nod.

"Dak," she repeated. "It's very nice to meet you, and welcome to . . . not my house."

"Whose house is it?" I asked. But before I could get that minimal amount of information, you cut in.

"We should probably get the car into a—"

"Yes!" Teresa exclaimed. "Yes. Let's do that right now. Time's a-wasting!"

THE GARAGE was spacious and uncluttered. The kind of garage you can find only at a house where nobody really lives. Teresa and I stood to the side while you pulled the van in. I was busy silently castigating myself, so she startled me a bit when she leaned over and asked:

"I'm sorry, can I ask you something really fast so I know how to act around you?"

"What?"

"Are you guys together?"

"Yeah." I was wary—how would she react to this, why was she asking? Was this a gauntlet being thrown or—

Her face lit up with a warm smile that almost physically changed the temperature in the garage.

"Great," she said. And meant it.

NEXT CAME the tour. Along the way I learned a little bit more: Teresa was a pediatrician ("mostly," whatever that meant), you liked to call her "T," and I was a petty, jealous, and insecure child.

Last, but distinctly not least, we made our way down carpeted stairs to the basement and I was struck immediately by the clutter. Thus far, it had been the sort of house you might assign to a rich, older bachelor. Clean, minimal, modern fixtures, straight out of a full-page color ad in a fashion magazine where people sit around all night talking about watches and cars. But the basement: nine beds, two cots, two TVs, board games, games for babies, air hockey, five mini-fridges. It was a completely different story.

The two of you were giddily reminiscing.

"This is *way* better than what you had before!"

"Right, God, when would that have been?"

"I mean, at least three years ago, right?"

"Yes! We would've still been in that old church! Saint . . . Whatever, I'm forgetting!"

"Yeah—wow."

"Right?"

Meanwhile, I'd finished a quick accounting of the contents of the room.

"So either this is the basement of a really fun granddad with like forty grandkids, or . . ."

"He's not really a fun granddad," Teresa smiled.

"This is a way-station," I concluded. "Who's the 'he'?"

Teresa sat down on one of the cots.

"Well, he's rich. Obviously. Part of the network—but really more of an angel, not so hands-on. He has a couple houses, so he's here like, I dunno, three weeks a year? He basically says, 'Just don't tell me, and if they raid, you're squatters. I knew nothing about you.'"

"What network?"

"It's called—" And then she interrupted herself, turning to you. "You are gonna laugh at this, it's a new name since last time." Back to me. "It's called . . . MATT 25."

Did you blush? I don't know. I know I did.

"The hell is that?" I spat out.

Easy, Dak. Come on. Stop being so stupid.

"It's short for Matthew 25. 'Then the righteous will answer him, "Lord, when did we see you hungry and feed you, or thirsty and give you something to drink? When did we see you a stranger and invite you in, or needing clothes and clothe you? When did we see you sick or in prison and go to visit you?" The King will reply, "Truly, I tell you—"'"

"'"... whatever you did for one of the least of these brothers and sisters of mine, you did for me."'" I stared at you, agape. Teresa clapped her hands.

"Right? How great is that?"

"You can just rattle that off?" I asked, feeling like I was looking at a stranger. You shrugged.

"I mean, it's the most famous thing in the whole Bible, right?"

"The network is churches, mostly." Teresa turned back to me. "Some here, some in California, a couple in New Mexico. ICE got a lot bigger when it went private, but they still can't cover everybody all the time. We find places people can live decently while they wait for the squads to lose interest. They're not all as nice as this. Actually most of them aren't."

"And you do this, what, on nights and weekends?"

"It's not regular. Just whenever this is the closest place."

"And I'm assuming a truckload of undocumenteds aren't showing up tonight."

"Nope! Or . . . just you, I guess." She laughed brightly, stood up, and looked at the two of us. "Anyway, sleep on any of the beds, there's like twenty of them. Oh, and showers, if—I mean I don't care, you guys smell great, just: if it makes you feel better."

A shower *did* sound amazing.

You stepped forward a bit. I was suddenly aware of the physical distance between the two of us. We were standing across the room from each other like . . . barrack mates, nothing more. "Um, before you . . . That thing we talked about?"

I was going to open my mouth to ask, "What thing?" but Teresa was already responding.

"Right! The van! I need to make one more call on that. And then—are you hungry? Ooh—more importantly"—she dropped her voice to a devilish whisper—"but do you guys need to get hammered tonight?"

You and I answered at the same time.

Me: "No, I mean, tomorrow's basically the biggest day of all—"

You: "Oh my God, yes, that would be amazing."

Teresa laughed again, delighted.

"Well, you guys decide. I'll put stuff out and we'll go from there. But definitely, eat." She headed for the stairs, turned back, and sighed. "God, it's so good to see you again. It's so good to see you happy!" She tipped me a wink and disappeared.

You caught my look right away.

"I was stationed near here. We met on a leave weekend and hung out whenever I—"

"'Hung out'?"

"I didn't tell you because I thought you'd . . . I dunno."

I did my best to rein in whatever the fuck was galloping through my chest. "How long?"

"Something like two years. Around there."

I continued to inspect the pretty ample inventory around us, as casually as I could.

"Cool. So we're holing up . . . with your crazy-hot hero-slash-pediatrician ex who you were with for like two years."

"Who has a garage and a hideout and no cameras and doesn't need a credit card and can maybe get us a van." I nodded. It was true. "There's a bunch of things I can say right now, but . . . I don't think you want to hear any of it," you added. That was also true. We were at an impasse—entirely my fault, but palpable all the same. You shrugged, gently, not wanting to make an issue out of my giant issues. "You wanted first or second shower?"

I wanted to say, "Who needs to take turns?" but suddenly I didn't want to be naked in front of you. I didn't want you to be naked in front of me. This all felt wrong and indecent.

What the hell happened to me? What's still happening to me?

"You go ahead," I said, idly fingering one of the air hockey paddles. "I'll . . . look at the map."

You held off for a moment, probably waiting for me to dispel the awkward tension. I didn't. You nodded and, gently, without judgment, answered, "Cool," before heading to the bathroom.

SO NOW: pasta and wine.

My first thought, ungenerous and judgmental, when she set out the dishes: *she's probably going to apologize for having to serve us something so humble.*

"Sorry, if I had more time, I'd actually make something, instead of just—"

"This is perfect," you stopped her.

"Home-owner-I-shall-not-name is obsessed with wine and pasta sauces, and sometimes I just decide, 'Hey, you know what? Tonight I'm gonna be the beneficiary.' I won't knock it too hard—it's the real deal."

We set to serving ourselves. You knew better than to serve me—that sort of chivalric condescension was likely to make me punch you in the arm—but I found myself wishing you'd try.

"Man, if I had access to this place I'd be here every night." You tore into a chunk of bread before passing the plate around.

You were grinning, but your eyes flicked at me, curious. Concerned.

"Actually, I'm still not sure what's best in terms of not attracting attention. I don't wanna stick out too much. I can only be 'the cleaning lady' so many days a month."

"I guess it's easier with a church." I was determined to be a regular conversationalist.

"In terms of cover, yeah, it's easier to explain why people are there all the time. But private homes are overall better 'cause if they come knocking you can make them go get a warrant and maybe buy some time. A little time, at least."

"You know that we—Matt and me—our employers also own ICE. Different division, but the same people at the top. You know that, right?" I poured myself a healthy glass of wine.

You stared at me across the table like I was insane. Maybe I was.

Teresa nodded. "Right, but . . . you're running away from them now, right?"

She had me there, I had to admit.

You reached over and topped your glass off. "It's okay to keep drinking this? Like, he won't miss it?"

"He doesn't remember what he has."

"Rich people are weird." I snorted, feeling like a fraud for playing along.

"Works for me." You smiled. "I won't hold back."

She laughed around a mouthful of pasta—still somehow impossibly graceful. "Just don't birthday drink, okay, that's all I—"

"Oh come *on*, come *on*—!"

"That's all I ask!"

"I can't live that down, what, how many years later is this?!"

Just like that, you both had exploded into some jubilant reverie, some delicious shared nostalgia, that made me feel like I had shrunk down almost to the point of invisibility. You would each direct something toward me, some excuse to dramatically explain the situation and groan and shout and laugh even further, but . . .

hell, I was like the moss. Observed, accounted for, steadily disappearing.

"It was your twenty-seventh or something! So, I take him out, right, the little brat—"

"First of all, first of all—"

"He gets so drunk, this one, right, he just starts singing. Like, singing. First in the restaurant, then all the way home. Now ask me what he was singing!"

"Okay, just for some context—"

"Steely Dan. Like, all of Steely Dan. Who still listens to Steely Dan?!"

"They were an incredibly important—!"

"It may have even been, like, in chronological order, but I don't know Steely Dan well enough to say. But, I mean, you know what he's like when he sings, right? Is he still—"

"No." I shook my head. I was eying both of you, polite and quiet, burning up and embarrassed at my fever.

"You haven't heard him . . . ?"

I shrugged, smiling tightly. My eyes burned inside my skull. I poured myself another glass.

"Well, I mean, actually that's a good thing, that's actually a lucky thing for you, 'cause it was like letting a genie out of a bottle or some shit, I couldn't cram him back in."

"Look, I was a young guy—"

"Steely Dan at the Mexican place, Steely Dan while I got the check, Steely flippin' Dan all the way home—"

"It was my birthday, I was happy, right, like 'Happy birthday!'"

"And you have to understand, Dak, at this time, whenever this was, I had two roommates I had to sneak him past—God, that apartment was a nightmare!"

"Right. Riiiiiiight. Oh my God."

"Which you'd think, you'd think, would make him stop singing Steely Dan, right?"

"Wait, I didn't stop? I thought I stopped!"

"No, no, your big concession to us being, you know, inside in the middle of the night, was to sing Steely Dan like ten percent quieter."

"Okay, I think there's like a lot of exaggeration happening—" I poured myself another.

"There's no exaggeration—"

"And there's slander happening, and I—"

"There's no slander, there's no—don't listen to him. Honestly, first thing I did in the morning was look to see if my stuff was on the curb."

And what about the part you skipped? I didn't say. *What about the part between the midnight singing and checking the curb? What about the last part of his birthday, where you took your clothes off and your thin bodies curled around each other like two snakes?* Instead of saying that, I remembered the map of Texas I'd taken out of my pocket and was now trying not to crush in my hands. I took it out and unfolded it on the table.

The two of you noticed and quieted down, which, while my goal, made me feel even more self-conscious. "No, no, I don't mean to be, like," I sputtered. "I'm saying before we hit bunks we should hammer everything out, but you can keep . . . talking about . . ."

Welcome back to puberty, you dumb chunk, some uncharitable voice cackled internally.

Teresa had taken a sip of wine, but hummed against the glass as she swallowed. As soon as she could speak: "So, okay, I talked to my guy, and it's sort of a good-news/bad-news situation."

"We don't really have a margin for bad news."

She nodded. "Well. He can get you the van—actually it's not a van, it's better than a van, it's a truck. More room in the back for . . . whatever. But." I braced myself. "He needs it back. After."

"He—" I began.

"I said we could pay for it," you reminded her.

"You said you could pay two thousand. He won't sell for two

thousand." Two thousand was all we had left in cash. We certainly couldn't risk stopping by a bank to make another withdrawal. "He's willing to let you borrow it, and he's willing to come pick it up when you're done with it . . . but only if you tell him in advance where you'd be leaving it."

You and I both sputtered over each other, trying to make sense of the situation.

"You could just tell me, if you want," Teresa offered. "You could show me on this map or—"

"Great," I growled, "and then, what, we give him a call? Shoot him an email? Maybe rent a fucking billboard?"

"I'm sorry, he has to have that first."

Distantly, I heard you say my name. Meanwhile, Teresa and I were staring each other down. The tiny amount of pasta I'd eaten was turning into concrete in my stomach.

"Do you have any idea how sensitive—"

"He won't leave the van here without that information."

"What if I hog-tie him and help myself, how 'bout that?"

"Then I'll tell him not to come," she said steadily. "He's a good man and that truck has sheltered a lot of people."

"What if you could tell him you're coming with us?" you asked suddenly. I pivoted in my seat.

"*What?*"

You continued. "That way you'd see the spot yourself and you could lead him back to it later, would that be good enough?"

"What are you talking about?!" I demanded.

Teresa considered it. "How would it work?"

"We take two vehicles. You drive the truck, I ride in the back, Dak drives your car. You see where we leave the van, drive home in your car, then bring your friend back to the spot the next day."

"Are you seriously suggesting she put eyes on the rendezvous?"

"They're watching the traffic cams, right? For large vehicles? But if they see her driving they won't care, and maybe they're not looking for us in regular cars."

"Why don't you ride with Dak?" Teresa suggested.

You turned back to her. "There's a . . . thing in the truck I need to keep an eye on."

"Okay . . ."

"Not like a—not like a bomb, I swear." Not like a bomb, but not unlike a bomb. So far the bumped hundred-hour clock theory seemed to be holding, but, hell, if this conversation was proving anything it was that we couldn't count on there not being any last-minute surprises.

"Hey! Excuse me!" I bellowed. "That still leaves her, who I've never met before in my life, putting eyes directly on our rendezvous point!"

"She's good for it, Dak."

"*I don't know that.*" I was aware of how quiet the night had been, how oppressively loud my voice had become. You looked at me, stung.

"Wait, so my vouch isn't good enough?"

But Teresa interjected. "You're right, Dak. You don't know me. You have no reason in the world to think you can trust me."

"Goddamn right," I grumbled.

"But that's also true of hundreds of other people who've been in my care, who slept in basements while I stayed awake. Matthew 25 says treat everyone who's on the run like they're God's children, because that's what they are. I didn't betray them. I won't betray you."

I wanted to put her face into the table. Not because I thought she was lying . . . but because I thought she wasn't. I leaned forward.

"You seriously . . . seriously . . . don't want to ask us a single question?"

She shrugged. "I never have. I never will."

I was suddenly exhausted. This would work. I didn't want it to work, but it would. And I couldn't think of any other solution. I sat back, breaking all eye contact. I gripped my upper thighs.

"Then . . . I guess . . . that's what we're doing."

"I'll square it with him first thing in the morning." Her voice was empty of any malice and I hated her even more for it.

You lifted your glass, relieved. "Okay! Okay, so we're good."

"We should hit the bunk." I scraped my chair against the concrete, folding the map back up as I did so.

You paused, mid-reach for the bottle. "What?"

I finally looked at you. You looked so young. "We should sleep. It's the biggest goddamn day of our lives tomorrow."

"But . . . there's still wine. I mean, we're having fun, right?"

"We're leaving first thing," I started to protest.

"Well," Teresa shrugged, "he probably won't get here *first* thing . . ."

"We can finish the bottle, though, right?" You said it to her, not to me. A minute redirection, but huge all the same.

I wanted to say, "Fuck you. Fuck you for bringing us here. For making me feel this way. For indebting me to your fucking secret ex-girlfriend and letting me get past so many obstacles before tripping me up this close to the finish line." Instead I said:

"Fine. Finish the bottle. Start another one after that." And I walked off the porch and back into the house.

I STOMPED down the basement, silently screaming at myself, "What are you doing, you're walking out on dinner like a teenager? Who are you?" I headed straight to the bathroom and closed the door. My face felt red-hot from wine and rage. I needed water, I needed to puke, I needed—

This is that scene in the movie where the character splashes water on her face, right? Try that.

I did. A little cold water. It was nice, but . . . the way it beaded on my skin. I looked pebbled and ancient. I looked covered in growths.

Where's my moss? Where's my life-force? Is it already gone?

You don't know that's what the moss is.

I don't know anything.

He's probably apologizing for me right now, like how she apologized for serving pasta. I'm the thing you apologize to friends for.

What are we doing?

It's not that I was never scared in the service. Sure, I was scared. Hell, I was scared even a few days ago—it was starting to feel like I would be some kind of scared for the rest of my life. But that scared had always seemed practical. "Okay, the situation's this bad, so I should be this scared. Okay, now it's *this* bad, so I'll ramp up to *this* scared." A sliding scale, adjusted in proportion, like a battery for focus. None of that—none of that—worked for the kind of scared pulsing in me now. If anything, my focus felt scattered to the winds. My mind wheeled and flailed: flashes of Lisa's face, of Teresa's face, of the woman I would only ever know as X. Why was I thinking of them? Because they were heroes, they were noble, they fought against the system. And what was I? Just a cog—a desperate one, a glorified middle manager who just needed some mission to lead. I wasn't roiling in agony because of your history with Teresa—not completely, at least. It was because I was old, I was small, I was weak, I didn't know myself as well as I thought, and I was so terrified of what would happen to me if you didn't come down to this basement soon and give me something to—

There was a soft rapping on the door. Your voice.

"Dak?"

Shit. ". . . Yeah . . ." Not a question, not an invitation, just an acknowledgment I was here.

The door creaked open. Your hand came in and found me.

"Let's get you to bed."

WE SPOONED in the dark. It helped a little. I was like the Harp, looking for security, I guess.

After a few minutes, you sniffed and gave a small jolt.

"Shit, where's the burner?" You must have fallen just a tiny bit asleep and then remembered something.

"In my pants pocket," I said into your neck. "Over by the rest of our stuff."

"Do we need it where we can see it?" you asked.

"Chinese don't even have the number yet. We'd be calling them, and hopefully not even that."

"And I guess if they've somehow tracked this one we're dead anyway . . ."

Silence for another few minutes. Maybe you'd fallen asleep. Maybe you were thinking like me.

"Matt."

"Mm?"

"Can we fuck?"

You rolled over to look at me. You were awake after all.

"What time is it?"

"It doesn't have to be—" *It doesn't have to be like before* is what I almost said.

"Do you seriously feel like it?"

"As opposed to what?"

"As opposed to, I dunno . . . you think we're going to die tomorrow and this is our last time?"

"I don't know." You ran your hand down my arm. "I don't feel like it."

"I don't either."

I kept trying to see you in the darkness. Wishing there was a light source. There weren't even windows. It was the belly of a much smaller bug.

"But we should," I whispered finally.

For a second I thought maybe you'd gone to sleep. Then I felt your lips on my skin. I prepped myself for it to be terrible, but it was actually okay.

IT WASN'T enough to put me out, though. I lay awake in the darkness listening to your slow and steady breathing, trying to run as clinical a diagnostic as I could on myself.

What was bugging me?

Jesus, what wasn't?

Was it anxiety about how tomorrow would go down? *It would go down however it went down, soldier, you know that.*

Was I worried about Patty and what Haydon intimated when he said he'd make her suffer? *He could easily have been bluffing—besides, she's squeaky clean.*

Was I worried Haydon had succeeded in planting seeds of doubt by making his offer over the speakerphone? *There might be something there, but . . . I trust the person sleeping next to me. I do.*

These worries were like waves upon a beach, crashing down but also then receding as another one came in. No one of them was more concerning than the others and there was almost a kind of peace to be found in their monotony.

All the same, something was sticking in me somewhere—a jagged edge, a loose tooth. What was it?

I wish I could take a long, hot shower right now—fill the room with steam, scald my skin until the heat rash took over like . . .

An answer came to me.

IN THE dark, ultra-modern master bedroom, Teresa was sleeping on top of the covers of the tightly made bed. She looked like an altar offering who'd finally decided to get some rest.

I sat down next to her and gently shook her awake.

"Don't yell, okay?" I whispered. "I don't wanna wake him up."

She blinked, rose up onto her elbows. "Is something wrong?"

God, she even responds well to being woken up by a stranger in the middle of the night.

This must happen to her a lot.

"You said you're a doctor, right?"

"For kids." Her voice was still raspy with sleep but I could tell she was alert now. "Is everything—"

"I need to show you something. In the garage."

"Okay." She rubbed her eyes. "You're not taking me to a dead body, are you?"

"That's actually what I want to find out."

. . .

THERE WERE a crazy number of light switches in the garage—it's like the guy wanted each square foot of this empty, utilitarian room to have its own dedicated spotlight. God, the things being rich must do to your brain. We turned on just a few, giving the garage an eerie, shadow-haunted quality, almost as if we had gathered around a campfire, but the campfire was upside down on the ceiling.

"Okay," I warned her, "I'm gonna open the van now. You did a good job not crying out before. This time it's gonna be harder."

Her arms were crossed and her mouth was set into a thin line. She was taking me seriously.

I went to the doors at the back of the van and pulled them open. The noise was ominously loud. Like a pistol cocking.

"Oh," I continued as I got into the van, "and I could use your help with his legs. Heads up: it will feel weird."

She came over and saw what I was propping up inside.

"Okay," she exclaimed quietly. "Oh . . . kay." She grabbed ahold of Moss's ankles, winced at their warmth, but didn't let go. "Okay," she said again, still low and cautious.

We got him laid out on the garage floor, at which point she stood over him and sighed, "I'm gonna get a few more of these lights." She was doing pretty well, though. She might've even passed her final training test at Quill. A few more lights came on, and the eeriness of the garage was beaten back a few steps.

"So." She was staring down at the lanky, grayish body. "This is what you and Matt do for a living." No question; an understanding.

"Did. But, yeah."

"Can I—?" she gestured to move down and handle him.

"Just be careful not to knock off any of the moss."

"Okay, so that's *supposed* to be there?"

"Yeah," I shrugged. "I don't know. I don't really know anything."

She began to run her hands over the entirety of his body,

careful to not disturb any of the rapidly diminishing wisps of kelp-like growth on his chest. The moss was now basically four vertical strands lying across his chest. Less already than when we got here. She lifted the body up in that practiced, careful way that only physicians seem to know, feeling for bones, weaknesses, anything under the skin that would make moving him a danger. But that wasn't all she was feeling for.

"No zipper, right? No seams."

She looked at me. Her eyes were wild with curiosity. It was a look I saw a lot on the floor of the Bazaar. It was the look of burgeoning scientific obsession.

"You know what my first thought was just now?"

"What?"

"He's such an *organism*," she laughed weakly.

I nodded.

"Why can't I touch the . . . that stuff?" She waved a hand over the strands.

"They had a theory where we worked . . . that when the last of the moss is gone . . . that means he's dead."

"He's not dead now?"

"Probably." There are times when the absurdity of any given situation is easy to ignore, and there are times when it begins to shriek desperately at you. This was one of the latter. I felt like a child, wrestling with the presence of something under my bed, now finally begging an adult for aid. It was a small, pitiable feeling. "He probably is. He's probably been dead for years. But. I don't know, I don't know, I'm . . ." She stood there, patiently, giving me room to say whatever it was I needed to say. There was nothing else I could say. "I'm all fucked up."

"Okay," she said plainly, sympathetically.

"I watched that moss recede for years and I didn't think anything about it."

"But now that he's in your custody . . ."

"But he's probably dead! I mean, what the fuck am I—"

"Do you not think he's dead?" She seemed more interested in

my emotional breakdown than in the unearthly creature on the floor between us.

"I'm asking you! Aren't you the, the . . ."

"Pediatrician? For human children?" She let out a small, dry laugh.

"Can't you like . . . examine him?"

She blinked at me, then knelt back down to the body. "Well, I guess I could do a couple things. I could feel around for places where I'd usually find a pulse, right? But—"

"But there's no pulse."

"And I could listen here, where I'd hear a heartbeat, or here, where I'd hear respiration . . ."

"But there's nothing." Embarrassment galloped through me.

"If I shined a penlight on these huge black eyes . . ." The more she stared at Moss the more rapt she became.

". . . nothing," I whispered. A shudder passed through me. An image of us preparing his long, thin body for funeral rites.

"Don't you already know all this?" she asked kindly, without accusation. I nodded. In the eight years I worked at Quill Marine, hundreds upon hundreds of tests had been performed on Moss. Lights. Noises. Gentle electrical prodding. Hell, one scientist tried the good old-fashioned shouting-at-Moss-randomly-through-a-bullhorn to see if that elicited any sort of response. Nothing did. But now . . . he was mine . . .

"The people you're taking him to," Teresa stood up, "do you have some reason to think they'll take better care of him?"

"No."

"Then why are you doing it?"

"He's our ticket."

"Yours and Matt's."

I nodded again. "I've hurt a lot of people. Getting this far."

"So—"

I couldn't stop myself; I had more to say. "But what was I supposed to do? I can't take care of them forever, I can't take care of everyone forever! At some point it has to be my turn to go home!"

"And . . . home is . . . ?"

We looked at each other. I didn't say it—I didn't say your name—but it was loud and clear all the same. She surprised me by walking over to the van, halfheartedly inspecting it, an artifact in a museum she wasn't quite sold on. We were silent for several moments.

"Dak . . . you have to be careful with Matt."

"What?" I swallowed.

"He's a beautiful man. Almost like, delicate. Even with all the things he can do, it's like he's helpless, he makes you want to . . ." *Save him,* I thought. ". . . save him. I mean, look at me. I'm still not past it." She gave a sad, self-incriminating shrug. "I mean, what's the first thing I did when you got here?"

I decided to risk voicing what had been pinballing through me. "What did you mean then?"

"Mean?"

"Right after you kissed him. When you said . . . 'Your call brought me right back to . . . .'"

She nodded. "He was stationed, so I couldn't see him all the time, we couldn't have a regular thing. He kept getting called away to do whatever. So we decided to make that exciting instead. We had a room we used a lot. I wouldn't see him for a long time, weeks or even a month, 'til I was totally wound up and losing my shit, and then my phone would ring. And I'd answer, right, and I wouldn't say anything. I'd just breathe. And he'd breathe. And we'd keep that going for as long as we could stand it, and finally he'd say: 'Get here.'"

And there in the garage, amid the smell of dirt and concrete and van and night, I started to hyperventilate.

"FUCK, SORRY, I'm—"

"No, it's okay—"

"No, I'm gonna stop, I'm."

"Can I hug you?"

I was mid-gulp, sitting against the wall, feeling tears prick the back of my eyes and desperately refusing to let them spill, so at first I didn't even think I'd heard her correctly. But when I looked up I saw her opening her arms just a little wider, palms upturned, ready to make good on her request.

"No!" I waved her away.

"Are you sure?" She stood there, still ready.

I could have caved. I could have let her. A not-insignificant part of me yearned for it—a connection, a feeling of acknowledgment, even forgiveness, for all that I'd done. I could see myself weakly nodding, her stepping over Moss, holding me in her arms, letting the tears I was holding back spill out against her chest, relieving the pressure that had been roiling in me like a boiler that needed dumping. I could be like Lisa—I could whisper, "I'm gonna stop in a second," over and over again until, eventually, it stopped. I had so little reason, beyond some damaged instinct, to distrust her at this point. I had so little reason to hold on to this creaking, straining, exploding pain . . .

But this was *my* pressure. These were *my* tears. She'd had enough of my things. I tamped it down. I forced my breath to slow, my heart to steady. I stood up.

"I'm sure," I muttered.

She dropped her arms and looked at me, concerned.

"My ex-boyfriend's downstairs. There's an alien on my garage floor . . . and what I'm most worried about is you."

I could say the same to you, I thought icily but didn't say.

A FEW hours later, the sun was up and so were we. I stood in the front hall of the house, watching as Teresa spoke outside with a man next to a large cargo truck—about the size of a fifteen-foot mover with an enclosed bed and a roll-up door. I hoped Teresa got at least a couple hours' sleep after we'd stuffed Moss back into the van. I knew I didn't.

Truck-Guy nodded a few times at some things I couldn't hear. At one point he looked back at the house. I wondered if he could see me but I couldn't work up a feeling either way. A few minutes later a taxi pulled up and Teresa said a couple more things to Truck-Guy before letting him go.

What the fuck are they talking about, I wonder?

"Whatcha looking at?" You came up behind me. I didn't turn around.

"Nothing. Probably."

"That's a hell of a truck. That'll work great!" You joined me, looking out. Something in your voice.

"You sound chipper," I said.

"Guess I'm just eager to hit the road."

And, as if on cue, Teresa bounded back into the house, beaming.

"We're good to go!"

There were a few more tiny logistical things to nail down before we hit that road, however. First, we'd need to keep in contact between vehicles. I asked Teresa for her number to put into the burner, except—

"Shit." My pockets were empty. "Where's the phone?"

"I think I saw it by the bed downstairs," you said. "Want me to grab it?"

"Yeah, we should just get all our stuff up now. Plus . . ."

"Right. Yes." You knew right away what I was referring to. Teresa, however, did not.

"What?"

I turned to her. "If you're driving the truck . . ."

"Right . . . ?"

"It's called a Lloyd Suit."

LESS THAN an hour later and we were ready to embark. Moss and the Turndown box–slash–Harp rig were safely secured in the luxuriously large cargo bed of the truck. Teresa had given me the keys to her modest, cozy sedan before getting into her space suit ("Life is weird," she giggled). She'd have to drive without the helmet, so we'd have to work fast in case there was an unexpected Power-Up, but it was something.

Before you got into the back of the truck, I pulled you aside. I needed to say something but I was completely unsure how to force it out in words.

"I'm . . . ," I began.

"What?"

I shook my head, at a loss. You let out a short breath through your nose, not quite a laugh, not quite a sigh, put your hands on my upper arms and kissed me on the forehead. Even though it was a perfunctory gesture, it felt like a benediction. I felt a weight lift and drift to the sky. Not all the weight, a tiny percentage of the weight all told, but enough for me to think a little straighter.

"It's gonna be okay," you said.

"I'm not always going to be like this."

"What do you—?"

"When we're in China and we're rich, I'll be"—I shrugged—"I dunno, easier."

"I think you should be . . . however you want to be," you said. Something was needling you, I could tell. I couldn't blame you. The last few days had been horrible and we were due for a mighty hangover. But I'd said all I could think of saying for now, so I left it at that.

"I think we're gonna pull this off," I winked at you, and then got behind the wheel of Teresa's car. "Don't get nuked."

FIVE HOURS later, we made it to the rendezvous point without incident.

I wish that's where we could end this.

25

I'LL GIVE her this much: Teresa knew a hell of a lot more than me about smuggling people.

After we'd pulled our cars over onto the dusty hardpan she waddled her way to the back of the truck, blessedly ungraceful in the Lloyd Suit, and called to you: "Matt! Cover your eyes! I'm gonna open the back and it's still bright!"

Your voice, muffled from inside: "It's okay, there's a light in here—!"

"Trust me, tough guy, it's way brighter out here." The sun was just beginning to dip toward the horizon and it was shining straight at us like a spotlight.

Good call, T, I thought. *I would have just yanked the door up and blinded him.*

The door came up and, as soon as the cargo was visible, Teresa put a hand over her eyes and moved around to the side. "I'm not looking!" she said earnestly. "I'm not looking at whatever you have in the truck!"

As soon as she was out of a line of sight, she took her hand away and her eyes met mine. I felt what could have been shame but was probably closer to admiration. I'd figured her wrong. Good for her, and good for me for realizing it.

Still. I was counting the seconds 'til you wouldn't be looking at her anymore.

Before that time came, though, I had to watch a few minutes later, after your eyes had adjusted to the glaring desert sun, as you unsealed her from her Lloyd Suit. She sighed with deep relief to be free of it. Meanwhile, I was trying not to think, *That's one more thing of mine I don't own anymore.*

"Can you find this spot again? For your buddy?" I asked. She looked around, shading her eyes with her hand, for any sort of recognizable landmark nearby. There was, decisively, nothing.

"I'm sure I can," she shrugged. We swapped keys and then she said, "Hey. Can I hug you now?"

Fuck it. In the light of day it didn't seem like a thing. I held out my arms and we embraced. Then she came over to you.

"I love you like crazy." She kissed your cheek.

"Thank you for everything." You smiled back. "Seriously."

She gave you a short, quick raise of her eyebrows, as if to say, "I know," and then got into her car. She gave us one final appraising look from her seat.

"I mean: look at you guys!" she cooed. Then closed the door, started the car, and drove away, kicking up gravel and dust that soon settled back down to the desert floor anonymously.

Watching her go was like . . . *Well, that's the last piece of normal for a long, long time.*

Neither of us moved for a small eternity.

"Let's set up camp," one of us finally said.

THE BACK of the truck was spectacularly spacious compared to any of the vans, but it got hot as hell inside fast. We waited with the roll-down door open.

It was maybe two hours from sunset. Then another hour after that for the contact, assuming they were on time. But here we were, undisturbed and quiet.

We didn't talk much; something about the expanse around us, the lack of enemies, the growing dread not only of failure but of now-possible success . . . how could either one of us have possibly known what to say? But at one point you took my hand and that was enough.

I looked at Moss, sitting in the back near his Harp. When we'd given him one final once-over, you had said, "Huh. Never seen that before." I came over to see what you were looking at and you pointed. "On his chest. You can see the moss swaying in the breeze."

It was true. His tiny skeins of moss were flitting about in the soft desert wind—little prisoners finally given some time to play outside. I'd had a moment of panic thinking maybe they might blow away, but the breeze was gentle and they seemed anchored enough for now.

It was noticeably less since the morning. The moss was almost gone.

There had been something hypnotic to it. Like kelp swaying on the ocean floor.

How far away the Marine Lab, the ocean, felt. How strange and varied this world was.

Did Moss ever get to appreciate it? Did he ever get a sense of it before he crashed, either willingly or not?

What sights would he want to see? What could he compare them to? What, even, was his mission?

What would his moss think?

Huh.

There was something I'd never considered before.

Did his moss feel? Was it sensate? Sensitive? Did it recognize this breeze and understand how well it meant—to cool, to comfort, to spread seeds and whip up the very weathers that made life possible? Was the moss as dumb and dead as hair, or was it alive like exposed nerves?

I thought of my own skin, of how it commingled with yours, together in motel beds, on kitchen counters. I thought of how I'd wished, wished so hard, that one day my skin could just spiral with yours into its own knot, its own intractable unit, undulating, as unstoppable as its own ocean. Perhaps we could even begin to grow and expand, you and me, pulsing out with tidal intent, until we covered the surface of the world. Nothing to fear, nothing to run from again, because we were everything, we were—

I woke with a gasp and a jolt.

There's nothing worse than realizing you nodded off mid-operation. That sense of waking up to every single factor left unattended for . . . how long?

Then I noticed you were gone. I was sitting in the back alone. And the sky was red. The sun hung low. The tops of the mountains had pierced it and dying sunlight flooded the sky like yolk from a soft-boiled egg.

I called your name, trying not to panic, and heard you shushing me, just outside. I climbed out cautiously and found you crouched low by the side of the truck.

"There's a car," you whispered. "Straight ahead. See?"

I did. Shit. About a hundred yards away. Barely more than a silhouette against the harsh, setting sun.

"If it was *them* it'd be like twenty vehicles with lights and megaphones, right?"

"At least," I nodded, squinting.

"What the hell is one car?"

"Is there even anyone in it?"

"I can't tell. But it wasn't there before."

I prepared myself to go investigate, red flags snapping curtly in the breeze once again.

"Stay here." I ordered. "Stay with Moss."

"You don't want me to—"

"Stay with Moss. Do not leave Moss. Close the back. Don't open for anyone but me. If I just knock, that'll mean I'm in trouble. If I'm fine, I'll say . . ."

" 'Open the goddamn door'?"

"Exactly."

You nodded.

"Look sharp, okay?"

"Fuck outta here." I kissed you. Both hands on the side of your face. I smiled at you. You smiled at me. You hopped back into the truck and slid the door down. I wished we'd thought to bring guns.

.   .   .

MY STEPS crunched like teeth grinding as I inched my way torturously toward the parked car. There was no way to sneak up
on it. We were in wide-open desert. All I could do was approach,
brazen as can be. If there was a sniper, I was done for—but also,
that had been true since the moment this car had gotten here.

The sun continued its descent behind the mountains. The sky
was awash in reds and golds, but a twilight blackness was close
at hand, seeping into everything. Soon it would be dark. Piteously
dark. Vulnerably dark.

*Could this just be coincidence? Someone dumped their car near
our spot and just . . . what? Where did they go?*

But the people after us don't set traps. They send tanks.

I reached for the driver's side door, touched the handle, tested
it, pulled the door open all the way.

It's empty . . . I think it's empty . . .

It was. Completely. Except for one thing. One thing I noticed
after it was too late, after I was awkwardly inside the car, kneeling on the seat, craning to look into the back. One thing, crumpled and discarded in the footwell. Probably thrown there by the
driver as they sped to this destination. They might have not even
noticed as they did so.

It was the wrapper to some beef jerky.

That's when the trunk flew open and someone sprinted to the
side of the car. I spun around, trying to scramble away, but then
a blast of fire hit me in the face, obliterating the darkening world
and leaving me blind and howling. Even under the confusion and
madness, there was no mistaking her voice.

"Hold fucking still," Patty growled.

26

IT WAS military-grade pepper spray. The pain was so intense, so world-obliterating, that realizing even that much was a major cognitive victory.

I was distantly aware of Patty slapping a pair of cuffs on my wrists, then throwing me in the backseat like I was a child. As soon as I hit the seat, face first, she closed a second pair of cuffs around my ankles. I could hear her coughing. The spray was hanging inside the air of the car—it was affecting her, too—but it didn't sound like she was slowing down even a heartbeat.

Doors slammed: the back door, then the driver's side as she settled in behind the wheel. The engine turned over, the windows all lowered. Meanwhile, I'd been moaning, impotent and wounded. My eyes felt doused in napalm, my nose ran with lava. Finally I formed some words.

"Patty . . . what . . . ?"

"What am I doing?" she snarled back at me. "I'm saving your goddam stupid ass."

"Wuh?"

She turned around in her seat, looking at me. "They have you. Somebody called it in. Exact location. You got sold out, Dak." She spat my name.

Sold out.

But only one other person knew—

Jesus fucking Christ. Saint Teresa. No wonder she'd been so chipper. No wonder she'd been so helpful.

I wanted to punch myself in the face until I didn't exist anymore. I wanted to shovel handfuls of dirt into my throat until I choked. Except I couldn't. I could barely move.

The car kicked into motion and we began to speed away.

"Patty . . . ," I whined.

She shouted at me over the engine. "I saw the roll-out orders! Coordinates and everything! I left while they were still mobilizing, got the best head start I could, but they can't be that far behind. So we gotta fly."

"Stop . . . stop . . ." I tried to flip over, to sit up, to see where we were going in relation to the truck.

"If whoever you're meeting doesn't get here fast Sierra's gonna get to him first. And they're coming with everything."

"Stop the car!"

"No." From the sound of the engine we were going even faster.

I tried to call your name. I was choking on snot.

"They'll get him," Patty replied. "They'll get Moss, they'll get the Harp, maybe they'll be satisfied."

I tried harder, screaming as if there was even the slightest chance you could hear me. "Matt! MATT! GET OUT OF THERE!"

"We're too far away now," Patty muttered. And she was right. I managed to pull myself up into a sitting position and the truck was almost a speck through the back window, sitting like an offering under the purple-and-black sky.

"Patty, I'm begging you, I'm begging you, we have to go back, we have to get him!"

"Shut the fuck up!" she snarled back at me.

"I'm begging you!"

"Just lie the fuck down and let me save your goddamn life!"

We continued picking up speed. I watched as the truck disappeared completely from view.

"Patty," I babbled, "I'm begging you, please, please, please Patty, Patty I'll do anything, Patty please I'LL KILL YOU! PATTY! I'LL KILL YOU IF YOU DON'T STOP THIS CAR!"

I beat the back of the front seats. I kicked at the doors. I squirmed like an undignified wretch. Patty wasn't impressed.

"Lie down and shut up, Dak, Jesus!" she barked back at me. "We should be at the main road soon. This no-other-cars crap is screwing with me."

"He's defenseless! They'll have him in a chem-zone by tomorrow!"

"Better than both of you."

"Patty, please," I moaned, I keened. "*Pleeeeease!*"

"Jesus, I didn't know you could sound like that." I didn't either. The pepper spray boiled inside my sinuses, it raked the back of my mouth. But I didn't know where the irritant ended and my own tears began. "I mean, you really . . . like you really . . . ?"

"Yes!" I cried. "Yes." And then, in a flash, the fight drained out of my voice as quickly as it had erupted.

Patty sighed in the front seat. Disappointed. Shocked. Probably a little horrified. It was quiet for a moment. She looked at me in the rearview mirror. "You done?"

I was done. For the moment. I'd suddenly realized two things.

The first thing was that I knew what cuffs these were. The second was that my hands could rotate inside them.

"I THOUGHT Haydon had you in a hole somewhere." I tried to sound casual, curious.

I saw her shoulders shrug. "I was confined to base. It wasn't pleasant."

"What happened?"

"I un-confined myself."

Outside the sky grew darker.

"So you're deserting," I said. Not a question.

"Yeah, Dak. I'm a real rule-breaker, huh?"

"They'll find out why you ran," I said. "They'll know."

" 'Will'? They already do; what do you think this is?!"

Understanding thudded into my gut. Patty didn't just think she was rescuing me. She wanted to run away with me.

"But we know how to lay low, both of us," she was continuing. "We'll stick it out 'til they stop caring."

Jesus. Patty. No.

"They'll never stop."

"Then that's how long we'll stick it out."

I was trying to be calm, but the indignity burst out of me like an assassin's bullet. "Fuck you, you can't choose that for me!"

"Like how you checked with me before ending my goddamn career?"

"I handed you Quill Marine on a plate!"

"You handed me an empty spaceship! You think these people give a solitary fuck for a spaceship that can't fly? You *ended* me! And I'm still here!" I could hear the implicit end of her thought, too: *I'm still here . . . would he be?*

Fuck that. Calm down. Combat ready. Go numb.

Go numb

Go—

I rotated my hands within the cuffs. Then I bent down to see if I could reach the pair around my ankles. I could. The restraints clattered together as I got to work.

"Jesus, Dak," Patty said from the front seat, "you know you can't break them; what're you doing?

"These are . . . these are Sierra cuffs," I said, bending forward. The pain was leaving my body. "The new series, the 2027s."

"Grabbed 'em on my way out the door," she said, suspicious. She was probably looking back and forth between the road and the rearview mirror, trying to see what the fuck I was doing. Good. Let her sweat.

"These are the kind we put on that prisoner when we Harp-nuked her." I remembered the sound they made as they clattered to the floor inside the amplified, N5-coated clear cube. The way the woman, X, rubbed at her wrists before pulling her hood off to see she was alone in the enclosure. No one was there to remove her manacles—they'd been released remotely.

"And before you get any ideas, Dak, I don't have the remote. I turned off the signal on the cuffs."

"Of course you did." Turning the signal off was easy, after all. It was just a switch near the base of one of the cuffs that you pressed down and slid forward. It wasn't the most convenient thing to try to access, but . . . my wrists could rotate inside the cuffs. First I found the switch on the ankle cuffs.

"We're on the run now, right?" Patty was saying. "No sense giving them a signal they can trace and hanging a goddamn 'Capture Us' sign on the car. Once you're ready, I'll take 'em off the old-fashioned way."

"What's the old-fashioned way?" I asked, painfully maneuvering my wrists down in the footwell, out of her line of sight. "A key?"

"No, with my dick."

"Well," I snorted back phlegm as I sat back up, "you better do it soon."

"What're you talking about?"

" 'Cause I turned them back on." And then I braced myself against the back of her seat.

SHE STOMPED on the brakes. The tires ground to a halt, skidding and sliding across the sand until we came to a stop.

"What?!" she roared.

"Both sets, wrists and ankles, I turned 'em back on. Sierra knows exactly where we are; we're singing out like a choir." I think I might have even been smiling.

"Why would you do that?!"

"One downside to keys: you have to get really close to use them." Yes, I was definitely smiling.

She didn't turn around. Even in the intensifying dark I could see she had the steering wheel in a death grip.

"Turn them off," she said flatly.

"No."

"You know what they'll do if they see cuff transponders going off?"

I sure did. Troop carriers were speeding down the interstate right now. Maybe even gunships. Helicopters. All headed straight for us.

"Throw me out and drive away," I sneered. "Or you could uncuff me. I'll take either one."

"Turn them off," she tried again.

"Come back here and do it yourself."

Her gun came out with almost unbelievable speed. The safety clicked off. The barrel hovered in front of my eyes as she twisted around in her seat.

"Turn. Them. Off."

Now I shrugged. "Shoot me."

"You're not gonna end up in some tropical paradise with your boyfriend, Dak—that literally never happens!"

"Uncuff me or shoot me." Honestly, at this point, I didn't care which.

"TURN 'EM OFF!"

"SHOOT ME!"

"I WOULD'VE FOLLOWED YOU ANYWHERE! I WOULD'VE FOLLOWED YOU INTO THE FUCKING SEA!"

Neither of us moved. We sat there, staring at each other, breathing, as the sky turned itself completely over to darkness. I knew what she was thinking. She could maybe turn the switches back off. It'd be a hell of a risk—she'd have to get between my hands, my legs, and she knew what I was—but maybe not if she somehow got me further incapacitated or even unconscious. The question was: would she try it?

She launched herself over the seat at me with a roar.

God, but she could put up a hell of a fight. She was younger than me. Stronger than me. Faster than me. I was wounded, exhausted, hobbled. But her objective was complicated and mine was simple. All I had to do in this struggle was get myself behind her. Once I managed that . . .

I threw my arms over her head and then jammed the cuff-chain up and into her windpipe.

I pulled tight—not so tight as to kill her, but the barest hair's breadth shy of that. I would do it if I needed to. She flailed and wheezed, rasping out protest and trying to swat me away.

"Keys," I said.

She made a noise that might have been my name.

"Keys."

I pulled tighter. Her eyes, her tongue, bulged out. Her skin began to turn the color of the black-and-purple sky. "I'm either bluffing or I'm not, Patty. It's your call."

She beat at me with all the tenacity of a windsock on a mild day. Finally, I heard a different noise; a noise that sounded like . . .

I loosened the hold around her throat by a fraction. She gulped air and tried again.

"Left . . . pants pocket . . . ," she gurgled.

"Put them in my hand," I ordered.

Weakly, awkwardly, she fished a hand into her pocket and pulled out a small, metallic key. As soon as it was in my hand I took the pressure off her neck entirely. I let her go and earth-wormed myself up and over into the front seat. I had about two seconds before she got enough air to be a problem again, so I didn't waste it uncuffing myself yet.

During the melee, she'd dumped her gun on the passenger seat. I grabbed it with my conjoined hands and made sure the barrel was the first thing she saw when her vision cleared.

"Facedown! Lie facedown! Do it now!" I hollered.

She nodded, unimpressed, rubbing at her bruised throat, and lowered herself into the footwell of the backseat.

This was the only chance I was gonna get. I kicked open the door and wriggled out of the car into the sand.

I unlocked my ankles first in case I needed to run. I kept the gun trained on the car as best I could while I freed myself. But she wasn't coming out. Next I freed my wrists. I thought wildly of X rubbing her wrists again—these manacles were no joke—as I dumped the heavy cuffs into the dirt. They landed with an almost delicate thwump.

I gave myself a nanosecond to look around. I had no fucking clue where I was, and night was upon us.

With a surer grip on the gun, I called out, "Patty?"

"Yeah," she answered from inside the car.

"I'm gonna open the back door. Crawl out. Hands and knees."

"Yeah," she said again.

I unlatched the door and stepped back, keeping the gun on her at all times. I was ready for her to try anything . . . but the door pushed slowly open and she poured herself languidly into the dirt, doing as she was told. The fight was out of her. The way I heard her sniff, just once, barely noticeable, I knew she was crying.

Once she was out of the car: "Stand up. Slowly."

She did.

It was the kind of dark that obliterated most visual nuance. Everything was its own shade of dark purple. Still, I could see the hate boiling in her eyes.

"Now run," I said, and ticked a direction with the gun. "That way."

"I'll . . ."

"Far and as fast as you can."

"I'll be alone," she said. In protest? In resignation? I wasn't sure.

"Go!" I jabbed toward her with the pistol.

"I'll just be alone," she said again. "I'll just have to run forever."

"I didn't ask you to come here! You did this to yourself!"

She staggered away a step, then came back, her body unsure of which suicidal impulse to follow: go to the woman with the gun or to the open, dark desert.

Her head was down, her face obscured in the black-and-purple smudge of night, so I didn't see her mouth move as she spoke. Instead, it was as if the words floated out on their own, independent of either of us.

"I would've been better than him," I heard her voice speak. "Not like a lover, but . . . every other way."

It almost broke me. So I screamed.

"GO!"

She nodded, took a step back . . . and then another one . . . and then turned her body to face the new direction.

"Jesus, Patty, don't walk, run!" She lumbered away, torturously slow. I fired the gun into the air. "I SAID RUN!"

She picked up the pace ever so slightly.

There were towns. There were roads. If she picked up the fucking pace she could be in civilization before sunup, before the desert became deathly hot again.

But the fastest she managed was a limping jog. And even if she sprinted like a demon, I wouldn't have time to watch her go. I hurried back to the car.

I could feel grief trying to happen. It needed to happen. The blighted skin around my eyes felt tight and foreign—maybe tears would have helped. But I refused to let it, no matter how unnatural it felt to press forward. Just as it went against everything inside me to leave one of my own in the wilderness.

They were coming for me. They were coming for you.

The best I could do was a private eulogy. "Thank you for trying," I whispered to Patty into the car as I turned over the engine. "Thank you for getting such a good head start."

Wait. How—

I spun the wheel and sped back in what I hoped was the direction of the truck.

The stars began to show themselves, as bright as streetlamps.

27

THE LOVELY thing about adrenaline is it drowns everything out. But it's only temporary: everything is still there once the tide has receded—in fact sometimes, if anything, things are clearer and stronger, like statues that have been washed clean in a flood.

Teresa sold us out, I had thought. But even in the moment, something about that rang false. It was too perfect, too obvious, too exactly what I wanted to believe.

There was this fact, too: she loved you too much.

Love makes you do stupid, reckless things, against all laws and better judgment.

Just look at Patty.

How had she gotten such a good head start?

As I drove back to the truck, I had two more realizations. It would be a night for such things, it seemed.

The first was that this had been Quill's plan all along. The fraternization policy. It was unnatural and cruel and worked exactly how they'd intended. I'd found myself wondering over and over lately why such a policy was in place; why couldn't we have friends or connections or love of any kind with the only other people who knew our secret? But now it was clear to me. Only the most hollow and pliable of employees could stay there with any real longevity. Anyone with even the barest hint of insurrection, of loneliness, in their bones—even if it was buried as deep as it had been inside me, so deep I never would have even suspected it was there—would eventually fuck up. That was by design. It was a self-cleansing mechanism that was brutal in its efficiency. Keeps the blood fresh, and as soon as it begins to grow stale and unsatisfied? Sic the white blood cells on it.

The second thing I realized, in my newly adrenaline-scrubbed brain, was less esoteric than that. It was just a memory, really.

Because, as I drove farther and farther away from Patty, I felt like I was coming out of a dream. And I remembered you, last night, as we lay in bed together. How you jolted against me in some sort of waking spasm. You had broken the silence to ask me something.

"LET ME in," I said to the roll-top door at the back of the truck. "I'm alone."

"Jesus!" You slid up the door. "I was losing my mind! What took so—oh my God."

I could only imagine how I looked right now. It was almost full dark but even in silhouette I must have looked like warmed-over death. And besides the physical damage, I'm sure you could sense something else about me.

"Gimme a hand up?" The truck suddenly seemed twenty feet tall. And apparently . . .

"What happened to your eyes?!"

. . . you'd been sitting in the dark.

"Pepper spray. Give me a hand up, please."

"Is someone here? Are they still—?"

"Fine, I'll climb up myself." I started to reach for the hand holds on the side of the doorway when you finally snapped to and pulled me in.

"Okay, you wanna tell me what the hell happened out there?"

"Turn on the light—why were you sitting here in the dark?"

"I was just . . ." You trailed off guiltily and flicked on the interior overhead cargo light. It cast a sick, yellow pall over everything.

I gasped.

"What?!" You jumped.

I was looking at Moss. He was still leaning up against the cold metal corner of the cargo area, next to the Turndown box. There was one strand of moss left on his chest. Even while I'd been gone he'd been wisping away.

"Look," I whispered, high and frightened. "He's almost gone."

You looked. You nodded. You swallowed.

"We need to worry about you, though," you said. "Your face looks like it's been thr—"

"Can I see the burner?"

"What?"

I held a hand out as answer. I didn't want to say it again. I kept my voice perfectly even—sweet, even—as if I didn't want Moss's final moments to be full of upset.

I don't want this to be true.

"Um . . . yeah, do you need to—have they signaled somehow? Wait, did they do this to you?"

"No. They didn't."

I want Teresa to have sold us out. Except—

"Dak, you need to tell me: are we under some kind of attack right now?"

Patty would have been coming from Quill. Which means—

"Give me the phone, please, Matt."

"Yeah, okay, um, it's, uh . . ." You dug into your pocket and handed it to me. I flipped it open.

Unless she hopped a plane or something—

"Do we need to get ready for, for an attack or—?" You were anxiously pacing in a very contained place, like a kid needing to pee.

"I'm looking at the call log," I said. I surprised *myself* saying it. You shut up instantly.

The call had to have been made last night.

And . . . there it was. Silence dropped onto us like a weight.

"Okay," you managed.

I stood there, breathing. The call had gone out around the time I was in the garage with Teresa. When I thought you were asleep.

The call lasted five minutes. There'd been plenty of time. And you knew where the phone was because you asked.

Some part of my brain refused to accept it, though. Some final, stubborn, childish part that was hoping for an obscure answer, a technicality that could excuse this. I wasn't really feeling it fully . . . until I finally looked at you and you whispered, your beautiful eyes wet with apology:

"Dak . . . we're never going to get across the border. You know we're not."

I SPRANG into action like a coiled thing.

"Okay we gotta move *now*. Where's your drill stuff—"

There were bags on the floor of the truck. I rifled through each one rapidly, dumping out their contents. One was snacks. One was our Lloyd Suits, another helmets.

You stood there dumbly. "What are you—my drill stuff?"

It wasn't here. It must be in the cab.

"Jesus, Dak, stop, we have to talk!" I heard you call as I hopped down out of the cargo bed and made my way quickly to the cab.

The stars were revealing themselves above us, bright and placid. You jumped down from the back and ran after me.

"It's the same deal, the same deal they offered us on the phone! We'll get a year each and then they'll let us go! Maybe we can find each other!"

The driver's side door was locked.

"Dak! We have to figure this out!"

"I am," I growled as I made my way around to the passenger side. You continued blathering on behind me, a pesky shadow in the darkness.

"They said they'll have papers, new contracts, superseding the old ones, guaranteeing one year in prison and then we're out. For good."

The fucking passenger side was locked too.

"If they catch us at the border we're dead, or in a hole forever, or overseas in a chem-zone, not even together!"

"Keys."

"Seriously: how is that better?"

"Give me your keys!" I expected my voice to echo, but it didn't. It just drifted up and away.

Our voices never had the chance to echo, I thought feverishly. *Inside the ship, now out in the darkness.*

I grabbed you and began searching your pockets.

"Hey—Jesus—what're you—"

I found them, pushed you away, and turned back to the passenger-side door. Once it was unlocked, I threw the door open, climbed in, and there it was: a bag between the seats. I could see the back hump of the drill peeking out, even.

As I went for the drill, you pulled me out of the cab.

"Dak! You have to stop and you have to listen to me!" I blinked back at you, willing myself to feel detached so I didn't do something emotional and stupid. I couldn't see your eyes, I couldn't get lost in your eyelashes, so I focused on your voice. Your voice wasn't echoing either. Of course, why would it, we were in open desert, the mountains were too far away to bounce off of. Still, I found myself thinking, *Maybe it's us. Maybe we're the reason. Maybe it was always us.*

"We made a bad call," you were saying. "We thought we could beat the world and we were wrong, nobody can do that, that's always wrong!"

But *you* were wrong. I'd never stepped a foot wrong in my life. I always followed orders. Even in choosing you, I was following orders, just finally from my own heart, finally I'd made the call, I'd issued the commands. It couldn't be wrong. *I can't let it be wrong; it's all I've ever done—*

"Dak, this isn't—it's not that I don't—"

"Please, stop," I heard myself whimper.

"I wasn't faking it, I wasn't using you, I wasn't lying about us, maybe there could still be us after—"

"Matt," I said, more firmly. You stopped talking. I let myself speak slowly and deliberately, still trying to feel divested from the situation. But the more I said the more I heard the edge of something sharp and steely honing into my voice. "Do you know what's really sad? What really upsets me? You didn't call it in after Haydon made the offer. If you'd just done it then, I could say, 'Sure, he's scared, people get scared.' But that's not when you did it. You did it after dinner with Teresa and barely fucking me. That's when you did it. And the most fucked-up part of all? *I'm still going to save you.*"

I reached back into the cab, grabbed the drill, and trudged my way to the back.

OF COURSE, I headed straight for the Harp. I heard you outside.

"All right, Dak, listen to me, yes, you're not wrong. Trip's call scared the hell out of me."

I got inside the Turndown box and set to unscrewing the Harp's rig. You climbed into the back of the truck.

"Get a Lloyd Suit on," I barked at you as I worked. "I won't trigger it 'til they're close."

"But the call wasn't enough to put me over the edge. It was that dinner with Teresa."

The drill felt heavy, deadly, in my hand. "Don't you dare say that to me—don't you *dare!*" I seethed.

"It's not that I want to get back together with her—I don't, that's not me anymore either. It's just . . ."

We didn't have time for you to fucking find yourself! "Spit your bullshit out and then get your suit on!"

"It just reminded me that there's all the rest of life, you know? There's life outside the service, outside Quill, Sierra. There's a whole world that's not life-or-death. And there's love that's not always, like . . . it doesn't have to eat everything, it doesn't have to be like, like—"

You cut yourself off. I stopped drilling.

"It doesn't have to be like me?" I finished the thought for you.

You were waffling and I realized again as you spoke just how young you were. I never really considered it to be such an issue before, but here it was. You were still practically a fucking teenager.

"Me and T didn't hold each other like we were drowning," you hedged, you whined. "Don't you wanna hold somebody and it's just *nice*? It's not, like, keeping you alive? Don't you wanna live in a world where, like, seconds don't make all the difference and love doesn't have to mean the world ends?"

I'd finished unscrewing the Harp and dumped the drill onto the bottom of the Turndown box. It landed with a sonorous, heavy thud. I leaned the Harp against the side and scrambled out of the box before heading straight for our suits.

"Put your suit on. We'll seal each other." I began stepping into mine.

"Okay—let's—why don't we put the Harp in the bag so it doesn't hurt anyone—"

"They might be ten minutes out, it might be less—put your suit on!"

"When they get here we need to be clearly unarmed with our hands—"

"Put it on!" I was almost completely suited up. I picked up one of the helmets and threw it straight at you. It hit the wall next to you with an outraged metallic clang.

"Jesus!"

"And I'll seal my goddamn self, I guess." I jammed another helmet over my head, and then worked on the seals.

"It's just too big," you were saying. "It's all too big. We were wrong, baby, we were just wrong."

The whoosh-buzzing of my seals wasn't loud enough to blot out your yammering bullshit. I needed it to stop.

"Put your goddamn suit on!" I bellowed.

When you spoke again, your voice was low and even.

"No," you said.

"What?"

"No, I won't do it."

"Matt . . ."

"We're not gonna get through the border, okay? We're not gonna be millionaires in China. And even if we were, we'd be scared they'd get to us for the rest of our lives."

"Please, please put it on."

"I wasn't faking it with you. I loved being with you. I don't wish it never happened. We tried, I'm glad we tried, but it didn't work. We have to be smart now. They're bigger than we are. All we can do now is get the softest landing we can."

"But I love you."

I said it without fanfare. Without hesitation. I didn't choke on it. I didn't cry. I don't even think I said it as a plea.

As soon as it was out of my mouth, though, I heard the Harp begin to hum. Faintly. Fainter than ever before.

"Dak—"

"I love you," I said again, raising my voice over the hum. "And that's gotten us this far. Just please: love me enough to get us the rest of the way. *Please.*"

You didn't appear in any way perturbed by the Harp making noise. *What the fuck?*

"I'm going outside to wait," you said. "I hope you'll join me. If you trigger the Harp, you'll take me down with them."

If I trigger the Harp—?! Is he not hearing it?

You turned and walked quietly toward the open back of the truck. You stood there, your back to me, waiting for something. The humming got louder. Some distant part of my brain was scrambling—neither of us was reacting to the Harp the way we should! We needed to protect ourselves!

"Goodbye, Dak," you said quietly—somehow I could still hear you.

I should have let you go.

It was your life. I should have just let you walk away.

The hum grew louder. I should have let it have its way with you.

Instead I picked up the Harp, which was as light as could be.

YOU KNOW what happened next. It would be your last memory. The final, fatal point of the knife that we'd been sharpening together. The culmination of everything I have been replaying in my mind as I sit here in the back of this truck next to your body.

I'D BEEN making the noise in the back of my throat.

I hadn't been aware I was doing it. I was so used to there being a low, steady, growing noise whenever we handled the Harp that I just took for granted where it was coming from.

But it hadn't been the Harp. It was me. And when it eventually culminated, when it broke through its insensible barrier, it didn't spread through the room and kill all the power. But it did echo through the back of the truck. And something did die.

I picked up the Harp, and it was me humming, moaning, it was me, and I bashed you over the head with it again and again. You did your best to avoid, to counterattack. At one point you swung a fist at my face but I ducked out of the way. I knew the rules for fighting someone bigger than me.

I brought the Harp sideways against your skull. You fell to the floor of the truck, onto where Moss was propped up against the wall.

You were saying my name. You were calm—none of these were death blows, of course; the Harp remained as formidable as balsa—but you needed to cool me down, to get me to stop damaging our payload.

The humming in my throat grew louder, a sustained howl.

"Do you know what I did?! Do you know everything I did?!" I heard myself shout over the noise. I thought of Lloyd, of Harrison, of Lauren, of Patty and how her face fell reading the letter from Haydon. I thought of Grant, tearing through his chest. That was what I was doing now: gouging out my own heart.

I hit you again and again and their faces flashed with every blow. Soon there was a splintering noise.

"Dak, careful, I think it's breaking!"

I hit you again and the Harp snapped in two.

HERE'S WHAT I was able to re-create from my memory.

The frame of the Harp shattered into two halves. The strings went limp and sagged, flopping over my wrist. There was a noise, a tremendous noise, an incomprehensible noise, like the sound of a piano dropping onto a bagpipe, and something bottled up, something pressurized, exploded outward. The air inside the truck rippled, like air over the highway on the very hottest day of summer. You and I were thrown backward. The last things I saw were you slamming into Moss and the Harp's ripple streaming out of the truck and rolling out into the desert beyond.

Then my head slammed into the back of my helmet and I was knocked unconscious.

I NEVER thought of myself as a violent person. I always thought of myself as someone who did what had to be done and tried her best to avoid unnecessary suffering.

I CAME to sometime later, slouched awkwardly inside my bulky suit. It was the second time that day I had the horrible feeling of waking up mid-operation, not knowing how much time I'd lost, or what I was supposed to be d—

You were lying in Moss's lap.

I might not have known I was speaking were it not for the muffled, hot feeling of my voice inside the helmet. Distantly, my hands unsealed the helmet, the suit (*like someone else is doing it*), and I tossed them to the side as I scrambled to you.

You were breathing, slowly, shallowly. Your eyes—those sweet, mind-obliterating eyes—stared up blankly. You were clammy; everything about you screamed *bleeding out,* but there was no wound to be found.

I begged. I pleaded. I sobbed. Nothing undid it. Nothing turned those eyes back to me.

You gave a soft, wet gasp, almost a polite clearing of the throat, and it was the sound of my heart.

My heart.

My everything.

Please.

I was so sorry.

I am so sorry.

Please.

But there was only silence.

Even my sobs, my wails, were silent. The echo-killing ambience of the ship had found us once again, only this time it squeezed off every noise. There was no need. The back of this truck became a tiny little world, and the world was as dead as the space beyond.

A MONTH ago I thought I knew what it meant to die. I thought I knew what it meant to become a ghost. But the thing about nothingness is you can't know it. Once you find it—once it finds you—knowing is no longer an option.

And that's how this story ends: with me sitting here next to you, next to Moss, reliving every moment I can, knowing nothing.

At some point later, there are sounds outside, far off in the dead of space: the sound of cars approaching. And a new story begins.

PART SIX

YOU

NOW

YOU DIDN'T know him at all, I think.

You can never know anyone, I think.

You get what you deserve, I think.

A VOICE shouts through a megaphone, distant, pixilated, and rough: *"Dakota Prentiss! Matt Salem!"*

I look up, mildly interested. I don't know how long I've been sitting here, just another body.

"Dakota Prentiss! Matt Salem! Exit the vehicle and wait for us on your knees with your hands behind your head! We'll be there in minutes!"

I walk to the rearmost edge of the truck and look out. One car in front, closing in; six pairs of headlights far off behind it; most likely even more beyond that. The full swarm will be here within two minutes at most.

"Do not attempt to leave! Wait outside the vehicle on your knees with your hands behind your head!" The voice gets clearer and closer as they approach.

"They found us first," I whisper hoarsely to no one. All that screaming has destroyed my voice.

"I repeat: wait outside the vehicle on your knees with your hands behind your head!"

I slide down the back loading door and lock it. I'm not entirely sure why—for cover? To hide? What is there to hide from? What if they have a medic with them who could save you? What if our contacts from the Chinese show up?

I know nothing. And now it's completely dark. During our scuffle we must have turned off the interior light, maybe even broken it. I feel around in the dark for the switch.

I'm floating in space again, and this time I'm completely alone.

That's funny, though, because it sounds like something is moving in here with me. A creaking, straining noise, like ancient tendons flexing for the first time in millennia.

The universe is expanding, I think, and that also strikes me as kind of funny.

But . . . a noise *is* there, isn't it? In the dark, in space, where there's not supposed to be any noise.

"It's a vacuum," my hoarse voice croaks. "There's no sound in a vacuum."

I stand still. Maybe the noise was just me again. After all, I've surprised myself quite a bit today.

It's quiet for a moment. That's when I hear . . . an exhalation.

Not a breath. More like a great squeezing of something filled with air. It's followed by an equally intense inhalation.

"Matt? Baby?" I squeak. Maybe you made your way out into space to find me! I desperately look for the switch.

"You . . ."

The voice stops me cold.

It's—

"You," the voice says again, unmistakable.

I call your name. For an excruciating moment there's no answer. "Don't try to move, baby," I beg, "lemme find the light, lemme—"

"You saved us . . ."

I find the light switch, turn it on, and gasp.

AT FIRST I think you're sitting up. But you're not. You're not sitting up.

"You saved us . . ."

You're being propped up, held up, by—

". . . we almost died . . ."

—by long, green strands of—

". . . we were at the very edge of death but you saved us . . ."

—moss. It's coming out of the mouth of the long, thin, gray-white alien and feeding, *creaking,* into yours.

"Matt?" I ask. My voice is barely recognizable to me now.

"No."

"Who are you?"

"WE ARE THE MOSS," the voice coming from your mouth intones. It's the sound of your voice, but it's not you, it's . . . it's as if someone carefully traced your signature, or surgically peeled your face off and wore it. An essential element is missing, however untraceable. "We've been dying, underground, in that Hangar, in indescribable pain, for eleven years."

I'm dimly aware of a megaphonic voice outside, shouting: *"Exit the vehicle and get on your knees."*

Your body convulses. I see ripples under your skin as the strands hungrily worm into you.

Your/its voice continues.

"We subsisted on the Ensign as long as we could. Held him at the very edge of life until we could hold him no longer. Another day, another hour, and there would've been nothing left, and our extinction would be complete."

"The Ensign?"

As if it's answering my question, the last of the green tendrils go into you and out of the thing we once so cavalierly named Moss. How wrong we were, I'm already realizing. The Ensign flops down onto the floor with a thick, dead thud.

"The warmth," I begin.

"Was us. Our colony. Hiding in his tissue, his cells, working together, rationing, trying to stay alive."

" 'Rationing' . . . like . . . *eating* him?"

"If we don't eat, we'll die. Like you. We never wanted to eat *all* the Ensigns. But if we didn't eat *some* of them . . ."

Outside, it sounds like an army of vehicles is pulling up around us.

"*Exit the vehicle immediately! We will open fire!*"

" 'Ensign' is the closest word we can find in Matt Salem's mind. Our prey. Our predators. Our exterminators. They built these Harps to kill us, to trap and starve us, keeping us from doing the one thing we need to do to thrive."

"*Exit the vehicle immediately!*"

"What's that?" I ask you/it.

"Add bodies to our colony. Our nutrient chain. Every time we grew strong enough to escape, to try to Add one of your human bodies at Quill Marine, the Harp sensed it and attacked. And every time we recovered enough to try again—roughly every hundred hours—the Harp attacked again, imprisoning us inside our Ensign. The insulation protects the Ensigns but it doesn't protect us. They killed our colonies by the billions."

"*We will open fire if you do not exit the vehicle!*"

I actually laugh. It sounds like a dying chew toy. "We thought the Harp was an engine."

"No. It's a weapon." Your arm jerks up, points at Moss's (*the Ensign's!*) body on the floor. "This Ensign became part of our nutrient chain. Our colony. His fellows saw that we included him, along with several others, and they cut our colony apart. Each body was put in a separate escape pod, with the insulation doors left open. They meant to kill us by killing them. The other pods were likely dragged into a star, a fate we expected to share. Instead . . ."

". . . you landed here."

I have a momentary flash of the video Lloyd showed us. We had thought that the flourishing amount of moss on his skinny, gray body meant he was at his healthiest—in fact, it had been him at his most overrun.

"Yes. And we were taken to your vault to starve to death a strand at a time. Until you saved us."

"*We're gonna count to ten, and if you do not exit that vehicle we will open fire!*"

There's the squawk of feedback and multiple voices, as if someone is struggling for the megaphone. Then another familiar voice is blaring from outside.

"*—sus Christ, you morons, the Harp's in there!*" It's our old friend, Trip Haydon. "*Dakota? Handsome Dak, I'm pretty sure you can hear me.*"

Your head jerks at the sound of his voice. It's an unnatural move.

"These are the people who rule the Hangar? The place where they kept us?"

"Yeah," I croak.

"*You've obviously cured your boyfriend of his bout of basic common sense, so lemme give you a rundown of what's happening out here. We're all wearing Lloyd Suits. Even I'm wearing a goddamn Lloyd fucking Suit. You know what that means? The Harp can't hurt us. Now, believe me, there's nothing I'd love more than to open fire 'til there's more holes than truck, but the bitch of it is you've got my toys in there with you. So, I'm gonna reluctantly settle for my second choice: cutting our way in and scooping you out like fucking clams. Now, if you come out first? You get the deal. If we get in first? You get hell on earth. So, y'know, talk amongst yourselves. You've got exactly as long as it takes for an acetylene blowtorch to draw a rectangle.*"

You—or whatever is inside of you—are listening intently, an ear cocked.

"Is . . ." I cleared my throat, but it was no use, my voice was torn to shreds. "Is Matt still alive?"

You looked back at me with shining, dumb eyes. His eyes. Your eyes.

What do these words even mean anymore?

"We don't know how you define that. But he has been Added."

"Added . . ." I rolled the word in my mouth.

Somewhere outside the door, a hissing sound, then sparks begin to spit and sputter into the truck. Someone's using a torch to cut through the door.

I look back at you and you're moving your shoulders and arms up and down.

"Your bodies are extraordinary," you say. "Maybe fifty times as fertile as the Ensigns'. You can't imagine how . . . how . . . *strong* we feel right now. And we owe all of it to you."

To you.

That word.

So much in that word.

So much power.

So much sadness.

So much distance.

You—I can't handle it—the separation. I never realized what a gulf it was before. Our entire relationship. It was always "you," never "we," never "us." Two separate worlds, hands straining over a chasm. And now it never will be—

"Stop," I beg in my broken voice. "I didn't do anything for, for you!"

"But you did. We were right there listening as you told Matt the whole story. The story of your love. The love that crossed the continent. The love that made bargains with Grant, with Lisa, with Zhang, with Haydon. The love that made you hurt people you didn't wish to, the love that hurt Lauren, Harrison, Lloyd, Patty. The love that brought you to this barren place, the love that would have cast you across the sea to a strange land, that love that brought you all this way brought us, as well. And even as that love curdled, spoiled, caused you to strike him to death." I'm groaning again, keening. The hiss from the torch outside gives me harmony. "Even in the act of striking him down, you broke our chains. We're free because of you, we're alive because of you, no one has ever loved us this much."

"But it wasn't for you! All that love, that wasn't for you!" I warble in paper-thin protest.

Your/its head tilts to the side. "We still received it. We still benefitted from it. Our duty is still clear. We are yours. Forever."

I try to laugh. It comes out more like a cough. "Great! Enjoy it, then! Enjoy 'forever' while it fucking lasts.'"

Behind us, the torch continues hissing.

Haydon comes back on over his megaphone. *"Hey! Is this seriously your plan? You're just gonna wait for it? You know what's gonna happen to you when we get in there?"*

I look behind me, still cough-laughing. They've cut half of a rectangle in the wall. Maybe a couple minutes more. A few hundred seconds.

"You're right, Dak," you say as if reading my thoughts. "If they get in now, Dak, they'll destroy us. We can't stop them. We're not quite strong enough." I look up, curious, and you/it reaches out with an almost stunning gentleness, takes my hand, turns it over, and touches one finger to the inside of my wrist. "We need one more body."

"You want . . . you want . . ." I hardly have breath enough to exhale the words.

The torch hisses.

"Both our fates are at your command. You can let them enter and destroy us both. Or you can accept what we have to offer. All our strength. All our life. A love equal to yours. A love as colossal and all-consuming. A love that is truly deserving of your own. If you want these things, we lay them down before you."

"How would you give me that?"

"We'd join you to our chain. Our colony. And we would hand power over to you. Utterly. Permanently. A new arrangement for both of us."

A marriage, I almost say, and feel like crying for the briefest of moments.

"They're coming in. I can't stop them," I say dumbly.

Your head jerks again, looking at the back wall with most of a yellow-red rectangle blazing into it.

"But we can. Together."

IN SCHOOL there was this boy I liked. I didn't know what to do, so I punched him. Once every day I went up and punched him on the arm. And that's everything that ever happened with us.

"HOW WOULD we . . . ?" But I already have an idea. I've already seen how the moss moved from the Ensign to your body. "Would it work if we . . . if we kissed?"

And my rational brain knows you're not looking at me with love, that you're not, in that paltry human sense of the word, *touched* by my request. But I imagine I see it in your eyes anyway. You nod your (*his*) head and I whisper, "Please kiss me."

I close my eyes.

"There will be pain," the voice leaning toward me says. "But then there will be strength."

DID THOSE newborn fish react to what was happening to them when they were speared as bait? I don't remember. I can't even remember if they flopped around.

I FEEL your lips press against mine. I remember how I used to clutch your head, wishing so badly in the heat of ecstasy that I could crush you with my hands, turn you into powder and breathe you in. Why is love so violent?

You open your mouth wide and I do the same. For the briefest of seconds it feels like your tongue reaching toward mine, so familiar, so welcomed. But it doesn't stop.

It doesn't stop.

I somehow find the air to scream.

"THE HELL is that?" the guy operating the torch outside shouts.

"Who cares?! Get us in, get us in!" someone else yells at him and the hissing resumes.

THERE IS pain. So much pain. Scalding, burning pain. The kind of pain that circumnavigates the entire spectrum of sensation and winds up becoming insensate, becoming white warm static. The static spreads throughout the nervous system and begins to focus itself, tune in to another frequency.

It starts to feel like paradise.

It starts to feel

We

We start to feel

We are together and we are electric.

"DAKOTA PRENTISS: you are the Moss," we say in Matt's voice.

"I am the Moss," we say in Dak's voice.

"Do you know what to do?" Matt's voice asks.

"Let's find out," Dak's voice responds. We let her take the lead.

The rectangle in the back of the truck clatters to the floor.

THEY WERE expecting to pour into the truck. They were not expecting us to pour out.

We open our Dak's mouth and gorgeous, verdant tendrils of ourselves, our moss, spread onto the person leaning into the entrance. He is wearing a Lloyd Suit but we know, Matt knows, Dak knows (*I know*), where the seals are and we find our way in.

Now he is Added.

We pull our helmet off and we turn to the man next to us. We open our newest mouth and now another is Added.

We are stronger. Stronger. We are pulsing with love.

BY THE time we bodily exit the truck we are five times larger, connected by thick, vibrant threads.

Now we are seven. One of us knows that is a poem and we are grateful.

Seven mouths. Seven new directions.

We Add more.

There are screams, the desperate pop of gunfire, but all is temporary. When we are Added we do not fight. We feel gratitude. We add another shelf of volumes to our library and are so very happy to read.

THE ENSIGN we thought of as Moss had a child. It liked to sing. Those memories got him through the lonely, soundless vacuum of space.

THERE ARE so many cars and trucks crowded into this empty patch of desert. Standing up in a jeep many vehicles away, Haydon is screaming into his megaphone, ordering people to put their helmets on, fall back in line.

We go to him.

We spit moss out of our Dak's mouth onto the ground, just tendrils at first, but they thicken and thicken, they become elephant legs, they become redwood trunks, and they lift us into the air high over the trucks. They continue to shoot at us but it makes no difference; they can't shoot all of us, and there are so few of them left. We Add more and more as we stride over to Haydon, who is screaming.

We remove Haydon's helmet, wrap moss around his waist, and lift him all the way up until we are face-to-face with him.

A memory occurs to us: a thing to say when picking someone up, gleefully appropriate.

"Is your Daddy a thief?" our Dak asks, and Haydon whimpers.

Our tendrils rush in, ready to Add him on instinct, but our Dak stops us.

I say who we Add, she protests. *I don't want him in our colony.*

But then she—we—realizes. Haydon has secrets. Haydon has

stories. When we feed, we feed on everything. We do not waste.
We can *use* him. Our leader, our Dak, consents, and we go in
through his tear ducts. His face contorts first in pain, then in pleasure, then in the deepest gratitude and joy, and we remember
something else together:

There is nothing more satisfying than seeing the look of joy
on the face of a friend.

WITHIN MINUTES there is something like forty of us, connected in
a vast web of green. Dakota's human body is high on a trunk
above us. We send moss down, build up a second trunk, and
bring Matt's human body up, as well. Our Dak reaches inward
and smiles, understanding love and all its noble attempts. Her
Matt did love her. As best he could. We celebrate them. This has
all been thanks to them.

We remember all our loves. We are stronger now. We are fear-
less now.

We remember our Dakota's fear of never knowing.

We think: she never asked him if he had the dream, the one
everyone has when they first met us in the building known as
Quill Marine. Of rushing blackness, a blackness so thick it's
almost monolithic and yet still that feeling of movement. The
dream that leaves them all with the conundrum: "am I rushing toward something alien . . . or is something alien rushing
toward me?"

They didn't know it was a fallacy. There is no binary. It can
all be one. It *is* all one. All fragments of *one* thing joining together
in a desperate lurch to be whole again. We are all sides of every
equation and that feeling of separation, of foreignness, is only as
vast as the separation of electrons inside an atom.

They didn't know. But we do.

We gather up our Dakota's consciousness and place it at our
vanguard. Our Dak has plans. Our Dak earned a life of peace
and we intended to give it to her—but our Dak is not so interested in peace now. Our Dak is still a soldier. And she knows, *we*

know, that some tours never end. Our Dak is elated to finally be in charge.

Our legs move in tandem, rolling like the invention of thunder through the desert, hands clasped together, an immense herd. We hunger for more: more stories, more life, more love.

We grow.

We ride.

And the stars seem so very close we could reach out and make them ours.